Rudolph Leonhart

The Wild Rose of the Beaver

and Tononqua, the pride of the Wyandots - Two border tales of the 18th century

Rudolph Leonhart

The Wild Rose of the Beaver
and Tononqua, the pride of the Wyandots - Two border tales of the 18th century

ISBN/EAN: 9783337349493

Printed in Europe, USA, Canada, Australia, Japan

Cover: Foto ©Andreas Hilbeck / pixelio.de

More available books at **www.hansebooks.com**

THE

WILD ROSE OF THE BEAVER,

AND

TONONQUA, THE PRIDE OF THE WYANDOTS.

Two Border Tales of the 18th Century.

BY

RUDOLPH LEONHART, A. M.,

Author of "Dolores," "Through Blood and Iron,"
"Tom, the Tinker," etc.

Printed and Bound by Werner & Lohmann,
printers, binders, and engravers,
Akron, Ohio.

THE WILD ROSE OF THE BEAVER.

CHAPTER I.

A VISION.

NINETY years ago! What a short period in the annals of the world, and yet how fraught with changes for the fair region now known to the geographer as Beaver county. Where schools and churches, where mills and factories, farms and villages now abound, ninety years ago not even the vestige of a building was to be seen. The river had not been dammed or spanned; the precious coal bed had not been tapped, nor the fertile field cleared. Indeed, one grand unbroken forest stretched from one end of the county to the other, and instead of the civilized white man, the dusky Indian, the greedy wolf, the blood-thirsty panther, and the awkward bear, thinly populated its sombre hills and valleys. Yet it was by no means void of beauty, only that this beauty in many places was of a serious, almost austere character. Through the dense foliage of its giant trees, and the denser one of its undergrowth, few sun rays found their cheering way, leaving fit haunts for poisonous serpents and beasts of prey underneath; but where rivers, creeks and runs intercepted the green canopy, the aspect was cheering enough. True, even here the forest strove for mastery, sending mighty tree tops obliquely over the water, or causing dense bushes to hang festoon-like into the clear flood; but the sun lit up the foliage to the brightness of burnished gold, and there was always enough of the limpid mirror left to reflect the azure of the sky. Yes, the water-courses of the country were then beautiful, more beautiful than now; for no ugly dam had as yet disturbed the rippling current, or the impetuous cascades of the rapids. Bridges and mill dams are practical improvements adapted to facilitate the intercourse and serve the purposes of man, but hardly calculated to enhance the beauty of the scene. Methinks I would gladly give a day of my life for the privilege of spending another on the waters and the banks of the Beaver river, as it appeared ninety years ago. I would, however, hardly fancy meeting the dusky savage that was then creeping along its bushy banks, following the trail of his victim with unerring certainty, and driving the tomahawk into its skull without the warning of a moment. Those were perilous times for the solitary pale-face wanderer, and none but men of nerves, strong sinews, acute senses, and great experience in the use of the rifle and the ways of the wilderness, could venture in with any prospect of returning.

The two men we see wending their way up the left bank of Beaver creek seem to be of that character. They are evidently backwoodsmen, or rangers, wearing the apparel of that class, which consisted of a hunting frock, Indian leggins and moccasins. While the frock of the older and smaller of the two is made of plain linsey, that of his younger companion consists of tanned deer skin, and makes some pretensions to taste and neatness. His leggins also, are fringed more profusely, and his whole suit looks as though its owner was thinking a little about his appearance, or as if it had but lately left the hands of one skilled in the art of tailoring. A fur cap sat neatly upon a mass of auburn curls, and the upper lip of the handsome, though sunburnt face, sported a short mustache in so saucy a manner that the young hunter would have done credit to the park of an eastern city. On the other hand, however, one need only notice his elastic, noiseless step, his keen, penetrating glance, that seems to take in and understand the whole surroundings with the rapidity of lightning, and the ease and skill with which he poises the heavy rifle on his left arm, while the right hand keeps in the neighborhood of the lock, ready for emergencies; we need only see all this to know at once that if the youth would grace the city, he is at home in the forest.

His senior is a man of smaller, but very compact build; one of those persons whose strength we are very apt to underrate. They have little flesh, but considerable muscle and sinew, a body which is best qualified by the epithet of wiry. His bronzed face has an honest expression and regular features, which possess as much comeliness as constant exposure to the weather, several ugly scars and the age of forty-five will allow. We guess him to be that old, though such faces as his are by no means tell-tale faces, while his companion can, in our estimation, scarcely have passed his twenty-third year. The smaller man, however, seems not only older in years but also in experience; for he takes the lead, his companion modestly walking in his footsteps and listening attentively to his words, without neglecting to use his own senses at the same time.

"It is as it is, Bob," the leading man said, in a guarded undertone, "and your disputin' it can't alter it, nohow; them critters are, to say the least, made of tarnation bad stuff. An inch is an inch, and a Delaware hardly better nor another. Don't talk to me about your *poor injured Indian!* all they're fit for is to be shot down, and no mistake."

"That is the general opinion here, Dave, I am well aware; but I cannot help thinking that the case might have been different if the red men had always been treated right. You can't deny now that he has not always been dealt with as justice would dictate, can you?"

"Well, I don't know. I guess you hint at the land question; but even there I ain't prepared to knock under. It ain't meet that them red devils should rove over sich wild tracts of land when white men want 'em for better purposes. We need corn, and wheat and terbacker, and you never saw the red man that would stoop to cultivatin', did you?"

"No, David; but it strikes me you don't like it much better. I have often heard you curse the plough and those that handle it, and turn these fine forests into fields and meadows. How do you explain this?"

The other was slightly embarrassed. His case, however, stands not alone, but is one of the many where rights and privileges cannot be proven except by the strength of the owner. The forester argued in that strain.

"Well, I don't undertake to explain it," he said; "but I know well enough that white ain't red, and that the white man wants these lands and is goin' to have them."

Such logic being irrefutable, the other kept his peace, but could not help smiling, a manifestation wholly innocent, as his comrade marched with his back toward him. It is impossible to state what turn the conversation would have taken, for it was interrupted, and that, too, in a manner which caused the two frontiersmen to seek the cover of a tree, and keep their rifles ready for immediate execution. The cause of this alarm was a noise emanating on their right, and approaching them with a recklessness truly startling for such a precarious time and place. It sounded like some human being or heavy animal breaking thro' bushes or other obstacles in the way, with a total disregard to secrecy or safety, and our hunters might have indulged in wondering calculations if the unknown being had not approached with such great rapidity. Five seconds had hardly elapsed since the first hearing of the noise, when a fine stag made his appearance, and with one tremendous bound precipitated himself from the steep bank into the clear water below. It just reached to his side, and half wading, half swimming, the stag endeavored to gain the opposite shore.

"What a fine animal," said the young man who had been called Robert by his companion. "Might we just as well kill him, and secure the good grace of our Indian friends by a savory morsel of venison?"

"No, no, Bob, don't shoot," the other exhorted. "A fellow never knows, in such ticklish times, what a bullet in the barrel may be good for. Besides we are too near their camp now to venture on so noisy a demonstration. I would rather—but there it goes. It seems we ain't as much to ourselves here as I would wish."

"The buck is down," said Robert, "and there comes the

lucky hunter. He, for one, don't seem afraid to show himself."

On the other side of the stream the bushes parted, and a young Indian made his appearance. The bank being low he stepped on the gravelly bar, where the stag was lying, and in doing so exposed a figure of much beauty and promise. I say promise, because he did not seem to be much older than fourteen or fifteen years of age. Still his conduct foreshadowed already the coming warrior; for in walking up to the deer he evinced a grace, dignity and self-possession peculiar to the Indian, especially when he knows himself the object of observation. The young hunter had, of course, noticed the pale-faces on the opposite bank; but instead of fearing them he seem to be rather pleased with their sight. Placing his left foot on the dead stag, he, with his right hand, made a saluting gesture which could be intended for no one but the rangers.

"That boy sees us," whispered Robert.

"No wonder," replied the other tartly. "We hain't tried our hand at hiding, to my knowledge."

"Well, I mean he beckons us."

"So it appears. Well, I suppose he has instructions. 'Tisn't very likely we could walk into an Injun town without being noticed, and here you have the proof of it. That young jackanapes has his orders to watch us, and caper about us like a young kid about a mother goat. You'll see if he don't."

"Do you intend to cross here ?"

"Yes, we may as well; the Injun camp is on t'other side, and this place is as easily crossed as another."

"Perhaps the boy can furnish us with a canoe."

"Yes, it would be a pity to spoil our suits by wading the creek," David said somewhat sarcastically. "Howsumever, we may as well ask him."

Upon this he stepped close to the bank and hailed the Indian, who might have been sixty yards off.

"Say, youngster," he cried "we want to cross this river, and hate to wet our breeches; can you perchance accommodate us with a canoe ?"

The youth evidently understood him, but before replying he turned his face towards the bushes behind him, as if expecting guidance from there. If so, his expectations were evidently realized, for nodding to the strangers he pointed to a bush at their feet, which was hanging into the water. They were men accustomed to take hints and read signs. Looking over the bank they saw footprints evidently made in the effort of climbing it.

"Aha, I understand it now," David said to his companion. "Do you see the canoe under the bush? One of their party crossed the river by it and stirred up the stag. He cannot be far off I'm sure, and though he is only an Injun, common politeness requires us to wait. Hark! there he is now."

It was even so. From the copse-wood lining the hillside a young Indian warrior at this moment stepped to the open river bank, at a distance of hardly a dozen paces from the white men. He was older than the boy on the bar, but hardly as old as the younger ranger. The exercise through which he had gone seemed to have called into play all the muscles of his body, and to have stirred him from that reserve which has become the second nature of the red man. His eye gleamed, a joyous smile lay on his lips, and he seemed to shout to the boy on the other side. But no sooner had his eye lit on the strangers than a change came over him, almost magical in its effect. The motions of the body ceased and he became as immovable as if he had been chiseled out of stone. The face lost its excitement under a mask of perfect reserve, and only the eye, incapable of belying its habitual fire, shone upon the stranger with an intenseness in which Robert imagined he saw the very essence of hatred. The older hunter now accosted the Indian.

"Good day to you, sir," he said rather roughly, and with no desire to conceal the contempt for the red man, which his former remarks have already betrayed to us. "I reckon this is your canoe; we mean to use it for the purpose of crossin' over. If you have the same notion you might as well come along."

Instead of an answer the Indian descended the bank and entering the canoe, untied the cord with which it was fastened to a projecting root. Holding onto the bush he looked

at the strangers with an inviting glance, but abstained from
uttering a word.

"Dumb like a fish," David muttered, half to himself,
and half to his companion. "I suppose our larned Captain
at the fort would call that mute illoquence. But we may
as well embark, without raisin' the fellow's dander. This
trip of ours is ticklish enough without making unnecessary
enemies. Here we are, Mr. Copperskin, and if you'll let
the bush go, I'll give the craft a shove, that'll send her over,
I reckon."

The Indian either understood his words or gestures ;
for he relinquished his hold upon the bush and the canoe
began to swing round with the current. When it stood at
nearly right angles with the bank, David, who had held on
as yet, gave the vessel so vigorous a push with his foot, that
it began to cross the stream with great rapidity, and grated
the low western shore with a momemtum showing that the
propelling power was not yet fully spent. When the trio
had stepped on the gravel David once more turned to the
Indian.

"I judge from your ways," he said in the tongue of the
Delawares, "that you know our character and guess the nature of our errand."

The Indian nodded an affirmative.

"Well then, if that is the case, you might as well tell us
where your camp is and inform your chief of our coming.
Not that we couldn't find it ourselves," he continued with
a derisive smile, "but a fellow hates to tumble in a hornet
nest unawares, and it would least way do no harm, to give
your folks a timely warning. What do you think of my
proposal ?"

The Indian raised his hand and pointed to the forest in
their rear. When they turned to learn his meaning, their
eyes beheld a sight, equally strange and charming. On the
second bank of the river, which rose about three feet over
the first, in one of the few apertures of the leafy seam, that
hemmed the water course for many a mile, stood the figure
of a young Indian woman. Now our rangers had seen
many an Indian woman, old and young, and the sight of
such alone would certainly have created no wonderment of

theirs, but the young maiden standing there was evidently no common apparition.

As a general thing, beauty, in our sense of the word, was a rare attribute of the Indian squaw of North America. True she, in youth, shared with the white woman that beauty of form and grace of motion, that seems to be the inheritance of the female sex the world over; but her features were generally coarse, the cheek bones projecting in a striking manner. Besides, her hair was coarse, and lacked that lustre, which forms such a charm in the Caucasian girl. The maiden on the bank, however, formed an exception to the rule, being entirely free from the defects of her race, and her figure and features formed an ensemble which would have created a sensation on the thronged boulevards of Paris. She stood there with the dignity of a queen, this dignity, however, tempered by the grace of her attitude and the smeet smile of a countenance, whose dark complexion was the only evidence of her origin. She was above medium size; her face formed a beautiful oval, framed by thick masses of waving hair that vied in blackness with the plumage of the raven. Her skin, though dark, was clear and transparent, showing the bloom on her cheek and the cherry color of her lips. Her profile was purely Grecian, and the most fastidious sculpter could have discovered no defect in it. Her eyes were large, brilliant, and yet moist, of that dreamy depth which reveals the corresponding nature of the virgin soul. Her graceful figure was well set off by the fantastic dress she wore. The frock or tunic in which her upper body was clad, consisted of doe-skin which had been exquisitely tanned, and then dyed with a brilliant scarlet. It reached to the knees, and was drawn to the waist by an embroidered belt of yellow leather. The lower edge was trimmed with white fringe of the same material, and so were the leggins, which shared the color of the belt. The small feet were encased in a neatly embroidered moccasin, in which the scarlet of the frock was repeated, showing that the Indian beauty did not only prize fine material and graceful cut in her apparel, but also understood the law of colors. A string of wampum around her neck and wrists, and a bunch of wild roses were the only ornaments she wore; but, indeed, the eyes of the spectators missed neither gold or diamonds, and so powerful was the effect of her unexpected appearance upon even the older hunter, that he gazed fully a minute before he collected sufficient composure to address her. As to the younger he gladly yielded to his companion the office of speaker, as this allowed him to continue feasting his enraptured vision upon charms he liked, which he thought never to have encountered before, which perhaps struck him with double force on account of the wild surroundings.

When the elder scout walked towards the maiden and began to speak to her, he showed none of that contempt which had become habitual with him in his intercourse with Indians. His tone and deportment showed, on the contrary, a respect which would perhaps have struck him as ridiculous, if he had been fully conscious of it. He went even as far as to borrow, in a measure, the flowery speech which the Indians use, but which accorded so little with his general blunt forwardness.

"I see a gay bird in the woods," he addressed the girl, "which I never noticed before; what may be its name?"

This was said in the Delaware tongue, but—was it for reasons of politeness or vanity—the maiden replied in tolerably correct English.

"My pale-face father is very good: he may call his daughter the Wild Rose of the Beaver Valley."

"That is a pretty name; does my daughter go by it?"

"She only claims what belongs to her; her tongue is not thievish like the magpie's, nor mischievous like the mocking bird's."

"I reckon not, and I shall therefore ask the Wild Rose a few questions: Does she belong to the tribe of the Beaver that sojourns in this neighborhood?"

"The Wild Rose is the old chief's daughter."

"Ah! no wonder then you look like the princess of a fairy-tale. But see here, would you trouble yourself to show us the way to your father's wigwam, and secure us a pleasant welcome?"

"The Wild Rose will do as her father wishes. She will

tell the young men what to do, and then go with her pale-face friends."

With these words she stepped to the young Indians, who had remained near the stag, and been silent but attentive witnesses of the above dialogue. She addressed them in an undertone, and although the older youth cast sinister glances from under his contracted brows at what he might consider intruders, he submitted without contradiction to the directions of the maiden. Both youths began to pull the venison towards the canoe, but when they came to lifting the dead carcass into the vessel, their united strength seemed inadequate to the task, and the girl was on the point of aiding in the effort, when the younger scout, with commendable zeal, sprang to their assistance. Bending his eye with undisguised admiration upon the fair creature, he cried eagerly:

"Don't, don't! you'll surely hurt yourself. This is no work for such tender hands. Come, lads, one good lift and the work is done. Steady! That's the style."

When the stag was in the canoe, the two Indians shoved it into deeper water and began to push it up stream by means of pole and paddle. The maiden, on the other hand, after casting a look of grateful acknowledgment upon the young scout, beckoned him and his companion to follow her. She took a northern direction, following the course of the creek, but cutting off the many curves which it describes, and succeeded in reaching the camp of her tribe at least half an hour in advance of the canoe. Little or nothing was spoken on the road, her capacity as guide necessitating a position in front of the hunters.

When the party reached the outskirts of the village, several sentinels were seen lounging about, and if alone, the white men might have found some difficulty in reaching the termination of their journey without molestation, or at least delay. As it was, however, the presence of the maiden sufficed to clear the way. She was not even questioned, either by the sentinels at the outskirts or by the groups of idling warriors they met and passed, further in the centre. At last the girl stopped before a hut, and turning to the scouts, said:

"You stay here a little while, me call father."

With these words she disappeared in the lodge, and the scouts found time to satisfy a natural curiosity by looking around. This was no common Indian town built on the spur of the moment, nor were the houses recently put up. They were regular blockhouses, erected and afterwards abandoned by the Christian Indians. Most of them were much decayed, having been deserted for more than eight years, nor did the recent improvements appear to be of a very substantial nature. To cut down, hew and square trees was too great a task for Indian patience to be thought of; so instead of renewing the wanting logs or missing shingles, the holes and crevices of the old buildings had been stopped up, and patched in a hurried and therefore careless manner, though may be well enough to answer the purpose. Even in their decayed condition these block-houses were superior to the general habitations of the Indian, and Robert imagined to notice a more than usual dignity in the warriors, as they walked in and out of their mansions, or through the deserted streets, in which shrubs, trees and grass had until recently struggled for the mastery. Still his chance of observation was very short, for a minute had hardly elapsed since the withdrawal of the maiden, when she reappeared in company of a man, whose appearance was as striking in one way, as hers in another. He was a fine specimen of the Indian chief, such as sketches and border tales have brought his picture down to us. Although his hair began to show streaks of gray, and more than fifty winters must have passed over his head, nothing in his appearance betrayed signs of declining strength. On the contrary, where the muscles and sinews of his body were exposed, they told a tale of strength and power of endurance, which made the thought of a hostile encounter with him rather unpleasant. But more than these signs of undiminished vigor did the noble, dignified deportment, the pleasant smile of his well formed countenance, and the great intelligence of his eagle eyes impress his visitors. He waved his hand to them in token, and then extending it to them for a grasp and a pressure, he said in broken English, which was hardly as good as that of his daughter :

"My pale-face friends are welcome at the wigwam of the Beaver. He be far from his home, and the pale-faces have not left him much : but what he has they are welcome to."

Both scouts took the proffered hand, and David replied :

"We thank you, Beaver, for your welcome. I suppose you kind o' guess that we are sent by the General in the Fort, to find out whether you have any notions to come to an understandin' or not. So if you will let us know whether you mean peace or war, we needn't bother you very long, but can return at once from where we came, and deliver your answer."

The Beaver smiled.

"You in big hurry ; but hurry no good. You rest first, then eat, then sleep ; when the great light come again into heaven, then plenty time to speak. Let my brothers step into the wigwam now."

The guests were conducted into a room, which, though bare of civilized furniture, contained bundles of moss or hay, which answered the purpose of chairs. When all had sat down, the Beaver filled his pipe, lit it, and after taking a few draughts handed it to his guests, who imitated his example, and thereby secured his protection. After a grave silence of nearly an hour, the Wild Rose entered through a back-door, and carried on a stick the savory steaks, which were probably cut from the venison recently procured. She had wisely changed her toilet ; but the young hunter thought her as lovely in her plain working suit as in the gaudy dress in which she had first presented herself to his eyes. Indian meals do not admit of much ceremony. The meat being placed on a bundle in the center of the room, each one of the party secured a morsel, and dispatched it without other implements than his fingers, teeth, and perhaps his hunting-knife.

The meal being over, the company arose. "My brothers must be tired," the Beaver suggested. "They may want to lay down and sleep."

"Not just at present, Beaver, thank you," replied David. "It don't agree with me to lie down right after supper. So with your permission I shall walk about a little and take a look at your town."

"Good," said the Beaver, with a smile, and the company stepped again into the street, where the dusk of evening began to gather.

"Stay with the chief," David whispered to his companion, in an undertone, when he could do so without danger of being overheard. "I'll go and reconnoiter the place. There is no tellin' how soon we may want a little information concarnin' it."

Robert nodded, and turning to the chief, drew into a conversation, while his comrade slowly and with seeming carelessness loitered through the village. Here and there he passed groups of warriors, who answered his good evening with a grave nod of the head, but made no attempt at farther intercourse. As the scout had started on his walk for the purpose of seeing, and not of talking, their reserve was very acceptable to him, and before the setting in of total darkness, he had well nigh finished a circle around the village, and fixed its most prominent features in his memory. He had no special reason for apprehension; on the contrary, the Delaware chief had smoked the calumet with them, a proceeding entitling them to his protection; but still the scout had lived too long in the wilderness not to know the instability of its affairs, and the wisdom of being prepared for the worst, while hoping for the best.

While he slowly wandered through and around the village, Robert remained with the chief, apparently to be entertained by him, but in reality to engage his attention and withdraw his eye from the movements of David. For a little while the two exchanged the unmeaning phrases, which good breeding seems to demand in savage as well as civilized society. After talking for half an hour on the weather, or making compliments to one another, the chief informed the scout of the necessity of his departure, as he had to see his brother chiefs, and prepare the tribe for to-morrow's meeting, in which the question of a treaty with the Americans would be discussed. This information was of course intended as an excuse for his departure, and the rough frontier man might indeed have learned many a lesson from his savage neighbor. as far as decorum and dignity of manner is concerned. Self-possession is the foundation of all civility, and this art the Indian was taught from his very infancy. The white back-woodsman, on the contrary, was very impulsive, and given to sudden outbreaks of his passions, a fault hardly calculated to improve his rude manners.

"Me back soon," the chief added; "but Wild Rose be at home; my young brother talk to her if lonely."

This hint Robert followed to a letter. The girl came from the house a few moments after her father had departed. She did not bring "her sewing" along, as a white girl would have done under similar circumstances; nor did she show that natural or artificial diffidence, which white girls frequently evince, when alone with young men; but for all that nature had taught the young savage the duties of her office to perfection. She knew that she was to entertain her guest to the best of her ability, and of this task she acquitted herself with admirable tact. Beckoning him to a rough bench before the house, and taking a seat there herself, she began talking to the young man with a self-possession and intelligence which would have done credit to the levee of a princess.

"You know my name; Wild Rose told you; will you not let her know yours?"

"Certainly I will, my good girl, and with pleasure, although in learning my name you will but get acquainted with a very humble and obscure one. They call me Robert Campbell."

"Robert Campbell," she repeated slowly, and with emphasis. "That very good name; me not forget it again."

"I hope you will not, Rose; I hope you will recollect me as long as I shall you, and I assure that won't be at a very early date."

"No, me suppose not," she said, with a touch of raillery. "You recollect Wild Rose until you return to the Fort, and see white girl; white girls much more beautiful than Indian!"

There, behold a coquette of nature's making! Who will, after this, condemn those who speculate with the talent which nature gave them?

"No, no, my good girl, there you are mistaken!" he exclaimed, with an energy which must have been gratifying to her, savage that she was. She smiled sweetly, but also archly. "Why you call me good?" she inquired, with a roguish turn of her head; "how you know me be good?"

"Oh, he who cannot see that must be blind indeed. Firstly, the Great Spirit would not have suffered the most perfect work that ever left his hands to be sullied by wickedness and depravity."

She looked at him as if she only half understood his meaning.

"Me fear your tongue be crooked," she said, with a tone intended to convey a reprimand. "Is that all why me call good?"

"No, Rose, I have another reason. I only need look into your eyes, and then I know for sure, that you are good."

She sat pensively for a few moments; then she nodded, and replied:

"Yes, me believe that, for me see same thing in your eyes."

The last words were spoken with emphasis and liveliness. They embarrassed the young man, or rather they caused his finger ends to prickle, and his blood to rush wildly to his heart, and then to diffuse over his whole face, with a burning blush. Perhaps this was embarrassment, for the young man could hardly summon courage to gaze again into her face. When he finally ventured upon this experiment, he found her eye, with a musing expression, fixed upon his countenance. There was no coquetry about her now. She was evidently studying a problem which, sooner or later, presents itself to the female heart, to establish either her felicity or wretchedness, according to its solution. This youth pretended to read in her heart, and she now discovered her ability, to fathom his. That was strange, but it was nothing stranger than the host of new emotions which crowded into her bosom. She had had many suitors amongst the warriors of her tribe, but invariably rejected their offers, the position of her father enabling her to do so with impunity.

She had also seen many pale-faces, who assured her of their admiration ; but in no case had their protestations impressed her like the simple, but fervent, statement of the young hunter, who was now a guest in her father's house. No doubt his handsome person and noble bearing had something to do with this impression ; but his superior address and the plain marks of an education above his companion's formed the greatest attractions in her eyes. Of this she was not clearly conscious, nor would she, on inquiry, have confessed to such a fact ; but it was nevertheless the case, while in a similar manner the suddenness of her appearance, the fantastic style of her attire, the contrast of her wild surroundings, and her romantic position as princess of this wandering tribe, deepened the impression which her beauty would otherwise have made on him. In the morning yet the victim of the aversion in which everything appertaining to the Indian was held by his companions, he now hardly asked himself any more, "Is she an Indian?" but rather, "Is she not the most beautiful and enchanting creature I ever laid my eyes upon?"

This being the condition of the enactors of the dialogue, the reader may easily guess the nature of the remarks exchanged. He will not miss the mark if he imagines anything ranging from the first timid advance to the final and complete declaration and acceptance of mutual affection. Perhaps this latter feature might really have been in the programme, if it had not been prematurely and—as Robert Campbell thought—cruelly interrupted by the return of David Anderson. This was, according to Robert's statement to the Wild Rose, the full name of his companion. David was rather in a good humor. He had eaten well, digested well, reconnoitered to his satisfaction, and this, together with the circumstances that one-half of the mission had been successfully executed, and that the other half bid fair to turn out like the first one, was certainly enough to create the good humor of anybody. When the Beaver returned, a few minutes later, David expressed himself as highly pleased with his host, and the whole village.

"Now, if you can manage to-morrow," he said, rubbing

his hands, "to make your redskins dance the peacepipe, everything will be right. But it is late, chief, and as I am unwillin' to deprive you of your sleep, I'll say good night to you and your pretty daughter. Come along, Bob."

CHAPTER II.

STARTLING NEWS.

The lodge chosen for the messengers was a blockhouse next to the one occupied by the Beaver and his family. It was as dilapidated as the rest; but, as they had summer then, with starry sky overhead, there was not much reason for dissatisfaction. If there was no lock nor latch, to keep intruders out, they were equally wanting to shut prisoners up. Both hunters stretched themselves, with a good conscience, upon the rude but comfortable bed prepared for them, and before the expiration of a quarter of an hour, were sound asleep. We shall see that they were destined to be awakened equally soon and in rather a startling manner.

A few minutes after their withdrawal from the lodge of the Beaver, an Indian scout or runner entered his apartment. He came without previous announcement, and from the breach of decorum, which only urgent exigencies could excuse, and the panting of his chest, the chief and his daughter drew the conclusion that the runner was the carrier of important news. The room was dark, the glimmering tobacco in the chief's pipe forming the only source of light. This probably suited the Beaver very well, as it enabled him to listen to the message with an unobserved countenance. His daughter remained very still. She was permitted mostly to share her father's important secrets; but occasionally he had thought proper to send her out, and it was for the purpose of avoiding this contingency, that she suppressed all signs of her presence.

This event, the description of which has filled nearly a page, filled in reality, hardly the space of a second. The scout, inferring from the presence of the pipe that the owner could not be far off, simply announced his presence by a significant "UGH!"

"I hear my young man," the Beaver replied gravely: "what would he want of me? He must have great news, or he would not have forgotten, that the lodge of the Beaver is generally closed so late at night?"

"I am aware of my rudeness; but my message must excuse me if I have done wrong: Is the Beaver prepared to receive it?"

"Speak."

"Well, then, listen. I come from the banks of the Ohio. I crossed it with eleven companions to obey your call for a peace conference. When we reached Virginian soil, we were wantonly assailed by men whom we had never wronged—of all the party I come alone to tell the story. I have spoken."

Truly, he had spoken; shortly, laconically, but with powerful eloquence had he told an awful tale of woe, a tale containing one of the many offsets, to what the historian pleases to term Indian atrocities. Well, let them loath them, but let him loath still more such actions, as the above related; actions, which scattered the productive seeds of bloody feuds all over the border country.

The chief heard the news, but while he preserved his outward dignity and tranquility, they struck him in reality with an almost crushing weight. There was first and uppermost in his bosom the sorrow at the untimely death of so many followers; but there was—and this was worse—the prospective destruction of many more, the ruin of his tribe. How could he after this dreadful occurrence continue to counsel his people, to maintain peace with the United States? And yet war meant nothing but their final destruction; of that he was fully convinced. His rival Maghpiway was for war, because it was in his interest to flatter the passions of the young warriors and thereby undermine the influence of the Beaver, who gave wholesome, but unpalatable counsel. Maghpiway would make capital out of these news, and yet the Beaver could not venture to keep them from him. He would rouse the ire of the tribe so as to overstep all bounds; he would—here the thought of his guests struck him for the first time. With this intelligence suddenly thrust upon the people, he could not answer for their lives. And yet they had smoked with them the pipe of peace; they had eaten at his table and were now sleeping under his roof. It would never do to sacrifice them to the passion of an infuriated mob. If he tolerated such breach of faith, he might as well hide his face forever from honorable men; he could never afterwards hold up his head. And yet how save them? How remove them from the premises without exciting the suspicion of his enemies? His daughter was the only person he could trust in this affair; to her and to her alone could he whisper his desires regarding the strangers. So after revolving these issues in his mind with a rapidity, which allowed a ready response to the runner's communication, he said:

"Your words are sad: they have brought sorrow to the heart of the Beaver. He mourns the loss of his children. You alone are alive; but you must be very tired. Before you tell your story to the tribe, you must rest, eat and sleep. There is a couch; throw your weary limbs upon it while my daughter prepares you some food. Will the Wild Rose attend to the wants of my young man?"

The answer, which the chief had expected, did not come. He repeated his daughter's name in a louder voice —but with no better success. He rose and felt for the seat she had occupied a few minutes ago—it was empty.

What did this signify?" Had she heard the sad news and like her father drawn the same fatal conclusions? Was she now at work to raise the unsuspecting sleepers? He hoped it sincerely; but matters of such importance must not be based on mere hopes and suppositions, and the chief prepared to leave the room, to convince himself of the correctness of his thoughts.

"The Wild Rose is not here," he said to the runner, who had obeyed his injunction with evident relish. "I shall go and find her. May the time meanwhile weigh lightly on my young man."

With these words he left the room and went to one generally occupied by his daughter. Although habitually slow in entering these premises, especially at night, he now set aside all ceremonies and stepping into the apartment as hastily as the reigning darkness would permit, felt for his daughter's bed and called her name. But both ear and touch failed to discover any signs of her presence and his original conjecture matured into certainty. Still he must extend his researches to the blockhouse containing the visitors, and turning in that direction he had already traversed one-half the distance, when he hears a slight noise within the blockhouse and sees three dark figures glide from it and disappear in the gloom of the night. Now he need doubt no longer. Heaving a sigh of relief, he turns towards his lodge, glad and willing to take upon himself the menial offices of a daughter, who has so cleverly released him of an irksome obligation.

Turning a corner of the blockhouse and striving to gain access to a back room, where he knew the remnants of to-night's meal to be stored away, he suddenly came upon a dark figure, which like himself started back with a low exclamation of surprise. This surprise having rapidly abated the chief looked keenly at the person thus intruding upon the sanctity of his home and to his greatest consternation discovered his foe and rival—Maghpiway. Of all the persons on earth none could have been less acceptable to him at that moment. At other times and under different circumstances the Beaver would quickly have repelled such uncalled for inroads into the privacy of his premises; but as it was he trembled at the thought of arousing his animosity. Wishing to retain the other sufficiently long to make a pursuit of the fugitives idle, he addressed him with as much urbanity as he could command.

"Ah! this is my brother, the chief!" he exclaimed with an astonishment, which he need not feign. "What takes my brother so late into the night air?"

"That is a question, which I might ask you with equal propriety."

"My answer might be that any movement of mine made on my own premises surely did not concern outsiders. But I want to oblige my brother and tell him, that I wanted to secure my back door against the dogs, fearing they might steal the meat standing there."

"And the runner in his house—is the Beaver stingy enough to deny him the food he so badly needs?"

The Beaver started, a motion which the darkness of night fortunately concealed from his adversary. So Maghpiway was informed of the presence of the runner. Perhaps the latter had dropped a word or two to one of the sentinels, so that the chief might have even an idea of the runner's communication. With this supposition secrecy was not only of no use, but might even injure the fugitives, who had as yet but a trifling start. By seeming candor he might still put the announcement off till the following morning : so he said :

"Ah ! is my brother aware of his arrival ?"

"Yes, why did the Beaver fail to tell me of it ?"

"The Beaver did not wish to rob his brother, the Red Feather,* the chance of a peaceful sleep."

"So the news are bad ?"

"They will put the tribe in mourning, for several of our braves have departed for the spirit land."

"Ugh ! were their scalps taken ?"

"I did not ascertain, because the runner was very tired. Let him eat and sleep to-night, and question him to-morrow."

"Red Feather will ask only one more question ; who slew our braves ?"

This question evinced as much sagacity as cruelty. The chief knew the answer beforehand, but it delighted him to see his formidable rival at his mercy. The friend of the white man was compelled to record the white man's shame. For that satisfaction Maghpiway would have lost the braves a dozen times over.

"Vinginians did it; the children of our father Penn would have refrained."

"Ha! paleface is paleface and scalp is scalp ! The blood of our braves cries for vengeance and the Red Feather will not turn a deaf ear to its cries. He will kill man for man and take scalp for scalp, until the spirits of our braves are satisfied. To-morrow he will burn two palefaces and send

---

*The English for Maghpiway.

their spirits to the blessed hunting grounds of the Indian, to tell our braves of his purpose."

The Beaver started again. Pretending not to understand the other, he inquired :

"What does the Red Feather mean? the Beaver did not know that he had two victims for the stake."

"The Beaver has, that is the same thing."

"The Beaver has not. The two palefaces in his lodge are envoys. They have smoked the calumet with me, and their life is sacred."

"And I say, they must die; the reeking blood of our braves cries for vengeance and when the Red Feather tells the Delawares they will think as he does and support him."

The Beaver was well aware that this was very probable, so he made a last effort to gain time at least, and said :

"Maghpiway had better consider what he is about. The honor of the Delawares has been kept bright through centuries—would the Red Feather sully it by treachery?"

"The palefaces slew our braves in bad faith, they are dogs, they ought to be tramped to death without mercy."

"Would the Red Feather be as mean? Let him listen to the Beaver; let him retire to his hut and sleep before he acts ; the good spirit will send him better thoughts over night."

The other mused a moment, then collecting himself like a man who has formed his resolution, he said :

"Very well, Maghpiway will do as the Beaver says ; but before he retires to his couch, he must place guards around the lodge in which the palefaces sleep, so that they cannot steal away in the gloom of night."

After these words he walked towards the blockhouse where he imagined the scouts still to be. The Beaver followed with a heavy heart—he saw the crisis fast ap-approaching and that too at a time when the fugitives had hardly cleared the skirts of the village. His courage sank within him and delivering himself to a silent despair, which paralyzed his energy and prevented all further attempts at warding off the catastrophe, he remained a passive spectator of the Red Feather's movements.

That chief evidently walked towards the blockhouse

without any suspicion of the real condition of affairs, and in softly opening the door and listening to the breathing of the supposed sleepers, he merely acted on these principles of precaution which a long and early practice had made his second nature. If everything had been right, he would probably have proceeded to the lodges of some of his braves and secured the persons of the scouts by placing half a dozen sentinels around the blockhouse. But unfortunately everything was not right. A violent start of the chief proved sufficiently that this discovery came unexpected to him. No breathing of any sleepers struck his ear and yet sleepers generally breathe rather noisily. Red Feather began to suspect that he had been outwitted, and when he hastily stepped into the apartment and found the couches empty, his suspicion became conviction. For a moment he stood confounded and seemed incapable of forming any resolution. But when his reasoning powers returned and told him that the flight of the scouts must be of a very recent date, he took his measures with a startling rapidity. He would no doubt have liked to vent his fury by hurling his invectives against the Beaver, but knowing the value of every second, he abstained from doing so and rushing past the chief, rent the air with one fearful yell, which drove the slumber from every individual in that village and caused the warriors to seize their weapons and rush to the place previously assigned to them as the rendezvous in emergencies. There they found Red Feather, who in spite of their rapid responses to his call, had meanwhile found sufficient leisure to acknowledge the truth of the proverb which says: the greatest haste does not always insure the greatest speed. His whoop had hardly left his lips, when he would gladly have recalled it. If it served to quickly collect his warriors, it was no doubt also instrumental in warning the fugitives of the discovery of their flight; and in putting them on their guard against pursuit.

The error once committed, he could now do nothing better than announce to his warriors the loss of their comrades, and the flight of the two scouts. By appealing to the passions of their savage nature, he might stir them up

to unusual efforts and thereby neutralize the injury likely
to accrue from his previous hastiness.

Nor was his calculation wrong. This address to the
tribe did not occupy more than five minutes, but at its
conclusion the savages rushed into the woods with the fury
of a pack of wolves, and a zealous haste forboding little
good to the fugitives. Red Feather, of course, led the
chase, while the Beaver stayed behind; for though his influence over the tribe was insufficient to restrain it from
the pursuit, he disdained to countenance an action which
he considered calculated to injure the reputation of the
tribe.

Before we now proceed to watch the movements of the
pursuers, we have to turn back a moment and acquaint
ourselves with those of the fugitives. When the Wild
Rose had learned the nature of the runner's message, she
knew at once that it was no longer safe for the white visitors to remain in the village. In slipping secretly from the
apartment she had been actuated by different motives. On
the one hand her great apprehension for the safety of her
guests had made her unwilling to wait for the termination
of the interview; and on the other, her sagacity had told
her that her father's position would be less embarrassed if
she could warn and hurry off the strangers without his
knowledge. So she had softly slipped away, entered the
other blockhouse, and by a slight shake recalled the hunters
to consciousness. The bordermen of the last century were
easily roused from their slumber. People who sleep with
their guns in their arms, and hourly expect the attack of a
savage foe, are apt to keep their ears open even in their
sleep, and not to pass through a state of semi-conscious
drowsiness to that of complete wakefulness. The first
touch of the girl had caused the scouts to rise to a sitting
posture, and a "hist" of her lips cautioned them against
making a noise.

"Who are you and what do you want?" Anderson now
asked in an undertone.

"It is me, the Wild Rose. You are in danger here, and
must not stay another minute if you value your lives."

"But how is this? What has occurred?"

"A runner came in just now, announcing the death of eleven braves by the hand of some wicked palefaces."

"Ugh! that is ugly. I reckon, they'll make us foot the bill for that nasty job, if we remain."

"Yes, even the Beaver could not save you."

"I guess not. We are ready for a start Miss Rosy, so if you'll show the way we'll follow in your tracks."

The maiden glided from the room, and by her perfect knowledge of the place was enabled to lead her proteges unobserved into the woods. Gliding rapidly and with the noiselessness of a spectre through the woods, she proved a most efficient guide. Fifteen minutes after their departure from the village the trio had distanced it more than a mile, and the girl now came to a halt for the purpose of parting from her companions.

"Me must go back," she said, "else them suspect us. You know way as well as me, and to-morrow when they find you gone, you far away and safe."

These words were accompanied with a noiseless laugh, in which the others joined. Then the hunters thanked the girl for her generous intercession. Robert grasped and firmly pressed her hand.

"I thank you, Wild Rose," he said, "I truly and heartily thank you for your kindness. I am your debtor and shall not rest until I have acquitted myself of my obligation. Indeed I would be exceeding loth to part from you now, if I did not entertain the hope of seeing you again. Will you keep a little place in your heart and memory for Robert Campbell?"

"Me shall think of you; indeed, the Wild Rose could not forget, if she would."

The youth was on the point of replying when a distant yell starled them from their fancied security.

"There, listen!" "Anderson exclaimed, "they must have discovered our flight."

"No doubt of it," Robert responded. "They'll start on our trail like a set of bloodhounds."

The maiden had remained still thus long. She stood as if the yell had transformed her to a statue; but after a few seconds she had regained the command of her limbs and tongue and urged her companions to a speedy flight.

"Run!" she said in her native tongue, which she seemed to prefer in moments of excitement. "Run, or they'll overtake you, and I will be forced to see you perish at the stake. Listen! the sounds are coming nearer. Oh, Robert, do not tarry!"

Thus urged by their guide, as well as by that instinct of preservation, which is innate to every human heart, the two hunters hastily withdrew from the spot and hurried through the woods as rapidly as the reigning darkness and necessary precaution would permit. They had to avoid every noise, for after that shout of exultant expectation with which their foes had started on their chase, the deepest silence prevailed over the woods. A careless step, the snapping of a twig, or the rustling of the foliage through which they passed, could bring their pursuers down upon them: and much as they longed to withdraw from that perilous neighborhood, they were too well schooled in the practice of the forest, to neglect the needful measures of precaution. An inexperienced observer of their flight might indeed have easily imagined that they were in no great haste at all. All their steps were calculated, all their movements measured, and every now and then they would even come to a dead stop and listen, with an acuteness which only a life like theirs can give to the ear. Speak they did but little, for so perfectly did these men understand each other and their craft that these words were superflous, especially when as in the present instance they might prove treacherous. Now and then, however, they bent their heads together, and conversed in the lowest whisper. This was the case, when all at once a small water-course intercepted their steps.

"What now?" said Anderson, turning to his companion, "I am for comin' to a clear understandin' of what we are about. 'Tis no use to run about like frightened chickens; but we must lay our plans and act on them. So let's have your opinion, Robert."

"You are the older and more experienced, David, and as such ought to speak first."

"Nonsense, don't let us waste our time by turnin' compliments. You have surely served your 'prenticeship, and are entitled to a hearin'. So speak out."

"Well, as you like, David. My opinion is this: The Indians won't try so much to catch us right away, which, on account of the darkness and some little maneuvering on our part, would be a pretty hard thing for them to do; but they are more likely to make all haste to outdistance us and draw a line of pickets between us and the Fort in order to capture us in passing it. This they can easily do, as there is not much need of secrecy and caution on their part."

"Aye, aye, there is reason in what you say. Go on."

"Well, this line of theirs, it strikes me, will follow the creek they call Connequenessing, on the east of Beaver river, and from its mouth across the woods to the Little Beaver on the west of it. There is no other line where a fugitive could be so easily intercepted."

"Well, grantin' as much; what are you drivin' at?"

"I was just going to explain. It will hardly do for us to strike off in a straight line for the Fort—"

"No, I guess not," David dryly interrupted. "They'd soon collar us, if we were fools enough to try that game."

"Well, nothing remains for us then but to turn their flank."

"Exactly."

"But there are two flanks to choose from."

"True as the Gospel."

Robert indulged in a noiseless laugh, for the coolness of his comrade in their trying plight amused him.

"You mean that statement requires but little penetration; still the choice is a little more difficult."

"Which side would you advise?"

"I hardly know. The country west of the Beaver is less cut up by ravines and water-courses, but as the Indians know this as well as we, they are more likely to expect us there and consequently keep a keen lookout. The eastern flank offers more natural impediments, but what impedes us hinders the enemy, and may in case of emergency be turned into a means of defense. After mature reflection I am therefore inclined to prefer the left flank."

"Reasoned like a larned judge; but without jokin', Robert, you have expressed my own view of the matter, and if you agree we may as well begin to carry out your plan. But wait, stop one more moment. It's very doubtful whether we'll have another such chance for consultation as the Doctors have it—and we had better come to a full understandin' concernin' our movements before we start. Supposin' we step first into the run and follow it to where it strikes the Beaver?"

"That would answer very well, for besides taking us in the right direction, it would be calculated to confound the savages if they should follow our trail."

"Well, then, so much, so good. After reachin' the river, I am for crossin' it at once, ford or no ford. Our course on the other side will of course depend on the nature of the ground. We shall likely find some run comin' from the east, which we may follow to its source. When far enough east we can change our course, steerin' south, until we strike the Ohio—wasn't that your idea?"

"It was, David."

"Very well, then we understand each other to perfection. But one thing more, we may get separated in our flight—what then?"

"You know the big knob about three miles from the Ohio?"

"Yes, very well."

"Would that not be a good point of rendezvous?"

"It would. In case of separation we strike for it then and wait there for one another—how long?"

"Until sundown to-morrow."

"Hardly that long. The distance is but short, and he that fails to reach it by to-morrow noon must be either dead or captured. In such a case we cannot reach the Fort too soon, to fetch a party of relief."

"You are right, let it be noon then."

"Very well, havin' come to a fair understandin' we may proceed. Will you take the lead?"

"No, David, I'd rather trust to your greater skill and experience."

"Well, as you please. The post in the rear is, in fact, as responsible as that in front; for there is no knowin' which way the Injuns may beset us. Are you ready? Off is the word, then."

With these words David cautiously descended to the bottom of the run, which, like most water-courses of that country, flowed in the bottom of a steep ravine. Robert followed at his heels and soon they were vigorously making their way towards the Beaver, a course which did not remove them any farther from the Indian village, but formed--as we know—a feature in the plan they had laid.

Their stopping place might have been about five miles from the Delaware town and three miles from the river, proving that in their flight they had taken a south-western direction. The bed of the run containing but little water and few impediments, they reached the Beaver river in less than an hour. Here, however, their progress necessarily became somewhat slower. Not knowing whether the river was fordable at that place, they had to construct a light raft of dry wood, on which they deposited their rifles, powder horns, and all such other implements, as would not bear the contact with water. Keeping this frail craft between them, they entered the channel, which they found less deep than they anticipated. The water at the deepest place hardly reached their hips; but as they resolved to follow the course of the river, until the mouth of some run coming from the east, they allowed the raft with their rifles to float on, merely guiding and controlling it by a projecting twig.

The eastern bank was steep and high, and overhung by dense bushes, whose shade still increased the darkness of the night, and thereby improved the chances of the travelers to remain unobserved. At times, however, the channel of the river lying on that side, and the water in such cases being deep and swift, they had, every now and then, to cross and re-cross, until at length the desired run on the eastern side made its appearance. They had lost so much time in desultory movements, that they could form no estimate of the distance they had marched in the bed of the river. They judged it, however, to be about two miles, and as they had left the village at a late hour, traveled some ten miles, and stopped at intervals, they concluded that the time must be considerably past midnight. In such a case there would be but a few more hours of darkness, and as they had still a long walk before them, rapidity of motion became as important a consideration as stealth and secrecy. Accordingly they proceeded up the run at a gait which now and then occasioned a slight stumbling, accompanied with more or less noise. At such times they would stop a moment and listen, but everything remaining quiet, start anew and bending all their strength and energy upon the task before them, climb higher and higher in the stony bed of the run, which flowed through a deep and winding gorge.

At length streaks of gray began to shoot across the sky, indicating the approach of day. The travellers had added ten more miles to the distance traversed, and began to study the propriety of turning to the right and striking for the stream, which even then went under the name of "Slippery Rock Creek." If the Indians had really done, as Robert imagined, and drawn a line of pickets across the country, it was hardly probable that this line extended far enough to intercept them here. They considered the greatest danger past, and resolved to rest a few minutes before they would undertake to climb the height on their right, and from there start on the new course. Selecting a mossy ledge, they sat down and despatched the remnants of their provisions, consisting of corn-bread and pork. The hospitality of the Wild Rose had enabled them to save this food and it came now very handy, as this forced walk had given them an appetite, and the neighborhood of their foes forbade the use of the rifle for the purpose of killing game. Their flasks, moreover, contained some of that good whiskey, which the western counties of Pennsylvania were famous for producing, and thus the scouts were enabled to make a meal, calculated to renew their waning strength. A quarter of an hour, however, was all the leisure they would permit themselves, and at the expiration of that time they rose and began to ascend the steep hill, constituting the southern side of the gorge. The darkness had by this time yielded to a grayish twilight, which much facilitated their ascent, and increased in strength, as they approached the top. The trees there stood comparatively thin, so that our adventurers obtained a tolerable view into the distance. The country was undulating or rolling, with here and there a higher knob projecting from the wavy surface. But high or low, far or near, there wasn't a foot of ground to be seen that was not densely covered with foliage.

As the two stood gazing upon this scenery, which at other times might have excited their admiration, the sun sent the first enlivening ray upon the leafy ocean. In this light they perceived a foggy streak at the distance of about four miles, which probably hovered over some larger stream of water.

"That must be the creek we're aimin' at," said Anderson. "It isn't over far away either, and an hour's tramp can take us there. I feel like a different man since takin' a bite, and if you agree, we may as well start without delay."

Robert consented, and once more the companions resumed their march. The ground favored a rapid and yet noiseless gait, and the progress of the two would have been entirely satisfactory, if the total absence of undergrowth had not somewhat alarmed them. Even the trees were so thinly scattered over the ground that they were able to see a considerable distance. This, of course, would have suited them well enough; but this' open view exposed them in an equal measure to other parties, a circumstance much less acceptable. However they had no choice, and so proceeded in that state of nervousness, which the fear of danger is more apt to engender, than the presence of it.

For half an hour everything went well, and they were just beginning to accustom themselves to their exposed condition, when all at once an outbreak of fiendish yells in their rear startled them, and for a moment threatened to paralyze their nerves. This condition, however, lasted but a moment, and when they turned to learn the number and position of their pursuers, they did not only intend to make

a final effort to escape, but also united with this intention
the firm hope of being able to do it.

Still their position was truly desperate. Some twenty
Indians came rushing down the slope, which they themselves had just finished descending. At the moment of
yelling they might have been 500 yards from the two scouts;
but as they ran at the top of their speed this distance was
of course rapidly diminishing. The fugitives saw, therefore, that no time was to be lost. Turning and dropping
the hand which held the rifle to their side, they accelerated
their motion to a rapid run. A casual spectator of the exciting race which was thus inaugurated, would have noticed that the Indians continued to gain on the whites; but
he could also have hardly failed to observe that the latter
were not yet exerting themselves to their utmost ability,
and that they were moreover laboring under a disadvan-
tage arising out of the nature of the ground. While the
Indians were running down hill, they were ascending the
upward grade of the next swell, which, though rather gentle, called forth greater efforts and at the same time allowed
less progress. This circumstance, however, gave our friends
no trouble. They knew that the Indians would have to
surmount the same difficulty, while they themselves would
soon enjoy the advantage of the coming slope. They also
understood the folly of wasting one's strength at the beginning of the chase, especially if it promised to be a long one,
The swiftest runner is apt to be beaten, if he does not add
endurance to swiftness. This thing was not new to them;
for if they had never before been in the same strait, they
surely had labored under similar difficulties. Running
formed a prominent feature in the education of the back-
woodsman. It entered into the plays of the boy from infancy, and as many a life had been saved by being skilled
in it, but few would neglect to possess themselves of so desirable an accomplishment.

"While our adventurers were thus running before a
deadly foe, they exchanged only the very few words absolutely necessary.

"We must part," said Anderson, "you are quick of foot
and can outrun 'em, I for my part shall dodge them."

"Why, David, I won't think of leaving you."

"Moonshine! I'll take care of myself. As soon as you reach the Fort, take out a party to scour the woods. I shall turn up somewhere or other, depend upon it."

"But, David—"

"Don't waste your breath. Mine is getting short already. Mind I shall take to cover, the first chance I get, so don't spile the game by any silly trick of yours."

Robert seemed inclined to make another effort at persuasion, but as his companion turned a deaf ear to him, and nothing is more apt to exhaust a runner than speaking, the young man kept his peace and began to arrange his movements in accordance with Anderson's wishes. They had by this time not only passed the summit of the swell, but nearly reached the bottom on the other side. The next grade was somewhat steeper, and this steepness increased as they approached the creek. The woods, moreover, in a certain measure lost their open character, the trees standing more closely and undergrowth here and there making its appearance. While this checked both the swiftness of the pursuers and left the chances of Robert and the Indians unchanged, it greatly favored the design of Anderson. When they reached the top of the next elevation, which was so densely wooded as to compel the fugitives to force a passage by pushing aside the bushes, he looked around for a place where he might hide himself, to let the Indians pass. Seeing the gigantic trunk of a tree lying at right angles with their course, he called a last adieu to his companion and after jumping over the log, hastened to conceal himself underneath. Circumstances evidently favored him beyond expectation, for the log being hollowed out in the middle, with the upper and lower ends less impaired, the scout found an excellent hiding place, of which he availed himself without delay. Creeping towards the lower end of the log, until he reached the part where only the heart had decayed and fallen out, he awaited the coming of the Indians. On they came, even sooner than he expected them, long before the wild beating of his heart had in a measure subsided. So loud did it knock against his ribs, that he for a moment fancied it might betray him to his foes. But on they went, more than half a dozen jumping on and over the very log that hid him, rushing wildly into the thicket ahead and never stopping to examine the trunk. Partly this was owing to the eagerness of the pursuit and the woody character of the place; but partly, mainly it was due to the noble conduct of Robert Campbell. When the young man imagined the Indians to be near the neighborhood of his friend, he, with utter disregard for his own safety, made the woods ring with one loud shout of defiance. This of course drew the attention of the savages upon himself and by increasing their fury made them less inclined to stop and examine the way.

After this act of self-denial he again bounded away with the swiftness of the deer and the elasticity of the panther, allowing none of the pursuers to lessen the distance between them. Of all the scouts of the Fort he had indeed the reputation of being the swiftest runner, and as the chase flew over the hill and valley, the hope of thwarting the expectations of his wild foes became stronger and stronger. Alas! he was not the first man whom cruel fate struck down at the very moment when affairs appeared to assume a propitious shape.

The ground over which the race was run, had, as we already know, gradually assumed a more hilly character. Not that the hills had become any higher, but they had, as it were, been shoved into a compacter form, causing a rapid passage across their brow to be accompanied with greater exertion and—consequently—greater fatigue. Under these circumstances two miles had been traversed, and Robert began to wonder why the creek in front did not fail to come in view, when all at once its bed yawned before him with such suddeness that the impetus of his rapid motion would surely have plunged him into the flood, if he had not fortunately checked it in the nick of time by seizing a sapling growing on the bank. The tree almost bent to the ground and would have broken if it had not been a tough hickory. Thanks to this circumstance, Robert was able to rise again and look for a place where a more sloping bank would permit passage. For this purpose he cast a rapid glance up and down the creek; but the sight that met his eye was well calculated to shake even as stout a heart as his. As far as he could see, the creek had contracted its bed into a deep and narrow gorge, through which the waters rushed with a fury, threatening instant destruction to any one bold enough to venture a leap into their mad current.

To risk a spring across was hardly less perilous, for the chasm at the narrowest place measured at least twenty feet. Yet the fugitive had only this alternative, for to stay behind and surrender himself into the hands of his relentless foes was out of the question. Nor had he much time to prepare for the fearful leap, for a single minute would bring his pursuers to his heels. Robert had, therefore, hardly taken in the nature of the ground, when he set upon the execution of this desperate measure. Selecting a place free of underbrush and stepping back sufficiently far to gain the necessary start, he ran towards the chasm with the swiftness of an arrow and with a powerful effort succeeded in sending his body safely on the other side.

The momentum of the leap caused him to drop on his knees and hands, but in a moment he stood erect again. and turning towards the creek, was on the point of sending another shout of triumphant exultation into the air, when a hand was laid on his shoulder and a voice whispered into his ear:

"Pale-face good jump! much good jump indeed!"

Although completely taken by surprise the scout turned to the person who had so boldly ventured within reach of his arm, fully determined to make him feel its strength, when—behold! his eyes fell upon fully a dozen of Indian warriors, who had formed a semi-circle around him, cutting off his retreat in every direction except that of the creek, to leap into which would have been worse than madness. To spring back upon the other bank was almost out of the question; for even if the Indians around him would have suffered such a step, the appearance of his pursuers on the other side cut off every chance of escape in that direction. So when the savages advanced on all sides, to secure his person, he suffered them to tie his hands upon his back, and to march him to their village, without the least resistance.

CHAPTER III.

LOVE AS A DELIVERER.

When they reached there the sun was near his meridian. In passing the lodge of the Beaver, Robert saw the chief standing in the door, a picture of sullen dejection. In the rear he perceived the Wild Rose, who looked at him with a glance of deep compassion. These signs were rather discouraging, for Robert rightly construed the dejection of the only friendly disposed persons in the camp, as indicative of certain and perhaps horrible destruction. The stake and its tortures rose vividly before his mind, and for a moment he regretted that he had not thrown himself into the waters of the Slippery Rock Creek, thus securing at least a rapid death. But youth is like cork-wood in water—it will not be depressed any length of time, and only surrenders hope with life. If Robert had no great expectation of escaping from the hands of his foes, he was at least confident of finding an opportunity to make the attempt, and in that attempt meet with a more speedy and less painful death than awaited him at the stake. The bordermen of that period were perhaps as fond of life as we are; but the constant expectation of death, in its most horrid shape, constantly nerved them in emergencies to an extent which seems truly wonderful to us. Although they did not carry stoicism as far as their savage neighbors, who would endure the tortures without uttering a sound of pain, they were able to, and in many instances did, for hours, bear torments, the mere thought of which causes a shudder to creep over our body. So, if the young hunter did not go to meet his fate with the boastful challenge of the Indian warrior, he was equally far from fear and dejection. His face was pale, but as he returned the exulting glances of the tribe, that had gathered on the way to the council ground, they became fully convinced that he would not increase their sport by vain expostulations, and appeals to their mercy.

The place, where the Indians met in council, was in the center of the village. The blockhouse used formerly by the Christian Indians for religious meetings was standing on one side of a kind of public square. It was in as dilapidated a condition as the dwelling houses, but still would answer well enough for holding a council. Into it therefore the prisoner was led, and placed in the center, while the warriors, entitled to a vote in council, ranged themselves on a number of logs lining the walls. When all were there, the Beaver arose and informed the tribe of the arrival of the runner, and the character of his news. He called upon the man to tell his story, and the runner acquitted himself of his task with the eloquence peculiar to the red men. He described the crossing of the river, the peaceful nature of their errand, and the cruel and wanton attack made upon their party. This part of the story was delivered rapidly, and in a loud tone; but when he related the death of his companions and enlarged upon their merits and respective virtues, his voice became deep, low and mellow. When he stopped and resumed his seat, a deep silence pervaded the assembly; but the furious glances which the warriors cast upon the prisoner, told him clearly that the silence was more ominous than any exclamations of wrath in which they could have indulged.

After the runner had retired, Red Feather rose and addressed the assembly. After recapitulating that part of the previous speech relating to the virtues of the murdered warriors, he bent his whole skill and energy upon rousing the passions of his hearers. He told them that the reeking blood called for vengeance, that the spirits of the slain would wander restlessly, until the blood of the white man would flow in retaliation. He then referred to the prisoner and told them that it was not only their privilege but their bounden duty to sacrifice him to the names of their murdered brethren.

When he retired, a dull murmur ran through the assembly, which might have swelled to more glaring manifestations of excitement and fury, if the Beaver had not risen to address them. No sooner became his intention manifest, when every sound abated, and the assembly prepared to listen, with every indication of respect to a chief, who, though far from absolute, had always stood high in the estimation of the tribe.

He began by lamenting the fate of the murdered party. He admitted that the tribe had just cause for indignation, and that this wanton act must be revenged, but he counselled the assembly to temper their wrath with prudence. He warned them not to punish the innocent for the guilty, but rather to delay their vengeance, until they could turn it in the proper direction. He reminded them that Virginians, and not Pennsylvanians, were guilty of this bloodshed. He reminded them of the good relation which had always prevailed between the tribe and the children of the good father Penn, and finally implored them not to suffer their better judgment to be blinded by wrath and prejudice, nor their honor to be sullied by murdering a man who had smoked the calumet in the lodge of their chief.

When this impressive harangue was ended, the assembly preserved the previous silence. The Beaver had appealed to the better nature, their reason, and that was an undertaking by far more difficult than that of Red Feather. Nor is this with savages alone—all the world over, people are more easily swayed by passion, than by reason ; hence the struggle of the true statesman with the demagogue, in which the latter but too frequently obtains temporary advantages.

Maghpiway rose a second time, but his speech contained nothing new ; it was simply a repetition of his former invectives in a more strenuous key. Beaver saw this ; he saw the resolution of the assembly fixed on their faces, and unwilling to waste his words on deaf ears, proceeded to take the vote. In answer to the inquiry : shall this prisoner die? a majority of the tribe struck the ground with their tomahawks, answering the question affirmatively. The Beaver, however, saw that this majority was not overwhelming ; that it consisted of the younger and more passionate, but less influential members of the tribe, and on this he based his hope of finally saving the prisoner, in spite of the resolution. So the Beaver once more addressed the men, asking them whether they had not better postpone the execution of the sentence, until after their return to their more western home? To stay here much longer, he said, was out of the question, for the companion of the prisoner, who had escaped them, would by this time, be at the Fort, urging the sending of troops against the village. He, the Beaver, had hoped that the journey of the tribe to this place would result in the establishment of peace with the people of Pennsylvania, but their decision having fallen the other way, he was prepared to respect it. Only this he would submit to their consideration : would the speedy execution of the prisoner not delay their departure, and thereby endanger the safety of the tribe?

The chief saw to his secret satisfaction that his words had made the desired effect on the older warriors : he might perhaps have carried his point without opposition, if Red Feather had not sprung up, and, in a furious strain, accused him of the design, to deprive the young men of the amusement in store for them. He demonstrated that the execution would only delay them a few hours, and that, moreover, in case of an attack, the tribe was strong enough to repel any number of pale-faces that might be sent against it. He was in favor of carrying out the sentence without delay, and would ask the decision of the tribe on the question. Again a majority of hatchets struck the ground, and although the Beaver perceived it to be lesser than the one with which the first motion had been carried, he was deprived of any pretense for further delay. He therefore ordered the prisoner to be removed from the building, and to be led to the center of the commons, where a beech tree, of about a foot's thickness, afforded a good opportunity to carry out the fiendish design of the tribe.

Robert Campbell had, in the meantime, been the prey of varying emotions. His knowledge of the Delaware language had enabled him to follow the speeches, which had been delivered in his case, and in proportion as they were friendly or hostile, his hope would rise or sink. Nothing is more calculated, as we have said before, to unnerve the heart than doubt and expectation. If Robert had at once been led to execution, he would have borne his lot without a murmur, but this debate upon his destiny had strangely increased his love of life and hope of ultimate escape.

When, therefore, after all, his doom was sealed and he was taken to the tree that was to support his body writhing in the agonies of death, a momentary faintness overcame him, and he might perhaps have dropped to the ground, if fear of the exultation of his foes at this display of weakness had not upheld him. He bit his teeth, and bearing, as it were, with all the energy of his will upon his tottering frame, succeeded in coming out victorious from this struggle with human frailty. His command over his nerves returning, he rose to his full height, and, looking proudly on the crowd that gathered for the welcome frolic, marched with firm step towards the tree. In gazing upon the multitude he noticed again the Wild Rose, who occupied a place in the rear, but never took her eye from his person. When his eye met hers she seemed to be greatly relieved, for a pleasant smile passed over her face, and nodding eagerly to him, she pointed to her bosom. It was evident she meant something, though Robert was unable to understand it. Still her sympathy did him good, and the picture of the lovely girl fastened itself more firmly in his heart than before. Having arrived at the tree some one cut the thongs that held his arms. This was the moment he had looked for ; in another second they would be fastened again, or he at least secured to the tree ; so, if he meant to make a desperate attempt at flight, this was the time. Looking around for a place where the surrounding crowd might be broken with some prospect of success, he snatched the knife from the Indian near him, and was just on the point of bounding away, when suddenly a sight met his eye that made him stop in extreme surprise, causing his body to remain immovable, as if it had been cut out of stone. Breaking through the foremost circle of spectators, a young maiden started into the open space, which had been left for the actors selected to play a role in the approaching tragedy. Her face, of course, was turned towards the prisoner, and it was the recognition of the lovely features of the Wild Rose that exercised so powerful a spell upon the young hunter. He saw indeed the lovely daughter of the Beaver, who, by her conduct, excited not only the astonishment of Robert Campbell, but the wonderment of the whole tribe. Nobody seemed to have anticipated such a movement, and the crowd stood, as it were, spellbound, in the eager expectation of what was to be the result of this. The Wild Rose, however, seemed to know fully what she was about. Hastening to the prisoner and pushing aside the warriors surrounding him, she seized his hand and led him a few steps from the tree towards the place where the Beaver was standing in the circle. There she raised her arm in token of her desire to speak to the tribe, a movement hardly necessary to secure a hearing, as her previous act had already produced such a silence that the humming of a beetle could have been heard all over the assembly.

"The Wild Rose would speak to her father, the chiefs, and her brothers, and the braves," she said, in a sweet, melodious voice. "They know that the Wild Rose is not given to chattering like the magpie; they know that she has never before thrust her presence upon the tribe. When she does it now, she obeys the command of the Great Spirit. Last night this young pale-face hunter met the Wild Rose in the forest, requesting her to lead him to her father's lodge. She did as he wished. She prepared a meal to appease his hunger, a couch to relieve his weariness. He spoke to her, and his words went straight to her heart. She could read in the depths of his soul and her heart lay open to him. It must have been the Great Spirit that led them together. Many a chief has asked Wild Rose to follow him to his wigwam and be his squaw; but her ears were deaf and her heart closed, so that their words could not enter. It must have been the Great Spirit that bade the Wild Rose listen to the words of the pale-face hunter. She cannot set her will against His. He made her forget the shyness of the maiden that shrinks from the gaze of the multitude. He gave her courage to stand up before her father, the chiefs, and her brothers, the braves, to claim an old privilege of her nation. She adopts this pale-face hunter as her husband, and asks her father, the chief, to release him from his bondage. The Wild Rose has spoken."

It would have been a subject worthy the painter's brush to depict the effect of this speech on the different parties around her. The captive at first listened with curiosity; but as her intention gradually developed itself to his understanding, surprise, joy, gratitude and love for this lovely and noble creature struggled for mastery in his heart. Forgetting his situation and his surroundings, he drew the bashful, blushing girl to his heart and cried :

"And nobly have you spoken, darling. It must indeed be the working of the Great Spirit that made my heart yearn towards you with such longing from the first moment I laid my eyes on you. Let come what will now ; you have made me very happy by your confession, dear, lovely girl."

But while the young hunter was thus revelling in the ecstacies of first love, the chief, Maghpiway, entertained sensations of a very different nature. Fury, envy, and jealousy were some of the ingredients boiling in his bosom.

Gladly would he have foiled the girl in her attempt to rescue the prisoner if he had only seen a way to do it. He knew well enough that the customs of the tribe sanctioned her proceedings, and, enraged as he was, he lacked the courage to dispute the privilege. He was one of the chiefs to whom the Wild Rose had alluded in her speech as having found no favor in her sight, and the former antipathy, which had filled his heart against the hunter as a pale-face, now assumed the character of the most intense hatred. He cast such furious glances on the young man that the Beaver deemed it prudent to step between them and to station some of his trusty followers in his neighborhood besides. On the whole, the tribe bore the disappointment of their savage sport with a better grace than the chief had reason to expect. There were some sullen faces on the part of the young warriors ; but their dissatisfaction did not go far enough to manifest itself in words. However, even if it had, the Beaver backed by the more prudent portion of the tribe, had sufficient power to quell any disturbances that might arise. Still he had been a ruler long enough to know that authority, like polished steel, gets rusty by exposure, and that the people seldom mind the rod, provided it is covered with velvet. So he would rather persuade than command, and, knowing that nothing is more calculated to engender bad thoughts than idleness, he directed the tribe to make without delay the necessary preparations for an early departure. To this they did not object, for they knew well enough that it was impossible to remain so near the Fort after this act of violence committed against one of the envoys of the commander. So they set to work with a good will, and in the general uproar soon seemed to forget the prisoner and his strange deliverance.

Robert, of course, accompanied the Beaver and his betrothed into the lodge, where he received back his rifle and accoutrements. Then the Beaver assured him of his hearty approbation of his daughter's conduct.

"I bear your people no grudge," he said, "although the red men have received many injuries at their hands. For that, however, I hardly blame them; they act the part of the strong against the weak, of the many against the few. The Great Spirit has willed it so. If the case were reversed, the red man would do as the white man does. I foresee the destruction of my race, and my heart is heavy at the thought; but I am too feeble to stem the current, and therefore ready to yield to its force. My people blame me for this; they set themselves against the progress of the white man, and in the foolish attempt fritter away their strength. They will kill a few, of course, but what does it all amount to? You cannot dry the ocean with a dipper, nor scrape down the mountain with the hunting knife. The white people are countless as the sand on the seashore, and the poor Indian must dwindle away before him—a few generations and you will see him no more."

The chief said these last words more to himself than to his young guest, who observed a respectful silence. After a few minutes the Beaver resumed:

"The Wild Rose has been the solace of my age. If you take her away I shall miss her very much. It is hard to think I shall no longer hear the sweetness of her voice, the silvery music of her laughter. Still I suppose it is all for the best; indeed I see in it the hand of the Great Spirit. The Wild Rose was not made for the wigwam of the red man; she would wither away like her namesake if plucked by his rough hand. But will she be better off among the pale-faces? Will the Yankee women not look down on her, the daughter of a chief? Will not my young friend finally tire of the Indian girl and repent of having taken her to his bosom? If I thought so 1 would sooner bury this scalping knife in her bosom, than let her depart from my lodge."

"Surely, the Beaver does not think so meanly of me!" the scout responded. "Has not the Wild Rose saved my life? Has she not bestowed upon me the most precious prize of her affection? No, indeed: the sun will sooner swerve from his path, than I from my fidelity to your daughter."

"So may the Great Spirit bless you as you are faithful to this vow!" the old chief said, with a voice so grave and solemn that his young hearers were deeply impressed. "But where do you intend taking the Wild Rose? They would scorn and scoff her in the Fort."

"I had not thought of it," Robert said, musingly. "All this has come upon me so suddenly, that I have hardly had a chance for reflection."

Now the maiden interposed.

"Will my friends listen to the counsel of the Wild Rose?" she asked.

"The pale-faces are at war with the Delawares now; but their enmity will not last forever. Robert has no wigwam for a squaw now; but when the war is over he will have one. The Beaver cannot spare his daughter now, because he wanders about from place to place, and has no one to prepare his food and fix his couch, if his daughter leaves him. But when the war is over he can come back to the banks of the Beaver, where the bones of his fathers lay buried. He can then spare his daughter, the Wild Rose, because he can live near his daughter's wigwam, and she can tend to his wants as before. Speak, is the Wild Rose right?"

"My daughter is very wise for one so young," the chief gravely replied. "What does my daughter propose?"

Robert asked no questions. His heart had already told

him the meaning of her words. He looked at her reproachfully; but the maiden smiled at him her sweetest smile, as if in that way she meant to ask his forgiveness, and then resumed :

"Why; if her husband cannot take her, and her father cannot spare her, what can the Wild Rose do better, than stay at present, where she is? Surely, the chief, her father, would not close his door against his daughter ?"

The smile stealing over and brightening the face of the Beaver was sufficient answer. Before he could reply in words, Robert exclaimed, half sadly, half reproachfully :

"Rose, you surely cannot love me, or you would not propose to leave me now! Is it fair to have shown me the garden of Eden merely to close its gates upon me ?"

The girl rose, and seizing his hand, knelt down before him :

"I not love you?" she said, with a deep convincing earnestness. "Have I not given myself to you before the whole tribe? Have I not violated the rules of girlish shyness to save your life? What must I do to convince you? Plunge your dagger into my heart, and expiring I shall bless the hand that struck the blow. Bid me leave my parent and my tribe, and I shall follow you to the uttermost ends of the earth. Oh ! what shall I do to persuade you ? I cannot make many words like the Yangeese girls ; but if you desire it, I can at any moment lay down my life for you. Scold me, abuse me, but oh ! never, never again doubt the fondness of the Wild Rose for her husband."

These words were uttered with an emphasis doubly impressive, because it was tempered with the sweet submissive resignation peculiar to the Indian female. On Robert it had a most powerful effect. He drew the kneeling form into his arms, and pressing it most fervently to his heart, merely murmured :

"Forgive me, Rose, forgive me."

The maiden gently disengaged herself.

"Will my husband now let me go with my father ?"

"Yes, Rose, I will. I will do anything you want me to do, for I am sure you are not only the fairest, but the sweetest and most sensible woman I ever saw."

The Wild Rose smiled. Savage or civilized, the woman that is not delighted to hear her praise from the lips of her lover, is yet to be born.

"I knew it," she said, emphatically, "for Robert is as good as he is wise—else he never would have gained my heart. But I hear the people getting ready for a start; will my husband shake hands with the Beaver, and allow the Wild Rose to accompany him a little distance on his journey to the Fort?"

"It is already time for me to start. Well, if it must be met, I'll meet it like a man. Good-bye, Beaver; you have won my esteem as well as my affection by your noble conduct towards me. You are but a poor Indian chief; but I am sure there are many potentates that may surpass you in power, but you outrank them in wisdom and goodness. Let us hope that we shall soon meet again, and that too, when the hatchet is buried between our nations, and these fair regions only echo with the shout of the huntsman and the chirping of the feathered tribes. Farewell to you!"

"Farewell," the chief replied, covering his emotion with the sternness of the Indian warrior. "May the Great Spirit smile on you and give lightness to your heart and strength to your body. Do not forget her, that now sacrifices her love to her duty, and who will never smile again except in anticipation of a re-union with her husband. In giving you my daughter, I have given you a priceless treasure; remember that and remember also, the vow you made before the Great Spirit."

Their hands united in a firm pressure, and then they parted. Wild Rose went with the hunter, and though there was not much danger of the couple being noticed by the Indians, bent upon early starting on their western journey, the maiden chose such by-ways as were least calculated to bring them in contact with the tribe. When they reached the forest, they wandered hand in hand, when the nature of the ground would permit it. Their hearts were too full and their thoughts too busy to speak much. The novelty of the situation might also add to their disposition to indulge in a pensive mood, and the fear of uttering the fatal word, "farewell," bind their tongues. Their hands firmly united, with now and then a loving glance into each others eyes, they wandered through the forest, until they put the distance of a mile between themselves and the village. Further than this Robert would not let his consort go. With a manly effort he suppressed all selfish feelings, and stopping suddenly, he said :

"Rosy, you must not go beyond this point. Much as it pains me to renounce the pleasure of your company, it would not be safe for you to tarry longer. The soldiers of the Fort are surely on the march, even now, and I tremble at the thought of your falling into the hands of these rude fellows."

"Her husband's will is law to the Wild Rose."

"Farewell then, sweet Rosy; will you sometimes think of your Robert ?"

"Wild Rose will have no thought but one."

"And will you endeavor not to tarry too long ?"

"I shall follow the tidings of peace as early as the wild swan does the arrival of spring."

"If I should not hear from you occasionally, Rosy, if peace delays too long, you may, sooner or later, look for my coming to your western home."

"My husband must not expose himself ; Red Feather is your deadly foe now. If you expose yourself to his fury, he will work your speedy destruction."

"I shall take care of myself. But, Rosy, is this separation really to be ? Can it be that you are to turn from me, and that in a few minutes I shall see your sweet face no more ?"

The maiden smiled encouragement.

"The Wild Rose can bear it—is her husband, the great scout-hunter, weaker than a woman ?"

"Ah! you are appealing to my pride? Well, then, of course I ought not allow myself to be outdone by a woman, though that woman be the bravest, cleverest of her sex. Farewell, Wild Rose of the Beaver, farewell, my own sweet darling."

The hunter drew her into a passionate embrace, which she returned with all the warmth of a nature unrestrained by the fetters of civilization. Seeing, however, that he would not summon the courage to tear himself away, she gently disengaged herself from him with the whole power of her affection shining on her countenance, and then turned to go, without looking back upon the youth whose fate had so suddenly become linked to hers. Robert gazed after her with a sharp sensation of pain, and if he had not been ashamed to betray before her a sign of so much weakness, he would have hastened after her and again clasped her to his heart. As it was, he admired her fortitude, but yet felt a pang of jealousy at the thought that her resolution had been greater than her love. At last he turned and plunged into the bushes with a haste, as if by physical exertion he desired to drown the throbbing of his heart, and the busy work of his brain. But this effort was not successful; in spite of his haste the lovely image of the maiden who had rescued him from death and assumed so intimate a relation with him, would not leave him; it adhered to him through the noisy scenes of a joyful meeting with his comrades, and was for many weeks the constant companion of his wanderings by the day and his dreams by night.

CHAPTER IV.

FORT MC INTOSH.

About two months after the above adventure several flatboats, or bateaux, could be seen approaching the landing at the foot of the elevation, on whose brow Fort McIntosh was standing. The garrison had espied them from their elevated position as they rounded the bend, which the Ohio describes in turning from a northwestern to the southwestern course, which it maintains to its junction with the "Father of Waters." Navigation, in those days, was not so brisk as at present, when the passing of the noisy steamer is a daily and even hourly occurrence, and the arrival of a bateau was the cause of much excitement at the Fort. Those of the garrison not on duty hastened down the covered way that led from the Fort to the river, and awaited impatiently the slow approach of the clumsy crafts, amongst whose merits speed surely was not to be enumerated. There were three of them, two laden with supplies for the Fort, and the third with a small detachment of soldiers and a number of other individuals, who had business at the Fort, and benefited by the safe escort of the expedition. Amongst them were also a couple of ladies, a sight calculated to create considerable curiosity and expectation amongst the men on shore, especially since one of them seemed to be young and handsome. This curiosity was shared by Anderson and Campbell, who both belonged to the crowd on the landing. The curiosity of the former, however, was destined to be turned into surprise bordering on consternation, when the older woman, on seeing the scout, ran up to him and, throwing her arms around his neck, began to cover him with the most affectionate caresses.

"Madam," he at last exclaimed, when he had succeeded in recovering his breath, "you are surely very kind; but still I do not understand you—you must surely be mistaken ?"

"Oh Dave, my dear, dear brother !" the woman exclaimed, reproachfully, "do you really pretend to not know your sister, your only sister."

The scout started. Holding her at arm's length, he said :

"Indeed, if I didn't know my sister Grace to be married and living in Philadelphia."

"Been living, Dave, you ought to say," the woman exclaimed, drawing forth a handkerchief and wiping away a solitary tear, which she had managed to press into the corner of her eye. "My dear good husband—pooh ! pooh !— is dead and buried, poor soul."

"He is—is he ?"

"Yes, Dave, and he left a poor, helpless widow, too. I had just enough to bury him and to travel across the mountains, and here I am, almost worn out with the hardships of this dreadful trip."

"Why, you look hearty enough, Grace; but you would not like to live here in this wilderness would you, Grace?"

"Alas! has a body a choice? What should we—poor Rose and I—do in the large city, without the means of livelihood?"

With these words she looked around at the younger woman, who had followed and stood behind her during this interview, a prey of confusion and embarrassment. When Anderson's attention was thus drawn to the girl, he started and evinced an emotion, which the meeting of his sister had thus far failed to produce.

"Why, Grace, you do not mean to say that this young woman is—"

In saying this he had taken a rapid step towards the girl; but, in consequence of his uncertainty, stopped both his words and motions.

"Indeed, Dave," Grace responded, with an eager tone and nod of her head, "she is nobody else but your own daughter, Rose, and a good, darling girl in the bargain, I assure you."

"And that you only tell me now, you silly woman!" the scout exclaimed, folding the hesitating girl into his arms. "My dear, my darlin' daughter stands near me without my arms openin' for a welcome! Alas, my poor Rose, many a year has passed since last my eye dwelled on your countenance. So 'tis no wonder that you have grown out of my sight. You have your mother's features though, Rose, and if I hadn't thought you far away, I would have known you after all. And so you have come to live with your old father in the wilderness?"

His tenderness had in a measure dispelled her shyness. Looking with a smile into his face she said:

"If you will let me, yes, dear father."

"Let you, of course I shall, I'd have called you here before this; only I was afraid you wouldn't like the wilderness. Say, Rosy, ain't you a little afraid of the red man and his scalping knife?"

"No, father, not as long as I am under your protection. They tell me the Indians stand in great awe of your skill and prowess."

"Tut, tut, it does not amount to as much as that. Howsomever, I should like to see the redskin bold enough to lay hands on your pretty curls, child. But we stand here gossipin' as if you had only come across the river. You must both be tired and hungry; so the sooner we get to our quarters the better you will like it, I reckon. Have you your trappings with you ?"

"Yes, brother Dave, these packages belong to us."

"Well, we'll shoulder them and then march up to the Fort. Robert will lend us a hand I reckon. Rose, this is Robert Campbell, a good friend and companion of mine. Shake hands with him, and you too Grace, for I want you to keep good fellowship with him."

The formality of introduction having been attended to, the company began to ascend the steep road leading up to the Fort. It was dug into the ground and then covered with brushwood as a protection in case of an attack by the Indians. Each scout loading himself with a large bundle and the women taking a smaller one themselves, they soon managed to reach the log house assigned to the use of Anderson. Hitherto Campbell had shared it with him; but the young hunter had cheerfully evacuated his apartment for the benefit of the new comers. The garrison never filled all the houses, as a surplus had been erected for outsiders in case of an Indian raid. In one of these Robert took up his abode, removing his arms and the few articles comprising his apparel and furniture. After that he returned just in time to act as guide and protector to Rosa Anderson, who was extremely anxious to explore the stronghold, which henceforth was destined to be her home. Her father had to make some slight alterations to suit the new character of the household, and, as his sister was anxious to unpack and arrange her clothes, neither of them felt disposed to join in the ramble.

"I am sure I have seen plenty of forts on the road," she said, "and between unpacking and getting supper ready—for I suppose that will be my business now—I hain't got a minute to spare, neither. So you must excuse me, Rosy. But if you ain't tired enough yet, and this young gentleman is willing to show you the sights—"

"Of course I will, madam, and with pleasure," Robert responded, and, leading the girl from the house, first conducted her along the inside of the works. It was of a quadrangular shape, the front being about doubly as long as the rear and the two sides cutting the former at acute angles of equal size. The front corners contained bastions, that were armed with a six pounder, while the balance of the enclosure consisted of strong palisades, about fourteen feet high. They were built bullet proof and built in a very ingenious manner. The requisite number of trees having been cut and split in the center, one row was erected with flat sides towards the interior, and so that a plank of the second row would cover a crevice in the first one. Iron nails being out of the question, the palisades were fastened together in a very simple but substantial manner by wooden pins. Nor did the buildings themselves show any more traces of iron. There were regular blockhouses with the roofs leaning against the stockades and slanting gently towards the interior, thus furnishing good standing places, from which the garrison could fire upon attacking foes through loopholes cut in the stockade. The center of the front stockade contained a small gate, which, together with the covered way, kept up the intercourse with the river. The interior of the fort consisted of a vacant square, lined by the blockhouses above mentioned, and containing a flag-staff, from which the stars and stripes were exposed to the breeze. This was the raw but serviceable fortification, called Fort McIntosh, erected only ninety years ago, which now has not only vanished from sight down to its very foundations; but also nearly from the remembrance of the town people living on its site.

The daughter of David Anderson examined everything with a scrutinizing eye, and the questions which she addressed to her companion, betrayed so much good sense that the girl rose from minute to minute in the estimation of the scout. That she was handsome, yes, even beautiful, he had noticed from the first : but the lively conversation in which the two engaged during the walk around the Fort, and the spark of intelligence kindled thereby in her eye, had the effect of considerably heightening this beauty. The young man was curiously affected by it. Not that his heart had evinced any sensation similar to that with which the Delaware girl had inspired him—no, this young stranger was more a subject for his reflections than his emotions. He could not realize that he had never seen her before ; her face was so familiar to him, and yet he raked his brain in vain to find the key to these queer imaginations. Perhaps the stories, which her father had, in long winter nights, related to his young friend, concerning his daughter, had been the cause of making her person familiar to the latter ; yes, this must be the case, for in vain did he search for any other solution of the mystery. This put him in a rather thoughtful mood, for he could not help recollecting how often Anderson had expressed it as his most ardent wish that his daughter and the young friend he so highly valued for his numerous good qualities, should become a couple. Formerly Robert had listened with much complacency to his proposition ; but his rencontre with the Wild Rose had, of course, changed his wishes in that respect. Thus far he had abstained from making his old and long tried friend a party to the new and sweet secret he had to hide ; but whether he was so reserved from reasons of prudence, or from regard for Anderson's feelings he had never accounted to himself. These former confidential communications of the father now, in a measure, influenced his feelings for the daughter, and though he can hardly be said to have even in thought violated his .vow of fidelity given to the Wild Rose, he certainly looked upon the girl at his side with that partiality which we are apt to entertain for persons or things belonging to us. This girl might be his, if he only chose to ask for her, and, although he was fully resolved never to do this, it certainly gave a warmer expression to the glance with which he looked at her, a warmer shade to the feeling he entertained for her.

After finishing the circuit around the Fort they were just on the point of re-entering the gate when they saw a young officer approaching them, over whose face, at the sight of the girl, passed a bright smile of recognition. Robert was struck with the manly figure and handsome countenance of the young man, who must have come on the bateaux with the troops, for he was a total stranger to the scout. His form, though perhaps less developed and indicative of strength, certainly showed fine proportions, and the regular features of his face were lit up by an expression of more than common intelligence.

When Robert noticed the stranger's look he turned rather abruptly to the girl at his side, and observed on her countenance not only the reflection of the other smile, but—as he thought—also considerable confusion. What could this mean? They surely knew one another.

His train of thought was interrupted by the officer's arrival in their neighborhood. He stopped and, bowing to the girl, said respectfully:

"Ah, there is our fair companion from the bateau; have you reconnoitered your future residence?"

Instead of answering, the girl introduced the two to one another.

"Mr. Campbell—Lieutenant Saunders."

"Mr. Campbell," he said gaily, "I suppose I have the advantage over you, for I have already heard ever so much about you and your doings, while you, most likely, have never heard my name mentioned—simply because I have done nothing yet to make it. Still, if you'll have the goodness to initiate me into the mysteries of border warfare, I shall try my best to do credit to your instructions."

Campbell merely bowed assent, not that he lacked words to make a suitable reply; no, it was rather a vague feeling of antipathy which filled him against the attractive stranger, perhaps for no other reason but simply that he was attractive. I do not mean to say that Robert was conscious of any such unworthy motive, but I am equally sure that he made no attempt at all to account for his dislike. Human nature is far from being perfect, and I have no desire whatever to draw the model of a perfect man. Even the best are subject to errors, and if the reader, in his further intercourse with Robert Campbell, meets with traits, which he does not like, I hope he will not forget that I depict in these pages men as they are, not as they ought to be. The officer did not seem to be discouraged by this lack of cordiality, taking the other's silence perhaps for the backwoodman's unintentional diffidence. Rose Anderson, however, thought differently. Was it that her woman's perception had disclosed to her the nature of the scout's feelings, or that she herself was particularly interested in anything concerning the young officer: she cast at Robert a rapid side glance, at once imploring and inquiring. Perhaps he saw it; before he had time to make a reply either in signs or words, the Lieutenant again drew the attention of both upon himself.

"I have just received orders concerning my men," he said, "and must now attend to them. So you will please excuse me. The adage, 'business before pleasure,' holds good in the wilderness as well as in more civilized communities. My duties will probably fill the rest of the day; but to-morrow, Miss Rose, you will, I hope, allow me to call at your quarters, and make the acquaintance of Mr. Anderson, who interests me as much on your account as on his own. Until then, farewell."

This meeting at once changed the nature of the relation between Rose and Robert. Instead of the gay, talkative persons they had left, they returned thoughtful, even pensive, he wondering what this could mean, she, how much he could possibly have discovered.

When they reached the blockhouse, the two rooms of which it consisted had already assumed a very different aspect. A woman's hand was plainly perceptible, and to judge from the amount of work Mrs. Jones—Jones had been her husband's name—had accomplished during the short absence of the young couple, she certainly deserved the name of an efficient housekeeper. She was on the point of finishing her preparations for tea—tea to be taken in the true sense of the word—when her eye fell on her niece.

"Well, Rosy, just in time to lend a helping hand," she said. "Put on this apron, and wash the china cups and saucers we fetched along. We'll show these savages what a real supper means. I suppose you haven't tasted tea these five years, brother, eh?"

"You come well nigh the truth, Grace. Howsumever you needn't take all that trouble on our account; we are used to rough treatment."

"So much the more you'll appreciate a change. I'll

just put on a decent table cloth, although it strikes me it will never lie smooth on this table. I declare, it takes a good stretch of imagination to recognize it as a table at all."

"Well, well, I suppose it is rough enough, Grace, but many a good dinner has stood on it, and as to appetite—it was never wantin' to those that sat around it."

"And that is the main thing, Dave, after all. Well, I am ready, so please sit down and try what we eastern folks can do in the line of making tea. I suppose this young hunter will do me the favor to accept a cup?"

"Of course he will, Grace," her brother replied instead. "I want him to consider himself a permanent boarder in my house. He was kind enough to make room for you women in the way of lodgin', so it isn't more than fair that you should compensate him in the way of boardin'."

"Oh, no, David, I can never consent to such an imposition on these ladies."

"Oh, it won't be anything of the kind," Grace exclaimed. "It ain't a bit harder to cook for four than for three."

"That's what I think, sister Grace; moreover, let me tell you that it will be well for you to keep on good terms with friend Robert; for a better hunter never pulled a trigger in these woods. If you want a piece of venison all you have to do is to let him know it; he can get you a turkey or a fat buck at any time, providin' he has a mind to."

"Ah! if this is so, we must endeavor to steal ourselves into his good graces—musn't we, Rosy."

"My father's friends will always be mine, provided they care about the friendship of a plain and stupid girl like me."

"Miss Rosa underrates her own merits. Her mirror will tell her that she is not plain and—short as our acquaintance is—I'll warrant she is not stupid either."

"Well said, my boy, for one not used to the company of women. But it strikes me we have had enough in this line of compliments now, and had better proceed to somethin' more substantial. Sit down Robert, and you Rosy, for I see Grace is bound to do the waitin' part. Laws, me! It makes me think of olden times to sit at a civilized table and enjoy the company of women. If it had not been for the cursed Injuns, Rose, your mother might be with us and complete our happiness.''

"The Indians?" Robert enquired. "Why, David, you do not mean to say that Mrs. Anderson came to her death at their hands?"

"Indeed I do, my boy, for it is the sad, lamentable truth."

"And you never mentioned it to me before."

"Well, Bob, you may perhaps wonder at that. We two haven't many secrets from one another, and it wasn't for the sake of secrecy either that I never told you. Somehow it never came up between us, and then to tell the truth, it is a sore spot in my memory, which I am loth to touch."

"If so, David, excuse my inquisitiveness."

"Oh, never mind that now ; it has been brought up, and I may as well tell you and be done with it."

After swallowing the morsel he was chewing, and clearing his mouth and throat with a sip of tea, he said:

"It is now nigh on twenty years since this horrible affair occurred. We had left the country east of the mountains and settled in Bedford county to better our fortune and to get more land for the benefit of our children. We had only two girls then, but entertained the fond hope that Providence would sooner or later favor us with the birth of a son. Instead of that, however, I was destined to the cruel fate of losin' my whole family, save this one daughter, by the hands of the savage foe, that was then makin' inroads upon the settlements on all sides. Unfortunately I was away from home on business when the news of their comin' first reached me. Leavin' my business unsettled, I hastened home with all speed ; but only came in time to witness the fallin' in of my house, which the savages had set on fire after finishing their work of butchery."

He stopped, and his hearers likewise maintained a sympathetic silence. Rose seized the hand of her father, who, touched by its token of affection, stroked hers in turn. At last, arousing himself from the gloomy mood into which the sad recital had plunged him, he continued:

"When the fire had died out, we found the charred remains of several grown persons and children, showin' that some of the neighbors must have taken refuge in my house, only to fall there victims to the fury of the Injuns."

"And Miss Rosa, how was she saved?" Robert eagerly inquired.

"She happened to be out with sister Grace huntin' berries in the woods. To be sure she was too small to walk herself, bein' hardly a year old, but Grace would carry her, you know. The child was fond of blackberries, and in her imperfect way made known her wish that mornin' to have some. So Grace humored her, and went out with her."

"What a narrow escape!" Robert exclaimed.

"Yes, you may well say so, Mr. Campbell," Grace remarked. "I heard the tumult in the woods, and not knowing what to think of it, ran toward the house. Reaching the edge of the woods I saw the savages at work, and came near losing my presence of mind, you may well believe. Fortunately they had not yet discovered me, so I pressed the child closely to my heart and fled to a thicket, where I remained until the voice of my brother roused me. After that I did not stay much longer in these forests, you may rest assured."

"And yet you have now returned a second time in the neighborhood of such dangerous foes?"

"Well, what could I do? We were without support and protection, and as Rose was anxious to go to her father whom she had not seen these ten years, we joined a body of troops that was to cross the mountains, and in that way we managed to reach this fort in safety. I suppose there is not much danger of the Indians here?"

"No, not very much, I guess. Still you had not better venture out alone, for though there are not many redskins in the neighborhood at present, we catch a few prowling about every now and then."

"I guess you won't catch me going out. I have got enough of Indian develtries for one. You had better address your warning to this young lady. She is young yet and romantic, setting great store on views and sunsets and moonshine, and all the like of that."

David Anderson laughed, while his daughter blushed more deeply than the occasion seemed to warrant. The gathering gloom of night, however, protected her from discovery, and soon the remark of the widow was forgotten over other topics of conversation.

CHAPTER V.

A TRIAL OF SKILL.

Our frontier men of the last century led simple lives; they retired early and consequently rose in time, and, when on the morning following, the sun shed his first light on the woody landscape, his rays lit on the figure of a maiden that stood on the bastions and cast an admiring glance upon the beautiful view below. It is hard for us to imagine every trace of civilization away from a valley that now teems with villages, factories, farms and cultivated acres. Still at that time not a single house was in view. There were woods around the Fort with the exception of a narrow belt that had been cleared away to guard against surprise; there were woods on the plain, which now contains Phillipsburg, woods on the site of Rochester and Freedom—in short, woods as far as the eye could reach up and down the river. There was also a beautiful wooded island in the Ohio right opposite the mouth of Beaver Creek, and the southern bank projected much further into the river, whose water even in times of drouth never reached the low ebb of the present day. Perhaps the narrower bed was calculated to keep the channel deeper; perhaps the endless woods occasioned more rain; this much is certain, that the Ohio river deserved at that time much more than to-day the appellation of "La Belle Rivere" or the "beautiful river." The girl on the bastion took in the beauties of the scene with a dreamy eye, until an approaching footstep startled her and caused her to look back. It was the young officer who had addressed her at the gate the evening before, and the smile with which she greeted him, lit up a countenance which had lost every trace of reverie. She returned his "good morning" in a gay voice, and when he extended his hands for a friendly pressure, she gave him hers without hesitation. The young officer seemed delighted at this favorable reception.

"Ah, Rosy, I see now that you have not changed as I was afraid you would last night," he exclaimed. "When I saw you at the side of that young scout, blushing and stammering in confusion, I was afraid my fair companion of the journey would be lost to me. Indeed, Rosy, if I had not been afraid to make a scene before this stranger, I might perhaps have taken you then and there to account."

"And it is very well you didn't, Mr. Saunders," she said, archly, "for if you had, I surely should not have recovered from my blushing and confusion yet."

"But what is this young man to you? How does it come that you explore the fort in his company the very minute after your arrival?"

"Who should he be but my father's friend?"

"And not your own?"

"You do not expect my father's friends to be his daughter's enemies?"

"Rose, do not avoid my questions, for I assure you I am very much in earnest."

"No, I hope you are not, William, or you would deserve a good lecture for your want of faith. This morning is so bright and cheering that I am inclined to look at everything from the bright side too. Come, tell me, you were merely joking."

"Well, even if I would, I somehow can not get this young hunter out of my mind. He is a handsome, noble looking fellow, and when I met him first I was much prepossessed in his favor. Your embarrassment, however, changed my notion, and I now look on him a good deal in the light of a rival."

"Why, it seems you are actually in earnest, William," she said, reproachfully. "I do not know what I have done to deserve this suspicion of yours. Perhaps I was wrong in giving such a ready hearing to your protestations of affection; for you now seem to think I might as readily listen to another as I do to you. This is indeed a proper punishment for my forwardness; only from you it comes with rather a bad grace."

"Rose, dear Rose, you wrong me," the young man said, earnestly. "I do not doubt your faith; but might not this hunter be my rival against your wishes? He is your father's friend, and as such—"

"My father is no tyrant to compel my inclination. Mr. Campbell is indeed his friend, and if a wish on my father's side to see him and me united constitutes him your rival, he may indeed deserve that name."

"Did your father really hint such a wish?"

"Not exactly, but he intimated last night after Mr. Campbell had retired, that the girl who could secure him for a husband would indeed have reason to congratulate herself."

"But you, Rose—I hope you contradicted such an unwarrantable assertion."

"Indeed, I did not; for I have seen enough of this young hunter now, to know that my father is right, provided the affections of both parties meet half way."

"And this proviso?"

"Is wanting. My affection happens to be fixed on a young military gentleman of rather fitful moods, and as for him—"

"Well, as for him?" the lieutenant exclaimed, eagerly.

"Oh, I merely meant to say, that thus far, no word or even glance of his face has intimated a desire of entering upon a nearer relation with your humble servant."

"Ah, Rosy, your statement greatly relieves me. Just let me have a little time to gain your father's good will, and I shall not fear a dozen rivals."

"But that task will not be a very easy one; don't forget what aunt Grace told us about his aversion to military men in general. Much as he venerates the rifle and the hunting knife, the musket and the sword are weapons he despises. I have heard that from his own lips, short as our meeting has been."

"Well, this is a deplorable defect in a man of whom I have heard so many commendable qualities. Still, I trust that he may be persuaded to make exceptions, and allow me to come in as such. How soon—"

A hasty exclamation of Rosy caused him to stop. "My father!" was all the girl exclaimed, and turning around the lieutenant saw a man approaching, whom the reader has met before, but who would have been a stranger to the officer, if Rosa's exclamation had not given him a clue. The face of the new-comer was rather morose, in spite of the respectful mien of the soldier and the sweet maiden. There is no knowing what he might have said, if permitted to start the key of the coming conversation, but his daughter, fearing a rude remark which might have made the hoped for understanding between the two much more precarious, hastened to anticipate him.

"Good morning, dear father," she said, running to meet him, and giving him an affectionate kiss. "I thought you were early risers here; but yet it seems that it does not require much exertion on the part of a town girl to beat you."

"Oh, perhaps you had extra inducements, Rose, and I think I see them. You surely must have plenty of leisure, or you wouldn't begin to form acquaintances so early in the morning !"

There was a thrust at the soldier, and Rose hastened to ward it off.

"Form acquaintance, father? Why, you would not think your daughter forward enough to gossip with strangers in so public a place, and at this time of the day! No, father, this gentleman is not a stranger; it is Lieutenant Saunders, who accompanied us all the way from Philadelphia, and to whose untiring courtesy we, in a great measure, owe the satisfaction of having reached this Fort without much detriment to limb or property. When I saw him this morning I could not resist the temptation of showing him that our gratitude had not ceased with the necessity of his attention."

"In that, child, you were but right; indeed I give my thanks to this gentleman for any favors he has shown you and your aunt. If he wants any assistance in my line, he has only to apply to David Anderson."

"I thank you, sir," the Lieutenant replied, "and shall not fail to benefit by your offer. My ignorance of the woods is only surpassed by the love I bear for them. I would therefore consider it a great privilege to be allowed to serve my term of apprenticeship under your direction."

"Well, if that is all, you can be accommodated," replied the scout, whose feelings of animosity against the young soldier had considerably abated since the avowal of his great partiality for the woods.

"I suppose you have supplied yourself with everything belongin' to wood-craft before leaving for the west?"

"Yes, sir, I have everything complete. Among other things, I boast of a rifle, which surely cannot be surpassed in all the frontiers."

"That is sayin' a good deal, Lieutenant," but I am not the man to contradict another without a show of reason. I shall be prepared to confirm your statement or dispute it, as the case may be, as soon as I have seen the gun."

"If that is all," the Lieutenant said, with a smile, "it will only take me a minute to produce it. I am really anxious to learn the opinion of so good a judge."

"Well, sir, if you will fetch your piece, I shall not withhold my judgment, I assure you. I am fond of seeing and trying rifles of uncommon merits."

The officer left them and in a few minutes returned with a rifle of exquisite workmanship. The stock was richly carved and the lock engraved with figures and implements of hunting. Anderson examined it with evident pleasure, although he took good care not to betray it.

"Fine workmanship, to be sure," he said, with a mien half admiring, half doubting,"but the finest guns are by no means the best ones. Did you ever try this rifle of yours?"

"Yes, sir, but only a few times. I have another for common use."

"But you have no objections to let me try it?"

"Not the least, sir. On the contrary, I am rather anxious to see what such a piece can do in hands like yours."

"Then let us go to work at once. I see the piece is loaded, and I would rather have you fire the first shot yourself. I am never sure of my aim unless I ram the bullet home myself."

"Well, as you please, Mr. Anderson. It makes no difference whether my want of skill leaks out a little sooner or later. What do you want me to fire at ?"

"Why, that matters little. Do you see that crow sitting in the tree about a hundred yards from here?"

"I do, sir."

Without further parley the young man raised the rifle, aimed, and fired. The woods echoed with the report, and the crow, after fluttering for a second with a broken wing, dropped from sight into the foliage below.

"Well done for an Eastern and a military man. You must pardon my bluntness; but my experience has taught me that the handling of the musket generally spoils a fellow for the rifle."

"But my weapon is the sword and not the musket," the Lieutenant said, with a smile.

"Yes, yes, I know, and didn't at all mean to detract from your merits; but what I said is nevertheless true. I have found but few officers who could boast of being even ordinary shots."

"But Mr. Saunders is an exception, father, is he not?" Rose inquired.

"Well, yes. For an officer he handles the rifle uncommonly well. But here, it is ready for a second trial; it is my turn to shoot now, and yours to set the mark."

"Exactly, and I shall choose one worthy of your skill. Down yonder towards the right stands an old decayed peach tree with one solitary fruit on the topmost branch. I know that I could not pretend to hit it, and if you think—"

The report of the rifle interrupted him. While talking he had looked at the peach in question, and therefore lost sight of Anderson's movements. The scout had lifted the gun carelessly and pulled the trigger, apparently without taking aim at all. Yet when the Lieutenant looked in the direction of the peach tree again, in order to ascertain the result of the shot, the fruit had disappeared. Rosy told him with a gay laugh that the bullet had sent it flying in every direction.

"It was a pity, too," she said, "and I could almost have wished that father had missed it. Peaches don't seem to be over plenty here—in fact, it's a mystery how they come here at all. The peach tree is not a native of these parts!"

"No, child," Anderson replied. "In former days there was a French-Indian town a little way below here, and from that time to ours the trees seem to have seeded themselves, as we find them all over the neighborhood. So you need not fret about that peach. If you coax Robert Campbell a little, he'll go with you no doubt, and give you a chance to gather a basket full. There, he's comin' now, as I thought he would, for he cannot hear the crack of a rifle without feelin' an itching to be present."

The young hunter was indeed seen walking up to the group; but he evidently did not come from his bed. The wet condition of his moccasins and leggins, and a fine turkey dangling from his hand to the ground, betrayed an early excursion in the woods. His face was all aglow, and he greeted the company with genuine good humor. Depositing the game at the feet of Rosa Anderson, he said:

"I heard this fellow gobble in the woods, and could not resist the temptation of stealing out to make him pay the bill for his own music. I suppose Miss Rose has eaten many a turkey, but may be none of nature's own raising."

"Indeed, I have not," the girl responded, casting a glance of admiration at the large bird. "What a fine, big fellow it is. Did you expect to finish him in one sitting, Mr. Campbell?"

"Indeed, I do," he said, laughing, "we are not given to picking bones very clean here. But what is going on here? I heard several shots while on my way back to the Fort."

"Your ears did not deceive you, Robert, and here is the piece we fired from. What do you think of it?"

Robert took the rifle with an admiring glance. Handling it with the same ease which a lady evinces in playing with her fan, he examined all its parts with the eye of a judge. After listening to the sharp click of the lock, and raising the stock repeatedly to his cheek, he said emphatically:

"Perfect, as far as I can see; this is indeed a splendid gun. Are you the lucky owner?"

"Yes sir," the Lieutenant replied. "Mr. Anderson has used it, and pronounced it good. I should be pleased to have you also try it, and confirm his judgment."

"What have you shot at?"

"A crow and a peach," the Lieutenant replied. Anderson shook his head.

"You oughtn't to have told him, Lieutenant," he said, laughing. "I know he will laugh at us. He'll consider that child's play."

A barely perceptible smile had indeed played around Robert's lips at the mention of the above words, but checking himself he said:

"I don't know about that, David. To hit a crow or a peach may be a difficult task, and again, a very easy one. Miss Rose, do you see anything that would justify the wasting of a bullet?"

"Oh, yes sir, I do. A good piece beyond the peach tree stands a large tree with little balls on?"

"You mean the sycamore—I see it."

"Well, on the branch standing out against the river I see a single ball, quite away from all the others. If you can hit that, I shall be inclined to credit all the stories the people tell each other about your skill in shooting."

This was said in a tone in which a trace of defiance was barely perceptible. The young girl was probably somewhat nettled at the skill manifested by these foresters, because they showed themselves much superior to one in whom she felt a deep interest. She forgot that the young officer would have come out victorious in a dozen other trials, and that he merely practiced as pastime what the others followed as a profession. It annoyed her to see him appear in an inferior character, and it was this undoubtedly that gave a touch of animosity to her words. Robert seemed to notice it, for he cast at her a wondering glance that made her blush. Then he raised his rifle with the determination to disappoint her, for he seemed to feel instinctly that a failure would have gratified her. Raising the rifle slowly and carefully, he pulled the trigger at the moment when the ball came into the line of vision. A shout of admiration from the bystanders proclaimed his success. Even in Rose it overcame the previous feeling of annoyance, and the Lieutenant could not tire of lauding his extraordinary skill.

"I must confess, this goes beyond my comprehension," he cried, "and I would give a great deal to emulate such skill."

"Oh, this is nothing, sir," Anderson exclaimed. "I have seen Robert split a dozen bullets on the blade of his knife, at the distance of a hundred yards."

"I believe it, though I fail to comprehend it."

"It is pretty hard to comprehend ; but difficult as it may appear, Lieutenant, the true grit of a man is only tested in the contest with another man, especially when that man happens to have a copper-colored skin, and there it is, where the merits of friend Robert shine in their true light. I tell you—"

"I tell you, David, that it isn't becoming in a white man to brag about himself, or his friend either." Robert interrupted him. "So, if you cannot desist, I'll go home, and help your sister get the coffee ready—I see her beckoning over yonder with all her might."

Anderson laughed.

"Well, you shall have your way, Robert," he said, "so don't go away without giving us another token of your skill. I wish you could show these people how you pick away a dusky Indian from behind a tree, when you see no more of him than what a copper cent would cover ; but as that cannot be, shoot at least somethin' that has life. Bring down one of those gulls that skip about the river.

Robert looked at him with a searching glance.

"Now, David, if I did not know you well, I might harbor the thought that you would catch me in a trap. To hit the sycamore burr is child's play, when compared with the shooting of a gull. They are nothing but bones and feathers, and I verily believe a bullet might strike through the center of their body without hitting a vital part."

"Why, makin' a speech !" Anderson exclaimed, while a smile of satisfaction passed over Rose's face. "I know well that the shot is a ticklish one; but I know also that you have made it a dozen times, and never failed. What then, in the name of goodness, are you afraid of?"

"I am not afraid, David, and shall try the shot; but as it is one where chance may sometimes play us a trick, I thought it but fair to save my reputation by giving you a fair warning. Give me a solid mark, and I am pretty sure to hit it ; but these gulls are most unsubstantial things."

During these words Robert had not been idle. He had carefully measured the powder, constituting the charge of the gun, and then rammed down the bullet in the most careful manner. The pan and flint were also subject to a close examination, and only when these measures of precaution had been taken, Robert cast his eye upon the river, and began to look for a fit object for the trial, to which the cunning of his colleague had exposed him.

"Look there !" Anderson exclaimed, "that white gull is almost on a level with us."

Robert shook his head. The uniform color of the bird offered a mark of insufficient distinctness. So he left the gull undisturbed, and waited until a second one with black wings and a white body made his appearance. This was at least fifty feet further than the first one, a circumstance to which Anderson called Robert's attention, when the intentions of the young hunter became manifest. He merely smiled, then raising his gun he aimed and fired in the previous manner, and with the same startling success. The gull did not flutter, as wounded birds sometimes seem to do, but ceasing its flight at once, dropped dead in the water with a splash that penetrated even to the ears of the party on the bastion.

"Well, I won't say anything after this," Anderson exclaimed.

"No, I think myself you had better not," Robert said, laughing heartily ; at least not before breakfast, for Mrs. Jones is making such speaking gestures of impatience, that I, for once, lack the courage to continue here against her wishes. This turkey must help me make my peace with her, so good morning to all !"

CHAPTER VI.

A SCUFFLE WITH BRUIN.

Life in the Fort was so monotonous, that a few weeks
sufficed to initiate the two women in their duties, and also
disclose to them the scope of all the pleasures which they
could reasonably expect. Grace positively refused to leave
the stockade, and was therefore reduced to the pleasure,
which a woman can find in the fulfillment of her duties,
and the intercourse with those whom destiny throws in her
way. Rosa fared a little better. Her father, in consequence
of his frequent scouting expeditions, would know tolerably
well when a walk in the woods was fraught with danger,
and when not ; but even under the most favorable circumstances she was strictly forbidden to leave the Fort, when
duty or other circumstances prevented Robert from accom-
panying her. Lieutenant Saunders had repeatedly prayed
for the removal of this restriction, but to no purpose. Anderson told him that he did well enough for an officer, and
would no doubt, sooner or later, make a right good fron-
tiersman. At present, however, he thought the Lieutenant was more serviceable within than without the Fort.

"A man that has lost two members of his family by
Indian develtries is not apt to expose his child to a like
danger," he said.

"But, Mr. Anderson, if there is really any danger in
going to the woods, you ought not to allow your daughter
to leave the Fort at all."

"Nor would I under ordinary circumstances ; but with
Robert Campbell I verily believe there is no danger, whatever. I never knew the Indian that did succeed in creepin'
within fifty yards of him, and he not aware of it. He must
have the power of scentin' them, else I am at a total loss to
comprehend it."

Thus, if Rose wanted to visit the woods she had to do
so in the company of Robert or stay at home. Now, she
could not deny that, under ordinary circumstances, this
would have been a very disagreeable condition ; for she

was compelled to admit that among her male acquaintances,
of the past or present, few could compare in point of beauty,
character or skill in their vocation with the young hunter.
Unfortunately there was another youth near, however, who
possessed her affections, and therefore in her estimation
outranked the other in every accomplishment, excepting
the use of the rifle.

The fact, that to him her father would deny what was
granted to the other without petition, was calculated to
produce antipathy, which otherwise would hardly have
existed. If Rose, nevertheless, continued to accept the attention of the scout, it was partly because her desire of
being out was stronger than her dislike, and partly because
she managed to draw her lover into the participation of a
pleasure, which she was prevented from enjoying with him
alone. That the relation between Campbell and Saunders
did not improve under these circumstances may be readily
imagined. A person not initiated in the customs of the
frontier might deem it strange that we speak of any intercourse at all between an officer and a mere scout, a character
somewhat resembling the light skirmishers of the present
day. Yet so important was this in a war with the wily
Indian, and in such high esteem were the occupants of it
held in estimation, that an officer was hardly thought to
lower himself by associating himself with the hunter and
the scout, especially, when as in this instance, the universal affection and esteem of the garrison was centered on the
man. Saunders, as we have seen, regarded the scout in the
light of a rival, and, in a certain sense, with good reason.
He knew from Rose that her father had made repeated
allusion concerning his desire for a connection between
her and Robert, and his announcement that his hints had .
lately gained in pointedness and frequency, was not calculated to diminish his uneasiness. True, he had no reason
to doubt Rose's fidelity ; but there was no telling what the
stern dictate of an unyielding father might accomplish.
Thus far Campbell had borne himself with commendable
moderation ; but the fear that he might sooner or later
benefit by the advantages of his position, not only tor-

mented the Lieutenant, but also blinded him in a measure
to the merits of his indulgent rival.

And Robert? He labored all the while under a confusion of sensation, which prevented him from understanding himself and makes it, therefore, surely excusable in us,
his biographers, to labor under the same difficulty. Of one
thing he was sure—the affection for his Indian bride, though
deeply buried in his heart, had not only not lost its itensity ;
but even gained in ardor. Perhaps the very necessity of
this secrecy was instrumental in keeping the recollection of
the lovely Delaware girl so bright in his bosom. We have
already stated that the frontiersmen held the Indian in su-
preme contempt, and that the mere announcement of a
nuptial connection with a girl of that race would have
exposed Robert Campbell to such an amount of raillery as
to make his position entirely untenable. In his first
enthusiastic acceptance of the fair girl's proposal, he had
not thought of this difficulty ; but on reaching his friends
and comrades he became aware of it, and praised the
thoughtfulness of the Wild Rose, which had indeed deprived him of the pleasure of her company, but also saved
herself from many a painful collision, which even he could
not have totally averted. True, white men would in many
instances associate with Indian women, without the formal
ceremony of matrimony ; but Robert, on the one hand, was
too pure for such a practice, which, from the ignorance of
the civilized habits on the part of the Wild Rose, might
have been practicable, and on the other, he bore too deep
and ardent an affecrion for that maiden to insult her
memory by even the thought of such a step. No, she was
too pure and lovely to be drawn into the mire of the world,
and while he rejoiced in her good sense that had given him
time to make the necessary preparations for her reception
to his heart and bosom, he was fully resolved to give her in
his future home the sacred position of a Christian wife.

While these feelings continued in the deeper current of
his heart, others of a rather contradictory nature floated on
the surface. They had all sprung from the arrival of Rosa
Anderson, the daughter of the man who up to the moment
of his recent love had held the warmest place in his heart.

He and Robert pursued the same vocation, hunted the same game, scoured the same woods for the same dusky foe, and in spite of their disparity of years, shared such a resemblance of opinions, hopes and aspirations, that a firm friendship must needs be the unavoidable result.

Rosa was the only object they had thus far not owned in common, and the desire of Anderson to see his friend and daughter united in wedlock, is sufficient evidence that he was willing to share with him the greatest treasure in his possession.

Before Rosa's arrival he had spoken about her only in general terms; but since this event his allusions had become so frequent and his hints so pointed that Robert labored under a constant embarrassment. He could not think of revealing to his friend his relation to the Indian girl, and consequently could not explain to him the impossibility of listening to his proposals. So he simply contented himself with preserving a total silence on the subject, never dreaming that Anderson would construe this silence as diffidence and bashfulness, which could and must be overcome by frequent allusions to and conversations on the subject. In that way the situation of the young hunter became more embarrassing every day, for beside the rupture with Anderson, which a mutual explanation was almost sure to bring about, there was the dislike of the daughter and the jealousy of the Lieutenant. Rosa and her opinion were by no means indifferent to our friend. He had from the beginning conceived a liking for the beautiful and clever girl, which might have changed into love if he had met her before instead of after the adventure related in the first chapter of this story. We are creatures of circumstances, and the much talked of decrees of fate mostly dwindle into the results of circumstances, when we examine them through the microscope of truth. Robert imagined he discovered in the daughter of the scout a softer image of the Indian girl, her beauty, intellect and character tempered as it were by civilization. Even the name reminded him of the Wild Rose, and he loved to hear and pronounce it. He looked at the young girl in the Fort much as we look at a mirror reflecting the traits and features of one we love.

Under these circumstances we need not wonder that the young man conceived a warm affection for Rose, and was considerably nettled at the indifference she manifested towards him. Man is at best a strange enigma. While our friend feared, and endeavored to check the disposition of the father to bestow upon him the hand of the daughter, he was at the same time eager, in a measure, to win the daughter's good will, although her coldness increased just in proportion to his eagerness. He had a pretty accurate idea of the relation between Rosa and the Lieutenant, and he felt a pang of jealousy without loving her. Perhaps this was not fair, nor approaching the noble and exalted feeling we love to read about; but I repeat it, that I draw a picture, and that he who expects no dross in the composition of human nature, however noble, shows a sad want of human knowledge. Robert did not love Rose Anderson, but he would not have objected to have been a little loved by her. Nor could he get himself to look with favor upon a man who ventured to aspire to something that had been set aside for him. Besides it was mortifying to think that Rose had bestowed her affection on the Lieutenant in preference to him, forgetting the all important circumstance, that she, like him, had fixed her choice before he entered into competition. Be this as it may, there is no denying the fact that Robert Campbell regarded the Lieutenant with rather an unfavorable eye, and the only thing we can say in extenuation is, that he was met more than half way by the latter. Rose saw the growing animosity between the young men, and in spite of the natural gaiety of her disposition, she could not help viewing the future sometimes with gloomy forebodings. Nor were her father's continual discourses on the merits of the hunter calculated to improve her humor, and so the six months following her arrival at the Fort were less fraught with comfort and happiness than everybody had anticipated. True the glorious season of the fall has many a pleasant walk into the forests.

Rose had witnessed the hunting of the turkey and the

deer ; she had with Robert alone, or occasionally in company of both the hunter and Lieutenant paid visits to the
old Indian town, situated about half a mile below the
Fort, and showing the ruins of many once substantial
houses. At some places the wooden walls were still standing, though ready to tumble at the slightest touch ; at
others nothing but the naked chimneys loomed from the
weeds and brushwood, telling a melancholy tale of the per-
ishable nature of everything emanating from the hand of
man.

The woods around the Fort abounded with wild fruit of
every description. Besides the peaches growing on the seed-
lings we have mentioned, there were wild plums and grapes,
and various sorts of nuts in the greatest abundance. Robert
and Anderson had made maple sugar in the spring, and a
considerable store of it being still on hand, Grace and Rose
tried their hands at preserving, the scarcity of jars alone
limited their industry in this direction. Anderson much
enjoyed the increased comforts of his household. He alone
seemed to be blind to the clouds gathering on the horizon of his domestic sky. When the tea which his sister
had brought with her was exhausted, he expressed such
regret that Grace was obliged to have recourse to such experience as her former frontier life had given her. She sent
her brother to the woods to gather a plentiful supply of
wild strawberry leaves, telling him that she intended to
dry them, and during the coming winter make tea of them,
strawberry leaves being an excellent substitute for the genuine article. It was amusing to see how readily he entered
into her plans, and if the members of the household had
been versed in ancient lore, the picture of Hercules spin-
ning at the feet of Omphale would undoubtedly have risen
before their vision. In his leisure hours he helped to lay
up great stores of nuts and fruit, and when Grace com-
plained of the scarcity of vessels for preserving purposes,
he went to the commander of the post and begged nim to
order, at the scout's expense, such a quantity of stoneware
to be brought down the river in the next flat-boat, that the
Captain wondered and laughed at his extravagence. This,
however, failed to annoy the scout, who probably thought

that two households would require supplying before long.

In Anderson's presence the whole family—in which we have to include Robert—put on their gayest faces. Grace, with true womanly instinct, would have soon divined the condition of her niece's heart and the state of affairs arising therefrom ; but Rose from the beginning had made her a confidant. Grace had, of course, shared the civilities of the Lieutenant on the journey, and consequently conceived a friendship for him, which induced her to receive the overtures of her niece with complaisance, and assume the character of a protectress of their love. Knowing her brother, and perceiving with a woman's instinct that an open avowal or direct opposition to his wishes would not answer, she managed, with considerable skill and seeming undesignedness, to advocate the interests of the Lieutenant. Nor had she a difficult task, for Lieutenant Saunders was in every respect a worthy young man , and as time passed away, the prejudice which the scout entertained against the order wore off in favor of the individual. He was glad to receive the Lieutenant in his house, for in the long and dreary hours of winter evenings the young man contributed his share to enliven conversation, by droll stories of his own eastern experience. They pleased the others in proportion to their novelty, and had about the same effect upon Dave Anderson, as the perusal of a book of fairy tales to the town-bred youth. Robert Campbell was more of a scholar, and consequently more proof against the intellectual charm of the Lieutenant, yet even he could not wholly resist the attraction, though the presence of the young officer would regularly make him taciturn. Rose, on the other hand, would brighten up on such occasions ; for then and there her lover appeared to a good advantage, excelling, as she thought, the other in wit, intellect and knowledge. It was easy for her to come to this conclusion, for Robert, as we have said before, consistently abstained from mingling in the conversation, excepting an occasional remark. This was not, however, from want of knowledge, for, like many of his profession, he had adopted it from choice, and only after having received the benefit of a good, earnest education. Since that, of course, he had not lost much of his knowledge in the rough, stirring life he led; but it is with a good education, as with the cutting of a diamond, that once accomplished its lustre will endure. If dust and dirt settles on the surface a good rubbing will remove them. Robert might, therefore, have easily competed with his rival, if he had only felt the inclination. Instead of that he remained silent, or at most said but little ; this little, however, being generally of a sarcastic nature directed against the Lieutenant, and calculated to widen the gap between them. Taking each of these remarks separately they seemed innocent enough, and Anderson enjoyed them, because they were uttered by his favorite against a man who was a member of the other order, which he considered with supercilious contempt. The Lieutenant, however, felt them keenly, and harbored them for final settlement, which, to all appearances, could not be delayed much longer.

Christmas had brought the usual festivities. and New Year their renewal. The men had brewed themselves a good glass of punch, and the women baked the customary cakes, and between the punch and the cakes, the fine turkeys, haunches of venison and smoked bear meat, our family had not only managed to enjoy themselves very well for the time being, but also taken softer feelings into the new year. Robert had been less sarcastic and more communicative, and when the Lieutenant, towards the end of January, proposed a common bear hunt, graciously gave his approval. The two hunters started soon after sunrise, with a couple of dogs. There was a layer of snow on the ground, just deep enough to show the tracks of the bear, in case he had been out during the night. His general abode was in a little cave situated about half a mile from the mouth of what is now called Brady's run. The Lieutenant had accidentally met him the day before while leading a scouting party of soldiers, that had been drawn out by a false alarm of Indians being in that neighborhood. The bear had taken to his heels and escaped into his den, where the Lieutenant had been obliged to leave him on account of pressing duties. It was the communication of these facts

that had brought about the expedition. The Lieutenant,,
as the one best acquainted with the abode of the animal,
led the way. It was a fine winter morning. The air·was
still and bracing, and the temperature just low enough to
keep the snow from melting. When they reached the ravine, into which the hole opened, the absence of all tracks
proved to a certainty that Mr. Bruin was safe at home.
The dogs got the scent and became restless, barking at the
hole. Robert told the Lieutenant to get his rifle ready and
then encouraged the dogs to enter. The two men took their
positions a little up and down the ravine, the opposite
ledge being too steep for even a bear to climb. Meanwhile
the dogs had kept up a furious barking, rushing in and out
of the cave in their eager endeavors to arouse and attack
their enemy. All at once the bark of one of them changed
into a howl, and the hunter saw him jump from the hole
in as great a haste as an injured leg would allow him.

"Now, watch, Lieutenant," Robert cried, "the bear has
broken Nero's leg. He is surely up, and I should not be
surprised to see him out."

The words had scarcely been spoken when two bears,
instead of one, trotted from the entrance of the cave, and, at
the sight of the hunters, began to growl in an angry manner. They saw that their retreat was cut off, and for a moment, seemed to hesitate as to the best course to pursue.
When, on a sudden, they wheeled towards the left, in the
direction of the Lieutenant, and tried to make their escape
down the run.

The ravine was rather narrow, and Robert began to
fear for the safety of the Lieutenant. He would gladly
have fired and thus dispatched one of the bears, but as they
turned their rear towards him, he could not reach a vital
spot with his bullet. At this moment the Lieutenant fired
and thereby, for a moment, checked the progress of the
animals. One of the bears was evidently badly wounded,
for he began to growl in the most savage manner, and, rising on his hind legs, marched towards the young officer
with his jaws apart, and his fore feet extended for a friendly
hug. The other bear imitated his example, thereby exposing the vital spot, where the neck joins the back. Quickly

the scout raised his rifle and fired, and the report had hardly died away when the bear fell, expiring almost at the same moment. Robert, however, took no time to examine him, for the other bear had meanwhile closed with the officer. Fortunately the man made no efforts to ward him off, or the wounded animal might have badly torn his shoulders in the attempt to draw him in a deadly embrace. Too brave to run, the Lieutenant had, on the approach of the bear, drawn his hunting knife and stabbed him in the belly. His want of experience, however, had caused him to miss the right spot, and the stab apparently had no other effect but to increase the fury of the animal. Hugging the Lieutenant, it endeavored to strangle him to death, and as the handle of the knife had broken off in the pressure, leaving the young man defenceless, there is no knowing how successful its attempts might have been without the interference of the scout. Running up to the struggling couple he drove his knife up to the hilt into the bear, piercing his heart, and causing him to relax his grasp almost instantaneously. In so doing he fell, drawing the Lieutenant to the ground. Robert, however, seized him by the arm and helping him to rise, inquired in an anxious tone whether he was hurt.

"No, I am not," replied the young officer, drawing a deep breath, "but I have an idea I soon would have been without your timely interference. I am indeed deeply indebted to you, and may congratulate myself for not having undertaken this adventure alone."

"Well, I don't know. If you had been alone, the avenue would not have been barred, and the bears would certainly have endeavored to give you the slip. The trouble was that we only looked for one bear, and yet found two. That was almost too much of a blessing."

"And what are we going to do with these fellows?"

"I think we had better skin and quarter them, and hang the meat in the trees. We can then, at our leisure, get assistance from the Fort to remove it."

"So we can. The men will be glad enough to get a chance at bear meat."

This programme was followed out, and from that day

a better understanding seemed to prevail between the two young men. There was no verbal explanation, nor did the connection ripen into a friendship. They spoke to one another occasionally, hunted together, and thus passed through the latter part of the winter more pleasantly than the first. The Lieutenant meanwhile perfected himself in the art of hunting and woodcraft generally, and more than once, by his aptness and docility, drew words of praise from the lips of Anderson, who seemed not only to have conquered his dislike, but even conceived a fondness for the young man.

When the first signs of mild weather showed themselves, the family made the most extensive preparations for the manufacture of maple sugar. In the leisure hours of winter Anderson and Campbell had cut and hewed troughs, destined to receive the sweet liquid, and their example had proved contagious to many of the soldiers. So when the sugar time arrived, the whole garrison was thrown into commotion. Hundreds of trees were tapped, and every kitchen of the Fort was stripped of buckets and kettles to carry and boil down the precious liquid, nature's spontaneous offering. The result was in proportion to the effort. Never before had so much sugar been manufactured in the Fort. The shelves of Anderson's kitchen showed large cakes without number, and as the first bateau coming down the river after the opening of navigation brought the ordered jars and jugs, the face of Grace shone with ecstasy of delight, and she was incessantly laying her plans for the preserving of immense quantities of every description of fruit attainable in that neighboroood. With these preparations and speculations time flew rapidly, and before the family was fully aware of it, every vestige of winter had disappeared, and a thin veil of pale green began to adorn the woods. Spring always gladdens the heart of man, and so it could not fail that at its arrival the Fort assumed a gayer aspect. To increase the gladness of its inhabitants, the above mentioned flat-boat also brought the news of the surrender of Cornwallis. It was rather late, the surrender having taken place fully six months before; but that did not prevent the garrison from enjoying it as much. The six-pounder was fired, and the forest made to ring with its report and the cheers of the men. Everything bore the aspect of a holiday, and the commander ordered the rations of food and drink, common on such occasions, to be distributed. Our friends, the scouts, were in the afternoon summoned to his quarters, and there informed that General McIntosh would, in the course of the summer, establish his headquarters at the Fort for the purpose of making a treaty with the Western Indians. He told them that the six nations had already signified their readiness to attend the conference, and that by them word had been sent to the Delawares and Shawanese. These tribes would no doubt, sooner or later, send an answer to the Fort, and he charged the scouts to exercise the proper vigilance, in order to learn the arrival of a messenger, or ascertain the approach of a larger body of Indians in the neighborhood.

With these instructions they were dismissed, a circumstance reminding us of the propriety of also dismissing this chapter, in which the reader has only received the outline sketch of the winter's proceedings. Although void of exciting incidents, it shows the secret working of the sentiments filling the hearts of the principal persons of this story, and therefore could not well be left out without depriving the reader of the link connecting the adventures of the first chapters with others still in store, the narrative of which we now begin without delay.

CHAPTER VII.

AN EXCUSABLE MISTAKE.

It was in the early part of April when, at the break of dawn, Lieutenant Saunders left the Fort. He had the evening before obtained leave for a day's absence, without stating to anyone the nature of his errand. While out that day with a party of soldiers, some three miles up the river he had noticed the large footprints of an animal on the moist ground near the bank, and on inquiry learned from his men that they originated with a panther. A panther! He had never seen, much less hunted this animal, and the stories which the soldiers told about its ferocity and strength filled him with the burning desire to meet and conquer it. So when one of his companions told him that a thicket near the river, about two miles further up, was the usual abode of a large panther, he at once formed the resolution to go out in-search of it. In the bear hunt Robert Campbell had borne off the palm, while the Lieutenant had run the greatest risk, and in order to avoid a repetition of this undesirable division, he resolved to keep the risk and the glory both for himself this time. However, as he had an idea that the reaping of glory was by no means a certain thing, he resolved to keep his intentions a secret until he could exhibit the skin and the claws of a panther as a trophy.

Once out of the stockade he pursued his way through the woods and along the banks of the Beaver as rapidly as possible, only followed by an old half lame dog, the same that had been used so badly by the bear, and since that encounter conceived a strong affection for the officer, perhaps in return for the kind nursing which he had then received at his hands. Silently the two followed the river bank until they passed the rapids. Then the former carelessness of the Lieutenant changed into vigilance, and looking carefully around for tracks resembling those he had noticed yesterday, he slowly proceeded on his way. The dog had by this time taken the lead, but for a considerable time failed to give signs of any game whatever, when all at once he stopped, and, with an eager growl, turned to a small thicket standing on a sharp bend of the river. Being flanked on two sides by the stream, and on the third by a small inlet or bayou, the small thicket was only accessible from the fourth, a narrow strip of land containing nothing but a few large trees. As the Lieutenant was standing on this strip he entertained the well founded hope to cut off the retreat of the game, provided the alarm of the dog was not a false one. True, the panther—if such it was—could leap into the river ; but the water was deep and the current rapid, and if the panther possessed only a small amount of the strength and fierceness awarded him on all sides, there was but little danger of his attempting a retreat without a show of fight.

The dog meanwhile approached the thicket with growling signs of an angry excitement, until he reached the dense undergrowth. There he barked furiously without, however, advancing any further, in spite of the encouraging words of the Lieutenant. At last the young man grew impatient.

"Well, you stupid brute," he exclaimed rather angrily, "if you can not chase him out, I suppose I will have to do it myself. So stand aside, Nero ; stand aside, I say."

The game held at bay in the thicket seemed to be capable of understanding these words, for no sooner had the Lieutenant ceased speaking them, than the bushes were pushed aside and a figure stepped into the more open neck, which made the young officer start in surprise. He came to hunt a panther, and now stood before him the human panther of these woods, infinitely more dangerous than the four-legged animal—"the dusky, savage Indian."

This was the first time Saunders had stood face to face with a hostile Indian, and on the first discovery he felt much inclined to raise his gun and without ceremony dispatch so dangerous an adversary. Still the Indian seemed so perfectly harmless—it was a youth of not more than sixteen summers—that the officer again dropped the barrel of his gun, merely keeping it in readiness for an emergency. The Indian was not armed, or, if so, had concealed his weapon from sight. With a wave of his hand and a gracious smile on his countenance, he saluted the white man, saying in broken English :

"Me good Indian—my brother no shoot."

"Brother? As, yes, exactly, I recollect that you are all one great big family out here. Brother let it be then, and if one of your propositions is correct, I suppose the other will not be far wrong either. You look young and innocent for it, anyhow."

The Indian seemed merely to have understood a part of the last sentence ; at least he replied to it only.

"Me no young," he said, gravely ; "me young warrior now—great warrior soon !"

"Granted, Mr. Indian, as contradiction is a violation of good breeding. Yes, sir, granting all that, I might take the liberty perhaps of asking you the question: What are you doing here?"

"Me here home; this Indian's land," he said, with considerable emphasis.

"Aye, aye! that assertion can hardly be gainsayed. But then having forfeited your claims by emigration, I must repeat the question: What are you doing here?"

The Indian saw from this repetition that his reply was not satisfactory. So shrugging his shoulders, he said very coolly: "Me take a little walk."

"Little walk? Why I know no Indian settlements twenty miles around here."

"Was not, but will be! Indian come make peace."

"Ah, is that the way! Still your people would hardly choose so young an envoy, would they?"

"No! Indian no send me. Old man on way—me come alone."

"That's what I expected. But you have not answered my question yet; if you cannot satisfy me as to your intentions, you must follow me to the Fort."

This the youth did not relish. He shook his head, saying eagerly: "No Fort! me good Indian, good friend of white man!"

"Of course you say so—still I am doubtful whether I can believe you."

"Yes, believe. Me friend, me run if like?"

"I guess not, my friend," the Lieutenant replied, drily. "My gun would soon put a stop to that."

"No, no, leaves thick, water deep. The Red Fox creep and swim. He gone much long, if wanted."

"And why didn't you then, my good friend?"

"Yes, good friend! much good friend. Me see brother, me like him. So come out, speak, shake hands."

With these words and a genuine smile on his regular, well proportioned features, he stepped nearer to the other and extended his hand with so much good grace and unmistakable uprightness, that the Lieutenant felt ashamed to show any more distrust. He received and shook the young Indian's hand and said :

"My young friend is welcome. Has he any of his people with him ?"

"No, Red Fox all alone. Him sly and cunning. Him creep through little hole."

"Well, I guess so ; but have you no gun with you ?"

"No, me take no gun. Me see big game, me want shoot !"

"And why shouldn't you shoot ?"

"Too much white man, not all good, some bad. Hear Red Fox shoot—come, take scalp."

"Well, yes, that might be the case. But, tell me, Red Fox, have you seen no sign of a panther here?"

"Yes, me kill one."

"The deuce, you did ! How could you kill a panther without a gun ?"

"Me knife, stick him in belly now."

With this he pointed to the thicket.

"In there ?" the astonished officer inquired. "You are making sport of me."

"No sport—all earnest. Come see !"

After this laconic invitation he stepped into the bushes, and parting them, exposed to view the body of a full-sized panther, which had evidently come to death by wounds inflicted with a knife, still sticking in the body.

"And you are not even wounded ?"

"No wounded—just scratched," he said, with a smile, exhibiting a gash on his arm, for which many a dandy of modern times might keep his bed for weeks.

"An ugly scratch, indeed, my boy," said the Lieutenant, with much more sympathy in his voice than before. "Come, let me bind it up a little better ?"

. The Indian seeing the kind intent, at once offered his arm, which the Lieutenant bandaged as well as he could. This done, he said : "You are a fine lad, that's sure, and I hardly know whether I am more pleased with your bravery, or vexed at your interference with my calculations. Are there no more panthers about here ?"

"Not very near; but me give skin to Blue Coat; me only want claws."

"Ah, you are smart enough, I see. You can more safely brag with the claws than with the skin. However, I accept your present, and may as well proceed without delay to secure it."

The Indian helped the Lieutenant, and in a few minutes they had severed the skin from the carcass. It was bleeding some yet, and so the young man hung it on the low branch of a tree to let the blood drip off. This required some time, and the walk having sharpened his appetite, he seated himself on an old log lying close by, and inviting the Indian to his side, offered him a portion of his breakfast. The Red Fox accepted the bread and steak with a good enough grace; but the Lieutenant's flask, with whiskey, brought a perfect radiance of happiness to his face. When Saunders saw it, he at once handed the bottle to his new friend, who put it to his mouth, and emptied it of part of its contents with a readiness, showing either considerable skill or great relish. When the Lieutenant noticed it, a thought struck him. Receiving the bottle from the Indian's hand, he merely pretended to take a dram, leaving, in reality, the whole contents to the Indian, who managed to finish it in the very short period of fifteen minutes. It was good, strong whiskey, and as the flask contained fully a pint, the young Indian soon began to show signs of a growing intoxication. For this the Lieutenant had only waited to draw from him any secrets he might possess, and would never reveal in any other mood.

"What tribe did you say you belonged to?" he began to ask.

"Me Delaware, great nation, grandfather of all Indians."

"Exactly, but you came here for a purpose, did you not?"

The Indian endeavored to look very cunning, but only succeeded in looking very stupid : "Me go see white brother at Fort."

"Ah, then you have acquaintances there! Who is it you know there?"

"Me know Big Jump, great warrior."

"Big Jump ! Who can you mean ? I don't know any such person."

"You not know? Big Jump, jump creek, twelve, twenty foot ?"

"When ?"

"Long while, then snow not yet on ground."

"Ah, now I know. I guess you mean Robert Campbell, the scout ; I heard he leaped across a creek in trying to escape from the Indians last year."

"That him, that him ; him great warrior !"

"You are right there, my lad."

"He have fine squaw, too ; take Wild Rose to his wigwam."

"Take whom ?"

"Wild Rose ; you know, too."

"I know a Rose, to be sure, though as to wildness, I can't see much of that."

"Rose very beautiful."

"I readily subscribe to that."

"She Big Jump's squaw soon."

"Indeed she won't !" the Lieutenant exclaimed, energetically. He knew only one Rose ; yes, it may be said in truth, for him there was only one Rose in existence ; so when the Indian spoke of Rose, he naturally thought him to allude to his Rose.. The reader may, therefore, imagine his surprise at the Indian's suggestion, and will not wonder at the vigorous denial of the statement. The Indian, however, did not suffer his opinion to be shaken or altered.

"Yes, him will ; Red Fox knows."

"How the deuce do you know ?"

"Me know, Big Jump love Rose."

"But how do you know it, stupid ?"

"Me see."

"See what ?"

"Big Jump take Rose and do so."

He made the pantomime of hugging and kissing.

"The devil he did !" cried the Lieutenant, who began to lose his temper. "Indian, you are dead drunk, or you would not talk such nonsense."

"Me sober ; me know what say ; Big Jump love Rose ;. soon take her to wigwam."

The officer looked blank. The Indian spoke with such positiveness that his faith began to be shaken.

"You mean to say that Campbell loves Rose ?"

"Me do."

"And hugged and kissed her."

"Me see."

"Well, now, my fellow, I hope you are prepared to prove what you say, or you might fare badly for your mysterious insinuations."

"Eh ! speak straight ; Red Fox not understand."

"I mean, can you prove what you say ?"

"What prove ?"

"Can you make my eyes see what you say ?"

"Yes, Red Fox can," the Indian said, eagerly.

"And how ?"

"My brother counts days ; one, two, three, four, five,. six—count six days."

"Well, what about it ?"

"Know big knob, three, four, five mile ?"

The Red Fox illustrated this question by pointing with his hand in a south-eastern direction.

"Big knob? yes, I think I do. A cone-like hill standing out from all the others."

"Yes, that him."

"But what has that hill to do with this thing ?"

"My brother go there—see Big Jump and Rose. See them one, three, six days."

"You mean six days from to-day ?"

The Indian nodded—the whiskey began to make him drowsy.

"At what time of the day ?"

"When sun stand there." ·

The direction intimated was the meridian.

"Six days from to-day then, at noon," the Lieutenant murmured to himself. "It is incredible, and yet this boy is so positive. It passes my comprehension how he should know, but I shall certainly not fail to act upon his hint.

I'll go to the place of rendezvous, and woe to him and her if
I find them."

Resting his head upon his hand and the elbow on his
knee, he preserved a mournful silence for more than half
an hour. Then recollecting himself, he rose with a sudden
start, and looking for his red companion, found him fast
asleep at the side of the log. The whiskey had done its
work in a double sense; but the officer had paid dear for his
information, thus extracted from the lad; so dear, that he
almost wished he had never obtained it. Without heeding
the panther skin, which the Indian had given him, he
gloomily wandered away, leaving the boy in a death-like
sleep. So deep indeed was the unconsciousness produced
by the fiery beverage, that the sun had well nigh completed its course when the sleeper awoke. He looked
around with a vacant stare, and in vain tried to obtain a
connected recollection of the morning's adventure. He
knew he had met a white man; he knew that he had drank
too freely of the dangerous fire-water, and he had a vague
idea that he had allowed his tongue to run at random. He
felt heartily ashamed of himself, for the Indian considers
the breach of trust one of the meanest of things, provided
the profession was not merely made as a ruse, to draw a foe
into a snare. Comforting himself at least with the idea that
he had revealed nothing of importance, and that the part
revealed would remain without serious consequences for
himself and his friends, he arose, and after adjusting his
simple toilet pursued his course towards the Fort.

It was night when he reached the brow of the hill from
which his eye could look on the plain on which the Fort
was situated. Fearing to draw too near in the darkness,
and knowing, moreover, that he could not then communicate with Big Jump—for such was his intention—he gathered himself some moss in a cluster of bushes, and stretching
his limbs on this rough bed, courted sleep to close his eye-
lids. But the nap during the day prevented the drowsiness, which usually besets us at break of night, and the
young Indian for several hours rolled restlessly about. It
was after midnight when he finally fell asleep, and so we
need not wonder that at sun-rise he still revelled in the

realm of dreams. The lad wondered considerably, when all at once he was recalled to consciousness by the rough contact of the stock of a rifle with his body.

"Get up, you vagabond," a voice sounded in his ear, causing him to spring to his feet with the rapidity of thought. A deep mortification filled his breast; twice within the space of a few hours had he suffered himself to be outwitted. If this leaked out to his Indian friends, would they not with contempt look upon him, so weak and unreliable a youth! Would they not hereafter refuse to even honor him again with any commission of trust and confidence? In consequence of these thoughts he preserved a sullen silence, not even looking at the man who had so roughly interrupted his sleep. A second inquiry uttered in a sharper tone, was necessary to make him raise his eyes. No sooner, however, had he beheld the person standing before him, when his mien of dejection changed, first, into one of wonderment, and then of joy.

"Ugh!" he exclaimed in his native tongue, "Big Jump."

"The Big Jump! Whom do you mean by such ambiguous appellation?"

"Yes, my brother is a Big Jump, he can leap the bed of rivers."

"Ah!" the other exclaimed, a smile stealing over his features. "You allude to the ticklish jump I made last summer. Well, I declare, I never thought that that leap would help me to a name, and such a dubious one. But I have it, and I suppose it will stick to me like pitch, so there is no use in trying to shake it off. But what are you doing here, my young friend?"

The reader understands already that the Big Jump is nobody but friend Robert. Obedient to the orders of the commander, he had as usual begun his morning round, and striking the Indian's trail, followed it to its terminus. This time the youth showed no hesitation in answering the question. Seeing in his neighborhood a bush of sweet briar in full bloom, he stepped up to it, and breaking off one of the flowers, with a smile presented it to the scout. Robert was too well versed in Indian customs not to interpret the meaning of the other in a moment. A joyous expression flew over his face, and making a rapid step toward the Indian lad, he said rapidly, and with emphasis: "The Wild Rose! It is she that sends you!"

"Big Jump is a great warrior. He jumps the beds of rivers; he follow the trail of the red man like a hound; he hears the message of the Wild Rose far off; he has spoken the truth; the Wild Rose sends the Red Fox to her white friend, the Big Jump."

The boy smiled.

The sensitive ear of Robert no longer shrank at that dubious name; in his estimation he had never heard a sweeter voice than that of the messenger while making his statement. He grasped the hand of the lad with a friendly pressure, and said: "My young friend, the Red Fox, is very welcome. It is well he has fallen in with his friend, the Big Jump, or he might have got into difficulties."

Now the Indian took great care not to reveal the disagreeable blunders of the day before. It suited him better to boast before the Big Jump, and so he did boast.

"The Red Fox is not afraid," he said, drawing himself up. "He can creep through the bushes like his namesake and avoid the gaze of the white man."

Robert smiled, for it struck him that a white man had without much difficulty, tracked the Red Fox but a minute ago. But paying no attention to this incongruity, he asked: "And what message does the Wild Rose send to me?"

"She loves Big Jump very much," the youth said with a cunning smile, at which the white man could not help blushing.

"Did she say so?" he inquired.

"No, but the Red Fox has his eyes open; he can see."

"But that is not the question now. I do not want to know what the Red Fox saw, but what he heard."

Thus corrected, the Indian resumed: "The Wild Rose will come this way before many days; when the sun appears in the sky the fifth time after this; she will be here to meet her friend."

The face of the scout became almost radiant with delight on hearing these pleasant news.

"Here!" he exclaimed. "The Wild Rose did not say that she would meet me here?"

"No, not here; she will be on the summit of the big knob yonder, when the sun turns its face towards the west."

"You mean at noon?"

"My brother has said it."

"Very well, I shall be there. Tell the Wild Rose I will be there, and if the trees tumble like reeds in a hurricane. But my friend must be hungry?"

"The Red Fox never get hungry."

"But a good breakfast will nevertheless be welcome, I reckon," the scout said, smiling at the extravagance of the boy's expressions. "If the Red Fox will stay here and take good care not to expose himself, I'll go down and fetch him something to eat."

Without awaiting the answer, Robert started for the Fort, and at the expiration of half an hour returned with a supply of such victuals as he had been able to procure in a hurry. The Indian had fasted since the breakfast he had shared with the Lieutenant, and therefore developed an appetite that did very well for one that never gets hungry. When he had done, the scout told him to arise and follow him, leading him by a roundabout way to the Beaver River, in the neighborhood of the falls. There all at once a canoe with two Indians attracted his sight. The vessel was coming down stream, and the openness with which the two inmates pursued their course was sufficient evidence that secrecy was not their aim. Still the scout thought best to conceal his presence from the strangers until they had approached near enough to allow a closer examination of their character. Motioning to his companion, he entered a cluster of bushes growing on an eminence, from which they had a full view of the approaching craft, and the falls or rapids of the river. The canoe was nearing fast, and the two Indians consequently came more plainly to view. All at once the Red Fox touched his companion's arm.

"Ugh!" he exclaimed, "I see the Red Feather and Turtle Heart."

"Upon my word you are right: one of them is the rascal that was so eager for a roast last summer. My fingers itch to send a bullet into his red carcass."

"Big Jump must not shoot," the Red Fox earnestly protested. "Maghpiway goes to Fort to make peace."

Robert looked at him indignantly. "What do you mean, sir? Do you think I shoot unsuspecting people from a cover? No, no, my boy, that is not my fashion. If I say my hand itches, it does not follow that I need yield to the itching. But see, the chief prepares to shoot the falls. That must be an interesting sight. I have heard that the Indians frequently did it, but I never did it myself, nor saw it done. Ah! the old fellow manages right handsomely."

While he was uttering these words, the canoe had indeed entered the rapids. The venture seemed perhaps more perilous from his elevated standing point, than to the men engaged in it. He could see the tossing waters madly rushing over and between the huge rocks and ledges constituting the bed of the river at that point. He could exactly calculate the course they had to take in order to avoid destruction, and involuntarily moved his body in accordance with his calculations. When the canoe had safely passed the tossing whirlpools, he felt greatly relieved, and drawing a deeper breath, exclaimed: "Well done, Red Feather! For this handsome piece of seamanship I forgive you your bloody intentions against me. But I must join them, Red Fox, or some one at the blockhouse might make a target of their dusky skins. So I must leave you now, which I well may, as there is no danger of your safety beyond this point. Farewell, my lad, and do not forget to tell the Wild Rose that I shall be on the Big Knob to await her coming."

The lad shook hands with him, and then taking a northern course started on his homeward journey. The scout, on the other hand, turned his attention to the canoe, which, at that moment, was swimming in the quiet current at his feet. He stepped from the bushes, and, by a single shout, drew the eyes of the Indians upon his person. They stopped the progress of their canoe, and, after a rapid examination of the white man, answered his signal by a cry of theirs. Then they paddled their canoe towards the bank, an indication that they had recognized him, and participated in his desire for an interview. Robert therefore descended the slope, and reached the bank at the moment the Indians landed.

"Good day, chief," he said, with a good natured smile. I am glad to see you back to the banks of the Beaver again. What brings you down to-day, if I may ask?"

"Me go see white father at the Fort. Delawares wish make peace now."

"Ah! you changed your notion then. I recollect a time, not very far back, when the Red Feather thought differently."

"Red Feather got older—got wiser. Him never too old to learn."

"That is a truth which holds good with the white man as well as the red; but if you want to visit the Fort, I may as well go with you. My presence may possibly save you some trouble and risk in passing the blockhouse."

"My brother is welcome. If him step in canoe, us paddle him down."

In obedience to this invitation the scout stepped into the craft, which shot back into the middle of the stream and then resumed its rapid course down the creek. On the present site of New Brighton a blockhouse had been erected, which, at that time, was garrisoned with a small body of troops. It commanded the river, and the two Indians might have found difficulty in passing it, if the presence of the scout had not protected them. It is more than likely that the commander of the post had been warned of the probability of a similar occurrence, but in those wild times the life of an Indian was no more highly valued than that of a dog, and the mere instructions of the commanding officers of the Fort might in itself have proved a very inefficient safeguard. When the canoe passed the building the men showed their heads at various openings.

"You have queer customers there, Bob," one of them accosted the scout.

"Will you give us leave to pepper away at them?" another added.

"If your own skin tickles you overmuch, why not? These men are under my protection, and I suppose you understand what that means."

"Proud like a duke," responded the man, laughing. "But, pass on. I have no inclination to have my body riddled, nor my bones broken."

This shows plainly in what estimation the Big Jump was held by his comrades. They knew him to be a steadfast friend, but also a dangerous enemy, and so it happened that his influence in the Fort was at least at par with that of the commander.

The canoe reached the mouth of the Beaver; and, after passing through the channel formed by the main land and the above mentioned island, shot up to the landing of the Fort. The vessel was fastened, and the party received by the few idlers who always, more or less, lounged about the Fort. The news of their arrival soon spread amongst the garrison, and when the Indians, in company with Campbell, had ascended the covered way, all the soldiers not detained by duty crowded to the gate to see them enter. They bore themselves with a dignified reserve, which never ceased until they stood before the commander. Maghpiway, being a chief, thought himself entitled to being received by his equal, and would have considered a contrary proceeding a slight, or even an insult. When the Captain, however, bade them welcome, he smiled graciously, and announced himself as an envoy of the Delawares, who had learned from the Six Nations that their great fathers in Philadelphia desired to make peace with them. The Delawares were ready to listen to their wishes, he said, and even now are on their way to the Fort to learn the propositions which their white brothers had to make.

To this the Captain replied that he was glad to learn the peaceful disposition of the Delawares. He was also glad to hear that the tribe was coming, and would do everything in his power to make them comfortable. He wanted the chief to stay and rest from the exertion of his journey, so that after a while he might be able to go back to his tribe, to inform them of the peaceful and friendly disposition of his own and of their great father, the Congress, in Philadelphia.

After this speech he delivered the guests to Campbell, with the request that they should be made comfortable, and receive every attention which could be shown them under the circumstances.

In obedience to this injunction the scout took them to Anderson's quarters, taking good care to inform the inmates beforehand of the character of the guests. In consequence of this precaution the women were enabled to suppress all signs of fright, with the exception of a nervous uneasiness, which worked itself off in an excess of civility and hospitality. The Indians were made to smoke, to eat, to drink and sleep to their heart's content, and their countenances showed plainly how much they appreciated the kindness of their hosts. Anderson was in a good humor, and evidently enjoyed the discourse with these savage children of the forest. He recalled numerous reminiscences in which he and Maghpiway had played a role, and laughed just as freely at his own discomfitures as those of his guest's; for he had not always been the victorious party in his encounters with the savages.

When he alluded to his visit at the Indian village the previous summer, Maghpiway exhibited the slightest possible trace of confusion.

"My white brother great warrior," he said, perhaps to coat the ugly reminiscence over with honey. "How he escaped Indians then? Maghpiway never find out."

"Ah, you would like to know chief, would you?" the scout said, chuckling at the recollection of his fortunate escape. "I supposed you never dreamed of the possibility of a fellow's dodging and giving you the slip that way?"

"Me not think it then. Me follow Big Jump. Big Jump give big cry; make Indians believe he much strong. Then go after Big Jump, catch him—Little Coon run away."

Robert broke into a laugh at this novel appellation of

his friend, in which Anderson himself joined, though he knew henceforth that name would adhere to him as tight as his skin. If he had been a young man and beginner, that name might have injured his reputation with his red neighbor; as it was, they would respect and fear him as much under the sobriquet of Little Coon, as if they had called him the Big Panther or Grizzly Bear.

Whiskey was then an every day beverage, without which no meal was considered complete. We need not wonder then that Anderson freely offered his guests of the dearly coveted fire-water. Nor did they refuse; but in remembrance of their dignified character as envoys, they for once abstained from degrading themselves into beastly intoxication. They drank enough to put themselves into an exceedingly good humor, a fact that showed itself by the numerous efforts at jokes they made. Red Feather also became aware of the charms of his female hosts, and attempted to sing their praise. Beckoning to Anderson, he said: "My friend has a beautiful daughter; what may be her name?"

"We call her Rose, chief."

"Rose?" the chief repeated, with unusual attention. "That beautiful name. The Rose make fine squaw some day. Big Jumb better take her—him very fond of roses."

The chief looked attentively at the young hunter, who could not help coloring slightly at this hint, which the others of course failed to comprehend. Anderson was well pleased to have a subject broached which he had thus far failed to bring up."

"Well, chief," he cried, "you are not so far wrong there, and your notion proves what I always believed, namely, that you are a clever sort of a fellow. The Big Jump, as you call him, is rather a little shy, but I shouldn't at all wonder if he would sooner or later act on your hint."

The rest of the company received these remarks with silence, which would have struck both Anderson and the chief as ominous, if it had come earlier in the day. Their frequent potations had indeed failed to upset the balance of their minds, but it had given them a wonderful capacity for dyeing everything to assume the color of their wishes. So

Anderson received the impression that the silence of the young people was equal to an assent; and Maghpiway would have sworn that the chance of the Wild Rose for ever becoming the squaw of the Big Jump was very poor indeed. Anderson wished a union between his daughter and Robert, because he was the hunter's friend, and Maghpiway, because he was his foe and rival. The discovery of this supposed new attachment of the hunter not only added to the chief's good humor, but also softened his animosity against the young man, and caused him to depart from the Fort the next day in peace with himself and the whole world.

CHAPTER VIII.

AN INVOLUNTARY BATH.

On the day of Maghpiway's departure from the Fort, the deserted Indian village, in which the reader has first met the Beaver, once more resounded with the noise of life. Again the chief had led his tribe towards the rising sun ; to the hunting grounds of their fathers. The same lodges were occupied by the same families, except where death with his merciless hand had made such an arrangement impossible. They did not find the dilapidated houses any better after their year's absence, and, willing or not, the men had to have recourse to the axe and tomahawk, or choose the alternate of seeing the roof tumble in over their heads.

The Beaver had done like the rest. As his house had from the beginning been in a better condition than most of the others, his preparations were less annoying; but the Wild Rose took good care to save him all trouble, small as it was. The chief had two sons, young men of seventeen and twenty, whose acquaintance we made a good while ago, without taking the time to state their relationship to the Beaver and the Wild Rose. One of them we have met lately again, for the Red Fox, the messenger of the maiden to the scout, is no less a person than her brother and the son of the chief. The other youth we know as yet but slightly, but may perhaps before long have an opportunity of improving his acquaintance. At present, we are much struck by the mien of deference, strangely contrasting with the ready obedience, which—contrary to Indian custom—the two youths observed towards their sister. She need only say a word to have it carried out, and so the few repairs are rapidly effected. The dutiful daughter still further attends to the simple wants of her father, arranging everything according to his well known tastes and habits; but at last having done this, she secretly beckons to the Red Fox and leaves the house. Striking for the woods in the nearest direction, she chooses a secluded spot and awaits the arrival of her brother. When she sees him coming, she points to a log opposite the one on which she sits, and begins to inquire about the results of his excursion. The youth had been home for several hours; but so great was the self-control of this rare girl, that she conquered her curiosity and only yielded to it, when she found it to agree with other and more imperative duties. She is still the brave, noble creature, that with a bleeding heart, turned from her lover, to save him the pain of a more protracted parting; as to appearance, she is even more beautiful than a year ago. Love brings out the charm of the maiden, as the sun does the color of the flower. The soul having lain as in a trance, awakes, lighting up the face with the fire of Prometheus, the spark from heaven.

Thus the Wild Rose has grown more beautiful, because she has grown more spiritual, and the smile spreading over her countenance, when she first begins to question her brother, is of a truly angelic beauty.

"My brother has returned from his errand," she said. "He has seen him then ?"

"The Red Fox has seen and spoken to Big Jump."

"Oh, do not call him so—it is an ugly name."

"I would gladly exchange mine for his."

"Ah, I suppose so," the girl replied, pleased by this praise of her lover. "To have his name the Red Fox would also have to have his qualities."

"He is young; but some day or other he will have them."

"I hope so. I know of no better pattern for my brother to go by. But what did the Big Jump say? Did he listen to the message of the Wild Rose?"

"He listened as the bear to the humming of the bee, the mocking bird to the calling of its mate. He said: 'I love the Wild Rose better than all other flowers, and shall be there to enjoy her sweet perfume.'"

The maiden looked delighted.

"And you are sure you gave him the right time and the right place?"

"The Red Fox did. Did the Wild Rose ever find him mistake the meaning of her words?"

"No, she did not, and I thank him very much. I want him to hold himself in readiness to go with me on the day appointed."

"The Red Fox will be ready."

"Will he also tell the White Wolf?"

"He will, if the Wild Rose is anxious to take him; but the White Wolf would hate to go: he is not very fond of the pale-faces."

"His feelings are older than his judgment. I want him to go, to rid himself of his prejudice."

"The Wild Rose has said it; the White Wolf will go."

"It is right. I will not forget how good the Red Fox is to his sister."

After these words, she rose, blending the dignity of the queen with the affection of the sister, in a manner which at once explains the great influence she exercised not only over her brother, but many other warriors of the tribe. Even those whose wooing she had rejected, remained her sincere friends and admirers, feeling perhaps, that their rough hands were not calculated to handle so delicate a flower. Of these the Red Feather formed the only exception. Although he was the oldest of her suitors, he had not suffered himself to be discouraged by her original rejection of his proposal. Perhaps he took the refusal for mere coyness, which would wear off with a riper age and understanding. It appeared to his conceit as a downright impossibility that a man of such reputation and a chief withal, should be jilted by a girl who had hardly passed her teens, and could surely not expect a more honorable connection in the tribe. The rescue and adoption of Robert Campbell on the part of the Wild Rose, had first startled him from his security, and opened his eyes to the possibility of a disappointment of his hopes and expectations. The rage which he felt at this unexpected *denouement* was, as the reader recollects, only equalled by the hatred with which from that day he contemplated his enemy, the hunter. True, the Wild Rose travelled in the same direction, which necessity compelled him to pursue, and so the chief could afford to defer his vengeance to a later day. That day—in his opinion—was drawing near, when once more the tribe turned their faces towards the east, choosing him as the messenger of their peaceful disposition. While acting as an envoy, he could not of course strike his foe, and therefore made no use of the various chances that offered to injure or destroy him. But he carefully studied the Fort and its surroundings, and would no doubt have matured his plans at an early hour, if the supposed connection between Campbell and the daughter of David Anderson had not suddenly turned his thoughts into a new channel, and induced him to strive for the consummation of his original designs on the Wild Rose in preference to the satisfaction of his vengeance. The reader recollects the good humor with which he departed from the Fort for his native village, where he arrived during the important conference held in the woods by the Wild Rose and her brother. Having no family to claim his attention at his lodge, Maghpi-way at once directed his steps to the hut of the Beaver, and was fortunate enough to find that chief at home. Per-haps his early return was unexpected, for the Beaver start-ed slightly at his sight.

"Ugh! the chief has travelled fast; but he is doubly welcome for that reason. Will he sit down and smoke a little before he tells me the result of his errand?"

The chief accepted the proffered pipe, and after finish-ing it, delivered the message of the commander at the Fort. The Beaver nodded like a man who sees a thing confirmed which he expected long ago. Indeed he was well aware that only the desperate opposition of the Red Feather had prevented the conclusion of a treaty a year ago, and his knowledge had induced him to send that chief, thus enlisting the sympathy of the only man that might again prove injurious to his plans, and detrimental to the best interests of the tribe.

At this moment the Wild Rose entered the room, and was ordered by the Beaver to prepare a meal for the hungry envoy. The Red Feather gravely saluted the girl, receiving in return a more gracious look and pleasant smile than had fallen to his share for a long while. This unexpected reception still strengthened him in his intentions, and thus led to the deplorable complication, which well nigh proved fatal to several of our friends, but to hear of which may not be unacceptable to the reader, as they furnish the material for the continuation of our tale.

We have often said that Indians were born statesmen, and have now a new opportunity to prove this assertion by the skill with which the Red Feather set to work. While eating he discoursed upon various topics in the hearing of the Wild Rose, touching here and there upon Robert Campbell, appearing unintentional and indifferent regarding the impression which his words would make upon his hearers. Yet he knew well enough that both father and daughter were earnest, attentive listeners, the former for political, the latter for personal reasons. It must be confessed that the chief talked well, like most of his race, who receive from nature what many a white orator has to acquire by long, patient years of study.

After describing the Fort, and the reception by the commander, he entered upon that portion of the narrative relating to his stay in the family of the scout. This, of course, was more interesting to the Wild Rose than all the rest, as she knew of the intimate relation between Anderson and Campbell, but she abstained from betraying her interest, thus showing the self-control not only of the individual, but also of the race.

Suddenly, however, her attention was destined to reach a painful intensity. The chief began to speak about a beautiful maiden, the daughter of his host. This maiden he purposely adorned with all the charms imaginable, and then suddenly followed with the announcement of her intended marriage with Robert Campbell.

This time the Wild Rose could not suppress a slight start. True, she had often seen Indian marriages between one husband and half a dozen of wives, but she also knew that such was not the practice among white men, and even if it had been, her ardent nature would not have contented itself with a share of her husband's affection. No, indeed, she, and she alone, wanted to be the wife of Robert Campbell, and woe to the maiden that would venture to cross her path! Certain destruction would be her fate!

But no! she merely raved and troubled herself for nothing, for only a short hour ago she had received her betrothed's message that he still loved her as fondly as ever, and that he would be sure to meet her at the rendezvous proposed. So this communication of the Red Feather must either be based upon a wilful falsehood or an innocent mistake. In either case it would be below her dignity to call him to account, or correct his error. She allowed him to finish his story, and to depart without uttering a single word about this or other matters. Still she could not prevent a certain dejection from spreading over her countenance.

The Beaver saw it. He had from the moment of disclosure sympathized with his favorite child.

"My daughter is sad," he said. "She must not take this too much to heart."

The Wild Rose quietly raised her head.

"The Beaver does not believe the Red Feather, his tongue is crooked, and his words are lies."

"I have never found the chief given to lies."

"Then he is mistaken. Surely Robert Campbell cannot be false to the Wild Rose."

"I hope not my daughter; but these pale-faces are at best a fickle race. If it be true, the Wild Rose must not wither and mourn her loss."

"If it is true, the Wild Rose will sink and die; but it cannot be true. The chief cannot prove his words."

"Shall the Beaver go and try him?"

"Yes, the Wild Rose will be thankful to her father. She would go herself, but she loathes to meet the Red Feather."

The Beaver rose, and without further parley, left the house. During his absence the girl neither spoke nor stirred, and when the chief returned after an hour's absence, he found her in the same place and position. His countenance looked troubled, and he seemed to shrink from making his communication.

"Let my father speak," the maiden said, with a steady voice "She knows he has bad news; but she can hear them."

The Beaver proceeded to give her the details of the Red Feather's visit at Anderson's house, neither adding nor omitting a single word of the account he had received from the chief. He also told her that the Red Feather had spoken of a trip which the family of the scout had agreed upon in his presence. They were to go to an island in the Ohio River, some miles above the Beaver, to spend a day there camping out. Campbell, he said, was to go along.

"And when do they propose making this excursion?"

"To-morrow."

"It is well," the girl said, with a determined voice. "The Wild Rose will go and see. To-morrow night she will know the truth."

The Beaver remained silent. Perhaps he knew his daughter, and was aware that persuasions would be of no avail; perhaps he thought himself that certainty was preferable to a state of painful doubt, no matter how galling it might prove. The girl on the other hand went to see her brothers, and bade them get ready for an early start the next morning. During the day she was taciturn, the Beaver humoring her like a spoiled child, but feeling the want of her sunny smile more keenly than he would confess to himself. When, on the rising of the next sun his three children, after a short farewell, left him for their trip to the banks of the Ohio, he looked after them with an expression more sad than his countenance had worn for many a day.

The trio followed the right bank of the Beaver to the

mouth of the Connequenessing. There they crossed over to the left bank, and pursuing a southeastern course, after a few hours walking, passed the foot of the Big Knob, at the sight of which the shade on the face of the Wild Rose deepened. No wonder! how could the poor girl gaze at the place of the appointed rendezvous with her lover without a keen sensation of pain at the thought of the peril threatening her prospects of future happiness? It took all the strength of her will to maintain the stoical, but deceptive indifference which had thus far marked her conduct.

From the knob the travelers changed their course for one due south thus striking the river at a point opposite the island, of which they were in search. The reader knows these islands now as Hog and Crow Islands, but he is mistaken if he thinks that in those days they bore an aspect similar to the present ones. They were larger and densely wooded, and their high banks projected so steeply into the water that their ascent was only practicable in a few places.

The girl and her companions had no canoe, and were unable to reach the islands; nor was this their purpose, but taking their position on the heights, lining the right bank of the river, so that they could spy any vessel coming up the river, they waited for the development of events with Indian patience.

It was about nine o'clock now, and a whole hour elapsed before the expected canoe came in sight. At last, however, they perceived a vessel of that description coming up stream with a rapidity speaking well for the skill and strength of the persons handling the paddle. They were still too far away to allow a recognition, but Wild Rose saw enough to know that one of the party belonged to the male and two to the female sex. The male was of the size and appearance of the young hunter, whose image she treasured with such fidelity in her heart, and she felt a strange thrill go through her body, as the canoe came nearer and nearer, and the eye sustained the anticipation of her heart. It was indeed Robert Campbell; but the pleasure which Wild Rose felt at this long-missed sight was embittered by the presence of his companions, in one of whom her keen eye, even at that distance, discovered marks of uncommon beauty.

When the canoe was abreast the first island it changed its course, heading diagonally for, and finally striking, the lower end of it, where it was fastened, and a landing effected. The hunter first helped his companions to ascend the steep bank, and then emptied the canoe of various articles, which he had evidently brought along to increase the comforts of the expedition. Wild Rose recognized several articles of apparel; also an iron kettle, probably intended for boiling tea or coffee. When everything was on shore the party disappeared in the bushes, thus forcing Wild Rose to draw upon her imagination for any conjectures of their doings. Alas! if her eyes had before done her bad service, her fancy now served her infinitely worse. She imagined her lover engaged in offering to another the homage so eminently due to her. She fancied him smiling upon his lovely companion, and whispering soft words of love and admiration. Ah! the agonizing tortures that filled those morning hours, as they slowly passed away. Wild Rose never moved, and her brothers, guessing the nature of her feelings, preserved a sympathetic silence. At last, when the sun was nearing the meridian, the scene once more assumed a lively aspect. A thin column of smoke slowly stole through the bushes and trees of the island, and figures could be seen gliding here and there in the pursuance of sundry occupations. All at once the younger woman came close to the water's edge, opposite the place from which Wild Rose watched her movements. She seemed to be gathering flowers for a bouquet. Wild Rose gazed at her with a painful interest. She noticed the coming of a danger, of which the stranger herself was ignorant. The bank of the island was not only steep, but the swift current had, with a greedy tongue, licked all the soil from underneath, until nothing but a network of roots kept the surface from caving in. This hollow ground was many feet in width, thus excluding from the mind of the girl on the surface all thoughts of danger, provided she kept reasonably distant from its edge. So she stepped out farther and farther, and, at last, in trying to pluck a cluster of roses blooming near the edge, leaned forward with the whole weight of her body. At this moment the suspense of the Indian girl reached its climax. Two principles, warring in her bosom, struggled for the mastery. While the demon of jealousy breathed into her mind the desire to see the bank sink with its precious burden into the treacherous flood, never to return, a better spirit whispered into her ears, the summons to challenge the girl, and warn her of danger. At last the better spirit prevailed. Wild Rose stepped from her cover, and, lifting her hand, uttered a warning cry, but it was too late. Her own voice was drowned by a more piercing shriek from the island, which the girl on the bank uttered on perceiving the bank give way. The poor maiden was the helpless spectator of her coming doom; for the piece detaching itself from the bank was so large that its fall consumed some time, landing her a considerable distance into the flood. Her shriek had caused the scout to start at once for the place from which it emanated, in order to ascertain its cause. He was by no means prepared for the full truth, and we can easily imagine his consternation when, on reaching the bank, he saw his companion disappearing in the water. Without hesitation he took a powerful leap, reaching near the place where the girl had sunk, and as he struggled powerfully to reach the surface, he emerged from the water at the same time with Rosa Anderson, and so near that she was almost within reach of his hand.

"Hold up, Rose, for God's sake! hold up one moment!" he cried to her in an encouraging tone, and striking out vigorously towards her, caught her arm as she was sinking the second time. Drawing her up with all his strength, he succeeded in raising her head above water, enabling her to breath, and preserve a shadow of consciousness. Having so far succeeded in his work of rescue, the hunter looked around for the best method of completing it. The current was fast taking them towards the end of the island, and once past that point the position of Rosa would again have become very perilous, as Robert could not have reached the main shore without a powerful struggle, and great loss of time. So he commenced to strike out for the

island with an exertion proportionate to the interests at
stake. For a while it was uncertain whether he would
succeed, as the burden of the half unconscious girl impeded
his progress. Nor would he, in spite of his most desperate
efforts, have reached the point if Grace Jones had not, with
great presence of mind, sprung to his assistance. She had
witnessed his leap into the water, and divining its purpose,
ran to the point to ascertain the result of his efforts. She was
filled with consternation, but her frontier experience had too
fully developed her mental and physical faculties to paralyze them beyond the power of control. When she saw the
hunter struggling to reach the point, she prepared to assist him to the best of her ability. Securing a long sapling she held it out to the swimmer, firmly grasping another with her unengaged hand. Robert eagerly benefitted by this unexpected aid. He seized the sapling and
suffered himself to swing around until he was out of the
strong current, and had reached the eddy below the point.
Once there, he found no difficulty in reaching the shore,
for telling Grace to keep a tight hold on the stick, he gradually pulled himself nearer the bank, until his feet touched
bottom. Then carrying the senseless body of the girl
quickly up the bank, gently deposited her on the grass.
Then both he and Grace began their efforts at resuscitation,
which was soon crowned with success, as the girl had not
been very long under water. When she opened her eyes
Grace broke out into a loud shout of delight. Nor could
the hunter abstain from loud expressions of satisfaction,
without having the slightest knowledge of the pain that
every movement of his sent to a loving heart. Wild
Rose had been a silent and immovable, but by no means
indifferent witness of the exciting drama enacted before
her eyes. She had struggled and conquered with the
hunter, exulting in the manly strength of one so dear to
her, and only when the faint body of the rescued girl
began to show signs of returning life, the whole consciousness of her own wretched condition returned to her
memory. She continued to watch the movements of the
party on the island; she saw them embark, and looked

after their receding forms until their last vestige had vanished from sight. Then heaving one heavy sigh, she turned to her brothers and said :

"You have seen the maiden ; would you recognize her again ?"

"We would."

"Very well ! within one week she must be a prisoner in my hands !"

CHAPTER IX.

A CRISIS.

The Lieutenant had led a miserable existence ever since his discovery of the imagined unfaithfulness of Rosa Anderson. He had shunned Robert Campbell as well as his mistress, greatly to the wonderment of the latter person. She had in various ways endeavored to intercept him, being exceedingly anxious for an explanation of his curious conduct ; but he had avoided her so doggedly that at last her anxiety gave place to indignation, and induced her to change her tactics. If her studied endeavors to meet him remained fruitless, perhaps the opposite extreme would be attempted with better results. So assuming a gay and unconcerned mien, to which her heart decidedly gave the lie, she feigned to find unusual pleasure in the company of Robert Campbell. She talked to him whenever she had a chance, and finally let her policy of defiance culminate in the excursion which we have depicted in the preceding chapter. The exposure to a watery grave was by no means the worst feature of this excursion. It had kindled sensations so fierce in two different minds, that the artless girl would have trembled at the knowledge. That Wild Rose had in consequence of it been confirmed in her unfortunate opinion, the reader knows; that the case of the Lieutenant had not been improved thereby he can imagine. Indeed nothing more injurious to the interests of both parties could well be conceived than this pretended indifference and flirtation on the part of Rosa Anderson. What she de-

signed for a cure merely aggravated the evil—a case not uncommon where the diagnosis is not well understood. Rosa
had not the slightest idea of the gloomy doubts regarding her
constancy that fevered the brain of her once light-hearted
lover, or she would have been slow to adopt a method
calculated to complete his delirium—for delirious he was.
Neglecting his associates, and, in a measure, his duties;
begrudging his associates the few words he was obliged to
speak, he wandered about the Fort a mere shadow of the
gay fellow he had been. The Captain noticed the change,
but attributing it to a passing indisposition indulged the
supposed patient. Had he known the dark projects of
revenge over which the young man constantly brooded, he
might have acted differently.

Yes, revenge! that was the only thought in which he
endeavored to drown a disappointed love. Revenge on
him and her! He might have immediately, by insulting
language, provoked a deadly quarrel, if the knowledge of
the near rendezvous on the big knob had not restrained
him. He resolved to wait and, like their evil genius, step
between them there, to fling his utmost contempt into her
face, and then drive a knife to his bosom; to fare afterwards,
he cared not how. His revenge once satisfied, the rest was
totally indifferent to him.

Time—generally so rapid in the estimation of the
many—crept with unbearable slowness to him. At last,
however, the morning of the rendezvous dawned, and after
providing for a more than liberal quantity of ardent drink,
he early sought the woods, taking the direction of the big
knob, and walking all over its summit hours before the appointed time. Every now and then his restlessness would
drive him away to wander in the woods, until at length
the fatal spot attracted him anew, merely to repel a
second time.

There was a second party to whom the big knob proved
equally attractive—Wild Rose. She had completely
renounced the sweet expectation which she had at first
entertained of the meeting. In coming now she had a very
different object in view—that of humiliating and punish-
ing her faithless lover. She would frown him down—but

no, we would violate the truth by saying what she would do. Her heart was a chaos of conflicting feelings, the only sensation of which she was fully conscious being a deep agony, bordering on despair.

Wild Rose was surprised at the presence of the Lieutenant; her surprise growing as she noticed his strange conduct. His frantic movement partly neutralized her excitement; but as noon approached, she became restless at the perseverance with which he adhered to the spot. What if he should take it in his head to stay! She would not tolerate the presence of a witness at the coming interview, yet she saw no way of removing him. She saw no other way but to resign herself to fate and abide the issue; but the irritation caused by the prolonged stay of this stubborn individual, had the tendency to soften her towards her lover, acting, as it were, in the capacity of a conductor.

Many impatient glances did the poor girl cast at the heavens, and when the position of the sun indicated the hour of noon, a nervousness agitated a body generally so firm. She knew the hunter was coming, for the frontiersmen imitated their Indian neighbors in the punctuality with which they observed their engagements. Robert would have hastened to the spot much earlier had he not thought his Indian bride would prize a manifestation of punctual firmness even more than impatient love. He had purposely restrained his impatience in order to appear at the rendezvous exactly at the appointed hour. In this he succeeded, but imagine his surprise at discovering the Lieutenant instead of another, towards whom he was drawn with all the ardor of a pent-up passion.

The appearance of the officer made him start. Robert had noticed his sullen looks before; but the anticipation of the happy interview in store for him had made him more indifferent than usual to this and other things not directly connected with his love. Now, however, the singular appearance of the officer struck him with double force, and for the moment he forgot his disappointment.

"Why, Lieutenant," he exclaimed, walking towards him with a concerned air, "what in the world ails you? You look very ill."

"And you, I suppose, would like to play the doctor ?" the officer inquired, with a sneer. "Well I do not object to the drawing of a little blood. I'll pay you on the spot, too ; for having so many little bills to settle with you, a little more or less does not matter."

"Bills to settle! Lieutenant, truly you are delirious and ought to be in bed."

"Yes, yes, I'll lay myself down to a long, deep slumber before long ; but first I must settle my accounts with you. But say, where is that hussy of yours? Is she going to break faith with you as she did with me ?"

"Hussy, Lieutenant! what on earth do you mean ?"

"How innocent!" the other sneered. "One would imagine you had always lived on mother's milk. I want to know where the heartless flirt is that stole my heart, and, after breaking it, threw it away like a worthless pebble!"

The hunter was too much astonished to get angry or even answer. He looked at the officer in blank surprise.

"Of course you will deny," the Lieutenant resumed. "Sneak and liar that you are, what could you do with more propriety than continue to do the same ?"

The hunter started. If the officer had spoken those words, in what the other considered a responsible state of mind, he would have resented them in a way that it would have been doubtful if the Lieutenant had lived to repeat them. The hunter, however, considered him delirious or mad—an opinion not falling far from truth—and therefore resolved to ignore the taunt.

"Lieutenant," he said, gently, "allow me to lead you hence to the Fort ; for it is evident that you need care and attention in the worst kind of a way. It does not suit me either to leave this place just now, but still—"

"Ah, he does not like to leave this place!" the other interrupted, with a bitter laugh. "No, I suppose you do not. Your paramour would cut a queer figure in coming here, and you away."

"Again that word! Lieutenant, you show method in your madness. You must in some way have got a glimpse of the nature of my errand here, else—"

"There it comes !" the Lieutenant cried. "I knew he could not hide it in his vile carcass !"

The brow of the hunter darkened. He made a rapid step towards the other, saying, "Enough of that now, sir! Mad or no mad, I want no more of your impudence!"

"Ah, finally !" the Lieutenant exclaimed ; "he's warming up. I had almost given up the hope of seeing his sluggish blood boil up."

"Yes, I see now what your intention is," Robert replied, coolly, having by this time fully recovered his self-possession. "But I am sorry to disappoint you. It shall not be said that I allowed a madman to make me angry."

"It shall not—shall it ?" the Lieutenant cried, fairly boiling with rage. "Well, then, they shall say at least that a madman was more than a match for you."

Drawing his knife, he threw himself with such rapidity upon the hunter that any one less used to the frontier and its warfare might have been taken unawares and fallen a victim to the sudden onset. Not so the hunter. He had learned to deal with the wily savage, and the thrust of the Lieutenant, therefore, did not take him by surprise. Springing aside and striking the lifted arm of the officer, he made him spin around before recovering his equilibrium. This disappointment, however, made the infuriated man only more eager for another onset, but just at the moment when he meant to make the spring, a strange hand was laid upon his arm, causing him to stop, more in consequence of the unexpected interference than by the force of the movement. Stopping in obedience to the check, and turning around, his eye caught a sight well calculated to upset the little judgment left him. Before him stood, in her majestic beauty, the maiden whom the reader has long ago learned to know as Wild Rose. To the Lieutenant it had almost the force of a heavenly apparition, so suddenly and unexpectedly did it break upon him.

"Who are you ? What do you want of me?" he asked, in startled surprise.

"It's all the same who me be. Me want to keep you from being kill."

"Are you so sure of that ?" the officer inquired, regaining his spirit of defiance in the same proportion as his bewilderment subsided.

"Yes, me is. If your eyes are not blind with fury—you see yourself. You not think you kill hunter?"

The last question was asked in a mixture of derision and exultation. Injured as she thought herself, she could not forget the skill and prowess of her lover.

"Yes I do think that, and if you stand aside I shall prove it. What business have you at any rate to interfere in this affair?"

"More business than you. Why come here when not called? Me sent for the hunter, not for you."

The officer started. "You sent for him? you?"

"Yes me—why wonder?"

"You sent an Indian boy, did you not?"

There was so much painful suspense in his tone, that Wild Rose was touched. So humoring him she said: "Yes, me did; ask any more questions now?"

But the Lieutenant was satisfied. A light began to dawn in his benighted mind, and he commenced to have serious doubts about the justice of his jealous suspicions. So much did the strong emotions of his heart overpower him, that he could neither stir nor speak, standing for a while the helpless prey of his excitement.

This pause was at once improved by the hunter. His first joyous start at the sight of his betrothed had yielded to the admiration of her splendid bearing in her encounter with his foe. He stepped, as it were, out of himself, losing sight of the lover over the enthusiastic spectator; but when the voices of the speakers died away, he returned to reality and himself. Never before had he been so fully conscious of the deep love with which this wonderful creature had inspired him, and extending both his arms toward the maiden, who all the while had kept her back to him, he cried with the thrilling accents of a powerful passion: "Wild Rose! my dear, my noble bride!"

The body of the girl quivered with excitement, but her face remained averted from the hunter as before. Now, for the first time, it struck him that this persistent effort on her part to ignore his presence was something more than casual. A fear of some impending evil, the thought of the possibility of losing this lovely maiden oppressed his heart with so much force as almost to deprive him of his breath. A pain shook his system, and finally found vent in an exclamation, fraught with all the conflicting emotions struggling in his bosom: "Rose!"

This time the girl was incapable of resisting the conjuration. She turned her head, as if driven by an irresistable power; but the glance she cast at him was evidently intended as one of crushing severity. Still all-powerful love lurked behind her indignation, as the sun behind the parting clouds of the thunder-storm. It also manifested itself in her voice, for though her words were words of accusation, their acrimony was tempered by softer feelings.

"What you call me for? Why you say with tongue what heart not know? You call me 'dear'—go to the maiden in the Fort—she dear, she listen to your words—the ear of Wild Rose is deaf—it cannot listen; her heart is closed."

Robert's grief was almost paralyzed by his bewilderment. "Rose what does this signify?" he cried, with looks and accents of injured innocence. "Has the world gone mad, and resolved to upset my reason too? Speak, what do your strange upbraidings mean?"

"You not know? You not know maiden at Fort?" Wild Rose asked, eagerly.

"If you mean Rose Anderson, certainly I do. Is there any harm in knowing the daughter of my oldest and best friend?"

"You not only know—you love her!"

"Again this strange insinuation. There must be a conspiracy to fasten this upon me, else how should you repeat the accusations of this crazy officer?"

"I accuse you no longer, Robert, and humbly beg pardon for my foolishness?"

The others were too much engaged with themselves to heed this exclamation.

"If you not love her, why go out in canoe?" Rose eagerly asked the hunter.

"Rose, how can you speak so?" Robert said, reproachfully. "Is a ride on the river an evidence of love?"

"When not love, why jump in river and risk your
life?"

"Well, this is really strange! My Wild Rose is evidently jealous, and that passion neutralizes all her virtues.
Rose, you want to know why I jumped into the river to
save one of you sex— a woman?"

Wild Rose looked abashed for a moment, but recovering rapidly under the impulse of a new thought, said
most sternly: "I fear Big Jump has a forked tongue. He
talks sweetly to the ear, but his words cannot enter the
heart of Wild Rose. Did not the father of the maiden say
the hunter would soon lead his daughter into his wigwam?"

"I will not deny but that he has often intimated such a
wish, though it surpasses my comprehension how you ever
heard of it. Tell me, Rose, what tale-bearer has thus pre-
judiced you against me?"

As the girl hesitated, the hunter continued in mournful
accents: "Rose, you have the heart to fling these accusations in my face, and yet refuse to let me know from
whence they spring. Do you condemn without a chance of
defense?"

"What good will it do to know? You cannot deny.
Red Feather no lie!"

"Red Feather!" Robert exclaimed in astonishment.
"Ah! now I know. While I kindly took that serpent to
my bosom, he endeavored to inflict a deadly wound. But
the day of reckoning will come. I owed him a grudge
before, but like a good natured fool, cancelled the account.
This time, however, he won't fare so well, for I vow to satisfy this injury with his blood!"

This was a savage threat, and would have alarmed a
girl of gentler education. With Wild Rose the case was
different. The words of the hunter were in accordance
with her notions, and her jealous indignation was gradually
overcome by the rising waves of love and admiration. She
looked at the hunter with a look of old, but in his excitement he failed to notice it.

"The chief did lie, Rose, but if you really believe his statement in preference to mine, I can prove my words. This officer is, or lately was, the lover of Rose Anderson until he began to labor under the delusion that I had meddled with his love. He can testify to this, if jealousy has not obscured his mind."

The Lieutenant winced under these cutting remarks, but without anger.

"I have acted like a madman," he said, "and therefore cannot complain for being so considered. But I have discovered my mistake. The Indian lad who betrayed this rendezvous, in speaking of a Rose meant not Rose Anderson."

The eyes of Wild Rose flashed fire. She stepped up to the officer, and said angrily: "Who told? What Indian lad do you mean?"

"I mean a youth going by the name of Red Fox."

The girl uttered a cry of indignation.

"You must not blame him," the Lieutenant replied, "for he never meant to betray his trust. It was fire-water that drew it from him."

"And so, your having been aware of this rendezvous all the time, I now understand your change of conduct. But why did you not speak? You came very near causing great distress by your mad jealousy."

"I know I am to blame; but if you knew what I suffered in these days of suspense, you would deem me amply punished for my want of confidence."

"Your face shows it, poor fellow. Well, Rose, do you want more testimony? Shall I lead you to the Fort, that you may learn from the lips of both father and daughter, how much you have wronged me by this cruel suspicion?"

Wild Rose was conquered. Stepping meekly up to the hunter, and taking one of his hands in both of hers, she said, with her face averted : "Wild Rose has been wrong ; she has bitterly wronged her husband."

"So, that will do !" the young man cried, with a joyous voice. "No more self-accusations, darling. Come to my heart, for that is where you belong."

He tried to draw her into his embrace, but she resisted,

keeping her face averted all the while. "My husband does not know all," she said, gently shaking her head. "When he knows all, he'll turn from Wild Rose and leave her."

"Rose, what can you mean? Do not torture yourself with idle fears! What could you have done to alienate me from you?"

"The heart of Wild Rose was angry; jealousy blinded her. She told her brothers to watch for the girl, and snatch her away—they are now on her trail."

"Did you really do that, Rose? And what would you do with the prisoner?"

"I hardly know. I wanted to strike the heart of my husband. I wanted to make him feel what it is to be deprived of one's sunshine, of all the prospects of happiness for a long, wretched life."

These words had been uttered in the Delaware tongue, as most all the words which Wild Rose had spoken in passion or excitement. At such time we use our mother tongue, and I have tried to imitate such passages by rendering them in their full flow, thus distinguishing them from the utterances made in broken English.

When Robert, after this confession, again endeavored to draw Wild Rose to his heart, she no longer resisted.

"Thus," the hunter exclaimed, the great happiness of his heart reflected on his face. "Our peace is made, my dear, beautiful wife. Henceforth I shall not allow you to leave me, for I do not want new differences to come between us."

Wild Rose shook her head and said: "My husband must let me go for a few days more. Wild Rose must take her brothers from the maiden's trail, and bid her father farewell. Her husband need not fear; she will not doubt again."

"So you want to run off again, you little vagabond? Lieutenant, do you think it safe to let her go?"

"Indeed it would! She is a wonderful woman, and if I had not my affection already fixed, I would feel inclined to turn the tables, and become your rival."

"Exactly my fix," the hunter said, laughing. "If I had not already loved Rose Number One, I should have fallen in love with Number Two. See how our Roses resemble each other, as if grown on the same stalk! Do they not?"

. "Rather as one grafted on the stalk of the other. They are both beautiful and lovely, and there is no cause for jealousy between us."

"Spoken from the bottom of my heart. Here is my hand, Lieutenant, and the offer of a firm friendship. There has been a cloud between us from the start; but now it is removed, and I do not see why we should not be friends."

"Nor I, Campbell. I always acknowledged your great merits, and now I shall love you as sincerely as I admired."

"And so will I. This is truly a gratifying conclusion to a perplexing difficulty. Instead of losing my little wife, as I thought I should, I gain a friend. But Rose is getting restless. What is the matter, child?"

"Wild Rose must go. Her brothers might harm the maiden."

"That sounds plausible. And when shall I call the Wild Rose my own?"

The maiden mused, and, with a slight blush on her cheeks, said:

"In one week from to-day Wild Rose will follow her husband to his wigwam."

"Agreed!" Robert exclaimed. "Let me seal this compromise with a kiss. And now, seeing that my little bird is eager to fly off, let us come to an understanding. You, Lieutenant, of course are eager to reach the Fort, to make peace with your pouting mistress. I can assure you she played the flirt all these days with a bad grace, and when I got her out of the water the first word after her return to consciousness was your name. So I suppose she is anxious enough to see you, though her face may possibly belie her feelings."

"Oh! thank you for this comforting assurance, Robert. But I suppose I shall have to make my way alone: for you will want to see this friend of yours at least a part of the way home?"

"You are not mistaken, sir," the hunter said, with a smile. "She is a wild bird, you know, and if I do not watch her some, her natural instinct may take her off to regions unknown."

After this they parted, the Lieutenant hastening with all speed towards the Fort, but the hunter and his companion wandering in another direction towards the place where the Delaware town was situated.

They had to tell each other so much, and were so completely wrapped up in their new born happiness, that for once the watchfulness of their senses left them. The hunter, who generally keeps his keen eye wandering all around, reading the signs of the woods, as the well-trained scholar does his A B C, in this instance had no thought but her who now walked at his side, and had indicated her willingness to soon light up his home with her beauty and loveliness.

We need, therefore, not wonder that after their departure the figure of an Indian rose from the dense bushes of the Big Knob, revealing the dark features of no less a person than Red Feather. The chief had stealthily followed the trail of Wild Rose, and thus became the witness of a reconciliation, which totally blasted his new-born hopes. His countenance, therefore, bore a sinister expression, and when he prepared to leave the place where he had endured a long mental torture, he balled his fist and shook it after the departing couple with a mien portending little good. Woe to them if his power of harming is equal to his desire of doing so.

Instant pursuit, however, did not seem to lie in the plans of the chief. Instead of following on the track of the couple, he took a more north-eastern direction, calculated to bring him to the Connequenessing about ten miles above its junction with the Beaver. He did not aim at speed, and therefore reached the creek about an hour of twilight. He wandered up and down the bank as if he were in search of something, until at last a look of satisfaction seemed to indicate that his intention had not been in vain. Stepping to the water's edge, he pushed some bushes aside, but starting back he uttered a cry of surprise, which showed that something very unexpected must have met his eye. This something at once rose from the bush in the shape of another

Indian, who ascended the bank until he stood opposite the chief.

"Ugh !" Red Feather exclaimed, "what does a Seneca chief do in Maghpiway's canoe ?"

"Eaglehead waited for his brother, the chief; he knew Red Feather was coming."

"Eaglehead must be very wise then ; for he knew something of which Red Feather himself was ignorant until this afternoon. What does Eaglehead wish of his brother?"

"He would borrow his canoe of him to go up the Nashannock."

"Is he alone?"

"No, there is a party of warriors with him, who will be here presently."

"But why do they not walk to the Nashannock? The water-course is winding and tedious. Surely Eaglehead and his companions are strong enough to go?"

"But he wishes to leave no trail behind."

"Ugh ! Is he not going to be at the conference ?"

"No! Eaglehead will never make peace with the white man ; he'll strike him unto the day of his death !"

"Ugh ! my brother speaks Maghpiway's heart ; but my hands are tied at present. The Beaver is going to make peace, and I must feign submission to his wishes, if I do not want to lose my influence with the tribe."

"Why does the chief tell this to his brother ?"

"To show him that he sympathizes with him. But listen, your men are coming."

This did not all seem to suit the Seneca chief, and he scowled at the Delaware in a very ugly manner. For a moment he appeared to entertain intentions of a decidedly hostile character, for his hand began to play nervously about the handle of his scalping knife ; but suddenly he seemed to change his notion, for the suspicious movements ceased, and with a bland and courteous smile he said: "Maghpiway is right. He'll soon see my young men coming. He'll also see a prisoner ; but Eaglehead would thank him to shut his eyes. It might hurt the chief to look too sharply."

Maghpiway nodded. "I understand my brother; he

need not be afraid. Maghpiway is accustomed to mind his own business. Is it a pale-face?"

Instead of an answer, Eaglehead pointed in the direction of the forest, through which several dusky forms were approaching. They were six in all, leading in their midst a white woman, who seemed to be much fatigued and in very low spirits, for two of the men more dragged than led her. When they were near enough to allow a recognition of her features, Red Feather gave an involuntary start, and he might have indulged in an exclamation if Eaglehead had not previously warned him. This was Delaware territory, to be sure, but Maghpiway being alone deemed it better not to put his finger into a pie that was not of his baking. So he not only remained silent, but also turned his face from the prisoner, leaving it uncertain whether he wanted to avoid seeing or being seen. Looking significantly at Eaglehead, he said in an undertone :

"Maghpiway now understands his brother. He does, indeed, well to destroy his trail; for if it is found the pale-faces will never stop until they find its end."

"Red Feather will not lend them his eyes?"

"Of course he will not ; for Eaglehead could shut them forever. Still he would ask the Seneca Chief a favor. If he will lend him his warriors for a little while he will show himself very grateful."

"Where are the warriors of Red Feather? They are not dead?"

"No, but I cannot use them for the work in store. Maghpiway wants to do like his brother: he wants to take a prisoner. After he has taken him, he wants to send him to his brother, Eaglehead."

"Egh ! Eaglehead has enough with one prisoner—he does not want to burden himself with a second one."

"My brother shall not keep him long. Maghpiway will come soon to relieve him. When he comes, it will not be with empty hands."

The Seneca left this tempting remark unanswered.

"Maghpiway has some fine red blankets he'll share with his brother, Eaglehead."

"Eaglehead has many blankets."

"Maghpiway will give him a good rifle."

"Our brethren, the English, give us all the rifles we want."

"Has my brother plenty of powder?"

"His horn is never empty."

"Well, let me tell him something: Maghpiway knows a lead mine."

This communication had conquered the Seneca's stoicism. A whole mine of lead! The thought was too powerful to be borne unmoved. Maghpiway resumed: "If Eaglehead helps his brother, Maghpiway will tell him the place."

Eaglehead mused a moment. "What will Maghpiway do with the prisoner? Will he let him escape to tell a tale?"

An expression of intense hatred passed over the face of the chief. Bending his head to the other's ear, he said: "He will hurn him at the stake; black bones tell no tale."

"Then Eaglehead will do it. When is Red Feather going to show him the lead?"

"When the prisoner sings his death song."

"It is well; how many warriors does my brother want?"

"Can Eaglehead spare four?"

"He can. How soon can they be with him again?"

"In a few days at least; where does Eaglehead intend to go?"

"Does the chief know the cave on the Neshannock?"

"He does."

"Very well—there Eaglehead will await his coming."

During this interval, the warriors had halted with the prisoner at a respectful distance from the chiefs. Eaglehead now stepped up to them and spoke a few words, after which two of them stepped into the canoe with the girl, the rest joining Red Feather. When the Seneca chief prepared to follow the smaller party into the vessel, Maghpiway saluted him, saying: "May my brother have a safe journey. I shall try to blind the eyes of the pale-faces."

With this the canoe started down stream, the chief taking good care to destroy all traces of the embarkation. It was not very likely that he would succeed in misleading a skillful pursuer by this alone ; but in addition to other measures it might considerably puzzle him. To accomplish this he now set about causing the four warriors to start in four different directions into the forest, and striking himself a fifth one, thus managing to create a profusion of tracks, which must necessarily perplex the party or parties, who, as he knew, would soon be in pursuit. He instructed the warriors to continue their course to the next run, and to turn off and all come back on the trail which they had made on their first passage through the woods. This they did, reaching the place of starting at a moment when the veil of darkness began to spread more thickly over the region, hiding them as well as the woods, in which, under the directions of the chief, they lay themselves in ambush. When everything was arranged they observed the deepest silence, listening with a sharp ear for the approaching footstep of the victim they were ready to ensnare.

CHAPTER X.

A TRAPPER ENTRAPPED.

When Lieutenant Saunders reached the Fort he saw Grace standing in the door of the blockhouse with rather a troubled mien. He walked up to her, and no sooner had she seen his countenance when her face brightened in a measure. Walking a few steps to meet him, she exclaimed: "Thank God ! there's one friendly face at last. I was near dying with restlessness."

"But what's the matter, Aunt Grace?" he inquired, slightly startled by her excited manners.

"The matter? Enough's the matter to set a person crazy. There's David to commence with. He fell this morning, dislocating his ankle in such a way as to lay him up for a week at least."

"That's bad indeed—may I go in to see him ?"

"No, indeed, sir, for there is other work at hand that wants attention. Rose has been missing ever since ten o'clock this morning."

"Missing?" the Lieutenant inquired, becoming also alarmed. "How can she be missing? has she left the Fort?"

"Of course she has, or surely I would be able to find her. She left the Fort, and, I guess, went on the river."

"But what makes you think so?"

"Well, she went fretting the whole morning about a necklace her father gave her when she was a baby. She dropped it on the island, she said, when she came near drowing the other day, and was only saved through the efforts of Robert Campbell; other persons who had a better right to do it being absent as usual."

"Aunt Grace, don't scold me now, but rather tell me how she went, so I may at once start in search of her."

"Ah! that sounds sensible. Well, sir, at ten o'clock I missed her first, and when I inquired, was told that she had been seen with Crazy Peter on the river bank."

"You mean Peter, the drummer boy?"

"Yes; it seems that, failing to find somebody else, the thoughtless girl went off with this half-witted drummer boy."

"Well, Peter handles a paddle as well as anybody; so, if that is all you fret about, you may rest easy."

"But it isn't all. It is nigh four o'clock now, and they could have been back long ago. If I could only paddle a canoe I'd go at once; but as it is, I can do nothing but stay at home and fret, as you express it."

"Well, Aunt, I can paddle, and I shall go without delay; so do stop fretting, and get a good supper ready, for I'll warrant you we shall fetch a monstrous appetite along, Aunty. Good bye."

After trying to cheer poor Grace in this way, the Lieutenant hastened down to the river bank, and jumping into one of the canoes that were always tied to the landing for general use, he shoved it into the river, and began to pull up stream with vigorous strokes. In the East he had spent a great portion of his time on the water, and had become an expert oarsman. The canoe, of course, was a different craft, requiring different handling; but with constant practice, and his previous knowledge, Saunders soon paddled his canoe as well as anybody in the Fort.

Like all his comrades in the Fort, he made it a practice never to leave it, except fully equipped, and he had on this occasion his rifle, knife, and tomahawk with him, never dreaming though that he might be called upon to use them.

Having started from the Fort about four o'clock, he reached the foot of the lower island nearly an hour later. He had every moment expected to see the canoe of Rosa and her companion; but thus far no sign of either craft or crew had become visible, and Saunders began to be a little restless. When he reached the southern point, he saw that a canoe had lately landed there, and on searching the bank, he noticed traces of what appeared to him a struggle. The ground was trampled down, and in a manner indicative of violent exertions on the part of one, or several individuals. All at once Saunders perceived a shining object sticking only a little out of the sand. Picking it up, he at once recognized a little lock of gold, with which a string of pearls was once held together. Now the lock was broken, thus accounting for the manner in which the necklace had been lost. Saunders had often seen it around Rosa's neck; but yet its discovery was by no means a certain indication of the girl's second visit to the island. Somebody had, of course, been there, and recently too; of that Saunders felt convinced. But to gain further information, his examinations had to be continued. The mark and tracks in the sandy soil led him to the center of the island, and there he discovered, to his greatest surprise and consternation, the bound, gagged, and almost lifeless form of poor Peter, the drummer boy. Now every doubt was gone. Rosa Anderson had indeed been on the island, and her companion had received a truly barbarous treatment at the hands of parties unknown. Would they remain to be so? How had the poor girl herself fared meanwhile? Was she still living, and, if so, in a condition to make life desirable? The first step to the solution of these problems must necessarily be an effort to revive poor Peter. After cutting the thongs that held his limbs, and the gag that tied his tongue, Saunders carried the senseless body to the water's edge, and by the constant application of the cool and invigorating liquid, had the satisfaction of seeing the boy open his eyes, and after a little while also begin the use of his tongue. The Lieutenant gave him a good dram of whiskey, and this restored the boy sufficiently to give an account of what had happened. The story was rather broken and incoherent, but what he told the officer in that way is substantially as follows:

The two adventurers had reached the island about twelve o'clock, and landed at the southern point. They had hardly ascended the bank and commenced a search, when several Indians rushed upon them, seizing the girl at once. The boy, however, according to his statement, had been taken only after a severe struggle, during which he tumbled down the bank with his captors. According to Peter's opinion, his resistance had infuriated the savages to such a degree that they treated him in the manner above described, leaving him in so painful and critical a condition, that a little delay would have made the work of rescue idle. More than this Peter could not tell; the savages had dragged him to such an impenetrable thicket, that he was even unable to inform Saunders on which side the Indians had effected their landing.

Strange change of feeling! A few hours ago the young man had looked upon Rosa Anderson almost with hatred, and tried to kill her supposed lover—and now he was deeply afflicted by her loss, and wished for nothing more zealously than the assistance of the hunter, in order to support him with his superior skill and experience in her recovery. But how should he inform him in the shortest way possible? There was no brooding, no hesitating in this instance; the loss of an hour might result in the loss of the girl, and feeling this, feeling also that a continued activity was the best antidote for a troubled heart, he set to work without delay. After helping the boy into the canoe, and seating himself, he began to propel the canoe down stream with a rapidity which promised to soon take them to the landing of the Fort. All at once, however, their progress was interrupted in a rather unexpected manner. A clear, shrill whistle emanating from the height above the right bank struck Saunders's ear, and caused him at once to stop his paddle. On looking in the direction of the sound, he perceived a young Indian making signs. The lad appeared familiar to him, and on a second glance, the Lieutenant recognized the Red Fox, who had borne so prominent, though unintentional, a role in the recent drama. If he had hesitated to answer the signal at first, this recognition put all doubts at rest, and beckoning to the lad, he turned the head of the canoe towards the shore. When he reached it, the Indian also stepped from the thicket, and with a nod of recognition, offered his hand.

"It is you, Red Fox, I see," the Lieutenant said, accepting the proffered hand, "and from your desire to communicate with me, I judge you know something of this terrible affair?"

"Me know—Indian steal girl!"

"You say that very coolly, my lad. If I was you, I would be somewhat ashamed of such kin."

"Me no kin, me Delaware, grandfather; they Seneca, good for nothing."

"So they do not belong to your tribe?"

"Seneca."

"You seem positive of that. How many did you count?"

"Counted chief and six warriors."

"Did they—I fear to ask you the question—did they do her any harm?"

"No, treated her very good—chief make squaw, me think."

Saunders hardly knew whether this announcement ought to relieve him or not. It made the girl safe for the present, but merely to open for her a most horrid future, unless her friends succeeded in rescuing her. This thought again reminded him of the necessity of speed.

"Which way did the Senecas go, my boy?" he asked.

"Up this way," he replied, pointing to the northeast.

"Had I not better try to overtake them alone? Alone, Peter could not rouse the garrison; but if you would go along and state the case, I might go after them at once, and check their flight."

A somewhat derisive smile played around the lips of Red Fox.

"May be: you go to Fort; let me go other way."

"Why, you do not expect to stop them any more effectually, than I?"

"No, not better check; but better find, better eyes for woods."

"Well, that may be; but I cannot bear the thought of going back, when I might just as well go on. I surely cannot fail to find so big a trail, after once knowing the direction in which it runs. So if you will do me the favor to go—"

"Me go; but Red Fox warn his friend, not put nose too deep in Seneca camp, or scalp—" A significant gesture finished the sentence.

In accordance with this new arrangement the Lieutenant and the Indian exchanged their roles. The former leaped from the canoe, and, after the necessary instructions, started on the chase. The Indian, on the other hand, took the vacated seat, propelling the canoe with a rapidity, which showed that he had equal skill with, if less strength, than the officer. The current being in their favor, they touched the landing before six o'clock. Their arrival created quite a sensation. The news of Rosa's absence had, by this time, spread all over the Fort, and so eager did the people press on the landing to ascertain the reason of Peter's return, and the absence of the girl, that the new comers could hardly disembark. A hundred questions reached their ears at once, making a reply impossible. But while Peter stared like one bewildered, the Indian looked on with a smile, showing his own convictions of superiority. He did not make an effort to answer, until the crowd were vigorously pushed aside, and Robert Campbell came in view. Their recognition was mutual, and Robert exclaimed : "Is that you, my boy? Your presence here is evidence that you know all about this affair. Let us have your story, quickly, for we ought to have been on the trail of these scoundrels a good while ago."

The Indian gave a short and concise sketch of the abduction, but when he related how he came to swap places with the Lieutenant Robert shook his head.

"He meant well, but I am afraid he will spoil everything by want of caution. Perhaps by starting without delay we may yet overtake him, and thus prevent mischief. As the scoundrels went northeast perhaps we may head them. Is Red Fox strong enough to take a message to Beaver without delay ?"

"Red Fox never gets tired."

"I reckon not, but it would be well if Red Fox talked less and acted more. If he wants me to think well of him let him go at once to Beaver and say: 'Big Jump sends me; he wants Beaver to send fifty warriors northeast as fast as he can, to intercept a band of robbers. Red Feather must not be with them. Did the Red Fox understand ?"

As the youth nodded he turned to one of the men and said : "Walker, will you take him to Mrs. Jones', and see that he gets a good supper. The most willing mind is worthless without a vigorous body to support it. Goodbye, my boy; God speed you ! And now to my men. You see how it is. A handful of impudent Senecas have stolen our comrade's daughter at our very threshold. If we suffer this they'll repeat the trespass. This must not be ; we are, therefore, going to pursue the thieves ! But to pursue is not enough. To catch so sly a foe requires all the ability you can muster. Let each man, therefore, do his duty. You will first take a substantial supper and then start. Sergeant Willoughby has been placed in command. He knows where I will meet him in the morning, for I mean to start ahead of you, and hunt up the lair of the game before you strike the blow. Farewell, lads; to-morrow we'll meet again."

There is something in a speech sometimes. That of Robert had the effect of electrifying his men, and caused them to enter cheerfully upon this duty. He himself did not wait to watch the result. After a hasty farewell to Grace and poor Anderson, who was doubly miserable on account of his disability and his mental agony, he started on his night march through woods, containing neither road nor path. Does the reader realize what it is to travel at night in a dense forest abounding with thorns, bushes, stumps, logs, rocks, ravines and the like. I have seen men lose their way at night in a newly ploughed field, with a few charred stumps standing about. Yet what a difference there is between such a field and the forest through which Robert Campbell had to trace his way. Robert, however, did not go quite alone. He was accompanied by a little dog, of insignificant appearance, but of his own training, and which he prized greatly. All he had to say was merely "Spy, look out now," and the dog at once knew what the matter was. He could distinguish the trail of an Indian from that of a white man, and once on the track would never tire until his work was accomplished. It was wonderful to see the complete understanding between master and dog. The least sign of the former, the most trifling motion of the latter was understood by each in turn, and more than once the dog had shared situations with his master so perilous that a single bark or the wagging of his tail would have betrayed them. But tongue and tail were still, and Robert's confidence in his four-footed friend was unbounded. When Robert started out on his trip he merely held a garment belonging to Rosa Anderson before the nose of the dog, and said: "Spy, stolen—seek!" Upon this the dog sprang to the door, and expressed great impatience to be off.

The first six or seven miles the dog remained inactive, but now and then snuffing the air as if in search of a scent. When they reached that distance from the Fort, Spy showed signs of restlessness. He ran here and there, but soon took a course lying a little to the left of the one hitherto pursued. The night was starlit, and the hunter was enabled to follow the little figure gliding noiselessly along. The dog was evidently on a fresh trail, though the wind coming from their rear prevented him from benefiting as much by his keen scent as he would have done under more favorable circumstances.

In this way they traveled a full hour, until a somewhat lighter streak ahead informed the hunter of the neighborhood of the Connequenessing. He allowed the dog to proceed to the water's edge, where, seating himself upon a log, he reflected on his course, speaking at the same time to his dog in a guarded way: "Well, here we are, Spy, and it seems our game has taken to the water."

At this moment Spy crowded between his legs, with the hair on his back standing erect. There was no mistaking these signs. Indians were near; perhaps he was already in an ambush. This was certainly a trying situation. A novice would have become alarmed and sought safety in flight, but the hunter knew the Indian to be of a cat-like nature, that is fond of playing with its prey before devouring it. If Indians were around—and of this he had no doubt—they would chuckle at his supposed security and give him all the play they could in order to strike the final blow, when least suspected. Instead, therefore, of betraying his knowledge of their presence, the hunter resumed his conversation with his dog: "We cannot swim like ducks or muskrats, Spy, and I guess we'd better stay here until morning, and then go on the trail of these rascally thieves."

With these words the hunter sank behind the log, which lay with its butt towards the creek. Another forest giant lying parallel with it, the hunter was in a measure protected on both flanks, and, benefited by these, he crept with the noiseless and rapid motions of the serpent into the deeper shade of the forest. His life depended upon the stealth and quickness of his motions, and he therefore brought to play all those admirable qualities for which he was famous, and five minutes had hardly elapsed before he reached the cover of the forest, and was enabled to stand up without exposing his person. Now he doubled his speed, and soon a full half mile lay between him and his dangerous foes. Here Robert checked his speed. He was not prepared to do battle single-handed, but it was still less his intention to run. He could do little or nothing during the night, the trail being lost in the creek; but he was determined to stay near his foes, in order to watch his chances for striking a blow.

The Indians in the meantime waited for the moment when sleep would render their supposed victim an easy prey. Maghpiway had at once recognized the voice of Big Jump, and he felt a grim exultation at the thought of so speedy a gratification to his vengeance. He touched the warrior by his side, fearing to engage his attention by a more noisy demonstration. Maghpiway might have made the signal for an immediate attack, but he well knew that Big Jump could not be taken without a desperate struggle; and learning from his soliloquy his intention of seeking sleep, he resolved to wait until a deeper breathing indicated his arrival at a state of unconsciousness.

Thus half an hour elapsed; but, in spite of the stillness, no breathing of a sleeper could be heard. The chief, therefore, gave the sign, and with noiseless steps the Indians drew near the place where they hoped to overcome the hunter. They had everything in readiness to bind him; but to their great surprise the place was empty. They searched all around, becoming gradually noisy in their demonstrations, but their search was unsuccessful. The Senecas had heard of Big Jump before, and this sudden disappearance on his part had filled them with a superstitious fear, calculated to increase the respect they already entertained for the hunter. Red Feather, on his part, was filled with rage at this disappointment, and would have vented it in a furious howl if caution had not dictated the maintenance of silence in so dangerous a neighborhood. Nor would he totally relinquish the hope of yet capturing his enemy, and was on the point of instructing his men when an approaching footstep became audible. There was their victim again! The eager expectation of securing the hunter's person made them forget the phenomena of his previous disappearance, and placing themselves once more in ambush they awaited his arrival. He was walking along the bank of the creek, and if the Indians had not been infatuated they would have noticed that his mode of proceeding was rather noisy for so celebrated a hunter. On the unsuspecting man came, and when he was opposite the ambush of the Indians, Red Feather pounced upon him with a force that sent him to the ground. The hands of the chief clutched his throat and prevented the utterance of the slightest sound. Nor was he allowed to use his arms, for he was immediately pinioned at both wrists and ankles. After that, a gag was applied to his mouth ; allowing the chief to withdraw and leave the prisoner prostrate in the most helpless condition.

"How feel now ?" Maghpiway inquired, as soon as his exultation and the recovery of his breath would allow him to speak. "You think marry Wild Rose now ? You think take her to wigwam soon ?"

The prisoner, of course, gave no answer, the gag preventing him ; but the chief expected none. There is a class of questions so significant that they carry the answer on their face. The chief wanted to glory over a fallen foe, and we are sorry to say that he did not merely confine this practice to his tongue, but also applied his feet vigorously to the body of his enemy. At last, however, he tired of the game, or may be the insecurity of the place induced him to desist. He certainly quit, and turning to the Senecas, gave them instructions for their future movements. He informed them that he had a second canoe concealed a little further up stream, which he would fetch down in order to enable them to reach the mouth of the creek, and from there start on their northward trip without delay. Then suiting his actions to his words, he really went in quest of the canoe, and after an absence of half an hour returned with the craft. The body of the prisoner was lifted in and the Senecas having embarked, the canoe was pushed into the stream and allowed to follow the current, the paddles in the vessel being used both to quicken its motion and to keep it in the channel. Maghpiway remained behind, glorying in the consummation of his vengeance. This meeting of Eaglehead had, indeed, been extremely fortunate. His own warriors would hardly have ventured to assist him just at this time, the whole tribe being really anxious to make peace with the Americans. He stood there on the bank, gazing at the receding boat and anticipating the moment when the prisoner would stand at the stake and in the most excruciating tortures expiate the crime of having thwarted so great a person as the Delaware chief. So deeply was he engaged in this pleasant pastime that he failed to notice the movements of a form stealing up to him with the noiselessness of a spectre. All at once a shadow passed before his eyes, a thong drew his arms to his body before he had fully recovered from his consternation,and he in turn lay prostrate on the ground,his life and destiny lying in the hands of the very man whom he imagined to have just now sent to a northern den for safe keeping. It was indeed the hunter, who had been a witness to the capture and embarkation of an individual unknown to him. Gladly would he have interfered, if interests of less magnitude had been at stake. He felt that the recovery of Rose Anderson depended mainly on his ability to lead the pursuit, and so in spite of a foreboding that nobody but Lieutenant Saunders had fallen into Red Feather's hands, he abstained from making a diversion in his favor. He had often battled against greater odds, and might perhaps have remained victorious in this instance; but the precarious position of his comrade's daughter induc- ed him to listen to the counsel of prudence in preference to the impulses of bravery. So the prisoner having been carried off, the chief alone remained on the bank, thus offering our friend an excellent opportunity of securing his person. Robert had been near enough to hear the questions of the chief to the supposed scout, and he could not now resist the temptation to retaliate.

"How feel now?" he inquired. "You think marry Wild Rose, now? You think take her to wigwam soon?"

On hearing this voice, the chief fairly quaked with con- sternation. This surely was the hunter whom he believed to be now a prisoner and on his way north. Believing himself the prey of some supernatural agency, he remained perfectly silent, awaiting the action of his captor, that would decide his fate. But the hunter was by no means sure of the best course to pursue. He knew Maghpiway to be guilty of conspiring against the whites, at least one of them, that individual being his own person. He knew that it would be dangerous to let him go again, saying nothing of the imprudence of having still increased his fury, and yet he could not help wishing to have him off his hands, as with such a foe to guard he could not think of continuing the pursuit of the knidnappers. If the soldiers of the Fort would only come; it was surely time that they should be here.

And hark! even as this wish shaped itself into a thought, he heard the tramp of many feet. Most of the soldiers at the fort wore heavy shoes, furnished them by the government, and their steps sounded, therefore, a great distance through the woods. The hunter had often execrated the clumsiness of these fellows; but in this instance his ear welcomed the noise with great satisfaction. He uttered a peculiar whistle, which had been previously agreed upon as a signal. It was promptly answered, and a few minutes afterwards the men crowded around the hunter.

"Whom have we here?" the sergeant inquired, as he came near stumbling over the prostrate form of the chief.

"Oh, merely a scoundrel chief belonging to the Delaware nation, who designed to favor me in like manner. It is the fellow who was at the Fort lately."

"Red Feather?"

"Exactly. I charge you to take good care of him in order to prevent his escape"

"We could leave a guard to watch him."

"That would answer the purpose; in fact the main part of the men might as well remain here at present for all the good their traveling to-night would do?"

"Have you discovered any signs of the stolen girl?"

"Not yet; but I have witnessed the taking of another prisoner."

"Another prisoner? Who in the world could that be?"

"I neither saw his face nor heard his voice; but I could almost swear that it was the Lieutenant."

"Saunders?"

"Of course. He was the first to start on the trail, without the necessary experience to avoid the snares of the red devils. He might as well have waited for all the good he did; and if he gets away with a whole skin, this adventure may do him good and take the conceit out of him."

"But they may kill him."

"Not just now—I overheard the conversation of the

rogues on that subject. They are on the creek now, going to its mouth, to start north from there."

"Perhaps they might be overtaken."

"It shall be tried at any rate. Pick me half a dozen fellows who can pull a trigger and set their feet down without shaking the ground for half a mile around."

The Seargent quickly set to work, and in less than five minutes presented the chosen party to the hunter. Robert led them at once across the creek and afterwards in a northern direction through the country between the Connequenessing and Slippery Rock Creek. The latter stream was forded by the party near the place where Wurtemburg is now situated, and then the northern course changed to one a little more eastward. At last they stopped.

"We shall soon know now," the hunter said, "whether the Indians are ahead of us or not. They cannot be far either way, and half an hour's waiting will decide the matter. If behind us they must pass here within that time, this being the only feasible course for them to take. If ahead of us we must let Spy find the trail and then trust to his sagacity."

After these words the hunter and his men retired to the thicket in perfect silence. The wisdom of this soon became apparent, as they had hardly been ten minutes on their posts when footsteps became audible, approaching from a southern direction.

"Make sure work of it," Robert whispered. "We cannot bother with prisoners just now. It's getting light, for the moon is rising. I will take the head man, and two of you the rest apiece. Don't make a blunder, though, and shoot the prisoner, nor waste your bullets on the wrong carcass, for it is important that none should escape."

This was all he said, or could say, for the Indians were drawing near. Robert had chosen his position well, calculating that the Indians would follow the most convenient route. The place formed a natural pass, rising steeply on both sides, and serving as a drain to the country, several little runs wandering through the bottom. The first quarter of the moon just then sent its welcome light over the tree tops to the bottom, revealing the forms of five men,

who were seen walking in Indian file, the prisoner march-
ing in the middle, his hands tied, and his mouth still
gagged. This arrangement suited the party in ambush to
perfection. Deliberately they took aim, feeling no more com-
punction at shooting these Indians than if they had been
so many dogs. The flash of the leader's rifle was the sign
for the men to pull their triggers. And the shots being almost simultaneous, not one of the Indians gained time to
secure a cover. When the smoke cleared away, the eye
saw four bodies on the ground, writhing in the agonies of
death. The work was done, and that rapidly, but so unexpectedly, that neither the victims nor the prisoner had
looked for it. The poor fellow stood like one spell-bound,
and he never moved until the voice of the hunter struck his
ear.

"Lieutenant Saunders, as sure as I live!" Robert exclaimed, running up to him, and without delay removed
the fetters from his mouth and arms. The officer could not
speak for some time, for the savages had applied the gag
with very little regard for the tongue or palate. Nor were
his wrists in a much better condition, the thongs having
completely rubbed the skin off. Robert resolved to stop a
while, and give the Lieutenant time to recruit his strength,
and recover from his injuries. His wrists were bathed with
whiskey, and the same stuff also used inwardly with the
best effect. After fifteen minutes Saunders was able to
speak, and give an account of his capture, without dreaming that Robert was pretty well informed concerning it.
The hunter said nothing, though, abstaining also from any
remarks on the somewhat rash exposure of his friend, as he
deemed the lesson the officer had received fully sufficient to
prevent a repetition of the blunder.

Under the salutary influence of his rescue, the spirits
of the officer at once revived, and, remembering the perilous position of the kidnapped girl, he turned with an
anxious mien to Robert for information. The hunter could
give him no other consolation than that a large force of
both soldiers and Indians were in pursuit. Having told
him this, Robert relapsed into a marked silence, evidently
revolving something of importance in his mind. At last

he started like one that has formed his resolution, and turning to Saunders and his men, he said: "I think I have it."

"Have what?"

"A good plan for the rescue of the girl. Standing behind a tree near the chief, when he instructed the warriors, I overheard and understood everything he said. They were to take the Lieutenant to some other chief in a cave. Now I know of a cave on the Neshannock; and should not be at all surprised if it turned out to be the same Red Feather spoke about."

"Then let us ascertain without delay; I am fully strong enough to stand the march now.

"Softly, friend, softly! The biggest hurry does not always secure the greatest speed. Just listen to my plan now. These Indians were to take the prisoner to the cave. Well, suppose we get up some mock Indians instead, leading you as a pretended captive—don't you think that would secure us the entrance of the cave?"

"Upon my word, that is a good idea, but it would not work in daylight."

"You are right there, and that is the very reason why we must go about it with due circumspection. It is too late to reach the cave before morning, saying nothing about the uncertainty of its being the right one. We are therefore compelled to delay the thing till to-morrow evening, when dusk begins to give our faces the right complexion."

"But think of what may befall poor Rose in the meantime."

"It is true," he said, "by waiting that long we give her jailor a good deal of leisure for mischief. Well, suppose we make a compromise of it, and set out at once. Rose must certainly have got tired in consequence of the long tramp over such rough ground, and there is a bare possibility of our reaching the cave before her."

"Then, for God's sake, let us try," the Lieutenant cried, and his conjuration finding an echo in the hearts of the soldiers, the whole party again started on its fatiguing journey. As they advanced towards the north, the ground became more level, thus favoring a more rapid progress, and diminishing the hardships of the march. At the first dawn of morning, they struck the Neshannock, a creek, on whose banks the cave in question was known to lie. Here they halted awhile, the men taking from their pouches the scanty breakfast, with which they supplied themselves at the Fort the evening before. The Lieutenant being without food whatever, received a small supply from each, relishing his cornbread and bacon much better than ever before in the Fort.

Our party rested for nearly an hour, and then resuming their march, reached the vicinity of the present town of Mercer, towards noon.

"We must be near the cave now," Robert remarked. "Although I openly confess my ignorance as to its exact location. From what I heard concerning it, it opens under a very large rocky ledge. Do you see yon hill? It looks rocky enough to answer the description."

"Then we had better go near and examine it."

"Exactly, only we must observe precaution and not expose ourselves to sight. If the robbers are in the cave, and catch a single glance of us, our chances of surprising them, of course, are gone. Fortunately, the country seems well timbered to the very foot of the ledge."

Robert now began to approach the hill in the most cautious manner. Keeping his party well concealed in the dense undergrowth with which the woods were mostly lined there, he managed to get sufficiently near the ledge to examine it closely. There was indeed a hole at its base, large enough to admit the figure of a man, and evidently reaching some distance into the interior.

"It must be the cave," Robert whispered, "but how we will learn whether it is tenanted or not, without exposing our bodies to the bullets of its garrison, is more than I can tell."

"Send Spy out and let him see," one of the men suggested.

Robert now drew the attention of the dog upon himself by calling his name. Then he pointed to the hole in the ledge, and said: "Spy, do you see that hole? Just you go and see whether you can discover any red-skins there. Go, Spy, that's a good dog."

The dog looked at him, and then in the direction of the hole. Robert repeated his order, and, all at once, the cunning little fellow commenced to walk slowly and carefully to the suspicious aperture. He smelled the ground before and in the entrance, but soon returned to his master without betraying signs of excitement. Robert patted him on the head.

"That decides the matter," he said. "I am as sure now that the cave is empty as if I had been through the whole of it. We may as well go in and take possession."

"Why, this seems to be a capital sort of a place," he said, "and we must manage to procure some pine knots in order to explore it. I think I noticed some spruce pines without."

He stepped out into the open air, followed by some of the men, who, by means of their tomahawks, soon procured a sufficient quantity of pitchy pine wood to last them through the proposed investigation of the cave. After striking fire with their steel and flint, they lit one of the knots, and, without delay, proceeded to the perpendicular descent above mentioned. It proved to be only a few feet deep, and, having reached its bottom, the explorers entered a large and spacious passage of considerable beauty. This, in turn, shrank into such dwarfish dimensions, that they could hardly effect a passage in single file. At its end the cave once more widened into a large and vaulted hall, echoing the voices of the visitors in a startling manner. After this hall there was another narrow passage, then a hall again, and thus wide and narrow places followed one another, until all at once day light mixed with their torchlights, and the cave terminated in a passage on the other side of the hill.

"This is indeed more beautiful than I expected," Robert said. "The cave is a citadel, which I would hold against a hundred men, provided I had plenty of food and a trusty companion. Without that this cave might turn out a very ugly trap, a splendid sepulchre withal. So the first thing for us to do will be to provide for sudden emergencies by killing some game or other, for Indians about or not about, we cannot live on air. Over yonder I see a nice buck ; just stay where you are, and let me try to get a shot at him.''

The hunter crept towards an opening in the bottom, where several deer were pasturing. In those days it was comparatively easy to steal up to them, as the few roving Indians were insufficient to disturb their feeling of security. Robert, moreover, was a skillful hunter, and before the expiration of a quarter of an hour his men heard the crack of his rifle. Going up to him they found a fine buck, which his bullet had killed on the spot. With their united strength they succeeded in carrying it into the cave, and having thus secured the needful supply for several days, they began to feel more at their ease. The cave was very cool, especially the interior department, and meat would keep here a whole week without spoiling. As they had a sufficient amount of food in their pouches and disliked to kindle a fire, the smoke of which might betray them to distant Indians, they merely dragged the buck into the second vault, and then divided their company, and, placing a party at each entrance, patiently and silently looked for the Seneca chief and his captive. Robert joined the party guarding the opening through which they had first entered, because he thought it probable that the Indians would appear there first. Nor was he mistaken. A little before sunset three red men were noticed to approach the cave, leading a female captive, in the highest state of exhaustion. Robert at once recognized Rosa Anderson, and a deep compassion filled his heart when he saw her frightful condition. Two Indians had to support her, and the hunter might have wondered at this complete exhaustion of so young and vigorous a constitution after a comparatively short period of suffering, if his experience had not taught him that mental agony is as fatiguing as physical exertion. He was glad that Saunders was with the party at the other entrance, partly because his absence saved him the painful aspect of his mistress in such a miserable plight, partly because it prevented any sudden demonstrations into which the Lieutenant might have been driven by his excitement. As it was, Robert could carry out the measures on which he had resolved during the hours of waiting. These measures, of course, depended on circumstances, and the hunter had instructed his companions with a view to them. If the Indians advanced in such a manner as to make the use of the rifle practicable, the men were to fire; but under no conditions was the life of Rosa Anderson to be endangered. If the rifle could not be used, they were to let the Indians pass and throw themselves upon them, to finish the work with the knife and tomahawk.

Thus instructed the party allowed the Indians to enter the mouth of the cave. The close proximity of two of them to the girl forbade the use of the rifle, and thus the silent steel must do the work. The sun was near the horizon, and was sufficiently shaded by the trees to hide from a superficial observer the slight marks left on the stony surface. The chief, eager to reach the cave, did not stop to examine the ground, but came on in advance until he reached the perpendicular descent. Here he allowed his companions to pass him, and prepared to light a torch, which he had brought along. The others turned to watch the operation, and they were facing Robert's party, which the lighting of the torch would have revealed to the Indians.

"Now," shouted Robert, and burying his knife in the chief's bosom. Eaglehead dropped with a blade in his heart, and the torch became extinguished by the fall. The companions of the scout moved a second too late, thus giving the other Indians a glimpse of their danger. They at once dropped the girl and commenced a retreat. One succeeded in merely making one bound, when he received a knife in his breast. His companion, however, merely received a flesh wound, and shaking off his assailant, succeeded in reaching the passage which led to the interior of the cave. The darkness greatly favored his escape and he fled with all speed. As he advanced without hearing signs of pursuit his hopes revived, and he was on the point of rushing into the last passage when the sight of the guards at the entrance checked him, but only for an instant. With a rush he felled the guard in his path, leaped his prostrate body, and cleared the entrance before the rest of the guard recovered from their surprise. Once in the open air, he quickly plunged into the thicket which covered a greater part of the bottom. Saunders and his men sprang out for a parting shot, but they were too late. After consultation they concluded not to go in pursuit until the arrival of the other party, which could be looked for with certainty.

Let us anticipate this arrival, and return to watch the movements of Robert and his party after the assault on the Indians. Robert at once lighted the torch dropped by the chief, and stepped to the girl, who half lay, half sat on the ground in a state of utter prostration. As they gently tried to lift her up, she freed herself from their grasp and sank upon her knees, and raising her hands in supplication said in heart-rending accents:

"Mercy! Oh, have mercy upon a poor forsaken girl!"

Robert remained silent for fear that his well-known voice would create a reaction equally dangerous. So one of the soldiers said: "Why, my good girl, we are friends, come to rescue you from the red-skinned devils. Don't you know me? I'm Sam Sullivan, and here is Pete Ingolsby, so cheer up child."

At first his words seemed to make no impression; but by-and-by the sounds of her mother tongue struck a kindred chord, and she began to look around with growing eagerness. Robert now deemed it time to show himself.

"Rose," he said with a low voice, "you may believe him. We—"

"Robert! Good God, is it possible?"

This was all she could utter. Her emotions were too powerful for her weakened frame, and with a moan she sank into unconsciousness.

"She has fainted, poor girl," said Robert. "Sam, bring her here to the water and let me bathe her temples. There, I can manage her now. Light the pine knots we left at the entrance, and then track the fellow that gave us the slip. It won't do to let him escape, for he might bring the whole Seneca tribe down upon us before we can move. Take Pete and the others with you."

His orders were promptly obeyed, and he was left alone with the unconscious girl. Patiently and gently he bathed her face and temples until finally she opened her eyes. After wandering a moment they fixed upon the hunter's face and showed both recognition and delight. Robert put his flask to her lips, pouring a few drops of the liquor down her throat. This acted as a powerful tonic, and with the hunter's assistance she raised herself to a sitting posture.

"'Oh, Robert, how grateful I am to you for this! You saved me from drowning; but in freeing me from the Indians you have done an infinitely greater favor."

"I am glad I could be of service to you, Rose; but I alone must not receive all the credit for what others did as well. There is one person here who would give his heart's blood to save you a pang of pain."

"This is not the moment to dissemble, Robert," Rose said, coloring, "so I shall not pretend I do not understand. I am very glad he thought it worth the while to come for me, though his conduct of late made me think differently."

"He was laboring under a delusion, Rose, which has now left him. But he may tell you that himself, for unless I am much mistaken I hear him coming."

The glimpse of a light and confused sounds penetrated the cave, and in a few minutes the whole party made its appearance in the passage. Saunders evidently had been warned beforehand, for he had no sooner seen the girl than he kneeled down at her side and enclosed her in his arms. Neither spoke, and the others turned aside, that the meeting between them might be sacred.

"Dear Rose," the Lieutenant at last exclaimed, "this is more happiness than I deserve; can you pardon my short-sighted folly?"

"I pardon your coldness without knowing its cause—does that suffice?"

"No, Rose, for I owe you an explanation which I shall give you at a later hour. Now we must not think of anything but your speedy restoration and removal from this place." Calling to Robert, he said: "I look to you for help; you have found her, and you will also devise means to take her to the Fort."

"I'll try my best, Lieutenant, but I fear the escape of the Indian will brew trouble."

"You mean the one that upset me? He came very unexpectedly."

"I do not blame you for the escape. I only say it was unfortunate. The country of the Senecas is not far off, and their bands often roam beyond their boundaries. If the runaway should fall in with such a one—"

"Well, what would be the consequence? They would not dare attack us!"

"Did this chief hesitate? They will dare anything when their passions bid them. If Eaglehead is any person of consequence, we may look for trouble."

"Then we had better start for the Fort without delay."

"With Rose in this condition? No, that would hardly answer. She'll have to make a good part of the way on foot, and I'd sooner wait here a spell than spend a dozen hours on the road."

"But, Robert, the joy of being rescued has refreshed me wonderfully. I think I could stand the fatigue of the journey even now."

"You think you can—I know you cannot. Excuse my bluntness, Rose; but my words are dictated by my wishes for your welfare. You must now eat and sleep ; to-morrow we'll see about the rest. Sam and Pete, if you will gather dry leaves for a bed, I will attend to cutting up and frying our venison. Two of us must guard the mouths. Lieutenant, you may watch here, and Isaac, you may come with me to the other opening. It would not do to suffer a surprise."

Again the men set to work to carry out these orders. A bed of leaves was procured and after Rose had partaken of the savory steak, which Robert prepared with rare skill, she stretched her weary limbs upon the soft bed and in a few minutes was asleep, thus verifying the hunter's opinion concerning her ability as to an immediate departure. The others also delivered themselves to rest and sleep, excepting the guards, who relieved each other every few hours. Robert was the only person who refused to shut his eyes. He had suffered too much from the blunders of others to allow himself to become the prey under such critical circumstances. He wakened the relief parties and kept everything in order until a faint streak in the eastern sky indicated the approach of morning. Then he waked the sleepers and convoked the guards.

"Friends," he said, "we must depart at once, for so caution and prudence dictate to us. If we gain nothing by our speed, we certainly cannot lose by it. One of you must go in advance of the main body, not so much for discovering foes as for finding friends. There is a large body of Delaware Indians between the Neshannock and the Slippery Rock Creek now, and this body must be hurried up as soon as possible. Sam, you understand their tongue; will you undertake the job for me?"

"Of course I will, Robert, and with all my heart. Shall I go now?"

"Yes; I suppose you'll have no trouble in finding your way?"

"I hope not, Robert. You expect me to lead them the same route we came?"

"Well, yes, that will do; the creek may possibly be of some service to us. You may lead them that way, Sam, but be quick. You understand."

"Aye. aye, sir. The sooner I'm off the sooner I'll be back."

"Now to the rest. Lieutenant, take charge of Rose. Keep close to her and adhere to her through thick and thin. That case being disposed of, there's six left including myself. Of them one may assist the Lieutenant. Isaac, you go with him. The rest may stay with me to cover the rear. Having no leisure for a breakfast here each man must take his share along, and trust to chance. Thus everything is arranged. Lieutenant, move forward with your charge."

Five minutes later the cave was empty, and away to the south a few miles could be discovered in the gray dawn a line of silent figures stealing noiselessly thro' the forest.

"I do not know what ails me," Robert said to his companions. "I am generally above forebodings; but this morning I can hardly keep from delivering myself up to gloomy thoughts. Just stay here a little while, I must retrace our steps and see whether there is any occasion for alarm."

Accordingly the men stopped and Robert returned on his own trail, examining everything with the greatest possible care and attention. At last he reached the summit of an eminence, which, though not very high, raised its top considerably above its neighbors. Not satisfied with this chance for a sight, Robert climbed into the top of a tall tree and thus obtained a very extensive view to the north and northeast. Although he was at that time nearly three miles distant from the cave, he could distinctly see the ledge containing its mouth: yes, more than that! at a second sharp glance he saw quite a number of human figures running up and down the hill, evidently excited like a swarm of bees into whose hive a foreign element has forced its way. To see it and to know that a body of hostile Indians had made their appearance at the cave, probably led thither by the successful fugitive, was the work of the same moment. Gliding rapidly to the ground, he returned to his comrades as fast as he could and in a few words informed them of his discovery.

"We have at best a start of them of two or three miles," he said, thoughtfully. "But what is that considering our slow progress? They can make two miles to our one if they choose, and of this you may rest assured. In two hours, at the farthest, they will be upon our heels, and then we shall be in a tight place if our friends fail in bringing timely succor."

The others looked at each other with rather serious faces.

"Couldn't we outrun them, Robert?" Peter inquired.

"We might for a short time, but not in the long run. We must try to reach a place where we can entrench ourselves until our friends arrive. If we can only hold out until to-night we may safely look for relief."

They now resumed their march, hurrying up to the girl and her companions. Rose read the state of affairs in the soldiers' faces, and turned to Robert, saying :

"I see your expectation has proved correct ; you have seen Indians ?"

"Well, it's no use to deny a fact that will become evident."

"If we cannot escape, I want you to kill me before I fall into their hands."

"Why, Rose, it is not so bad as that. If we succeed in reaching a place where we can hold out against the odds, our friends will rescue us in due time."

"And do you know of such a place ?" the Lieutenant inquired.

"I know of one ; but we'll have to move lively in order to reach it in time. Here, Lieutenant, take Rose's right arm, and Isaac take the left one. Now forward, but steady, for we have several miles to go."

The others acted in accordance with his instructions, and for more than two miles the party kept up a rapid gait. The hunter kept watch in the rear, and when they reached the foot of a long ridge running parallel with the creek, he deemed it prudent to make another reconnoisance. Suddenly he started, and well he might, for the Indians whom he imagined at least a mile behind, ran at that moment across an opening not quite one-fourth of that distance away from them. They were so numerous, and seemed so full of confidence, that they disdained to conceal their approach from their supposed victims.

"You seem very sure of catching us," the hunter soliloquized, as he hastened after his companions ; "but you may be disappointed."

"Friends," he cried, "now run for your lives. What we have done is child's play to what we must do. Follow this ridge until you come to its end ; there stop and wait for me. I'll stay behind with Pete and teach these fellows better manners than following white people."

The Lieutenant and Rose, with four soldiers, quickened their flight, while Robert and Peter dropped somewhat behind. They could hear the forerunners of their foes coming nearer and nearer.

"Now, Peter, watch what I am going to say," the hunter said as coolly as if he meant to enlarge on rabbit shooting. "I'll show you what I call a running fight. I picked you in preference, because you are the steadiest man, and have the best rifle. Mind, I say rifle, because I intend to do the shooting part myself. We cannot afford to waste a single bullet, and though you shoot well enough under ordinary circumstances, you will allow that I do a little better yet. Well, I shall shoot at the foremost one of these dusky devils, and, of course, bring him down. That will stop them for a minute or two, I warrant you. In the meantime, we swap rifles, and you load. If the vermin become troublesome again, we give them another dose, and so on, until we are in camp. Do you comprehend me, Peter?"

"I think I do," Peter said with a chuckle, and greatly increased confidence in the issue of the fight.

"Then we may as well begin the dance. Do you see, they begin to pepper away at us, although they only waste their bullets. Take that tree, Peter."

Peter obeyed orders, and Robert took his station near him behind another tree. The Indians, meanwhile, advanced unconscious of their danger, until all at once the rifle of the scout cracked, and the foremost Indian dropped dead upon the ground.

"Do you see how they run, Peter? Just like a flock of sheep. Now give me your gun and load mine; but don't put in too much powder—I hate a kicking gun."

During these words they leisurely retreated from tree to tree, now and then sending a deadly shot into the ranks of their enemies whenever they were bold enough to show themselves. By and by, however, the bullets of the Indians began to fly in various directions, showing that the savages had begun to spread, with the intention of cutting them off.

"Now it is time, Peter," the hunter exclaimed, taking to his heels again. "They must not circumvent us, and if we stay here much longer, such a thing is not impossible. So, here is our redoubt, and unless they have some six-pounders with them, we can laugh at their efforts for the next eight hours to come."

The place which they now reached was well adapted for the purpose of the hunter. The ridge did not only come there to a sudden end, terminating in a steep ledge of at least twenty feet, but it also narrowed on both sides, running like the backbone of a huge animal to a dull point. The thin soil of the ridge produced nothing but here and there a scanty bush, thus preventing the capture of the place by surprise, while the defense of the point was greatly facilitated by large boulders surrounding it in a rather irregular curve, and enclosing a space of some twenty feet in diameter. Here the hunter and his companion found the rest of the party, Rose being in a great flutter over the shooting occasioned by what he called his running fight. She therefore welcomed his arrival with a sigh of relief, and a deep felt "Thank God!"

"I hope you will have a chance to thank God for many future blessings yet, that is if you protect your head a little better than you did just now. A few lines to the right, and your lovely face would now lie low, penetrated by an ounce of lead. Lieutenant, you try your luck, and see if she will mind you."

Rose smiled, but obedient to his hint, assumed a position where she would be safe from the bullets of the Indians. The others stationed themselves according to the directions of the hunter, and for more than four hours an incessant fire was kept up by both parties. The besieged sustained no loss whatever, and as the assailants took good care not to expose themselves, only now and then a shot from the rifle of the scout took effect.

"This is extremely tiresome," Robert said, with a yawn. "If the Indians are as sick of it as I, they will surely stop this useless waste of lead and powder."

"But do you think they will, Robert?" Rose inquired.

"That's hard to say. If they stop shooting now, however, you must not take that as an indication that they will stop trying to get us in their clutches. No, indeed, you must give them credit for more perseverance than that, especially at a time when their chances keep on improving."

"Improving? how so, Robert?"

"Why, don't you see, the afternoon is nearly spent,

and that we can never hope of holding this place if they are determined to make a night assault? It would cost them some men, to be sure, but would undoubtedly put them in possession of the Fort and its garrison."

"Then we must try to escape from them in the dark."

"That would be the best; but that is easier said than done. If we only had a canoe, we might possibly escape by water."

"A canoe! Let me see. The chief took me in a canoe up stream; but I do not know exactly where he landed. It cannot have been far from here either, as I remembered most of the country on my return."

"Well, we must make the attempt at any rate. To remain here would be madness, for the Indians can attack us on all sides. The slopes are steep, but not enough so to prevent a skillful climber from reaching the top. I am afraid they will hardly give us time to perfect our arrangements."

"And you mean to try it on the river side?" Saunders inquired.

"Yes, there lies our best chance, poor as it is. We may run away from them a little ways, but in the end they are sure to capture us, if our friends do not succor us before long. Indeed, I wonder—"

His words were cut off by a loud hurrah and huzza, evidently emanating from white throats. At the same time Indian war hoops sounded through the woods, creating very different feelings in the hearts of the hearers.

"Cheer, Saunders! Rose! cheer, boys!" the hunter cried, setting himself up as an example for his summons.

"But there are Indians, too, Robert?" Rose inquired.

"They are Delawares, child. I know their war-cry too well to be mistaken. Yes, our men and the warriors of the Beaver have come together, thus accounting for their lateness. But come, friends, let us go and give a sign of life, else they may think us dead, and butcher off the whole tribe of Senecas in their rage."

The hunter let the neighboring slopes vibrate with the ring of his powerful voice, and the others joining in the chorus, their voices were at last heard by the soldiers and

Delawares. The apprehension of the hunter was not without good reason. Anderson, whose foot had recovered from its lameness, was there boiling with rage, and, as the Delawares were greatly incensed at this encroachment of their privileges by a neighboring tribe, they felt but too well inclined to wreak their vengeance on the unlucky Senecas. The latter, stupefied by the suddenness of the attack, attempted hardly a defense, and their retreat being cut off, a considerable carnage was already going on, when the appearance of the scout gave to affairs a new turn.

"Here we are, all of us, hale and hearty!" he cried. "We have already killed a heap of them, and so I think we could afford to let the rest slip."

A new hurrah was the answer to his remarks, and the surviving Senecas benefiting by the joyous uproar, slipped away as well as they could. Anderson had, meanwhile, made his way to the ridge, where Rose was standing. With a shout of joy she sprang into his arms, laughing and crying in turn, while numerous tears trickled over the bronzed cheeks of the hardy pioneer.

"Back at last!" he said, when his power of speech had returned. "Rosy, Rosy, if you try that trick again, I'll get some jailor for you, who shall keep the restless bird caged."

Rose knew what he meant; but she knew what she meant and desired. Not wishing, however, to jar the present harmony by an untimely declaration, she kept quiet, praising to her father Campbell, Saunders, and all the other men who had assisted in her rescue.

The hunter meanwhile had gone to the Delawares. They greeted him with signs of respect and admiration. The Beaver himself was at the head of the troop, a sign of respect which Robert fully appreciated.

"I thank the Beaver for his ready assistance," he said, skaking his hand. "Big Jump will never forget his kindness."

"My son can pay the Beaver by paying his daughter. But will my son tell me what he means to do with Maghpiway?"

"I hardly know; the rascal fully deserves death."

"The Beaver knows; but if he answers for Red Feather in the future, will my son forget the injury received at his hands?"

"Of course, I will, Beaver. To oblige you, I would do even more. But it is getting late ; does the Beaver intend to encamp here?"

"He does. It is too late to reach the village of the Delaware to-night; so one place is as good as another."

"Exactly, Beaver; but you would much oblige me by letting me know where and how you left Wild Rose?"

"Wild Rose is no longer sad: Big Jump has cured her. She told me to go and help you, fearing for your safety. She will be happy to receive you at her lodge to-morrow."

"Well, I shall go with you, and with your permission take the soldiers also. There will soon be peace now between the white and red men, and the more frequently they meet the sooner they will lose the hatred, which, as yet, animates them to some extent."

Thus it was arranged and carried out. Venison being plentiful, there was an abundance of food, the first and indispensable condition for man's good humor. A good bed these hardy frontiersmen valued much less, and both Indians and white men passed what they considered a very pleasant night.

In the morning, after a very informal breakfast, the bodies began their march to the Indian village. The canoe of Red Feather being found, Rose and her friends made the trip by water. The weather was beautiful, and the company as gay as could be expected, a certain gloomy recollection of the past trial still remaining. Saunders was also in the canoe, but less gay than all the rest. He kept thinking of the obstacles still in his road to happiness, and only the affectionate glances of Rose were able to rouse him from his reverie. All at once the Lieutenant started. He had felt in his pouch, and discovered the necklace of Rose, which he had carried ever since his visit to the island. He showed it to the girl, whose joyful exclamation was the best thanks he could wish to have. Anderson also evinced his satisfaction.

"This chain I gave her when a child, and it has always been a source of mournful pleasure. I bought two of them, one for Rose and the other for her sister, and I can never look at this chain without thinking of her dreadful death. And now my surviving daughter came near sharing her fate. I feel, indeed, most grateful to the Almighty, who has so visibly protected her."

Rose tied the necklace around her neck, and the canoe sped on its way until the Indian village was reached. The party landed, and the hunter led them to the house of the Beaver. Wild Rose stood in the door, playing the hostess, instead of her father, who had not yet arrived. Robert ran to meet her, and before the whole company drew her to his heart.

"Welcome, Robert," she said lovingly, and with a shy grace, extremely beautiful. "Wild Rose is glad to see her husband safe home."

"Her husband!" Anderson exclaimed, being unable to control the expression of disdainful disappointment, which the sight created in his heart. "I declare you are a sly dog, Robert, and henceforth—"

"Henceforth you will oblige me by treating this lady with the respect she deserves. She will be my married wife in a few weeks, and as such, command universal regard, I hope."

It is doubtful how Anderson would have replied if nothing had interrupted the conversation. As it was the arrival of the Beaver drew upon him the attention of the party. He shook hands with all, and cordially invited them to the hospitality of his house. When he came to Rose Anderson, he started, and his eye fixed itself steadily upon the girl. A close observer, however, would have noticed that it was no less than the necklace of the girl which attracted his attention. After a few minutes the chief recovered from his emotion. He turned to Anderson, and said: "Is that your daughter?"

"Yes, chief, my only daughter."

"And this necklace—how did she get it?"

"Why, of course. I gave it to her; how do you come to ask such a question?"

"You shall hear. Did you live on the western slope of the Allegheny Mountains twenty years ago?"

"Yes, I did," the scout said, becoming more attentive.

"Was your house burned by the red men?"

"It was, and I never forgave the red men either; for my wife and child were cruelly butchered on that occasion."

"Did your other daughter wear a like necklace?"

"She did, Beaver. But why torment me with such useless questions? They only grieve me, and unless you give me the key to them I shall refuse to answer."

The chief stood the prey of a powerful emotion. His body shook under the powerful struggle. At last, however, he conquered. Leaving the astonished company, he stepped into the house, and shortly returned with a necklace, at the sight of which Anderson started.

"Is this the necklace of your lost child?" the chief asked, in a dejected manner.

"It is. See her name engraved on the lock, 'Mary Anderson!'"

The scout stared at the trinket, but his emotions were not altogether of a joyful nature. With a sinister glance at the chief, he finally exclaimed: "Chief, I ought to thank you for this; but, indeed, I cannot. Perhaps you know the murderers; perhaps you—"

"Yes, I knew them, for I was there; but I did not participate in the deed. I can proudly say that I never steeped my hands in the blood of women and children," replied the chief, with a proud and noble mien.

"You say you cannot thank me for the necklace," he resumed. "Perhaps you can and will thank me for your daughter—there she is, take her. The lodge of the Beaver will be lonely now; but he wants to be just before he is happy."

During these words he pointed to Wild Rose, who stood by an attentive listener. After he had spoken, he wrapped himself in his blanket and turned aside, presenting a picture of dignified grief and manly resignation more than which the history of Rome never furnished. On the company this communication acted like an electric shock.

Anderson started, and seizing the chief's arm, said imploringly: "Can this be true? Is it not a cruel mockery merely to deride the feelings of a father?"

"The Great Spirit is my witness that I have spoken true. With my own hands I carried the child from the house, and never for a moment has she left the lodge of her foster-father. Now the Beaver will see her no more—she will go to gladden the home of the stranger, that never knew or loved her."

Anderson was satisfied. With steps trembling with emotion, he turned to Wild Rose, and with outstretched arms, exclaimed: "Mary! my child!"

But Wild Rose did not stir. When he made an effort to embrace her, she simply took his hands, half in spirit of remonstrance, half in that of a caress, and said with a sweet smile, but in a firm voice:

"My father? I am glad to have found one among the pale-faces; but if I thought he would want me to forsake my *first* father, I should feel exceedingly sorry. The Beaver has nursed me in the helpless days of infancy, should I now repay good with evil, and forsake him in his age? Wild Rose cannot be so base."

Anderson listened to his daughter with a mixture of surprise and love. Wild Rose could not read nor write, nor do all the other things which her sister understood; but in the exercise of high and noble virtues she was her superior. Not that the girl at the Fort had not possessed these virtues, but they compared with those of Wild Rose as the bud with the full blown flower.

' Anderson, as we said, admired the magnanimity of his daughter.

"How can you have so poor an opinion of your father? You shall not only continue to love the Beaver—nay your white father will vie with you in your love for the red one. Is my daughter satisfied?"

"My father is very good, but Wild Rose has other favors to ask. My father has two daughters—will he allow me to give him also two sons?"

"Two *sons!*" Anderson exclaimed. I have an idea where one of them might be found, but the other—"

Wild Rose took Robert by one hand and Saunders by the other.

"Does my father now see his sons? Could he wish for better ones ?"

Anderson was taken in. For a moment the shadow of a frown passed over his face, but he was unable to preserve a serious countenance. Drawing Wild Rose to his heart with an ecstacy of delight, such as had not lit up his face for many a day, he exclaimed :

"You are a perfect little vixen. You are fair to look at ; but you are more cunning than fair, and more good than cunning. Here, Rosy, don't you want to hug this sister of yours?"

"Yes, father, as soon as I get a chance. Thus far you have kept her to yourself."

"Well, go ahead, child, and in the meantime I'll look at this other son of mine. How comes it, Sir Lieutenant, that you never spoke of this wish before ?"

"I did, sir, begging your pardon."

"So? You did? Well, that makes your case only worse, for as far as I can see you applied at the wrong door."

"How could I come to you, knowing your inveterate hatred for all the uniformed servants of the common-wealth ?"

"Aye, aye, true enough. But still I preserve my opin-ion concerning them. If I make an exception in your favor that does not affect the rule. But I see the girls are through with the huggin' process, and you will most likely want to come in for your share now. Or have you already tasted of forbidden fruit ?"

In that way father Anderson endeavored to drown the excitement to which he had fallen a prey. By and by he cooled down, however, and so did the whole company, which entered the Beaver's lodge and partook of the hospi-tality of the chief; the plainness of which was still sur-passed by the genuine suavity with which it was dispensed.

And now, what else shall I add ? That the two couples were married in due time you may imagine. That Wild

Rose never deserted or neglected her red father is a matter understood. That the Indians, in the summer of 1782, gathered at Fort McIntosh and there concluded a peace, which like all Indian treaties was merely made in order to be broken, the reader knows from history. Therefore he will kindly allow me to withdraw from his presence, thanking him kindly for his patient attendance to

THE END.

TONONQUA, THE PRIDE OF THE WYANDOTS.

CHAPTER I.

THE DECOY.

THE month of May of 1785 had arrived. Nature wore its festive dress, and so did Fort McIntosh, the small stronghold which crowned the banks of the Ohio, a short distance below the mouth of Beaver Creek. Its days of desolation were over; the barracks were still thronged with the four companies of soldiers which had protected the commissioners in their negotiations with the Indian tribes. The treaty with the Six Nations, the Delawares, and Wyandots had been signed on the 21st of January, but as the delivery of the stipulated presents to the tribes required some time, Colonel Harmer continued to occupy the Fort as his headquarters.

So great was the demand for the blockhouses which lined the inner walls of the stockade, that several new structures had been erected outside of the fortifications by those who had no valid claims to be accommodated within, so that such measures could be entertained and executed without much danger of life or liberty.

Most prominent among these houses were those belonging to Campbell and Anderson, the two scouts of the garrison. True, *they* could justly claim the needful lodgings in the Fort, but they had yielded by compliance what others had rendered by compulsion. Campbell had a family, consisting of his wife and a little daughter, and as the pacification of the Indians made a removal to the pleasant environs feasible, he gladly humored their request, and, with the assistance of Anderson, his father-in-law, built a snug cabin on a spot of the river bank, which allowed a splendid view upon the sweeping Ohio, and the romantic mouth of the smaller Beaver.

It is his house which we now take the liberty to enter. Of course, it was rude like other log cabins, but as it was new, and evidently finished with unusual care, it bore a character a little above its kind. It faced the river, and was surrounded by a garden which, in turn, was hemmed in on three sides by the majestic forest. The front alone was open, allowing an unimpeded view upon the numberless charms which nature, with a lavish hand, had scattered over this favorite spot. The garden contained many signs of care and cultivation, for all around the charred stumps the eye discovered spaded ground, from which various crops were springing, nursed by the generous fertility of virgin soil. The workmen, however, seemed absent, for of the three persons in view, none seemed to have either the strength or the skill to wrest such fruits of husbandry from the wilderness. Two of them, a little girl and a half grown boy, were playing on the lawn before the cabin. The girl was a little creature of exquisite beauty, which was heightened by the fantastic dress she wore. Her body was wrapped in a frock of finely tanned doeskin, with fringes of swandown around the upper and lower edge. A belt of wampum held it around the waist, and displayed the lithe, slender body to great advantage. The feet were encased in moccasins of fine workmanship, with down round the upper edge, like the gown, while prolific curls of auburn color were allowed to fall untrammeled upon her shoulders, and to encase an oval face of exceeding beauty and angelic sweetness.

The companion of the girl, on the other hand, was as plain as she was pretty. He was not downright ugly, but his features bore a look of so much vacant simplicity that it was difficult to calculate his age. To judge from his looks, he seemed to be no more than 16 years old, while in reality his age reached almost double that number. Still, if not a child in age, he surely was so in spirit, for he joined in the sport with a glee that showed his whole soul to be engaged in it. This sport consisted in the playing of an old drum, which the lad handled with so much dexterity as to draw shouts of delight from his mate. No sooner did he suffer his hands to rest a minute, when the child exclaimed:

"No stop, no stop, Peter; more drum, a great deal more drum!"

And Peter, obedient to the order, set his hands again in motion with so much satisfaction in his ungainly countenance that its good natured expression involuntarily gained him the favor of the spectators.

Of such spectators there was at that moment but one, but this one evidently gazed at the children's sport with her soul in her eyes. We allude to the woman who, as already mentioned, could be seen through the cabin door. She sat on a short log fashioned into a stool, and seemed to have dropped, a moment ago, her previous work for the purpose of enjoying the prospect. She was a woman of about twenty-five years of age, and displayed such a resemblance to the girl before the cabin that we, without hesitation, set the two down as mother and daughter. She had evidently expanded from a bud, such as the little one was then, into the fullest bloom of womanhood. Every leaf was developed, every source of fragrance tapped, while on the other hand, no sign of decline, of decay, as yet reminded the spectator of the frailty of human beauty. The woman in the cabin, however, did not only resemble the child in feature, even their dresses were of a like cut and material, with the difference that the delicate fringe of swandown had been replaced by a more substantial one of scarlet-colored leather.

It was a strange sight which these two women presented. An inhabitant of an Eastern town would hardly have expected so much loveliness, such an expression of real refinement in the wilderness, and yet there was in them so much of the savage, combined with the beautiful and refined, that they did by no means appear to be out of place. The garments they wore, their free and easy bearing, the absence of every sort of restraint—all this reminded the spectator that he saw beings who lacked nothing but a skin of deeper hue, to make them in every respect real, thoroughbred children of the forest.

The lovely scene above described was interrupted in a manner as startling as unexpected. In the excitement of their sport, the playmates had overlooked a slight rustle in

the woods, they had even failed to observe a dusky figure
that glided from the forest, and now stood in close proximity, watching their sport with an eye from which emanated
a smothered fire. The newcomer was a tall, athletic Indian, clad in a woolen frock, leather leggins and moccasins.
His belt of wampum contained a tomahawk and scalping
knife, while a rifle was thrown carelessly into the hollow of
his left arm. His head and face were shaved, the former
presenting nothing but the scalp-lock, a trophy which, in
the estimation of the Indian, forms the equivalent of the
laurels, the stars, the orders, and the medals of their more
civilized comrades in arms.

The Indian had been standing and gazing for several
minutes when, on an accidental turn of his head, Peter
caught sight of him. The boy seemed to stand in considerable fear of the red man, for his eyes dilated, and jumping
to his feet, he uttered a cry of alarm. The child followed
the direction of his look and, on discovery of the savage,
manifested similar symptoms of alarm, though in a milder
form.

The woman in the cabin could not see the Indian from
her seat, but, judging from the gestures of Peter and her
daughter that something was amiss, she arose and hastened
to the door with a natural alarm. No sooner, however, had
she noticed the Indian, when every trace of anxiety vanished from her features, making room for a smile, which, a
moment afterwards, assumed the character of recognition.
She seemed to know the Indian, for, stepping from the
door, she advanced towards the newcomer and said in the
dialect of the Delawares:

"Is that not the Black Snake? My friend is welcome
in the wigwam of the Wild Rose."

The Indian replied with a grave nod of his head, and a
graceful wave of his right hand, but when his lips remained silent, the woman resumed:

"Will the Black Snake not enter and partake of some
food? He has no doubt walked long, and his feet must be
tired. He has not breakfasted, and food and drink will be
welcome to his palate. Let my friend come into the lodge
of the Big Jump and rest and eat."

The Indian gravely shook his head.

"The Black Snake will neither rest nor eat until he has delivered his message to the Wild Rose."

"So you are the bearer of a message? Well, let my friend speak, the ears of the Wild Rose are open."

The Indian hesitated.

"The Wild Rose has turned into a pale-face," he resumed. "Is her heart red enough to bear an evil tiding?"

The Indian was evidently well enough versed in Indian customs to know that this preface veiled a calamity of no trifling nature. Yet the placing of her right hand upon her bosom was the only gesture by which she suffered her new-born anxiety to manifest itself. Endeavoring to maintain the even tenor of her voice, she said firmly:

"If the skin of the Wild Rose is pale, her heart is red, and her nerves are strong. She is prepared to hear the message of the Black Snake. Let him proceed."

The Indian let his glances drop to the ground. His face assumed an aspect of sadness, and when he responded he had in his voice all that melancholy depth of which the red man's tongue is capable.

"Ten suns ago," he said, "the Black Snake left the western home of the Delawares. He walked in the wake of the Beaver and the Red Fox."

"Ugh!" the Wild Rose exclaimed, indulging in the favorite exclamation of surprise or pleasure of the Indian. "Has the Black Snake lost the trail of the chiefs?"

"He has not. He followed their trail to the desolate village of the praying Indians. There he left to seek the wigwam of the Wild Rose."

"And the chiefs—are they less strong and cunning than the Black Snake?"

"An evil spirit has seized upon the body of the Beaver and withered the strength of his limbs."

"And the Red Fox?" the woman inquired, struggling hard to maintain her composure.

"He is too good a son to desert his father."

"Of course he would not leave him," the Wild Rose resumed, still using the Indian tongue, but assuming the more vivacious mode of speaking of the whites. "The

Beaver did well to keep the Red Fox and send the Black Snake; but what message sends he to his daughter?"

He said: "Go to the Wild Rose and tell her that the Beaver is dying with the disease which the white man brought across the Great Salt Lake."

"You mean the small-pox?" she inquired, wavering between curiosity and distress.

"Thus the white man calls it."

"But this is dreadful!" the woman exclaimed. "The Beaver dying with this dreadful scourge, and no medical assistance near! Fortunately there are physicians in the Fort; if the Black Snake will tarry a moment, I will go and summon one to go with us to the sick bed of my father!"

She turned to execute her intention, evidently to the dissatisfaction of the Indian, for no sooner had her eye ceased to dwell on his face, when an ugly scowl passed over his features, and an expression of intense ferocity lit up his eye. He had, however, been raised in too severe a school to lose the control over his passions any length of time. Repressing them with a powerful effort, he uttered the "ugh" of his race which intended to bring, and act- ually brought, the departing woman to a stop. When she turned to learn his meaning, he extended his arm towards her with a grave dignity and said:

"Let the Wild Rose stay and listen to the words of her father."

"Well, then, proceed; but be brief, so that I may go for help and depart at once for the village."

"The Beaver has forbid it. 'Go,' he said, 'and bring my daughter, that she may close my weary eyes; but let her come alone. I have lived in peace with the pale-faces; but it is enough that I have suffered them to encroach upon my footsteps during life; I shall not want them to disturb me in the hour of death. Untrammeled with their rites and admonitions, will I start on my journey to the blessed hunting grounds.'"

The woman paused. She had been reared among the Indians—the adopted child of him who was now reported as laying on his bed of death—and the chief's desire was therefore fully comprehensible to her. She knew that he had always turned a deaf ear to the advances of the missionaries, and she well understood how he could now wish to be sáved the sight of a race which at best had been insincere to his and his nation's interests. Much as she wished to procure medical assistance, could she secure the attendance of a white physician in the face of the patient's direct interdiction? No; it would not do. And, having come to this conclusion, she retraced her steps and said to the messenger :

"The Beaver's wishes are commands to his daughter. If the Black Snake will step in and partake of some food, the Wild Rose will get ready to accompany him to the deserted village."

So eager was she to carry out this intention, that she turned at once and entered the house, leaving the Indian to follow her steps. No sooner was her eye off his face, than his passions once more broke all bounds of control, and a flash of almost fiendish joy lit up his face. He entered the cabin and seated himself upon a stool, and when the hostess returned with some corn-bread, some smoked meat and a bottle of whiskey, his face had resumed its customary composure.

While he was eating, the Wild Rose hastily arranged her house and person for a speedy departure, an occupation in which she was interrupted by the questions of her little daughter.

"What doing, ma?"

"Fixing up the house, Grace."

"Fixing up you, too, ma. Where you going?"

"I am going to see poor Indian grandpa, who is very sick."

"Annie wants to go along."

"Oh, no! Annie cannot go; she is too small and feeble."

"No me not. Me very strong, ma. Me want to go."

"It will not do, child. You cannot walk through the woods, and it is altogether too far to carry you. I shall leave you and Peter with Mrs. Sullivan."

But the little one would not listen to any such arrangement. She began to cry and to plead with all the strength of her little tongue. While her mother was trying to persuade her, Peter made his appearance as the little child's second, and said:

"Take her along, Mrs. Campbell. I'm sure she'll fret herself to death if you don't. If you can't carry her I know somebody who can."

"That's you, I suppose, Peter?" the woman inquired, when the fellow ended with a broad grin.

Peter nodded, and would undoubtedly have continued to advocate the cause of his playmate had she given him a chance. This, however, she refused to do. Animated by the unexpected succor, she renewed her supplications with so much effect that her mother at last yielded to her and Peter's going.

The Indian had been an attentive listener to the controversy, and, though it had been carried on in English, he seemed to have understood its principal features, for when it was ended, he thought fit to interfere in the arrangement by saying:

"The white boy must not go; the Beaver would loathe to lay his eye upon him. The Black Snake can carry the Budding Rose."

The mother smiled at this appropriate appellation given to her little daughter; but though pleased by the compliment it conveyed, she seemed not at all willing to submit so far to the dictates of the messenger.

"The white lad will go," she said, positively. "The Budding Rose is not used to the Black Snake, and his voice would frighten her. The Beaver need not see the lad."

She turned to complete her preparations, and, although the dark glance of the Indian showed that this arrangement did not suit him, he, for reasons of his own, abstained from arguing the point. After finishing his meal, he sat with stoic indifference, or rather sullen silence, and awaited the moment when the Wild Rose would give the signal for departure. Her preparations were simple and soon completed; but before she started for the woods, she took her daughter's hand and paid a visit to the cabin of her next neighbors, an Irish couple by the name of Sullivan, rude and illiterate but honest people. Mr. Sullivan was absent, but his wife being in, Mrs. Campbell at once stated the nature of her errand. She begged Mrs. Sullivan to watch for the arrival of Mr. Campbell, who would be back from Fort Pitt in a day or two, and to tell him that she was called to her foster-father's death-bed—a summons which both her conscience and disposition forbade her to neglect. She expected to be back before long; but should circumstances prevent an early return, she would beg her husband to hasten to the forsaken Indian village, and give her both his assistance and protection. Mrs. Sullivan was considerably startled at the idea of making such a toilsome journey with so inefficient an escort.

"But this won't do at all at all, mum !" she exclaimed, clasping her hands, "for yer such a delicate lady to go through them woods in such like fashion. An' sure yer ought ter taike a corporal and a dozen men wid yer."

"It is not necessary, Mrs. Sullivan, and might not please my foster-father. So please resign yourself, and speak of this as little as you can. I may be back before my husband comes ; and should I not, a message to him is all that's necessary. Good-bye, madam !"

"Good-bye darlin', and may all the saints and the Howly Virgin taike ye in their howly kapin! Good-bye, good-bye !"

Mrs. Campbell now returned to her cabin. After resigning Annie to the care of Peter, and taking herself a small bundle, in which she had tied up such medicines and dainties as were in her reach, she manifested to the Black Snake her readiness to depart. The Indian arose and, without further parley, led the way. With his gun thrown in the hollow of his left arm, he entered the woods, and proceeded at once at as rapid a gait as he thought his companions capable of maintaining.

The deserted town lay at a distance of about a dozen miles, midway between the Big and Little Beaver, and as only a few hours of the early morning had been spent, they might reasonably expect to reach their place of destination before evening. So, when the hour of noon arrived, the Wild Rose signified her intention of making a short stop.

Peter had acquitted himself admirably, but although he professed to be as fresh as ever, Mrs. Campbell ordered the rest mainly on his account. A few morsels of food were eaten by all with a relish, and when an hour had elapsed the march was resumed with renewed vigor. The day was beautiful. The heat of the sun was just sufficiently broken by the leafy canopy under which they walked, to lose every vestige of oppression. The birds kept up a constant carol, and every now and then a deer or other animal would glide across their path to the great delight of Peter and his charge, whose spirits rose to a great exuberance under the influence of the beautiful day.

Mrs. Campbell would undoubtedly have also yielded to the powerful persuasion to be happy, which poured in upon her from all sides, if the anxious expectation of a distressing meeting with her foster-father had not dampened her spirits. She was the prey of a thousand calculations, wondering now at the stern dispensation which had caused the Beaver to fall sick so near a place where aid and comfort would have been in his reach. At other moments she pondered on this strange freak of the chief. What could have caused him to leave his new home on the Muskingum so soon and against their mutual agreement, the fall having really been set down as the time of his visit. If her guide had been a white man she would have asked a hundred questions; but, knowing the reserve of the red man's character, she forbore to trouble him. Once or twice she actually made the attempt to draw him out; but the information elicited was so meager and so vague that she soon gave it up in despair. The silence of her tongue, however, favored the busy working of her brain. Strange fancies would, every now and then, rise in her mind, and an evil foreboding, for which she could not account, would oppress her heart like a weight, and cause her bosom to heave as with the effort of one who cannot draw his breath. When her eyes fell incidentally upon her guide, these strange fancies assumed a definite shape. He appeared to her in the garb of a human fiend, a monster, bound upon, and leading her to destruction. So vivid was her horror at such moments that she shrank back in fear,

and had to have recourse to her reason, in order to break
the spell of the powerful hallucination. In this she generally succeeded. A moment afterward she would call herself a cowardly fool, joke with her little one, and press with
greater zest than ever towards the accomplishment of her
task in view.

Thus the day passed on, and as they now approached
the deserted village, in which she had spent so many happy
days of her child and virginhood, the undefined visions of
her fancy gave way to real ones. She saw with her mental
eye the old time-worn blockhouse, whose humble roof had
faithfully sheltered her from sun, rain and frost. She saw
the dignified form of her worthy foster-father, then believed
to be her *real* father ; she saw the lithe and agile figures of
her dusky brothers, the grave and haughty White Wolf,
and the merry, playful Red Fox. She pictured to herself
her former forest life, so void of care and fetters, so highly
calculated to please a nature in which the animal instincts,
rather than the mental qualities, have been developed.
Much as she loved her husband and her child, for a few
minutes she felt a real yearning for this savage existence,
and when at length the first dilapidated cabins of the deso-
lated village met her view, she greeted them with a delight
which, for a moment, drove even the recollection of her
father's sickness from her mind. No sooner, however, had
the joyous exclamation passed her lips, when this recollection returned, and cast a deeper shadow over her face than
any that had dwelled on it that day. The guide hardly
walked fast enough for her now, and when she caught sight
of the cabin, which, for many a day, had been her abode,
she actually forced him to a quicker gait. She even endeavored to pass him; but this he would not allow her to do,
until she was close at the door. Then he stepped aside,
half yielding to her pressure, and when she opened the
door and entered the front apartment, he gazed after her
with a smile which would have done credit to the chief of
demons.

CHAPTER II.

A FEARFUL DISAPPOINTMENT.

But let us adhere to the footsteps of the Wild Rose. On entering, she cast eager glances in every direction, expecting every moment to discover the Beaver dead or dying. The room, however, was empty, and so she hurried to enter and examine the next one, to which a door in the rear wall gave access. She was just on the point of opening this door when a piercing shriek, emanating from her child, and a second one from Peter, caused her to stop short and turn, for the purpose of ascertaining the cause. But what was this? What strange change had that room undergone in one second! The former solitude had vanished, and the space so dreary and vacant but a moment ago, now contained a dozen Indian warriors, who stood like marble statues, but, in reality, acted as so many sentinels between her and the open door.

The Wild Rose was more bewildered than alarmed. The sight of the red man had, as we know, no terror for her, and when she stopped short, it was from the sheer perplexity into which so sudden and unexpected a sight had thrown her. The wail of her child, however, soon recalled her to her senses, and gave back to her the control of her limbs.

"Stand back!" she cried, in the Delaware tongue, trying, at the same time, to push the next warrior aside, and break through the line. In this, however, she failed, for the savage foiled her in a manner which, though gentle, was so determined that she lost all hope of effecting a passage. Now it was that her former training came to her assistance. Unlike some white women, bred in the settlements, that would most likely have broken down at once and taken refuge in tears and entreaties, she collected all her faculties, much like the horseman who draws short the reins preparatory to a desperate leap. Recollecting the door in her rear, and being fully acquainted with the nature of the house, she wheeled and, with a sudden bound, endeavored to reach the aperture and, by means of it, escape into the open air. The gloom of dusk had, meanwhile, begun to gather in the building, which received the light merely by the open door. This prevented Mrs. Campbell from seeing in the aperture the figure of a man, who evidently stood there prepared to stop her flight. But, even if she had seen him it would have been too late now to check the impetus of her start. She bounded against him with the velocity of a dart; but, as he was well prepared for the onset, he had time to open his arms, and to receive her on his bosom. A low chuckle, in which he then indulged, showed clearly the satisfaction which her disappointment occasioned him. On the Wild Rose. however, this manifestation of delight acted as the spur on the flank of the sensitive steed. Gathering all her strength into one effort, she pushed her captor back, and then made a retrograde spring in order to withdraw from the loathsome neighborhood, and view the form of her enemy. With sparkling eye she scanned his features, which gradually became visible to her as her sight became accustomed to the reigning gloom. A fierce and savage eye sparkled from under brows, which a low and cruel nature had habitually contracted. The thick and sensual lips were now drawn into a scornful smile, and the whole expression was such as to cause this pure and innocent woman involuntarily to shrink back. Still her aversion was not merely dictated by the antagonism of their natures; there was a fearful meaning in the look of growing intensity with which she gazed on him. She had seen these features before, and, in proportion, as the light of recognition dawned on her mind, her anxiety increased. Yes; for the first time that day this brave woman gave way to fear. Slowly but surely the enervating feeling crept into her heart, and when at last her lips parted it was with a convulsive shudder, that she exclaimed :

"Maghpiway ! the Red Feather !"

"The Wild Rose knows me still," he said. "I thought she had forgotton her red friends."

Her courage instantly revived under the taunt.

"Friends," she retorted. "Is this the action of a friend ? What does the Red Feather mean by such conduct ?"

"He means that the Wild Rose has been long enough with her white friends, and that she must in the future tarry with her red ones."

"Then the message of the Black Snake was a snare to decoy me from my home?"

"It was the song of the mocking bird; the Red Feather knew that it would bring the Wild Rose to the desert village."

"Yes: with fiendish cunning has he worked upon a daughter's feelings. Still, shocked as I am at his treachery, I rejoice that the Beaver still lives to avenge his daughter's injury. Let the Red Feather tremble at the wrath of my friends; when they find him they will tear his limbs asunder, and give them to the beasts of the forest and the birds of the air to feast upon."

The Red Feather again smiled contemptuously.

"Maghpiway is not afraid," he responded. "Does the Wild Rose think he will, like a fool, remain where they can trample upon him? Maghpiway is brave like the panther; but he is also cunning like the fox, and when his enemies become too strong for him he slips away from them and strews sand into their eyes, so that they cannot see his trail."

"But the Wild Rose does not wish to share his flight; why, then, has the Red Feather decoyed her from her home ?"

"An Indian warrior does not ask his squaw. He motions to her and she obeys."

Horrid thoughts these words awaked in the soul of the Wild Rose ! She understood the allusion of the chief; she knew that he meant to renew his former wooing, and take by force what she had often denied his prayer. The fearful prospect might have caused her to tremble if her indignation at such an outrage had not surpassed her anguish. As it was, she rose rather than succumbed under the cutting irony of the chief, and cried with accents of defiance:

"His squaw! The Wild Rose scorns the thought !

While she lives she will refuse to enter the wigwam of so
dastardly a being.''

The brows of the chief contracted until a deep furrow
ran up the center of his forehead.

"Let the Wild Rose beware !'' he hissed between his
teeth. "The Red Feather has means of making refractory
women conform to his wishes.''

"The Wild Rose is none of them. She can die, if necessary, to escape his grip.''

The face of the chief became more demon-like every
second : with a fiendish triumph shooting from his savage
eye, he exclaimed :

"The Wild Rose can die, I know, but can she deny her
child ?''

A convulsive motion of her hand to her heart was her
only reply.

The chief saw the effect of his words, and continued
without the least symptom of compassion.

"Is she prepared to see the brains of her little one
dashed out before her very eyes ?''

"Monster !'' the frightened woman exclaimed : "can
you be inhuman enough to contemplate such an action ?''

"The Red Feather can do anything to consummate his
plans.   Does the Wild Rose still refuse to follow him ?''

Mrs. Campbell stood the prey of a fearful struggle. She
knew this chief, who, amongst all the warriors of the Delaware tribe, had enjoyed the reputation of the greatest re-
lentlessness and cruelty. She knew that he would not hesitate to execute his threat, and her mother's heart revolted
at the thought of such a sacrifice to escape the clutches of her
foe. And, after the murder of her darling child, would she not
remain within the reach of his arm ? No, no, she could not
suffer her little one to be cruelly tomahawked by this savage
chief; while, on the other hand, it was equally impossible
to humor his brutal passion, and grant his preposterous
demand. What was to be done ? In vain did she torture
her brains to discover a remedy, an outlet from the fearful
dilemma. To escape from the hands of her captors just
then was an impossibility. Would prudence, then, not
counsel the attempt to make a compromise, and thus delay

the fearful crisis long enough to give her friends a chance of rescue? She knew that but a few hours would elapse before her husband and father, if not others, would be on her trail. Their skill and prowess would compensate for their small number ; if she could only gain the necessary time, she felt confident that her loved ones would sooner or later neutralize and overcome all the cunning which the Red Feather might exercise. These thoughts whirled through her brain with the rapidity of lightning, and, supported by that self-control which her former training had given her, she answered the question of the chief soon enough to avoid the suspicion of dissimulation.

"My little daughter must not die."

The face of the chief brightened.

"The Wild Rose speaks with a cloven tongue," he said. "Can she not give a straight answer to my question?"

"She will follow the chief."

"Into his wigwam?"

"I did not say that. The Red Feather asks too much. Does he expect me to forget my friends so soon? If I said yes, he would know that I spoke with a crooked tongue."

"What will the Wild Rose consent to do, then?"

"She will follow the footsteps of the Red Feather without resistance."

"Will she make no attempt at flight?"

"Is the chief afraid to be outwitted by a squaw? He holds her heart in his hand: does he think she would escape without her little daughter?"

"It is well. Let the Wild Rose now follow the footsteps of Maghpiway."

"But my child? Is it not to be given back to me?"

"It is not. The Red Feather wants to retain the heart of the Wild Rose in safe keeping. One of my young men shall carry the child."

"She will get frightened. Let the white lad have the charge of her."

"It would not answer. He might remember that his skin is pale, and that he does not belong to the Red Feather's party."

"The chief need not fear, the Great Spirit has benighted his soul and deprived him of his cunning."

The chief meditated a moment, then he replied :

"It is well. The Jack-'o-Lantern may take the Budding Rose. Let us depart."

With the readiness of Indian oratory the chief had given the drummer boy a fitting appellation. He now left the house, followed by his band and Mrs. Campbell who, having made the compromise, as far as it went, with good faith, meant to fulfill all the obligations she had assumed, and not only followed the footsteps of the chief without resistance, but entered into the spirit of his directions with a readiness which evidently pleased him. It is not to be presumed that he put implicit faith in her professions— indeed, such an assumption would have done his discrimi- ·nation and cunning little justice, but he had just then obtained as much as he had ventured to expect, and, consequently, could not help feeling elated with his success as far as it went. The decoy had been successful. The coveted prize was in his possession, and even if that prize should not surrender without a protracted struggle, he trusted to his craft and cunning for its safe keeping. As yet there was no enemy on his trail, and by the time his foes would be in pursuit, he' expected to be beyond their reach. As this may be, his face had certainly lost a portion of the gloom which the resistance of the Wild Rose had gathered there. He suffered Peter to retain little Annie, and to come so near to Mrs. Campbell that mother and daughter could speak with one another. At first the child cried loudly for her parent, but persuasions on the part of her friends, and a few savage threats on the part of her foes, soon succeeded in hushing her lamentations. The journey of the day had evidently fatigued her, and before the expiration of many more minutes her head dropped on Peter's shoulder and she forgot for a while the consciousness of her perilous position.

Meanwhile the chief had called his men around him, and while he earnestly discussed his intended movements and assigned to every man a part to execute, the Wild Rose had a good opportunity to study their number and

character. She counted just a dozen warriors, and familiar
as a long contact with the Indians had made her with the
barbarous traits of the savage, she was shocked at the
amount of brutal ferocity which the faces and manners of the chief's followers exhibited. They did not belong to one tribe particularly, but rather seemed to be the
scum of half a dozen. The Black Snake, who had been
instrumental in decoying her into this dilemma, was the
only Delaware, beside the chief, she could discover, and
oppressed as she was in consequence of her perilous situation, she retained enough of the pride of caste to feel gratified at this discovery. The other Indians belonged, as
mentioned, to various tribes, representing the Shawnees,
Wyandots, Senecas, and others. They were just such men
as a lawless chief could gather around his person for the
purpose of exciting lawless deeds. That Maghpiway had
severed the bonds which formerly bound him to the Delawares, was clear to her. If he had still been a member of
the tribe, or intended to remain one, he would certainly not
have committed an act which was sure to bring the direst
vengeance of the tribe down upon the perpetrator. The
chief now, evidently, acted on his individual authority,
backed by a handful of men whom their own interest had
gathered under his command. These reflections, however,
did not, in her estimation, lessen the perils of her situation;
on the contrary, she had every reason to apprehend extreme
measures from a man who had cast aside nationality, tra-
ditions, rank, title and influence, to accomplish the one
great purpose of his life. But while her thoughts were
calculated to open her eyes to all the dangers of her lot,
they also gave birth to the resolution to meet determination
by determination and never to cease the struggle, and to
defend treasures more precious even than life, as long as
one single spark of vitality remained in her veins.

The deliberations of the Indians were as short as they
were earnest. After the expiration of fifteen minutes, they
began to carry their plans into effect. The Indian village
stood on a low ridge which separates the water-courses of
the Big and Little Beaver. The party was divided into
two divisions of unequal size. While the larger party

started for the Little Beaver, taking care to make as conspicuous a trail as possible, the smaller one, containing the prisoners amongst its number, entered a little rill which started from the center of the village and took its course in a northeastern direction towards the bed of the Big Beaver. This party was ordered to proceed in the most cautious manner, the Red Feather walking in the rear and watching with a jealous eye the movements of the prisoners. Mrs. Campbell was strongly tempted to feign stumbling, and, by stepping on the bank of the rill, produce a mark which would facilitate the researches of her friends; but as it was too light yet to do this without detection; and as, moreover, such a movement might have endangered the good terms on which her seeming readiness had placed her with the chief, she abstained from yielding to the temptation. This self-denial was greatly facilitated by the absolute confidence she placed in the sagacity and skill of her husband and father. So certain indeed was she of their discovery of the Red Feather's artifice that she could not abstain from smiling at the care which the chief took in disguising his course. Her former training had left a sufficient impression not only to fit her for the hardships of her trial, but also to give her a keen and lively interest in the chase, the excitement of which caused her to forget at times the tragic role she played in it.

The rill soon widened into a run which, after a course of a few miles, emptied its waters into the Beaver. Near the mouth one of the Indians pulled a canoe from under the bushes which lined the bank, and into it the prisoners were now summoned to embark. The chief, however, took good care to keep Mrs. Campbell and Peter separated by causing two Indians to place themselves between them. He himself took his position in the stern, while the fourth and last member of the party stationed himself in the bow. On a sign of the chief four paddles were dipped into the water, propelling the canoe up stream with considerable swiftness, the strength and skill of the rowers overcoming the resistance of the current. It was nearly dark now, and as the dim outlines of the banks flew past Mrs. Campbell's eyes, the unexpected rapidity of their progress startled her,

and in a measure destroyed the confidence of a speedy delivery, which she had thus far maintained.

After the expiration of an hour, the chief gave a signal
which brought the canoe to a sudden stop. On his direction
it was then paddled to the right bank, where the warrior in
the bow seized the overhanging branches of a willow bush
and kept the boat stationary. Not a word was spoken, and
Mrs. Campbell had to form her own conjectures concerning
this early delay. As far as she could judge in the gloom of
night they were at the mouth of another little run, and this
induced her to believe that they were waiting for the
arrival of the other party, which would most likely choose
the bed of this water-course in order to hide their trail.
The result soon proved this conjecture to be correct; for,
after waiting an hour, they were joined by a second canoe
which came out of the mouth of the run, and in which
Mrs. Campbell could count the dim outlines of eight warriors. When it came in sight, the Indian in the bow let go
his hold, four paddles sank into the flood, and again the
craft shot into the deep gloom of the night and the deeper
one of an uncertain future.

CHAPTER III.

On the morning of the following day a canoe shot
around the bend of the Ohio near the place where the village of Freedom is now situated. It was paddled by two
men dressed and armed in border fashion, and as it rounded
the projecting southern bank, Fort McIntosh and the
mouth of the Beaver river burst into view.

"Isn't this lovely, father?" exclaimed the younger of
the two paddlers, a handsome, stalwart young man of
about twenty-eight years. "I have seen this scenery a
thousand times, and yet I cannot lay my eyes on it after an
absence of a day without experiencing the same delight."

"Aye, aye, Bob, it is even as you say," responded the
other man, who might count double the years of his companion without being any the worse for it in regard to

strength and activity. "The Ohio is a long-necked fellow from its head to its mouth, but there ain't many such purty bends on it as this, I warrant. True, I hain't seen the whole of it, but I have conversed with them that has, and every one agrees on this here point."

"No doubt, father, no doubt of it. Some times, however, I fancy that we love this spot so much because it is our home. Just look at yonder spot, you can just see the chimney of our cabin peep over the bank. Does it not look beautiful?"

"It does pretty well, Bob, considerin' that it was fashioned by such hands as your'n and mine, which are more given to pull the trigger than the plummet. Howsomever, it would look much more agreeable to me, if a good honest smoke would curl from the top. I am afeared Rose is poorly prepared to fill the orful caverty which this trip has created in my stomach."

"True," said Robert, casting a keen glance at the chimney. "There is a poor prospect for an early dinner. But it could hardly be otherwise, father ; breakfast is over, you see, and for dinner and its preparations the hour is rather early. But I tell you what we can do, I'll land you at the point, and while I paddle on and deliver my dispatches to the Colonel, you climb the bank and have the calf slaughtered for the celebration of our return. Don't forestall the news, though, for I want to see how Rose enjoys the prospect of an early reunion with her sister. I think it was very clever in the Colonel to recommend Saunders for promotion, and have him assigned to duty in the Fort."

"It is, Bob ; and Rose will enjoy the news as much as I. I must own up I have considerable hankering after Rose number two and her little boy."

"I'm sure, father, you'll be glad to see the captain, too?"

"To be sure lad, to be sure. Uncle Sam's regulars ain't my favorites exactly; but Captain Saunders is a pretty decent sort of a fellow, leaving alone the fact that he is the husband of my daughter."

By this time the canoe had reached the point which projected between the Ohio and the Beaver on the western side of the latter river. The conversation was therefore dropped, and the elder man landed, after which the younger paddled down stream with a rapidity that betrayed his impatience to reach his home and join his family.

Five minutes after the separation from his companion he reached the wharf erected on the river below the Fort. The loungers on the bank greeted him with great cordiality, and endeavored to learn the news, which a person coming from Pittsburgh was always known to possess. The scout, however, plead pressure of business, and, after promising an early gratification of their curiosity, rapidly ascended the bank. Having reached the Fort, he sought at once the presence of Colonel Harmar, and delivered a package of papers which had been handed to him in Pittsburgh for that purpose. The Colonel seemed to divine the feelings of the scout, for, after a few general questions, he said, pleasantly:

"That will do for the present, Campbell. You must be impatient to see your wife and child. These papers will occupy me a couple of hours, and if you will call again after dinner to give me any particulars you may have for my hearing, that will answer every purpose."

Campbell thanked his chief and, benefiting by this indulgence, withdrew from the Fort and with hasty steps advanced towards that part of the woods where his cabin lay. In passing the log house of Sullivan he was surprised to see his traveling companion standing in the door and holding an eager conversation with the inmates. Anderson was still accoutered as he had been during the journey, a clear proof that he had not tarried at the cabin of his daughter. More startled than alarmed at this strange freak of his father-in-law, he hastened to the door and inquired:

"What now, father? Has your appetite vanished in a hurry, or has Rose sent you off again to shoot a possum first?"

On being thus accosted, Anderson turned around and showed a face not only puzzled, but even considerably alarmed. Now Campbell knew that it was not in the other's nature to become alarmed for nothing, and he could, therefore, not help catching the emotion, although ignorant of its cause. Before he had time, however, to ask a second and more serious question, Anderson answered the first.

"No Bob, Rose couldn't well have sent me away, considerin' that she ain't there herself."

"Not there herself; what do you mean?"

"I mean what I say, lad. Finding our door locked, I came over to learn the cause, and 'tis a pretty story Mrs. Sullivan is telling me."

"What did she say, father?"

"Well, ask her yourself. I'm so puzzled that I kinder think my ears have cheated me."

At this moment Mrs. Sullivan made her appearance.

"An' 'tis no wonder ye should think so!" she exclaimed. "'Tis enough to skeer inybody to go a travelin' wid sich a bloody, skulkin' Injun. But 'twas'nt Mrs. Campbell as would take advice; 'twas'nt Mrs. Campbell as would listen to an ould neighbor's warnin'; not her at all, at all."

"I don't understand you, Mrs. Sullivan," said the bewildered scout. "Do you mean to say that my wife left home in company of an Indian?"

"And sure I do. Did'nt she come here and tell me all about it, bless me soul?"

"What did she tell you, madame?"

"Well, sir, she tould me as how an Injun had come and tould her that her father that wus—I main the ould Injun chief—I can't mind the name now———"

"The Beaver, you mean?"

"And so it wus the Baiver, sure enough. Well, she told me as how an Injun had come and tould her that the Baiver wus dyin' in yon Injun town that was."

"Dying, you say?" inquired Campbell, exchanging at the same time a quick glance of intelligence with Anderson.

"An' sure it wus dyin' I said, I warned her not ter go, or least-ways to take a dozen soljer men along. But Mrs. Campbell has a head of her own, she has, and off she went as if her road had a run through the settlement and not through them orful woods as is full of bloody Injuns and savage baists."

"Did she assign any reason for not taking some of the men along?"

"I think she said the Baiver wouldn't like it; leastways, I think she did."

"And so she started all alone with little Annie?"

"No, sir; Peter, the drummer boy, was to go along and help to carry the little one; but for all the good the crazy lad will do her, she might as well have left him home."

"And did she not leave a message for me?"

"An' sure she did. 'Mrs. Sullivan,' said she, 'when Mr. Campbell comes back, just tell him where I went, and that he must come and meet me there.'"

"And that was all?"

"That was all, as sure as I hope to be a good Christian woman. She didn't stay a minute, that's the truth of it. She looked kinder skeered and seemed orful anxious to go and see the ould chief, the Baiver."

Campbell saw that he could learn nothing more, so he took Anderson's arm and led him into the woods, in the direction of the Fort.

When they were out of hearing distance, he stopped and faced his companion. His mind was greatly troubled, and he looked at Anderson as if he expected to read encouragement in his eye, and have his fears dispelled by one of greater age and experience. In this, however, he failed; his gaze met a countenance on which there was—if possible—more consternation depicted than on his own. At last he summoned sufficient courage to inquire:

"Father, what does this mean?"

"It means devilment, I fear, Robert; Indian devilment. The Beaver is not sick————"

"He was'nt at least when he dispatched the runner that met us at Fort Pitt."

"Nor had he any notion to come east so soon."

"His message was that he expected to meet us in the fall."

"Then somebody else must have played possum and borrowed his name and character."

"Father, I have a thought that makes my blood curdle."

"You need not mention it, Robert, I also have a thought, and mine reads *Maghpiway*."

"Just my idea. We must be right, else the same thought would hardly have struck us as it did."

"It aint so very strange, Bob, when we remember what the runner told us."

"That the Red Feather had braved the Beaver's authority and become an exile by the unanimous decree of the tribe ?"

"Even so. Now, when we brush up our memory, lad, and recollect how the red scoundrel used to bother the child with his vile attentions,—"

"Oh, stop, father! Your words call up such horrid fancies!"

"Well, that cannot be helped. Let us think the worst, then we'll be prepared for the worst."

"Oh, Rosie! Rosie! Why hast thou done this to me?" the poor fellow exclaimed in the agony of his distress.

"Stop! Don't blame her !" Anderson interposed, laying his hand upon the other's arm. "This red devil of a chief knew her weak spot, the tender regard for the honest man that nursed and raised her when her kindred could not do it. It was the plot of a demon, and therefore successful. A mind as pure as Mary's was incapable of fathoming it."

"It is true, father, but all that does not restore her to my arms."

"But something else will, Robert; these strong hands and active feet will ; so will these well trained senses, and the craft which time and practice have bestowed upon us. Be a man, Robert. If you have lost a wife, I have lost a daughter. Cease thinking how you lost her, and rather bend your energy to the task of recovering her."

Campbell started up as from a dream. He passed his hand over his face, as if by that gesture he meant to wipe away the excessive grief which for a while had almost unmanned him. When Anderson could see his face again, a great change had taken place. The lips were no longer expressive of anguish, but determination. The brows were knit and the eyes shot forth a fire which foreboded little good to those who had dared to tamper with his dearest interests.

"Pardon me, father," he said, seizing Anderson's hand and giving it a firm pressure. "You have seen me weak— you will never see me so again. Henceforth I will have no thought but one: how to rescue my wife and child, and then to invent a torture keen enough to punish this fiend in human form. Once before I had vowed him vengeance, but relented at the intercession of the Beaver; this time nothing short of providence will save him from his well deserved doom !"

"Amen !" Anderson chimed in. "I pledge firm and unwavering support in this your undertaking. But time is precious, Robert. Let us cease speaking and consider how to act. Shall we apply for help at headquarters?"

Campbell reflected a moment.

"I think not," he replied soon afterwards. "These clumsy fellows are of no account in the woods, and often spoil more than they benefit. Let us go to the Colonel, though, and state the case ; it would hardly do to leave the Fort on so long and serious an errand without informing him."

"You are right, lad; so go at once. Meanwhile I can take all needful measures, so that on your return everything may be ready for an immediate departure."

They parted accordingly. Anderson hastened to the cabin, in order to collect such weapons, utensils, and provisions as the intended expedition would require. Robert Campbell, on the other hand, hastened to the Colonel, who was surprised at his speedy return. A second look showed him the troubled countenance of the scout, and when he had listened to the short but shocking tale, he not only expressed his sympathy and indignation, but also offered all the assistance in his power.

"Take as many men as you want, Campbell," he said. "I can spare you a whole company if necessary."

Robert shook his head.

"I thank you kindly, Colonel, for your good will," he answered, "but in this instance the men would be of no account. I have not to deal with a whole tribe, but with an outlawed chief who, at best, has gathered a dozen similar spirits around his person. What we need is speed and cunning, and the soldiers, therefore, would be a hindrance rather than assistance. If you will give Anderson and myself the necessary furlough and the privilege of shaping our course according to our own judgment, we have nothing else to ask."

"Of course, I will, Campbell; how can you doubt it? Depart at once, and God speed you on your way. I shall have no quiet moment until I see you all back safe at the Fort again."

Campbell thanked him again and after a hasty farewell joined Anderson at the cabin. The latter had meanwhile completed the necessary preparations. He had collected some provisions that would keep and also filled two flasks with genuine whiskey, an article which they might badly need in the emergencies of the expedition. He had, moreover, spread a simple meal on the table; and Robert, whose experience had taught him that only a strong body can keep up a strong spirit, sat down to partake. of sufficient food to sustain him during the day. Anderson followed his example. During the meal not a syllable was spoken ; nor was their departure marked by a frequent interchange of words. These two men had known one another for many years, and during that time had learned to understand the slightest signs and gestures of each other. They had passed through numberless adventures in company, and many a time their situation had been such that a single word would have drawn their dusky foes upon them and terminated their existence. Such situations are apt to create great caution, and a language of signs and signals had as a matter of necessity been agreed upon between them. Habit, however, at last became a second nature, and often these signs and signals were exchanged when there was no special need for such a practice. So to-day their hearts and minds were full and few were the words that passed between them as they rapidly traveled the

country through which we accompanied the Wild Rose on
the day before.

It may be easily imagined that they strained every
sinew to make their progress correspond with their anxiety,
and as they were perfectly familiar with every foot of
ground over which they passed, they reached the neighborhood of the deserted village shortly after the sun had
passed his meridian. Then their progress became slow,
as a matter of necessity. They did not, as intimated, expect the party of the Red Feather to be very formidable in
number, but it might after all be possible that some
wandering tribe had joined his fortune and embraced his
cause. In such a case, it was more than probable that an
ambush had been laid to ensnare pursuers, and against
such an emergency it was now their duty to prepare. Half
a mile from the border of the village they parted, and after
describing the segment of a circle, approached it from the
east and west respectively. Cautiously they advanced,
keeping well in the cover of the bushes and examining the
ground with that acuteness of the senses and perfect circumspection which only a long practice and great familiar-
ity with nature can engender.

Nothing, however, met their view and obstructed their
progress, and so nicely had their motions been calculated
that they emerged at the same moment from the bushes
which lined the outskirts of the village. Knowing now
that there was no danger of a surprise, they laid aside their
former caution and boldly walked towards the center of the
place. They met before the Beaver's lodge, and a glance at
each other's countenance sufficed to inform them of the
similar result of their investigation.

" 'Tis as I thought," Anderson commenced. "It was a
small party, too weak to think of any resistance here."

"Have you formed any idea of their number, father?"

"Not exactly. The trails cross each other in such a
manner as to make an exact estimation difficult. It hardly
exceeds a dozen, though."

"That is my estimate. Nor is there any doubt about
Rosie's capture. It must have taken place in or near the
cabin. Look at these tracks she made. The impressions

are deep and far apart, showing the excitement under which she labored. Ah! how she must have suffered in the hands of these red-skinned devils! Come, father, I tremble with impatience to begin the chase and hunt the scoundrels down. Woe to the chief and his tools if they fall into this hand of mine!"

"Nay, Robert, do not suffer your wrath to run away with your judgment. The pursuit of so wily a foe as Maghpiway will take all the circumspection we can muster. I'll wager, the cunning rogue has used all his craft to hide his trail."

"Then let us lose no time to look for it."

"Agreed. Let us commence by describin' a circle around this place, startin' in opposite directions. He as makes a discovery, may signal it by the cry of the raven."

Campbell indicated his consent by starting on his tour without a single word of comment. His companion left in the opposite direction and a minute afterwards both figures had disappeared in the bushes. Their progress was slow; for, as it was their purpose to discover the direction in which the party of the Red Feather had departed, they carefully examined every foot of ground through which the line of the designated circle ran. The signs of the presence of the Indians were numerous enough, their tracks running in every direction; but when the scouts followed them, they soon discovered that they ran at random and had been made previous to the final departure. After the expiration of half an hour they met on the opposite side without having found a clew.

"I thought as much," said Anderson, "the chief has n't his reputation for cunnin' for nothin'."

"We must try again," responded Campbell, with the irritation of a man who has been balked at the very beginning of an undertaking. "The Indian does not live who could eventually conceal his trail from us, unless he understood the art of flying."

"Perhaps he couldn't, and if we try the game a second time, we may come out winners. Let us widen the circle though, so as to take in more ground. Off is the word and better luck."

They went a dozen steps further off from the center and then started a second time, describing a larger compass and devoting to its investigation the same patient research which had been bestowed upon the first. Still they were very nearly through and already in seeing distance of one another, before the preconcerted signal from Anderson's lips brought Campbell to his side. The scout was leaning on his gun, and something like a smile broke through the cloud which the abduction of his daughter had spread over his countenance.

"The adage is, he cannot see the forest for the trees," he said. "But I never knew its truth until this very minute. Behold, Robert, is this not a trail that would do honor to one of our companies at the Fort ? "

"It would, father, and if we had made our circle a little larger from the start, we could not well have missed it. This seems to be a trail indeed, although I see no trace of either Rose or Peter."

"Why, Robert, you did not expect the Indians to be so reckless as to expose the footmarks of their prisoners? A big red-skin walking at their heels could hide their marks with very little trouble."

"True, father, and you must think me very much the worse for this unhappy blow, to deem such a hint necessary. What I meant is this: The fellows have taken so little trouble in hiding their trail that I am very much inclined to consider it a sham, and to look for the real one in another direction."

Anderson mused a few seconds :

"There is sense in what you say," he remarked, at last; "and I would give in to your reasonin', if I could discover the least indications of another trail."

"There is one, nevertheless, father; I feel sure of it. A chief so cunning as the Red Feather could not have betrayed the direction of his flight in so blundering a manner."

"But, supposing he counted upon our taking this very view of it ?"

Campbell started.

"Yes, that is possible,".he said. "The chief may have left so broad a trail, thinking that we might deem him incapable of committing such a blunder, and we would waste precious hours in seeking for a hidden one."

"Then shall we follow this ?"

"It might not be amiss to examine it at least a little. Come, let us hurry, to settle the point, while the light of day assists us in our search."

CHAPTER IV.

AN UNEXPECTED MEETING.

They started without further parley, and, as the trail was too plain to be mistaken, they made considerable headway for the next half hour. It is doubtful how long they might have followed this blind trail, if the figure of an Indian had not all at once come to view. This discovery seemed to come entirely unexpected, for it caused both the scouts to spring behind a tree, and put their rifles in readiness for immediate use. At the time of discovery the stranger had stood in the deep shadow of the bushes, a circumstance which, together with the distance, prevented a close scrutiny of his person; but as he came nearer, and stepped out into the light of the sun, the scouts at once recognized him as a Delaware, a tribe from which, with the exception of the Red Feather and his adherents, they had nothing to fear. Still, the habitual caution of their calling induced them to remain in their covers, until the Indian was near enough to allow a careful scrutiny, and even a recognition of his features. Then Campbell gave a sudden start :

"The Red Fox, as sure as I live !" he exclaimed. "What on earth can bring the lad here ? Come, father, I am exceedingly anxious to know what this means."

With these words he abruptly broke from the bushes, closely followed by his comrade, who fully shared his curiosity in regard to the unexpected appearance of an individual whom they had every reason to imagine far away.

Their previous movements of concealment had been so quick that they might well think their presence had escaped the notice of the Indian. Such a belief, however, would have been fallacious, for in spite of their abrupt appearance the youth betrayed no vestige of surprise. He smiled pleasantly, and showed his gratification at this unexpected meeting as clearly as his conception of dignity would permit. He nodded in a friendly manner, and offering his right hand for a salutation, received a grasp from the white men which left no doubt of the friendly relations existing between them.

"We are glad to see the Red Fox," Campbell addressed him in the Delaware tongue; "but we are also much surprised at his appearance; what has turned the footsteps of the Red Fox towards the rising sun?"

"The heart of Red Fox was with his white friends. When the Beaver said to him: go and deliver the greeting of a chief to his daughter, the Red Fox was not slow to obey his order. He is glad to meet the Big Jump and the Little Coon in the woods; has game begun to be scarce in the neighborhood of the Fort?"

"No, lad, that is not what brought us out," said Campbell, the cloud on his face deepening with the recollection of his loss. "Prepare for something worse than that."

"The face of my brother is troubled; let him pour his troubles into the ear of the Red Fox—it may relieve him."

"Then listen: the Wild Rose has been decoyed from her wigwam."

"Ugh!"

"A mocking-bird came and sang a lie in her ear. He sang: Come to the deserted village of the Delawares; there the Beaver lies on the point of death, and wants to see you."

"Ugh!"

"Shall I breathe the name of the mocking-bird into your ear?"

The Indian shook his head. His eye flashed fire, and a quick flourish caused his scalping knife to sparkle in the sunlight.

"My brother need not tell me; *Maghpiway* is his name !"

"You are right, lad. Your tongue has spoken the name of a wicked chief."

"It will never speak it again; but the knife of the Red Fox will strike the heart of a truant Delaware. It will cut out the tongue of a liar, and show to the red men and the Yengeese that it was cloven."

"Do you mean that you will lend us your assistance in recovering my wife and daughter ?" Campbell inquired, with an eagerness which showed clearly how highly he valued the proffered aid.

"The Red Fox has spoken. He only speaks once. If he lives he will make good his word, and if he dies in the attempt, he will let his deeds vouchsafe the earnestness of his intentions."

Campbell again seized and pressed the Indian's hand.

"I thank you, lad, I thank you from the bottom of my heart ; your help comes very opportune; for, though I re-fused the help of those clumsy fellows in the Fort, I set great store upon the service you can render. Your senses are keen, like those of your namesake ; your heart is brave, and as to shooting, I never saw the Indian that drew a sharper bead."

The Red Fox showed by his pleased looks how much he valued the praise of so competent a judge. Yet he main-tained his full composure, and said :

"Will the Big Jump tell his brother all about it ? How long is it since the Wild Rose disappeared from his wig-wam ?"

"It was a day this morning."

"And she left word that she meant to go in this di-rection ?"

"She did, lad, but that matters little, since we have found plain traces of her trail. My wife and daughter have been here; that is a clearly proven fact."

"Were they alone ?"

"No, Peter, the drummer boy, was with them."

"It is well. The Red Fox knows enough. Let the Big Jump lead, and he will follow."

"But, lad, I should like to get your opinion about this trail first. It is the only one that leaves the village; do you think it was made by Maghpiway's party?"

The Red Fox at once did the bidding of the scout. He not only examined the trail closely at this place, where they had met, but followed it a considerable distance. At last he pronounced his opinion:

"It is a blind trail; it was made to strew sand in the eyes of the Big Jump."

"Do you think so? If that is the case, it came very near reaching its purpose."

"Well, Mr. Fox," Anderson now interposed, evidently somewhat nettled at the Indian's assurance, and using English in consequence. "It is easy enough to make assertions; but a good deal harder to prove them. Now, what are your reasons for deemin' this a blind trail?"

"It too thick, too broad," the Red Fox responded, using as a sign of respect the language in which he had been addressed.

"Couldn't the Red Feather have tried to fool us by such a trail, wishin' us to spend precious hours in huntin' for another?"

"Maghpiway knew better," the youth replied, shaking his head, "he know who be on trail; he know Big Jump and Little Coon not spend much time, like fools."

"But you see that we were on the very point of doing so," Campbell resumed in Delaware, as in that language the Indian expressed himself with much greater fluency, if not force and perspicuity.

"It would not have been long. The Red Fox does not claim to be any wiser than his white friends; if they knew what he knows, they would think as he thinks."

"And what do you think?" inquired Anderson; his curiosity overcoming his vexation.

"I have followed this trail up from the Little Beaver."

"Well, what of that, we did not expect it to run any other way?"

"But there it stopped."

"Exactly; we are old enough to know that water leaves no trail."

"My father is angry with the Red Fox ; let me ask him one question ?"

"Ask away, then."

"When does he think this trail was made ?"

"Well, I don't know exactly; but I reckon it must have been towards dusk."

"And then you think the party went down the creek ?"

"That is my opinion ; anything else ?"

"Yes, if my father will not get impatient at one so much younger than he ; how soon could their canoe have reached the Ohio ?"

"Why, if they went on as quick as they might have went, they could have touched the Ohio early this morning."

"It is well. Now let my father listen : I camped last night at the mouth of Little Beaver. Does he think the Red Fox could have overlooked so big a party? An owl would have heard, a mole seen it."

Anderson looked puzzled, while Campbell could not abstain from a glance fraught with a sort of triumph, as if he·meant to say :

"Now, didn't l tell you ? Wasn't I right, after all ?"

Anderson nodded.

"Just stop a moment!" he exclaimed with a good-natured smile. "You must not forget that I was by no means certain of my case. Only it seemed reasonable to stick to this trail until we found a better one. If you can discover one, I shall be quick enough to own up to my mistake."

"Well, we have to seek for it until we find it," Campbell answered. "You must admit that such a party could not have passed *us* without detection, and what I know of the senses of this lad, inclines me to the belief that they are pretty acute. Had we not better, then, retrace our steps and make a final search? This trail is as open to us in a couple of hours as it is at present."

Anderson at once consented, and the two now retraced their steps even faster than they had first made them, accompanied by the Indian, whose advent Campbell was inclined to consider in the light of a special providence.

When they reached the place before the deserted lodge, they stopped for a short consultation.

"Do you know anything about Maghpiway's band?" Campbell inquired of the Indian.

"I do not. There is only one Delaware with him: his cloven tongue could find no more renegades."

"And of the others you have no idea?"

"The Red Fox has an idea; he believes most of them to be Senecas."

"Ha! then would he not likely seek a refuge with that tribe?"

"That strikes me as very probable," Anderson chimed in. "In such a case, his trail would be opposite to the one we followed."

"And so we shall surely find it. Let us examine all the water-courses running to the Big Beaver. Is there no run about in which they might have concealed their tracks?"

"There is a rill beyond that ridge," the Red Fox informed him. "If my friends will follow me, I shall hunt the spot."

He led the way up a gentle slope, which fell more abruptly on the other side and formed a small kettle, from which the above mentioned rill issued.

The trio reached the spring and examined the ground with their wonted care; but, although they discovered numerous footprints, they found nothing calculated to betray the wished for trail and the direction in which Maghpiway had accomplished his flight. When Campbell saw that their efforts proved unsuccessful, he said:

"Now one more trial before we give up this spring. The bed of this rill is rather muddy, and if we could lay it dry for a few moments, we would surely discover the prints of any party that lately used it as a roadway. If you will lend me a hand, we can soon put the matter to a test."

He set to work without delay and, with the assistance of the others, succeeded in damming the spring and leading its waters into a small hollow, the filling of which would require ten minutes or more. Thus they gained the much coveted insight into the bed of the run; but, as the ground was rather muddy, it required several minutes to dry sufficiently to display any impressions it might have previously received. The improvised basin was already full, and its water on the point of overflowing, when an exclamation from the lips of the Red Fox suddenly brought the scouts to his side. He had, indeed, made a discovery which at once set aside all their former doubts, and corroborated the conjectures of Campbell. At a place where the ground was more than usually soft, the marks of several feet just then became barely visible, but increased in distinctness as the ground increased in dryness. The approaching flood made further investigations impossible, but they had seen enough to satisfy themselves as to the identity of the party. They could clearly recognize the small footprints of the Wild Rose, and the unusually large ones of Peter, and as this was the principal knowledge to be gained, and the existence of a second party made the conjectures of the size of the band at best very precarious, they took up their march and proceeded down the banks of the rill, without subjecting the environs of the village to any further search. As they traveled faster than the water, they were gratified by seeing here and there new impressions step faintly into existence, to be erased by the following flood even faster than they had been born. They lasted, however, long enough for all purposes, and by means of them our friends were enabled to follow the trail with certainty until the rill entered a larger run, whose waters of course had never been affected by the building of the dam. From this point they watched both banks of the run with great attention to guard against the danger of losing the trail in case the chief should once more have taken to the woods. But though they observed these measures of precaution, they were morally certain that the Red Feather had trusted to the cunning concealment of his trail, and confided his fortune still further to an element so generally decried as fickle. So when they at last reached the mouth of the run without discovering the least additional indication of the trail, they only felt their convictions confirmed, and without delay, consulted on the further measures of the pursuit.

It was now about five o'clock, and as the season would only grant two more hours of daylight, the trio felt it not only necessary to agree upon a plan of operations, but also to enter upon it while the remaining light would make this feasible. So, when they gathered on the point projecting between the creek and run, they felt more than usually impressed with the solemnity of the occasion, and looked and spoke in accordance with their sentiments.

"Father," Campbell at last broke in upon the silence, "I call upon you first to give your opinion of this matter. True, we have discovered the right trail, and that is much, but we have yet to recover our dear ones, and that is more. One false step, and they are irretrievably lost. We naturally look to you, the oldest and most experienced, as the first one to express his opinion."

Anderson nodded like one lost in thought, then, collecting himself, he said:

"Well, you shall get it as freely as you asked it, and must take it for what it is worth. You have just seen that I am as apt to err as anybody, and if I speak, nevertheless, it is with the assurance that you will attach no more importance to my opinion than it deserves."

Campbell merely nodded, and the other continued:

"In considering this case we must take all the bearings into view. First, there is this wicked Delaware chief, who has been ousted from the tribe and vagabondizes about the forests. Being full of devilment, he steals your wife, my daughter, and takes her down the bed of a run to this here place. Of this we are assured; but we know neither the direction in which he has continued his flight, nor the place to which he finally means to take his captives. Still, a body is apt to form an opinion of some sort, and I'm now ready to account for mine. First, let me ask how many places has the Red Feather to go to? And, second, which of them is he likely to choose? Now, as to the places, it strikes me that the east and south are pretty effectually cut off, and as to the west, the Delawares and Shawnees are not likely to give him the very pleasantest reception just at present. Well, if south and east and west are barred to him, the north remains as the only likely direction, does it not?"

His companions limited their reply to a nod, and Anderson continued :

"In the north he finds two water-courses, the branches of this creek, one coming from the Wyandots, or Hurons, in the northwest, and the other bearing more to the hunting grounds of the Senecas. Now, both these courses being open, the question is: Which of the two is it the interest of the Red Feather to choose? From what I know of him, and from what the Red Fox has told us concerning him, I feel inclined to lean towards the second tribe."

"You mean the Senecas?"

"Exactly. Don't you remember the scrape into which he brought the Lieutenant and his wife four years ago? It was a Seneca chief that then assisted him. Last winter, when the tribes met the Commissioners at the Fort, I saw the chief more in company with the Mingoes than his own tribe ; and taking these facts into consideration, I am of the opinion that he has taken his prisoners up the Beaver Creek, and from there to the country of the Senecas."

A little pause ensued, during which the two hearers evidently pondered upon their comrade's words. After its expiration Campbell asked for the opinion of the Red Fox. It was given in these words:

"The Red Fox has but little to say; what he thinks, his white father has said a great deal better than he could say it. The Great Spirit must have opened the bosom of the Red Fox, to let the Little Coon look in and discover his most secret thoughts. My white father has given my opinion; why, then, should I waste time and words? I have spoken."

"Well, lad, you have spoken my own mind. There is not the shadow of a doubt that the Red Feather leans considerably towards the Mingoes, and if it had been my turn to speak first, I should have expressed myself very much in David's manner. I am glad to see that we agree so well, for this agreement looks to me like evidence in favor of the correctness of our opinion. But to know the intentions of the Red Feather is one thing, and to follow him is another.

Have you any suggestions to make, father, as to the course we had better pursue?"

"Well, yes, Robert ; and as we have no time to lose, I shall give them as briefly as possible. We seem all to agree in this, that the chief is bound for the hunting grounds of the Senecas. If that is so, our task seems very simple. We must either overtake him on the way, or, if we fail in that, bring him before the council of the Senecas, and in that way recover his captives."

"But, father, do you think they will be inclined to humor our demands ?"

"I don't know about their inclinations, Robert, but it strikes me that they will hardly dare to retain the prisoners so soon after the ratification of their treaty with our government. The Mohawks have been ousted from the Union for their hostility during the late war, and their fate will be a sort of warning to the others, I should think."

"It may, father, and it may not ; but, as you said before, it would be much preferable if we could overtake the desperado on his route, or at least press him so closely that the Senecas could not deny his presence. It would be an idle undertaking to go to them and demand the surrender of the Wild Rose without the most positive proof of the chief being with them."

"Why, yes," Anderson chimed in; "they could hardly be expected to make out a case against themselves."

"Very well; expedition then seems to be our first consideration. Red Fox, which is the nearest route to their village."

"By water ? The chief could go up the waters of the Shenango and come down those of the Venango."

"True; their sources lie not far apart; but such a voyage would take time."

"It would hide the trail so well as to compensate for that."

"But is there no nearer route? Could he not go up the Slippery Rock Creek ?"

"He might in high water, but he would strike the Allegheny below the village. That river winds like a serpent, and could not be navigated without much loss of time."

"Moreover, that route would lie too near the settlements," said Anderson. "I think the chief would much prefer the other."

"But there is a third one yet. Is not the Neshannock big enough to float a canoe?"

"Not if weighed down with a large party."

"The chief may have embarked in two or three canoes."

"True; still I think the first so much the best, that I have no doubt the chief has chosen it."

Robert was evidently the prey of conflicting thoughts.

"You may be right, father," he replied, "indeed I think you are; but yet I fear to start on the pursuit in that direction. If we shall go so far to the north, and the Red Feather has taken to the right, we may arrive too late to liberate his captives. I do not know what ails me; but it seems the yearning for my wife and child have affected my judgment. I used to reach conclusions rapidly enough when others were concerned; but now, since this calamity befell my own household, I have to trust to the counsel of my friends."

"Not so, Robert, not so. It is merely a momentary weakness, a passing cloud. Don't you think I am similarly affected? If you lost a wife, I lost a daughter. No, no, do not give up. The cloud will pass and leave your judgment brighter than before."

"I trust you may be right, and yet I cannot come to any definite conclusion. As there are three courses, perhaps it might be well to separate and follow them all with the agreement to meet at a certain rendezvous."

"But supposing we meet the enemy before? What can a single man effect against a dozen?"

"True enough, I thought of that objection before I spoke. There is odds on both sides of the question, take it as you will."

The Indian had thus far preserved a respectful silence. He was young and the customs of the tribe were such as to forbid the young to speak in council, while others of greater age and experience deliberated on important questions. But, having waited until then, and seeing his companions unable to arrive at a conclusion, he drew their attention to himself by an impressive gesture of his hand and said :

"Will my friends listen to the words of one so young? When the Red Fox hunted in the valley of the Beaver, he possessed many canoes. But his tribe had to leave and as he could not take them along, he stored them away for future use. One of them is very near."

"And what would the Red Fox do with this canoe?"

"He would go up the creek for a little piece. The Wild Rose possesses the cunning of the Indian maidens, and will leave signs on her trail if she can elude the watchfulness of the Red Feather. Might it not be well to follow the river for a while? If my white friends want to strike across the country to the waters of the Allegheny, they can do so at any time."

"That sounds reasonable, Robert, does it not?" Anderson remarked, after the Indian had ended. "The Red Fox wants to make a compromise of it, and that is perhaps the best way of solving the question. It is as he says: when we think we have gone as far north as we ought to go, nothing hinders us from turning our faces towards the rising sun. What do you say, Robert?"

"I say, let us move by all means. This inactivity is rapidly unmanning me. Motion may cool my feverish blood and enable me to exercise my judgment as of old. Where is your canoe, Red Fox?"

The youth pointed up the river, and starting without delay, led his companions to a place where a hollow tree of huge dimensions lay prostrate on the ground parallel with the bank. From it he drew a neat canoe, which was not only well preserved, but also contained sufficient paddles to allow the entire party to join in propelling it up stream.

CHAPTER V.

SIGNS ON THE TRAIL.

The canoe was at once carried into the river, where it swam like a duck, the moisture soon closing up the narrow fissures which the long exposure to the air had created. When the three friends saw the craft fit for use, they embarked without delay, and soon caused it to fly up stream with a rapidity which spoke as well for their strength and skill as for the expertness of the hands that built it. The Indian canoe was fashioned like our present dug-outs, its form being long and narrow, so as to admit only one man into its width. Our adventurers, therefore, sat one behind the other, their faces turned up the river and their paddles describing a dipping motion, with handles nearly perpendicular, thus forcing the vessel through the water with a power surpassing that of the current. They were thoughtful, and therefore silent, and a whole hour was suffered to elapse without any interchange of words whatever. The Indian had the seat in the bow, while Anderson occupied the center and Campbell the stern, the latter position requiring not merely strength, but skill in steering, a quality which the younger scout possessed in a superior degree.

The day was nearly spent, and the first shadows of twilight began to sink upon the region, when all at once an exclamation of surprise from the lips of the Delaware caused the two scouts to start and to cease rowing. The Red Fox did not wait for a question, but pointing to a spot on the water, drew their attention to the object which had caused his exclamation. It was small, but floated erect, and bore on the top a crest of scarlet. As it was getting dusky, the scouts had to look twice before they recognized the object ; but when this was done, a ray of pleasure lit up their faces almost simultaneously. Campbell was the first to give expression to his feelings.

"A sign from Mary, father, as sure as I am living. Let us paddle up to it and see what she has to say."

The paddles were lowered accordingly, and a few moments afterwards the Indian held the object of their curiosity and delight in his hand. It was a small phial, such as druggists use for liquid medicines. The bottom was filled with a substance which looked like camphor, and which, in this instance, had served as ballast. Above that was a green substance which had been rolled up to allow its passage through the narrow neck, and bore a close resemblance to a willow-leaf. The opening was closed by some material of scarlet color, which had been instrumental in attracting the eye of the Indian. The youth looked at the bottle with great curiosity, but that deference to his older companions which we have noticed before, forbade him to retain it long in his possession.

With a self-denial worthy of imitation amongst the youths of white skin and civilized habits, he handed it to Anderson, who in turn subjected it to a close investigation. Campbell gazing eagerly over his shoulder.

"Sure enough!" the older scout exclaimed, after a moment's scrutiny. "It is the camphor bottle from the shelf above the cabin door. She must have taken it in hopes that it would benefit the Beaver."

"No doubt of it, father, and the scarlet fringes of her skirt have answered for a stopper."

"There was a cork in that bottle, though."

"Very likely, father, but she may have put the fringes in to attract attention to the bottle."

"Why, yes, that's possible."

"It is certain, father," Campbell cried, with a voice to which this discovery seemed to have restored a portion of its former buoyancy. "Captive though she is, Mary seems to have kept up her spirits ; and if she, a poor lone woman, was capable of doing this, why should we show less fortitude? Away with despondency, father. It seems as if the fact that my darling wife co-operates with us, restores to me my wonted energy."

"I'm truly glad of it, Robert, for to tell the honest truth this moping mood did not become you much. But what is this in the bottle, I wonder? It looks like a willow-leaf, and yet I can see no sense in sticking that in."

"Well, take the stopper out, father, and pull the leaf out. I warrant you, Rose has not put it in for nothing."

This, however, was more easily said than done. They did not want to injure the leaf, and as the bottle had done its mission, it was decided that its neck should be broken to relinquish the coveted leaf. This was done without delay, and when Anderson held the leaf in his hand, they could plainly see that it had been punctured with a pin or a thorn, and that a large Latin S had in that way been rudely produced. Anderson was no great scholar, and the awkward figure considerably puzzled his ingenuity. Campbell, however, had enjoyed good schools in his youth, and therefore found no difficulty in unravelling the mystery.

"It is an S!" he cried; "a large S. Now, father, what do you think that means?"

" 'Tis hard to-guess, Robert. It might mean Shenango, and Slipperyrock and Senecas."

"Yes, Seneca; there you hit it, father. Rose, no doubt, intended to inform us of the destination to which the Red Feather was bound."

"It may be so, but in either case our course will not be much affected by this discovery."

"That is true, father; but to me this message is a great comfort. I take it as an omen of success, and only wonder that the trick escaped the notice of the Red Feather."

"Mary must have done it in the night. You see the holes are made considerably at random."

"Yes, that is probable. She stripped an overhanging willow branch, and then set to work like the clever woman she is. The Red Feather must have sharp eyes if he will frustrate her designs."

"Well, she is clever enough, and no mistake; but had we not better bestir ourselves? We ought to be many miles up the river to-morrow morning."

The others at once consented, and a minute afterwards the canoe had resumed its course, cutting the water and passing the banks with a rapidity at least equal to that of the crafts in which the party of the Red Feather had begun its flight about twenty-four hours before.

Night now set in, and slowly her silent hours passed

away. No sleep came to the eyes of the three oarsmen, who paddled with the full consciousness of the great stake at issue. The only allowance they made to frail human nature, was the occasional eating of a few morsels taken from their pouches, the supper of the evening having been forgotten over the excitement of the chase. Yet when the morning dawned, they were ready to continue their efforts, though in a different direction. A council had been held at break of day, which resulted in the resolution to abandon the river, and to strike through the country in such a way as to reach the Venango a few miles above its junction with the Allegheny. Deeply and maturely did they consider the subject before they arrived at this conclusion; but as the trio held the opinion that the Red Feather intended to link his fortune with that of the Senecas, and that he was bound for their nearest village, though selecting a circuitous route, the resolution mentioned was the natural result. They concealed their canoe under a heap of dry brush, and then started at a brisk gait in a north-eastern direction. At noon they halted just long enough to partake of a scanty meal, and then renewed their march, only stopping a second time when the dusk of evening spread over the earth, and the waters of the Venango glided beneath their feet. It had been a forced march even for hardy pioneers, and it was with a feeling of relief that they stretched their limbs on the soft moss, and snatched a few hours of sleep, one of them, however keeping watch, as the close neighborhood of the Senecas, and the possibility of an early passage of Maghpiway's party made such precaution necessary. In turn they slept and watched, and when another morning broke upon the world the three hunters were fully restored and ready for the work which they knew to be close at hand. They had been thirty-six hours on the way now, and considering that the chief had the advantage of a start of an entire day, they could look hourly for his arrival.

It has already been stated that their belief of the Red Feather's probable movements amounted to conviction; but as they were fully conscious of their liability to err, they took their measures in such a way as to counteract the consequences of a mistake. As the Red Fox was best acquainted with the country, he received the charge of crossing the creek and following the steep ridge that ran along its eastern bank to a point, from which he could gain a sight of the Seneca village at its junction with the Allegheny. There he was to remain concealed and to watch for the arrival of the Red Feather, in case the chief should have taken a different route from the one anticipated by his pursuers. He was to report any discovery without delay, and as the computed distance from the village to their present station did not exceed five miles, the communication could be made without much loss of time. If he did not discover anything during the day he was to rejoin his comrades nevertheless in the evening, as the absence of light would prevent close observations and new developments might make the renewal of a consultation desirable, if not necessary.

The darkness of night had only partially disappeared, when the Red Fox started on his mission. He benefitted by a fallen pine tree, which lay across the channel of the creek and formed a natural bridge. This he passed with the light and elastic step peculiar to the red man, and after reaching the opposite bank vanished in the forest. The two scouts on the other hand set to work to carry out such measures as their situation and the character of the place they occupied suggested. The struggle with a strong party so near the Seneca village was exceedingly hazardous. The report of a gun could be heard three or four miles off, and might under favorable circumstances even reach the village. If then a conflict was to take place, it must be under circumstances which would neutralize the advantage of greater numbers and secure the victory to the whites, before any interference on the part of the Senecas could deprive them of its fruits. For this purpose it became of the greatest importance to stop the passage of the canoes and let the rifles play upon the savages, before their first consternation on falling into an ambush had vanished. Fortunately their place of concealment favored such a measure, or—to do the scouts justice—it had rather been selected with such a view. The huge pine had—as above mentioned—fallen across the river bed in such a manner as to leave a space of some five feet between the tree and the water. As there were no branches on that part of the trunk which spanned the channel, the tree really was no obstacle to the passage of a small canoe, and if there was to be a stoppage, it had first to be created. To accomplish this the two scouts now set to work. They had noticed that the pine tree had struck a second and higher bank receiving a fracture, which threatened to result in a complete separation of the parts in case of a further strain upon the injured spot. Nor was the hold with which the roots of the tree sustained the position of the butt end much more secure; an old decaying log supported it more than the roots themselves. The scouts noticed on the spot that a small lever applied to this log in the proper place, would cause it to swing around in such a manner as to deprive the pine tree of its support, and therefore force it into the creek, the few small roots being apparently insufficient to uphold it. It was at least worth trial and seizing a couple of young hickories which a whirlwind or other cause had uprooted, the scouts set to work. They had both strength and experience which aided them in the effort, and the result more than justified their expectations. The supporting log was set in motion with comparative ease, and as it changed its place the roots of the pine tree commenced to snap, and it began its downward career with an uproar that startled, while it gratified the scouts. The butt struck the water with a, splash that sent the spray to the highest tree-tops, and hardly had the agitated element returned into its wonted state, when the fractured end on the opposite bank followed suit, and fell in such a way as to leave only the narrow space of a few inches between it and the lower bank and the surface of the water. The roots of the near end also kept the butt from sinking to the bottom of the creek, and thus the trunk formed the most effectual boom which the scouts could have wished or fashioned. ·

When they saw that their design had so well succeeded, they obliterated the signs of their presence as best they could, and then concealed themselves on a spot, from which their rifles could command the creek above and below the boom, while they themselves were effectually protected from hostile bullets. They did not know how long they would have to wait, but they were prepared to wait for days if necessary, their frontier training having taught them a patient perseverance, which we find but rarely in more densely settled and more highly civilized portions of the land. Their experience and—if I am allowed the expression—their instinct had led them to believe that their foe would approach the Seneca village on the water-course, which they just then had barred in such an effectual manner. A life like theirs is not only apt to sharpen the senses, until they reach an acuteness truly miraculous to the dweller of the city, but to bring out all the animal propensites of the human nature, and to awaken that strange guide of the lower animal, commonly called instinct, but often the result of observation and experience. The following pages will show the reader how close the reasoning of the scouts came to the truth, and that nothing but additional circumstances to grasp, all of which is beyond the power of the human mind, caused a disappointment of their expectations.

About the same time at which the construction of the rude but effectual boom took place, an Indian warrior left the village of the Senecas. He followed the right bank of the Venango, preserving, however, a straight line and approaching or leaving the creek in proportion to its curvatures. The creek describes a slight curve, deviating from its south-eastern course to one a little more due south, and as the warrior proceeded on a line as nearly straight as circumstances would allow, he crossed the trail of our friends about a mile from their place of concealment. He started at the sight of foot-prints which were evidently of recent date, and partly made by white men. His practiced eye found no difficulty in ascertaining this fact, since the white man puts his toes outward, while the Indian places his foot straight, and sometimes even slightly inward.

The discovery of the trail seemed to puzzle the Indian considerably. Perhaps the nature of his errand was such as to make the neighborhood of pale-faces very undesirable; perhaps his feelings were merely those of curiosity; however this may be, it is certain that he deserted his original route, and began to follow the trail with all the caution which the red man is apt to exercise on such occasions. He proceeded with the greatest circumspection, creeping from shrub to shrub, and taking particular care to protect his body from the gaze or bullet of an enemy in front.

When the high ridge of the opposite bank came in view he stopped, and spent full fifteen minutes in scrutinizing the entire region with an eye rivalling in keenness that of the falcon. He was still a considerable distance from the creek, and therefore failed to discover the well concealed bodies of the scouts, but the habitual caution of the Indian prevented him from following the trail in a straight line. The creek was too natural a stopping place as that he should have ventured to approach it just at the intersection with the trail.

Fearing an ambush, he turned towards the left and approached the river in a curve, which enabled him to maintain an equal distance from the suspected point. The movements of a serpent could not have excelled those of the Indian in stealth and secrecy. His body was almost always concealed by some dense bush or other, and if he had to expose it to view for want of a cover his motions were so noiseless or so rapid, and the color of his dusky form blended so well with that of the ground that one would have had to look a second time to distinguish its outlines.

To make the circuit consumed fully half an hour, when the warrior at last reached the line of bushes which fringed the creek and, with careful eye, viewed the river, a sight met his gaze which fully paid for his trouble. He seemed to be familiar with the region, for no sooner had his eye met the boom, when it remained riveted on it with a steadiness which showed that something unusual had attracted his attention. The splinters of the fractured spot were too fresh to have been exposed to the sun and weather any length of time. Nor had the roots of the pine tree and the bank above lost that darker shade which an immersion into or contact with water always leaves behind. Perhaps the spy had recently seen the tree in a different position; perhaps he possessed the knowledge of facts that gave him a clue to the change; however this may be, a look of intelligence flashed from his dark eye; a smile of contempt passed over his dusky features, and without the loss of another minute he began to retreat with the same caution which had characterized his advance. Instead, however, of returning to the trail, he pursued a course which formed an acute angle with the creek until he had reached a point which was fully a mile from the bank. Then and there his caution greatly diminished, his gait merely retaining that stealth and noiselessness, which is habitual with the red man, even under ordinary circumstances. He now pur- sued the direction which we saw him originally maintain, and so rapid was his progress that after the expiration of two hours he was fully ten miles from the scene of his late exploration.

His own course had been nearly as straight as the flight of an arrow; but as the creek described the above mentioned curve he had again reached its banks. Stopping a moment, his keen eye swept up and down the leafy seam that fringed the water-course, as if he was in search of some land-mark or other. When he failed to discover what he searched, he followed the bank in an upward direction, stopping every now and then and renewing his gaze with the former keenness. In this manner he turned a sharp bend of the creek. and then at once perceived a little island, which was densely wooded, the branches of the trees and bushes hanging in large clusters over and dipping their ends into the limpid flood. At the sight of this island a look of pleasure lit up the Indian's eye; he stopped abreast of it, and in rapid succession uttered three shrill sounds which were such close imitations of the cry of a crow that numerous responses from those birds awakened the echoes of the hills. There was, however, another response from the island, for which the Indian evidently had been waiting, for, when the bushes parted of a sudden, and allowed a canoe to glide into the current of the creek, he seemed neither surprised nor alarmed. There was one warrior in the vessel, who, with one vigorous stroke of his paddle, sent it across the creek, and caused it to land in a little cove densely fringed with bushes. These he parted, and, after securing the canoe, stepped upon the bank. The new comer advanced towards him with every mark of respect, and raised his hand in greeting. The warrior from the island returned the salutation by a nod of his head, then he said:

"The Bouncing Deer is welcome; what news has he for Maghpiway?"

"He has good news. The ears of the Senecas are open; they expect the chief at their council fire to smoke with him the calumet, and to share with him their food and drink. The chief is welcome at the lodges."

"Good!" the other ejaculated. "Let the Bouncing Deer follow me into the canoe. My warriors are impatient to depart."

The Red Feather was on the point of turning, but when he saw that the runner preserved an unaltered position he knew that there was other news in reserve, which might, perhaps, not be quite so acceptable. But, whatever its character, he had to learn it: so he again turned towards the runner, and said:

"The Bouncing Deer has something else to communicate: let him speak."

"The Bouncing Deer crossed a trail."

"Well, the woods around the village must be full of them."

"This trail was the trail of pale-faces."

"Ugh!"

This exclamation contained the elements of both surprise and alarm. White men near the Seneca village, and at such a time? A guilty conscience is always ready to bring events into bearing upon itself.

"Is my young man sure?" the chief resumed.

"The Bouncing Deer has eyes; he can distinguish the trail of the pale-face from that of the Indian."

This was uttered with a sort of wounded pride: but it showed at the same time that the authority of this outlawed chief was based on a feeble foundation. He knew this, no doubt, for, changing his tone into one of commendation, he replied:

"It is true, and Maghpiway might have known. Is, the trail large?"

"Two pale-faces and one Indian."

"Did the Bouncing Deer follow it?"

"He did."

The tone of the runner was surly, and the chief thought proper to apologize.

"Let the Bouncing Deer forget the words of Maghpiway. His skill and prowess are above suspicion. If he will speak, the ears of a chief are open to hear his words."

Thus mollified the runner related his story, which was received with the most marked attention by the chief. When it was finished the latter pondered a few minutes, and said:

"The plans of the Red Feather have been betrayed. He does not know how this was possible; but he cannot doubt the evidence of the Bouncing Deer. My young men must leave their canoes, and strike for the village, through the forest."

The face of the runner assumed a slight touch of derision.

"There are but three men," he said; "if the Red Feather will give the Bouncing Deer six warriors, he will take three scalps before the evening."

It was now the turn of the chief to look contempt. He stepped up to the runner and said, impressively:

"My young warrior does not know what he says. Does he know the men that made the trail?"

"He does not," the runner replied, subdued by the manner of the chief.

"Well, Maghpiway does; he will tell the Bouncing Deer. Has he ever heard of the Little Coon?"

"Ugh!"

This exclamation was sufficient evidence that the reputation of that person had penetrated to the runner's ears.

"Has he ever heard of the Big Jump?"

"Ugh!"

This time the sound came out with redoubled emphasis, and while uttering it the Indian looked involuntarily around as if afraid that the owner of that formidable name might show himself.

"The red man's name Maghpiway does not know ; but the Bouncing Deer may be sure that the pale-faces have a companion worthy of their fame. Is my young friend still bound to take their scalps ?"

"I still think it could be done; six Indian warriors ought to be a match for two pale-faces."

"Well, perhaps they are," the chief said, thoughtfully ; "but it does not suit my plans to seek strife. Let the Bouncing Deer follow me into the canoe : it is time that we should start."

The runner obeyed without contradiction, and a few minutes later the canoe, with its two inmates, shot back under the leafy canopy overhanging the water around the island. There it joined another, in which the prisoners were stationed. They observed pretty much the same order which we noticed when we parted from them a few days ago. But if the dim, greenish light of the leafy cover does not deceive us, their faces wear a much more dejected mien. The eyes of the child look red and inflamed from weeping, and while the countenance of Peter shows all the concernment in the welfare of his ward, of which his dull nature is capable, the pale, careworn features of the Wild Rose betray the double interest of the mother in the fate of her child, and her own doubtful destiny.

On the arrival of the canoe, half a dozen warriors emerged from the bushes of the island and took their seats in the two vessels. When this was done, the chief whispered a few orders to his men, and then gave the signal for departure. One stroke of the paddle forced the canoes into the current, and when they had assumed their intended positions, powerful, but noiseless strokes forced them down stream with a rapidity which quickly diminished the distance between them and the boom. The Red Feather had given his orders, and now waited for their execution, seeming totally unconcerned in regard to the perilous neighborhood. All at once the Bouncing Deer, who had taken the front seat in the first canoe, raised his hand. No sooner had this signal been given when the canoes turned their bows toward the left or eastern shore, and once more glided under the fringing bushes that overhung the water. The chief stepped on the bank, and by motion of his hand invited the captives to disembark. This was done without difficulty, as the shore consisted of a sandy beach which rose so gradually to the second or higher bank, that its ascent presented no obstacle whatever. The canoes were securely fastened, and then the company began to climb the steep ridge which rose in close proximity to the river, and reached a considerable height. The ascent was rough, but on the summit they struck an Indian path, and proceeded with comparative ease. The greatest silence was preserved by the whole party, nor did the chief allow even the shortest halt, although the sun had reached the meridian and was sending down his hottest rays. The captives began to show signs of fatigue, especially Peter, who was greatly troubled with the management of his fretful charge, when all at once the woods opened before the party and allowed the view into the narrow valley of the Allegheny. At their feet flowed the Venango, effecting a little to the left its junction with the Allegheny, and on the opposite bank of the lesser stream lay the small and artless village of the Senecas, at which the destiny of the captives was to be decided. A steep path led into the bottom, where the party at once embarked in a couple of canoes, and by this means crossed over to the western bank. The Wild Rose entered the village with a heavy heart, but in spite of her dejection she could not prevent a feeling of relief from stealing over her heart at the thought that the fatigues of the day were at an end, and that a temporary rest at least would follow the shifting scenes of the flight.

CHAPTER VI.

INDIAN POLICY.

We must now return to the two scouts, who remained in their cover patiently waiting for the arrival of their foes, when all at once the cry of the raven, three times repeated,

and emanating from the opposite ridge, startled them, and
caused them to break the deep silence into which they had
sunk. Campbell answered the signal, and shortly afterwards the Red Fox made his appearance on the bank, and
beckoned them to join him. As they knew that he must
have weighty reasons for this conduct, they crossed at once
and ascended to the point where he awaited their coming.
No sooner had they cast a look upon his face when they
saw that he had important news in store for them. Still
his gravity would not permit him to divulge his information with an unbecoming haste, and he therefore preserved
a dignified silence until Campbell, somewhat impatiently,
inquired:

"Well, lad, what is the matter? Has a panther broke
in upon the Senecas and frightened their women?"

"Not a panther," the Indian responded, with pointed
significance, "but the Big Jump was not altogether wrong;
the Red Fox saw a renegade chief and some prisoners enter
the Indian village."

"Ugh!" both scouts exclaimed, uttering the sound
which the red man used in moments of excitement.

"The Red Fox cannot mean the Red Feather?" Campbell continued, showing by the eagerness of his voice that
he feared an affirmative, but wished the contrary.

"It is as my brother says; Maghpiway is in the village
of the Senecas."

"I cannot understand it; which way did he arrive?"

"He passed my cover so closely that my tomahawk
could have cleft his skull."

"He must have received a warning then and left the
creek," Anderson suggested.

"Very likely, though it passes my understanding how
that was possible. Well, it has been done and cannot be
undone, and we can do nothing better than to start for the
village without delay, and trust to Indian honesty."

"It is as well so, Robert," Anderson remarked; "the
fight against such heavy odds was exceedingly doubtful,
and if we had failed in liberating the captives, our chances
for an appeal to the Senecas would have been gone, leaving
alone the risk of our falling into their hands. Don't get

down hearted, lad, I have an idea that our mission will not be in vain."

"I trust it may be so; indeed, I think that you are right. But let us hasten to reach the village before the chief has time to hatch new mischief. We ought to cross the creek so as to avoid all further delay when we get in sight of the place."

He descended the slope with a rapidity that showed the earnestness of his purpose. The others followed without further comments, and soon the tree was crossed and the forest on the western bank reached.

"We crossed an Indian path a little ways from here," said Campbell, resuming the conversation. "It leads probably to the village, and will facilitate our progress. Let us search for it."

With these words he again assumed the lead, but he had proceeded but a short distance when the discovery of a new trail on the top of their old one caused him to come to a second and sudden stop."

"Look here, father!" he exclaimed. "Now I understand it all. Some sneaking Seneca has discovered our trail and reported to the chief. It is no wonder he evaded the trap we had laid for him."

"Indeed it is not, Robert; but from this I judge the chief has been expected in the village, else how could he have received the news of our presence?"

"I am afraid you are right, father. If Maghpiway is aware of our neighborhood, and was expected at the village, our case grows truly desperate, and nothing but great speed and resolution can carry us through. Come, let us see whether the determination of a white man cannot overcome the cunning of this crafty chief."

Campbell gave the others no chance for a reply, but plunged at once into the forest, and proceeded at a gait which had more the character of a run than of a walk. Anderson and the Red Fox, however, were equal to the emergency, and the trio traversed the forest at a rate calculated to bring them speedily to the village. The Indian path greatly facilitated their task, and enabled them to reach the outskirts of the place in a little more than an

hour. Here, however, they moderated their haste, knowing full well that nothing would injure them and their
cause more, in the estimation of the Senecas, than the appearance of an unbecoming hurry. They adjusted their
garments, and suffered the excitement of their rapid walk

subside, and only when they had fully recovered the appearance of dignified reserve and self-possession, which Indian decorum demands, did they emerge from the woods,
and enter the open arena on which the village stood.

This entrance was unobstructed. The Senecas were then
at peace with all their red and white neighbors, a circumstance which made sentinels superfluous. But even if this had
not been so; if the tribe had waged a savage warfare with
pale-faces and hostile Indians, guards would hardly have
interfered with the progress of our friends. The Indians
were exceedingly cautious on the war-path, and their expeditions into hostile regions were always guarded by van and
rear guards, by ambushes and stratagems of every description ; but no sooner had they returned from the expedition
when every trace of restraint was thrown off, and the tribe
confided alone in that readiness for emergencies, and that
self-control in moments of peril, for which the red man was
always noted.

The two scouts and their Indian companion found,
therefore, no difficulty in reaching the village, which consisted in lodges rudely constructed, and preserving no other
order but that a cluster of small ones was placed in irregular profusion around a central one, of superior size, though
hardly superior workmanship. The arrival of the strangers produced but little apparent curiosity, and still less excitement amongst the tribe; for although there was some
running and whispering amongst the women, the warriors
visible at that moment preserved their grave dignity and
reserve, and hardly nodded in answer to the salutations,
with which the newcomers greeted them. The strangers
continued their advance until they reached the larger
dwelling of the center. There they stopped and looked
around for somebody to whom they might state their
errand, and their desire to meet the tribe in council. The
Indians had their ceremonies as well as the white man,

and according to them it was unbecoming in a chief to address a person of inferior rank. The scouts, therefore, abstained from talking to the common warriors, who began to gather in their neighborhood, and to betray, by their keen sparkling glances, the interest which their gestures so peremptorily denied. It could hardly be otherwise, and the scouts knew it. They knew that the Senecas were aware of Maghpiway's arrival, and that they could hardly help bringing the sudden appearance of the trio in connection with the visit of the Delaware chief. They had seen the captives, and probably knew their relation to the Red Feather, and, taking all this in consideration, it would have required superhuman self-control to suppress a curiosity whose power over the Indian was always in just proportion to the efforts he made to conceal it.

The crowd around the strangers increased from minute to minute, and Campbell was already deliberating on the propriety of waiving further ceremonies and addressing one of the warriors, when all at once the door of a neighboring lodge opened, and a person stepped to the ground whose garments and bearing at once betrayed the chief. On seeing the strangers he stopped, appearing to take cognizance of a fact of which he had undoubtedly been apprised only fifteen minutes ago. He was a tall man of almost thirty-five years of age, and his features were finely moulded. His forehead was high, looking even higher than it was, on account of the hair being shaved away to the scalp-lock. His nose was large but of good proportions, and the finely set lips of a well shaped mouth betokened resolution. The eyes were dark and brilliant, their natural fierceness much softened by a look of uncommon intelligence. On the whole this chief was as fine a representative of his race and rank as any that roamed the forests, and the impression which he made on the scouts was favorable, for they exchanged a glance of pleasant intelligence.

"It is Red Jacket, father," Campbell said, in an undertone. "You are the oldest and had better address him."

"Well, I will. It is fortunate that we made his acquaintance at the Fort. Come, let us walk up to him."

Anderson led the way, and in a few moments they stood before the chief.

"Good day, Red Jacket," the spokesman began to address him. "How has the chief of the Senecas fared since his visit at the Fort?"

A smile passed over the features of the Seneca, and his hand met the extended palm of the scout with civil readiness.

"Red Jacket has been well," he replied in an English which bore a foreign accent. "He is glad to welcome the Little Coon in the village of the Senecas. What does my white brother bring his red friend?"

"Nothing very particular, exceptin' a complaint which we have to make against a vagrant Delaware chief. This here is my son-in-law, Mr. Campbell."

The chief smiled.

"Does not Red Jacket know?" he inquired, offering his hand to the younger scout with a bland courtesy that would have done credit to an emperor. "The fame of the Big Jump reaches from the salt lake to the father of waters; could Red Jacket be ignorant of it?"

"Thank you for the compliment, chief," Campbell replied, shaking the proffered hand. "I might return it and say I knew you by reputation before I had the pleasure of making your personal acquaintance at the Fort."

"Red Jacket recollects it; he remembers the pleasant hours spent there. Is my young red brother also from the Fort?"

"No, chief, he is from the village of the Delawares. His name is the Red Fox, and he boasts of a father who has few equals among the red men."

"Docs Red Jacket know his name?"

Campbell replied by another question.

"Does Red Jacket know the name of the Beaver?"

The chief continued in this style by saying:

"Does Red Jacket know the sun, the woods, his own people? What Indian lives that has not heard the praise of the Beaver? The Red Fox is welcome in the lodge of his father's friend. Will not my friends step in and refresh themselves after smoking the calumet with a Seneca chief?"

"They will after a while; but first we would beg the Red Jacket to send for his brother chiefs and the braves of the tribe to meet in council. We wish to address them on the nature of our errand."

The chief looked slightly discomfited, but he was both too crafty and polite to allow this feeling to assume the definite form of words. He bowed consent, and said :

"Let my brothers then step into the council lodge, while I send my young men to convoke the warriors. Red Jacket would have liked to entertain his friends first with food and drink, but their wishes are laws to him. Let them proceed."

He pointed to the central lodge, and when the visitors had done his bidding, he turned to some of the younger Indians and in a low voice gave them an order which caused them to scatter over the different parts of the village.

The scouts and Red Fox meanwhile entered the open door of the council lodge and seated themselves on some of the bundles of brushwood which lined the walls. Here they waited in silence for the arrival of the warriors, who either for age or bravery, had gained a voice in the council of the tribe. They arrived one by one, each one taking a seat and awaiting the opening of the session with the immovability of a marble statue. After the expiration of an hour more than a hundred warriors lined the walls, forming an assembly as formidable as striking. There were no doubt chiefs and braves of great reputation amongst their number ; but Red Jacket had thus far failed to make his appearance. At last, however, he stepped into the lodge, and with him another chief, who was in every respect his equal in looks and bearing, but over whose head at least twenty more winters had passed, streaking his scalp-lock with the first streaks of gray. It was Cornplanter, a half-breed, well known to both the scouts then and afterwards as a centenary chief to the entire white population living on the Allegheny. He always was the friend of the race, to which on his father's side he belonged, and the kind, glances which he bent on the visitors in passing them, fully corroborated the reputation which he bore for being the white man's friend.

When the chiefs had taken their seats the calumet was passed around, each taking a few whiffs of the coveted herb, and sending forth such a cloud of smoke that by the time the pipe had passed around the entire circle, the air had assumed a hue of blue.

When this formality was over, the assembly for a while maintained their previous immovability and silence. At last, however, Cornplanter arose and began to address the assembly.

"I have been informed," he began, in the Seneca language, which all the visitors understood, "that our paleface friends and the young Delaware have come to meet the Senecas in council. The Senecas are the friends of the Yengeese, they have met them and have formed a treaty of peace and friendship. They are glad to see their visitors; they are glad to listen to their words. They have met in council and smoked the calumet; their ears are now open to the wishes of their friends."

Thus summoned, the scouts prepared for a reply. It had been previously arranged that Campbell should make the speeches, and in accordance with this understanding, he now rose and said, in English:

"We thank the Cornplanter for his kindness; we thank all these warriors for the courtesy which they have manifested by granting us a ready hearing. We are now summoned to lay before the council of the Senecas the nature of the errand that has turned our footsteps in the direction of their village. If my red friends have no objection, I shall tell them a little story."

Here the orator made a short pause.

"On the banks of the Ohio," he continued, "near the Fort which witnessed the late treaty of friendship between the Senecas and the Yengeese, stands a cabin. In that cabin peace and contentment had an unbounded sway until a few days ago, a serpent crept into the open door and crushed the happiness of the inmates between its poisonous fangs. There was a beautiful mother—the flowers of the forest hide their faces in dismay when a smile lit up her countenance. There was also a daughter, a budding flower only, but full of promise. The serpent snatched them both in its folds and tore them from their homes. When the husband returned from an expedition, the smile of his dear ones did not greet him; they were gone, snatched from the protection of their home and carried into the depth of the wilderness. But the husband started in pursuit, aided by the father of his wife and a young Indian friend. The three united their strength in order to follow the trail of the captives, and recover them at the peril of their lives. The trail ran northward and led into the village of the Senecas. The Senecas have given countenance and protection to a vile Delaware chief; but they have acted in ignorance and not in malice. They did not know that he stole his captives from the friends of the Senecas; when they see the truth of my assertions they will drive the Red Feather from their village like a scabby dog, and restore the prisoners to the rightful owners. I have spoken."

The deepest silence had been preserved throughout this address; but the intensity of the gaze with which the eyes of the whole assembly hung upon the countenance of the speaker, betrayed the great interest which his words had awakened. When he had ended, several minutes were suffered to elapse before a reply on the part of the tribe was attempted. But finally Red Jacket arose and said:

"We have heard the story of our white brother; we are sorry at his loss, and if it is true that he has traced the perpetrators of the deed into our village, we must take measures to redress his wrongs. The Senecas are just; but impartial judges will not render a hasty verdict. They must sift all the evidence and then decide. Has my white brother seen the robbers enter the village?"

"I have not, but this young Delaware has. He was stationed on yonder ridge, and so near did the Red Feather pass his cover that his tomahawk could have cleft the skull of the thieving renegade."

"The Red Feather? My friend names a great name; has the Delaware seen the prisoners in his possession?"

"He has; but there is no use in beating around the

bush in this manner, Red Jacket. The renegade chief is here, and you know it. The question now is this: Do the Senecas wish to retain the reputation of being honorable men, or do they wish to become offensive to the nostrils of the righteous by upholding the miserable cause of so miserable a man? We are plain spoken men, and want a plain answer."

The eyes of the warriors sparkled more fiercely at this bold language, but the chiefs preserved their former equanimity; or at least the outward appearance of it, and when Red Jacket again arose for a reply, he said, with the most faultless urbanity:

"My white friend suffers under a keen smart; the loss of his wife has raised his anger. If it were not so he would see that the Senecas are disposed to do right. They believe the words of their white friend, but to be just they have also to listen to the defense of the Red Feather."

"It is well," replied Campbell. "I have no objection, indeed I would like nothing better than to meet the dastard face to face, and to fling my defiance into his countenance. If he was a man, instead of being an ensnarer of women and children, I would throw the gauntlet at his feet and challenge him to single combat. But it is hopeless to look for courage in the heart of a poltroon. The Seneca women ought to take switches and drive him from the camp; that would be the proper punishment for such a dastardly thief."

The undoubted courage breathing from these words was so much in keeping with the sentiments of the assembly, that they involuntarily suffered their eyes to express their approbation. They went even further than this. A low murmur flew through the lodge, and proved beyond a doubt that Campbell had gained their respect, if he had failed to enlist their sympathy. Before Cornplanter or Red Jacket were ready to meet the new point presented by the scout, an old warrior arose and thereby signified his intention to address the assembly. He seemed to be no chief, but yet a man of note and consequence, for the eyes of the assembly at once turned to his tall and dignified form with an expression of respect which only the powerful and influential are apt to exact. His bold features bore an ex-

pression of ferocity which sixty years had not been able to
quench. His face was literally covered with scars, memen-
toes of a stirring live, which by no means softened the savage character of his mien, but was a ready index to the
reverence paid to him by his associates. They now probably waited for his remarks with double interest, because
they anticipated a suggestion for the solution of the difficulty which was in keeping with their own savage disposition.

"The Thunderbolt has a stiff tongue," he now began, in
a gruff, hoarse voice, "his voice has neither the sweetness
of the whip-poor-will, nor the charm of the mocking-bird.
He can strike fiercely in battle, but is slow in making himself heard in the council of the nation. He feels backward
now : but what he has heard forces him to raise his voice
in the debate. The Big Jump has spoken bravely ; he has
used big words, but they are not empty sounds, for the rec-
ords of his exploits prove them to be true. He says the
Red Feather is a poltroon : if this is so, the Seneca women
ought to drive him with switches from the village. The
Senecas do not know; they thought Maghpiway to be a
warrior and a brave ; they will think so still until the contrary is proven. Nothing is easier ; give the Big Jump
and the Red Feather a knife and pit them in deadly
combat against each other. They quarrel about a squaw ;
when two stags meet on the trail of the hind they clinch
their antlers and fight for the mastery ; the victor takes the
hind. Let the Big Jump and Maghpiway do the same, let
them show their strength and prowess ; the best man may
take the squaw. Thunderbolt has spoken."

Again an approving murmur passed through the ranks,
and the glances of the warriors gave sufficient evidence of
the satisfaction with which they received a suggestion so
calculated to gratify their savage passions. With the two
highest chiefs, however, this was evidently different.
Both Red Jacket and Cornplanter showed miens in which
solicitude, rather than approbation, formed the chief element. If they had merely consulted their personal inclinations, they might have discovered sufficient ferocity in
their hearts to rejoice at the prospect of the deadly struggle

proposed; but in their capacity as chiefs they had to consult the interest of the tribe, rather than their own desires. If the defeat of the Red Feather had been certain, they might have given a ready consent; but of this they had no assurance. If the Big Jump was strong and agile, the Red Feather had the reputation of possessing both these qualities in no small degree. The conflict then might result in the death of Campbell, and this death would surely be followed by evil consequences. The commander of Fort McIntosh was aware of the nature of the expedition of the scouts, and would sooner or later be informed of any mishap that might befall them. The fate of the Mohawks was too fresh in the memory of the chiefs to make them wish for any complications with the American* government. These considerations induced them to conteract the proposal, and council a postponement of the matter to the following day. This, they said, would give the rivals time for rest and preparation, and the tribe a chance for deliberation. But their prudent counsel was not to the taste of the warriors. The chiefs of the Indian tribes were by no means absolute in their power, and in this instance Red Jacket and Cornplanter had the mortification of seeing the will of the assembly prevail over their own. This result was considerably prompted by the effort of Campbell, whose intense hatred against the destroyer of his peace and happiness, caused him to hail the prospect of a deadly struggle with fierce satisfaction. He repeatedly professed his readiness, and when at last the council passed the resolution to summon the Red Feather to the lodge, and inform him of the result of the deliberations, he turned to Anderson and said :

"Now we have him, father. Prepare to see me mete out to the scoundrel the punishment he so richly deserves."

"Don't be too confident," was the reply of the older and less sanguine scout. "It is not always the justice of the cause that decides the struggle ; and then this Delaware chief is no contemptible adversary. I cannot help thinking that you have pushed yourself rashly into a peril which might have been avoided."

"Don't you believe it, father. Red Jacket bears us ill,

or has at least no sympathy for us. If he could have helped the renegade with any show of good grace, he would undoubtedly have done it."

Before Anderson had time to answer the messenger re-entered the lodge closely followed by the Delaware chief, who had been the subject of the recent debate. With proud and lofty bearing the Red Feather stepped into the circle, which had debated on his destiny. After casting a glance of scorn at the men who had so doggedly tracked his steps to the refuge of imagined security, he turned his gaze towards the chief, and, folding his arms tranquilly over his breast, awaited in silence the communications they had to make to him. It was the duty of Red Jacket to communicate to him the decision of the council, and the hesitancy of his movements showed clearly how irksome he considered the task.

"Maghpiway is welcome," he began. "He sent word that he would come, but he forgot to mention that he intended to bring captives belonging to the Yengeese. If the Senecas had known it they might have acted differently. Now it is too late to change it; Maghpiway is here; the Senecas have said he should be welcome, and he is welcome."

The speaker stopped a moment; but when the Red Feather merely acknowledged the address by a nod of the head, he continued:

"Will Maghpiway tell us where he took his captives?"

The Delaware straightened himself up to his full height and said:

"Maghpiway will; he has nothing to conceal; he took the captives from the accursed Yengeese, the inveterate foes of the red man."

"Maghpiway forgets that the red man and the Yengeese have smoked the calumet and buried the hatchet. He had no right to take the prisoners."

The Delaware's eyes flashed.

"Maghpiway has," he said. "He did not smoke the calumet: he did not bury the hatchet. He hates the pale-faces, and wants them to know it. He will be on their trail, and take their scalps, as long as there is breath in his body and strength in his limbs."

This fierce invective, no doubt, found many a secret response in the bosom of the swarthy warriors that lined the walls of the council-lodge ; but nothing but an occasional glance was suffered to betray their approbation. The relation which the Six Nations then held to the union forbade all hostile manifestations. and Red Jacket hastened to express this :

"Maghpiway is a great chief," he said, "but he is alone. Can he swim against the rapids of the Niagara? He had better give up his wrath and follow the example of the Senecas. They have made peace with their white neighbors, and are determined to maintain it. They cannot harbor and protect men who are the enemies of the Yengeese."

It was evident that the Delaware was burning with an inward rage, and that he would have liked nothing better than to burst out into a torrent of furious invective, and hurl defiance into the faces of everybody present, if his interests had not demanded a different course. His tribe had cast him off, and if he offended the Senecas, they would not only deprive him of his captives, but set him adrift to wreck somewhere on the great leafy ocean, which the Western States then presented. So he curbed his temper ; but in spite of his efforts he could not force his compliance beyond a sullen silence.

"The Senecas have pondered on Maghpiway's case," Red Jacket continued, "and they have found that it would be best for his interest to surrender the captives. Are his ears open to the counsel of a friend ?"

The Delaware shook his head, while a sinister smile played upon his countenance.

"Why does the Red Jacket use so many words?" he said. "The Senecas have the power ; let them do their worst. If they are bound to rob a guest, why do they cleave their tongues and mock him by asking his consent ?"

The brows of Red Jacket darkened.

"The tongues of the Senecas are whole," he replied ; "they only say what they mean. They ask the Red

Feather to surrender his captives; if he refuses he will not be compelled."

The Delaware at first seemed uncertain as to whether he could trust his ears. Then, however, a smile of malignant triumph lit up his face.

"Never!" he exclaimed, with an emphasis that showed his determination. "When the Allegheny flows up stream; when the she wolf sucks the fawn; when the thistle bears ears of corn; then you will find Maghpiway ready to give up the captives—never before!"

An ominous silence followed these words, which was not interrupted until the Red Jacket finally replied:

"It is well: the Red Feather can do as he pleases; but he will now listen to learn the resolution of the Senecas. They will not compel him to give up his captives; but they will compel him to fight for them. The Big Jump claims them as his; when the sun has reached the turning point to-morrow, the Red Feather will meet him with knife and tomahawk in single combat. I have spoken."

This announcement evidently struck the chief as a flash of lightning from the azure sky. He started, and the blood withdrew from his swarthy countenance, leaving there a dingy hue.

Still his feelings seemed more to partake of the character of consternation than of fear. He recovered his self-possession in a moment, and when he addressed Red Jacket for the purpose of signifying his assent, his voice betrayed no weakness.

"It is well," he said. "I am ready to meet the Yengeese. I shall give his flesh to the wolves of the forest."

CHAPTER VII.

DISAPPOINTMENTS.

The council had been dismissed, the warriors had left the lodge and either returned to their wigwams, or were standing in little knots here and there through the village, eagerly discussing the recent occurrence and expressing their opinions in regard to the merits of the combatants and the probable issue of the duel. The scouts and the young Delaware had been led into an empty lodge which had been erected for similar occasions, and on paying them a visit we find them engaged in partaking of such viands as the hospitality of the Red Jacket had furnished them. We who live a more civilized life, are apt to have our appetite impaired by mental agitation, joyous as well as mournful; but these children of the forest who were continually exposed to the keen bracing air, very rarely suffered joy or sorrow to interfere with those meals which their exhausting exercises imperatively demanded. And yet they were in a state of excitement. Even the Red Fox could not think of the struggle of to-morrow without his blood coursing more rapidly through his veins. Anderson, who was more nearly concerned, of course took a still deeper interest; but neither of them showed the excitement of the younger scout. Not that he had been alarmed or dejected—his feelings were rather those of a joyous anticipation at the chance of striking an early blow for the recovery of those to whom he was attached with all the ardor of his nature. His feelings, however, were now and then tinged with a shade of sadness at the idea that his wife and daughter were so near and yet so totally beyond his reach. If he had been less acquainted with Indian customs, he might have made an attempt to see and speak to them; but as it was, he practiced a self-control which lost a portion of its merits by the conviction that all efforts to that effect would not only be vain, but calculated to injure them for whose deliverance he would gladly have sacrificed his life.

These sentiments colored the conversation which the trio kept up during the rest of the day. They had entered their lodge at dusk, and soon darkness wrapped their forms in its sombre veil. This, however, did not deter them from conversing, although their voices were lowered sufficiently to make the attempt of eaves-droppers a very thankless task. At length Campbell remarked:

"It is getting late now and I must sleep to gather strength for to-morrow's trial; but before I close my eyes, I want your solemn pledge that you will take up the cause of Rosie and her child in case something human should befall me. I do not look towards the combat with gloomy forebodings ; but the issue being doubtful, it would ease my heart and spirit if you would pledge yourself to guard their interests in case my condition should be such as to prevent me from doing it myself."

"Robert," Anderson replied, in a feeling manner, "I suppose this is all well enough for the sake of form, for as far as I am concerned you did not, I hope, seriously doubt my willingness to stand by my daughter and her little one, as long as I can draw my breath. I hope you didn't doubt this, Robert ; still, for appearance sake, you may now receive my solemn pledge to stand by Rosie and her child as long as life is in my body and strength in my limbs. Yes, more than that, Robert, if the chief should overcome you —which God forbid—I shall take your place and fight him for the liberty of the prisoners, so help me God !"

Red Fox now seized Campbell's hand :

"Little Coon has spoken my feelings," he said, "as long as the hand of Red Fox is able to hold a knife and strike at Maghpiway's heart, the Wild Rose will not lack a brother to protect her and provide for her. Let my brother sleep in peace !"

Campbell was deeply moved—he was greatly comforted ; for although he had really not doubted the readiness of his comrades to continue faithful to the interests of Mrs. Campbell, he now knew that three lives would have to be sacrificed before the Red Feather could carry the captives further into the wilderness. Three against one ; there was indeed comfort in the thought. It caused him to lay his head upon the rude couch prepared for his benefit and soon lose the consciousness of a troubled presence in the dreamy visions of a brighter future.

The Red Feather had meanwhile returned to his lodge where his followers kept a strict watch over the captives. This watch, however, was rather superfluous, for no sooner had Mrs. Campbell and her companions partaken of a simple supper, when the fatigue engendered by the long and hurried march of the day threw them into the arms of a deep and lasting slumber. The Red Feather did not care to disturb them; so he threw his blanket around him and seated himself upon the ground, leaning his back against the wall and indulging in a long train of thought, all of which bore more or or less upon his situation. When the twilight darkened into night, he suddenly started and felt for the handle of his knife, for in the aperture of the door he perceived the tall figure of a man. He could not discern his character, and therefore prepared for the worst; but when the visitor had uttered a single word he dropped the knife and dismissed all thoughts of danger, for his keen ear recognized the voice of Red Jacket.

"Is Maghpiway awake?" the Seneca inquired, "a friend would like to speak to him."

"Maghpiway is awake; what would Red Jacket say to him?"

"My brother has a keen eye and a sharp ear; he knows a chief in the darkness of night, he must clearly see that a *friend* comes to whisper in his ear?"

"My friend is welcome; what has he to say to a Delaware chief?"

"Are no idle ears in the neighborhood? Red Jacket's words are poison for meddlers."

"He may rest easy; the prisoners are asleep and my young men are outside of the lodge."

"Well, let Maghpiway listen to my words," replied Red Jacket, cowering closely to the side of the Delaware. "Is the heart of my brother really bent upon the possession of the prisoners?"

"Ugh! how can Red Jacket doubt? Does he think Maghpiway's tongue is cloven and that he speaks one way in the council and another in a private interview?"

"I did not doubt, but Maghpiway's answer was necessary to shape my advice. If he values his captives let him arouse them without delay and leave the village as soon as possible."

"Ugh! is that the council of a friend?"

"It is, and Maghpiway will see it when he ponders well."

"Would a friend advise me to withdraw in the dead of night and forever bear the imputation of a coward?"

"Maghpiway forgets my previous question. If his heart is bent upon the possession of his captives, I see no other way; to stay would be to lose them."

"Have the Senecas so little faith?"

"They have and mean to keep it; but they cannot lend strength to Maghpiway's arm in the coming combat."

"They need not," was the proud reply. "Maghpiway has enough strength to fight two Yengeese."

"Does the Red Feather know the power of the Big Jump? Red Jacket has seen strong men wither before him as the grass before the noonday sun of summer."

Maghpiway remained silent.

"There need be no cloud between two chiefs," Red Jacket continued. "Let the Red Feather boast before the crowd. He cannot deceive a Seneca chief with idle words; if the combat takes place to-morrow, Maghpiway will be a dead man."

"Red Jacket has little faith in the prowess of a friend," the Delaware remarked bitterly.

"He has not, he knows the courage and strength of his brother; but he also knows that the hickory is tougher than the beech; the panther stronger than the wild cat."

"But supposing my brother should conquer," he continued, when the other remained silent. "He will never take the captives away from this village."

"Ugh! who will hinder him? Are not the Senecas honorable men?"

"They are, but they have to look to their own interest. A tribe ought not to suffer for a man."

"Nobody will blame them. Maghpiway will take the Wild Rose away, and when the Yengeese come they will blame a Delaware chief, and not the Senecas."

"Maghpiway knows better," was the cool reply, with a touch of irony in the voice of the Seneca. "But supposing my brother were right, he forgets that the Big Jump has two friends."

"Maghpiway will fight him alone."

"He may have to fight the three if they desire it. Would the Senecas deny them the privilege?"

Maghpiway remained silent. The weighty reasoning

of Red Jacket had driven him from position to position, until the Delaware could no longer conceal from himself the truth of the fact that he must either sacrifice his reputation or his prize. Nor had he much time to make up his mind. Even if the Seneca chief assisted him in covering up his tracks, his absence could not remain a secret after the early hours of morning. The scouts would then, of course, throw themselves upon the trail without delay, and as his progress, with the burden of the prisoners, must of necessity be slow, a conflict would be the certain consequence. But Red Jacket had certainly laid his plans; perhaps he had to offer valuable suggestions, and it was with the view of sounding him on this point that Maghpiway now addressed him:

"The white men will follow my trail even if I go," he said.

"Well, if they do?" Red Jacket asked, derisively. "Has not Maghpiway a dozen men to meet them? It was a mistake of the chief to run into the village of the Senecas. If he had laid an ambush he could easily have quieted his enemies·"

The Delaware swallowed the bitter pill in silence.

"I can give my brother my advice if he will listen to it," the Seneca continued. "He is welcome to all I can do for him."

"Maghpiway thanks his brother. Let my brother speak; the ears of a chief are open to receive his words."

"Very well; does the Red Feather know the place north-east from here where the Great Spirit has scattered mighty rocks like pebbles over many acres?"

"Maghpiway has heard of them; he knows the way."

"Good. Now I will tell my brother what a Seneca would do. He would first embark and paddle up the Venango to the mouth of the creek which winds through many sugar trees."

"Maghpiway knows it."

"There he would divide his party, and send the Budding Rose and the Vacant Head with three or four warriors up the smaller creek as far as a canoe could be paddled."

Red Jacket paused; but Maghpiway listened with too

much eagerness to think of an interruption.   So the Seneca continued:

"From that point he would send the party across the country to the place of many rocks, leaving a trail distinct enough to be traced with readiness."

No interruption yet; but the fiery eyes of the Delaware seemed to dart flashes of lightning in the darkness of the lodge.

"In the rocks are places where a small party could withstand the attack of hundreds for many days.   To such a place Red Jacket would send the two captives, and bid his warriors await the coming of the pale-faces.   They would arrive and lay siege to the rocks, and a day or two would be spent in useless efforts to carry the position.   Perhaps the pale-faces would be killed in the fray—this would be well.   At best they could only possess themselves of the captives after many hours.   These hours Red Jacket would use to escape with the Wild Rose."

"Ugh!"

"Does my brother understand?   The plan is good—it cannot fail.   What does Maghpiway care about the Budding Rose?   What about the Vacant Head?   They are a burden on his hands; they will be a burden on the hands of the pale-faces."

"Ugh!   Where would the Seneca chief go with the Wild Rose?"

"To the country of the Wyandots across the fresh-water lake, to Canada."

"Ugh!   The path is long and dangerous; what should a Delaware do among the Hurons?   They do not love the children of the Lenni Lenape."

"My brother forgets that the Mohawks live near the Thundering Waters.   Red Jacket is the friend of Joseph Brant, the chief of the Mohawks, and if he takes to him this belt of wampum, he will be welcome, and be awarded a position in the tribe in keeping with his merits."

In saying these words he offered to the Delaware the above named ornament, and the eagerness with which the latter received it showed plainly that he had fully entered into the views of the Seneca.

"Red Jacket has not finished," he said; "let him proceed, his words are music in the ears of a Delaware."

"Red Jacket has nearly done. His brother must take his captive as far up the Venango as practicable. Then he must leave the canoe and strike northward through the country until he reaches the shore of the big lake. Has he ever been up there?"

"No, but he has a warrior in his party who is familiar with the country."

"It is well. Let my brother proceed to the eastern point of Presque Isle; there he will find in the sand of the beach a couple of canoes large enough to cross the lake with. My brother is welcome to the canoes; he takes with him the wishes of a Seneca chief, who hates the pale-faces as fiercely as himself, but has to hide his hatred under a smiling countenance. Red Jacket has spoken."

The chiefs arose.

"Maghpiway is very grateful to his brother," the Delaware said, in the undertone which had marked their previous conversation. "He sees now that Red Jacket is his friend. He will act upon his hints and depart at once. The service of the Seneca chief will never be forgotten."

The two chiefs now stepped from the lodge, and while Red Jacket went to the Venango and paddled a couple of canoes to a place above the village, which would be convenient for the embarkation of Maghpiway's party, that chief himself approached the place where his warriors lay stretched upon the ground, some of them watching, and others indulging in a refreshing slumber. A slight touch aroused them all, and when they had crowded around the chief, he communicated to them his intentions in a low and hurried whisper. This done, Maghpiway returned to the lodge and awakened Mrs. Campbell and Peter. They were at first considerably confused, as one is apt to be when roused from profound slumber. When the former, however, had fully recovered her consciousness, she gave expression to the indignation which the interruption of the needful rest had aroused.

"What does this mean?" she inquired. "Is the Red Feather not satisfied with tormenting me in daytime?

Must he rob me of the sleep and rest of the night? If he means to kill me, must he do it by inches?"

"Maghpiway cannot help it; he wants to continue his journey this very minute."

"Ha! what does that mean? Is my husband near? Cannot even the presence of the Senecas save the Red Feather from his vengeance?"

"The Big Jump is not near; but the Wild Rose is not safe here; the Senecas look upon her with covetous eyes."

Mrs. Campbell shuddered. Could the assertion of Maghpiway be true? His actions seemed to indicate it, for what else but jealousy could be the cause of this sudden departure from the village? If Campbell was near, it would rather be to the interest of her captor to remain than to flee, as the rescue from the center of a populous village would be a far more difficult task than another, in which the hostile party would be comparatively small. Mrs. Campbell was ignoront of all the circumstances attending the case, and so we need not wonder that the explanation of the chief appeared reasonable to her, and filled her with a desire of aiding, rather than resisting his movements. If the Senecas seriously thought of retaining her, there was but little prospect of a final rescue, while her deliverance from the small party of the Red Feather could only be a matter of time. So she prepared herself for an immediate departure with a haste and readiness which surprised the Delaware chief as much as it gratified him. A violent resistance on her part might have frustrated his plans; but as it was, he could hope to withdraw from the village without discovery.

In a few minutes everything was ready for a start. Peter was bid to load himself with the sleeping child, and under the double cover of night and the surrounding warriors of Red Feather, the way to the canoes was made without discovery. Silently the party embarked in the two vessels, preserving much the former order, and then the ascent of the creek was commenced in a noiseless but yet effective manner. From the mouth of the Venango to that of Sugar Creek, the distance can hardly exceed five miles, and was therefore traversed by the expert oarsmen of the crew in a comparatively short time. When the mouth of Sugar Creek was reached the two canoes were stopped, and Peter received the order to take a seat in the other vessel. This was a new arrangement which could not help filling the heart of Mrs. Campbell with fear and consternation.

"Why is this?" she exclaimed, in a voice so loud and thrilling that Maghpiway contracted his brows in the most threatening manner. "The Red Feather must not rob me of my child. He promised not to. Has the Wild Rose failed to keep her word?"

"The child will not be harmed," the chief responded, "unless the Wild Rose screams like an owl and draws the enemies of Maghpiway upon his trail. Maghpiway takes the Great Spirit as a witness of the truth of his words."

But a mother's anxiety cannot be easily assuaged. Mrs. Campbell did not heed the words of the chief; she only saw that the transfer was effected in spite of her remonstrance, and rising rapidly she prepared to spring into the water and escape from her captors, or perhaps rejoin her child. Quick, however, as her movements were, they had been anticipated; and before she had time to make the intended leap, a strong arm encircled her waist and held it as in a vice. Mrs. Campbell was no weak woman, nor did she lack courage, and the struggle for her liberty soon began to rock the little vessel in an alarming manner. It was not likely that her strength would have prevailed against the strong arm of the Red Feather, but still her efforts might have sufficed to upset the canoe and precipitate the crew into the water, if the struggle had not come to a sudden end. The noise of the altercation and scuffle had awakened the child in the other canoe, which had never ceased to ascend Sugar Creek, and had therefore reached a considerable distace from the one containing Wild Rose and the chief. On awaking, the child began to cry and to call her mother's name. These calls were evidently made at the top of her voice, but to the ear of Wild Rose they sounded distant, and revealed to her the terrible fact that she was even then on the point of losing a treasure, the possession of which had greatly assisted her in bearing up under her calamity.

This discovery set her mind in a whirling motion, and strong though she generally was, this new stroke was too much for her. A cloud gathered before her eyes; she groped for a moment wildly in the vacant air, and then, with the name of her child on her lips, sank into a swoon, which, for a spell, robbed her of the consciousness of all her misery.

CHAPTER VIII.

MORE DISAPPOINTMENTS.

The dawn of the next morning had not fully set in when a hurried footstep approached the lodge occupied by the scouts and the young Delaware. The inmates were fully awake, but had abstained from making their appearance in the village, because they knew that such a step would be construed as a sign of excitement unbecoming a warrior. They of course noticed the approaching footsteps, without, however, bestowing much attention to them ; but when the figure of no less a person than Cornplanter appeared in the door, bearing upon his face the unmistakable signs of great perturbation, they knew at once that something was amiss, and sprang to their feet to learn the nature of the trouble. The chief looked at them a moment with a mien that held the middle between compassion and indignation. Then extending his arm he said :

"The Senecas and my pale-face friends have been deceived. They thought there was a Delaware chief in the village, but they have been mistaken; it was no chief; it was no warrior ; it was a vile cur ; for in the dead of night has he stolen away from the village of the Senecas !"

"Ugh !" cried the Red Fox, while a similar sound emanated from the lips of the scouts.

"He escaped, did he ?" cried Campbell. "Indeed, we might have expected as much. We might have expected as much, Cornplanter, and taken our measures accordingly. But let the vile dog slip, and take us to the prisoners Our soul thirsts to bring them the news of their deliverance."

A cloud passed over the face of the chief. He averted it and said, in a husky voice :

"Cornplanter cannot do it; the Red Feather has taken them along."

A simultaneous cry of indignation burst from three pairs of lips. Campbell sprang forward and snatched the arm of the chief.

"It cannot be, Cornplanter," he cried. "Has the spirit of honor deserted from the Senecas?"

Cornplanter turned to face him. He raised his right hand, and said, in a conjuring manner:

"It has not left the breast of Cornplanter. I take the Great Spirit as a witness that I know no more of this than you."

"But the others, Cornplanter?"

"For them I cannot answer. The tribe, I think is innocent; but there may be a serpent in the fold that played us false."

Campbell clenched his fist in a threatening manner, and cried:

"If I knew him, I would slay him before the eyes of the whole nation."

"It would not recover the captives," the chief admonished him. "Had my brother not better prepare to find their trail?"

"You are right, chief, and thanks to you for the hint. Come, father; come, Red Fox, let us leave a town which shall henceforth be a stench in the nostrils of honest men. How could we be so foolish as to look for justice at the hands of the Mingoes? Let us be gone!"

A flash of anger passed over the face of Cornplanter. For a moment he seemed inclined to give way to the feeling which agitated his mind; but obeying a second and maturer thought, he checked himself and said:

"My friend is angry. Cornplanter will not listen to words dictated by wrath. He feels for his white brother, and to prove it he will assist him to find the trail."

"Will you, chief?" Campbell eagerly exclaimed. "If you are sincere in this I will exonerate you from the blame which justly rests upon your tribe. Yes, I will do more— beg your pardon for my hasty words. But if you want to speak, speak quickly, for there is something burning in my bosom which urges me to pursue the renegade, and never rest, or eat or sleep again until I have torn his treacherous heart from out his body."

"I shall not detain you long. I would hardly have left my lodge if a runner had not brought me a message from the Seneca village at the headwaters of the Allegheny. He came down the bank of the creek, which passes through maple groves not far from here, and told me he heard the sound of paddles and the weeping of a child that spoke the English tongue."

"It must have been the voice of Annie, my little daughter."

"I think it more than likely. The information of the runner startled me, and I resolved to go and search the lodge of the Red Feather and his band. I need not tell you that I found it empty."

"Where is this creek you spoke about?"

"It empties five miles from here into the Venango, coming from the north-east."

"That is enough, Cornplanter. I am indeed indebted to you for this news, for it will enable me to pounce upon my foe with the rapidity of the eagle when he swoops upon his prey. It gratifies me to see that you are in no way tainted with the treachery that lurks in this affair. But they say you have white blood in your veins—that may account for it."

"At least I bear your people no grudge. But now come on, I mean to take you to the bank opposite, so that you can start without arousing the gossip of the village."

"And you will set us right before the tribe? You will not suffer us to come under the imputation of sneaking cowardice."

"Rest easy, friend, Cornplanter will set you right before his people."

After these words the four men walked to the river bank, taking care to make their progress as secretly as possible. Cornplanter's eye scanned the row of canoes.

"Two are wanting," he said, "the runner was not mistaken. Strike across the hills in this direction; a tramp of two hours will bring you to the spot."

The party embarked, the chief softly paddling the canoe to the other side. There the visitors once more shook hands with their host, and a minute afterwards ascended the steep ridge lining the river bank.

"Now for the north-east," said Campbell, when they reached the top. "The creek is more due north; but if they are in for the village on the headwaters of the Allegheny, we shall strike their trail in this direction. Red Fox, your eyes are young; suppose you take the lead and watch the ground with all the sharpness of an Indian vision. Anderson and I will meanwhile scan the bushes right and left, to see that we do not fall into an ambush, which the rogues may have laid for us."

They started accordingly, walking in single file, the Indian leading, with his looks rigidly bent upon the ground, while the scouts swept the surrounding forest with eyes from whose vigilance but few things were suffered to escape.

For two hours their search remained without result; still they were not discouraged.

"Cornplanter intimated as much," said Campbell. But if I am not mistaken, we are nearly in range now, and must double our vigilance. Let us follow this ridge; if they really went north-east they had to pass it somewhere or other. Attention, now."

The ridge alluded to was that which divides the watercourses of the Sugar and Oil Creeks, and strikes the latter in the neighborhood of Titusville. The trio followed it with redoubled caution and watchfulness, and before the expiration of thirty minutes their efforts were crowned with success. The Indian, as he was the foremost one, of course discovered the trail first, and informed his companions by his favorite exclamation. Hastening to his side they saw a number of foot-prints, so fresh and deep that the persons from whom they originated must have passed very recently, and been very indifferent in regard to the trail they left. This, however, might only be a ruse; indeed, it seemed to be, as Peter, whose trail the scouts at once recognized from his peculiar swinging style of walking, had been compelled to exchange his shoes for moccasins. There was no sign from Mrs. Campbell's feet whatever, nor did the number of trails exceed five; but this was neither proof of the absence of the Wild Rose, nor of the weakness of the party guarding the captives. The scouts knew that the Indians could and would often for miles walk in the foot-prints of one another, either to disguise their number or to hide the presence of captives. The scouts were therefore determined to follow their trail, and as the marks were so very fresh and plain, they made considerable headway in the course of the next hour or two. Their confidence was still incréased when all at once they discovered the trail of a little child running parallel with Peter's. True, it stopped as suddenly as it had commenced, but for this they found a ready explanation.

"The lad must have got tired and made the child walk a while," said Anderson. "This is not more than fair; only I wonder the Red Feather tolerated it. It left these telltale marks and must have greatly retarded the progress of the party. Just see how the steps have been reduced in length to accommodate themselves to those of the child."

"It is difficult to account for," replied Campbell, "but as they have so short a start, we shall find out before long. Heaven guard us against a second disappointment."

"Amen!" said Anderson, and relapsing into the previous silence, the trio plodded over hill and valley, following the trail which increased in freshness and perspicuity as they advanced. It crossed the Oil Creek and struck through the center of Allegheny township, until it finally entered the rough wild region which lines the banks of the West Hickory a few miles southwest of Tidioute. The most dreary portion of the Allegheny Mountains can hardly show a spot so truly grand and wild as the spot alluded to. A few hundred acres are covered with rocks of gigantic size and fantastic form, as if they were as many dice from the cup of his Satanic Majesty, thrown there in a fit of anger at a lost game. At some places these rocks are crowded closely together so as to form dark, gloomy passages, overhung by laurel bushes and scrub oak, in which the hissing of the rattlesnake is as frequent as the buzz of the mosquito in a river bottom. At others they stand more thinly scattered, gaining however in size what they lose in number, some of them reaching truly formidable proportions and overlapping occasionally in ledges, which threaten death to any one venturing below.

It was noon when the pursuers reached this wilderness. No sooner had they cast a look upon it when they simultaneously expressed their belief that the Red Feather had taken refuge in its rocky recesses.

"It isn't a bad place for such a purpose," said Anderson. "If Maghpiway has plenty of provisions, we may spend many a day before we succeed in making an impression on his ramparts."

"Perhaps he is not there, though," said Campbell. "The place is not overlarge; how would it do to go around and make a sure thing of it?"

The others consenting, Campbell's suggestion was at once carried into effect. Keeping within the dense seam of crippled pine trees, which surrounded the rocks at a distance of several hundred yards, and thus guarding against a premature betrayal of their presence, they slowly described a circle around the wilderness and examined the ground with their usual circumspection. After the expiration of an hour, they again reached the point from which they started, and as they had failed in discovering any signs of a continuation of the trail, their original belief changed into absolute certainty. Maghpiway is in the rocks, and as the success of the enterprise depended on their next movements, they sat down to deliberate upon the course which they should now pursue. The spot which they had chosen for this purpose was secluded in the highest degree. The sources of the West Hickory lay amongst the rocks, the country shelving towards the southwest and breaking into the ravine which contained the bed of the above named stream. While the immediate environs of the rocks were generally free from trees, containing merely laurel bushes and crippled shrubs of various descriptions, the pine forest crept on both sides of the ravine into the very rocks, thus forming a secret and secure passage into their gloomy recesses. It was not this, however, that the trio thought of. They sat in a dense cluster of young pine

trees, through whose center the infant creek was sending
its cool and prattling waters. While they dispatched the
remnant of the food with which the Senecas had filled their
pouches the night before, and washed the dry morsels down
with an occasional sip from the waters of the brook, they
earnestly exchanged their views, which evidently were at
variance with one another.

"It would be foolhardy, Robert, to make the attempt,"
said Anderson, shaking his head at a previous remark of
the younger scout. "How can three men expect to carry
such a strong position against a dozen?"

"But what would you do, father? We cannot afford to
watch them for a week and finally let them give us the
slip? Strong or not, the attack must be ventured at once,
or be abandoned altogether. You would not entertain the
latter alternative, would you?"

"No, Robert, I would not; but I must confess I do not
like the idea of making this foolhardy attack either. The
Red Feather is no idiot, and will benefit by any advantage
that you may give him. I know this much; if I were concealed in yonder rocks with a dozen men at my disposal,
and three enemies of mine were so tired of life as to poke
their noses into the muzzle of my gun, I would soon blow
their silly noddle-heads into a thousand atoms "

"What you say stands to reason, father; but circumstances alter cases. There is something in the conduct of
the Red Feather I do not comprehend. If he has half a
dozen warriors at his command, why should he hide like
a timid chicken before the hawk?"

"You forget, Bob, that we counted full a dozen foot-
prints on the trail."

"We did before their arrival at the village."

"Maghpiway did not leave anybody at the village, I am
sure."

"I know he didn't; but he started with two canoes—
what if he had divided his men and instructed some of
them to allure us to this spot, so that he might have a
chance to escape in the meantime?"

"Ha! you never mentioned that before; what makes you
think so? Did we not see the footprints of the little one?"

"We did, father; but we failed to find the trail of Rosie. The Red Feather is wicked enough to tear an infant from its mother's breast, if that will help him to secure his purpose."

Anderson did not reply; the suggestion of his comrade seemed to rob him of his breath.

"God forbid that I may be correct," Campbell continued; "but during the last hour many ugly thoughts have risen in my mind in spite of all my efforts to suppress them. The absence of any sign of Rosie's presence, the regular continuance of those four trails, the character of this gloomy mass of rocks—all this combined inspires me with the belief that there is mischief brewing, and that we will fall into a snare unless we watch and keep our eyes open."

"You may be right, Robert," Anderson replied, after a considerable spell of silence. "I hardly know what to think of it. Come, Red Fox, you have not spoken yet; give us your opinion. Young as you are, your eyes are sharp, and your judgment ripe beyond your years; what would you have us do under the circumstances?"

Thus addressed, the Red Fox prepared to answer. He extended his hand towards the rocks and said:

"Big Jump thinks there are four warriors in the rocks; Little Coon says there are three times that number. Red Fox does not know; but if his friends will wait until the night sets in he will go and see. He will not return without knowing the exact number of his foes. The Red Fox has spoken."

"There now," said Campbell, "two against one; you have to give in, father."

"I do so cheerfully, Robert. Besides, there is a difference between a stealthy expedition in the dead of night and a wild, foolhardy rush against a foe whose number and position we know nothing about. If the Delaware can creep into the hostile camp, I can do the same, and you may depend upon it I shall not stay behind."

"Well, that's settled then," said Campbell. "Let us wait until the night sets in, and then explore the rocks on three different sides. Meanwhile we are condemned to idleness, and can do nothing better than to take time by the forelock and anticipate the slumber of which this mighty expedition will deprive us. I, for one, shall snatch some sleep, if my thoughts will let me. Good night, friends."

With these words Campbell stretched himself on the swelling grass that lined the bottom, and closed his eyes. His friends followed his example, and soon the regular breathing of the trio betrayed the fact that they had not in vain practiced the difficult art of maintaining their self-possession even under the most trying circumstances.

CHAPTER IX.

A TRIAL AT SCOUTING.

When Campbell awoke from his slumber the stars had already begun to sparkle through the pines. A gentle breeze caused the slender trees to swing gracefully in the night air, and to produce that melodious soughing so apt to sink rest into the troubled heart. The frogs kept up a grand chorus, a whip-poor-will uttered its sad notes, and the night owl chimed in with her peculiar but not unpleasant cry. All this gave an idea of such perfect peace that Robert had to think twice before he could realize the fact that he was on the point of entering on a perilous undertaking, which would probably terminate in strife and bloodshed. He was still trying to free himself from the magic spell, when his companions started up, and, like him, cast wondering glances around themselves. A few seconds, however, sufficed to put them in full possession of their faculties, and to complete their preparations for the intended exploration. It was agreed that the Red Fox should proceed up the ravine, while the two scouts were to branch off in opposite directions, and to take the rocks from the flank. It was agreed that the rifles should remain behind, and that even the knife and tomahawk should not be used, except in cases of absolute necessity. Two hours were fixed as the utmost period allowed for the expedition. These expended, the three scouts

pledged themselves to return to the place of rendezvous
and report, no matter how the exploration had turned out.
These principal features having been agreed upon, the three
adventurers parted, the Indian stealing up the ravine and
the scouts ascending its sides, all three proceding with the
noiselessness of spectres.

The night wore on, its shadows deepening gradually,
until the sparkling stars assumed a truly golden color.
Slowly the minutes passed away, although to the daring
men, so dangerously engaged, they may have seemed quick
enough. At the expiration of the preconcerted time the
chirp of the squirrel three times broke the silence of the
night, and a moment afterwards three forms stepped from
the deeper shade of the pine trees, and again stood face to
face on the spot which had witnessed their deliberations.

We cannot doubt but that they were eager to learn each
other's experience, but yet nothing of the noisy demonstrations with which town people often endeavor to snatch the
words from one another's mouth, became apparent on the
occasion. Age had the preference with the red man, and
those influenced by their intercourse, and so Campbell and
the young Delaware both looked for Anderson's explanation. The latter, however, shook his head:

"I have but little to say, lads," he began. "The truth
is I got into such a jumble of rocks, and cracks, and briars,
and laurel bushes, that I completely lost my way, and for
more than an hour wandered at random to escape from my
prison. If the rocks are all as intricate as the portion I examined, then good-bye to the prospect of exploring them
at night. But what have you to say, Campbell; have you
been more fortunate?"

"Not much, father. It wasn't the rocks and brambles
that bothered me; but I have been compelled to listen to a
concert, the like of which I never desire to hear again. I
was making excellent headway, and had entered a narrow
passage between two towering rocks, when all at once a
sharp rattle in front caused me to arrest my step. I was
once bitten by a rattle-snake when a boy, and the narrow
escape I had at that time did not make me very anxious to
repeat the experiment; so I wheeled, and was on the point

of leaving the cleft, when again the fatal sound met my ear, and caused me to stop in dismay. I need not boast of my nerves, for I think they have stood pretty severe tests, but I must confess that just at that moment a disagreeable sensation crept over my skin. If I could have seen the reptiles, a well directed blow or kick would have made them harmless; but not knowing their exact position, I feared to make a step, lest it would put me just in reach of their ugly fangs. If I made the slightest movement, or started the least noise, their rattles were at once set in motion; and fancy or no fancy, the musicians seemed to increase in number, until at last a hundred snakes appeared to choke the entrance of the passage on either end. I do not know how long I stood there, for the continual stain on my nerves prevented me from keeping a very strict account; but this I know, that when the ominous sound at last died away, and the withdrawal of the reptiles allowed me to think of my own retreat, I fancied the trial to have lasted half a century. The nasty creatures have actually unnerved me, for the thought of them makes my flesh creep even now. I was prepared to meet and fight a bloody Indian, but this concert of rattlesnakes was more than I bargained for. That is my story, friends, and now you may laugh at me as much as you please. I'll have to endure that trial of my patience, too, and have but little doubt that I shall stand it better than the last one."

"You were in a bad fix, Robert, and no mistake," said Anderson; "but thanks to my brambles and your rattlesnakes, our expedition has a fair prospect of proving a total failure. I have my serious doubts that the Red Fox has fared better than we. Am I right, lad? Let us know the truth at once."

"The Red Fox has seen the enemy," replied the Delaware, as coolly as if Anderson had ask him merely the time of day.

"Ugh!"

"You don't say so!"

These exclamations broke forth simultaneously. Campbell seemed to have lost all recollection of the rattlesnakes, and plied the Delaware so eagerly with questions that the youth found difficulty in answering them.

"How many did he count?"

"Four warriors."

"Was a chief amonst them?"

"The Red Fox did not see the face of Magbpiway."

"But he saw the prisoners?"

"He did."

"How many—did—he—count?"

Campbell's voice trembled when he asked this question. It was indirect in its character, but yet he feared to learn from the reply a fact of which he had been apprehensive all the while.

"He counted but two."

This answer of four words, so innocent in themselves, struck the heart of Campbell with the force of a thunderbolt. He laid his hand heavily upon the Indian's shoulder, and gasped:

"The Wild Rose—did my brother see no trace of her?"

"There is no trace whatever in the rocks of the Wild Rose."

This answer was given in that sweet, sympathetic voice of which the Indian alone is capable. Still, the soothing voice could not break the sting of the information. The scout groaned deeply, and for a moment he seemed to sink under the weight of this new disappointment. Just then Anderson inquired of the Indian:

"But the Red Fox saw the child; is it well?"

"It is as well as the flower can be without sunshine, the fish without water. The Budding Rose yearns for her mother."

This allusion to the child came much in season; it roused the unhappy scout by reminding him that he was father, as well as husband.

"Poor little one!" he cried, the tears streaming copiously over his bronzed cheeks; "if I cannot give thee thy mother, thou shalt at least no longer want thy father. Delaware, lead the way—show me the road to the miscreants that hold my child; if this blade will keep its edge, this arm its strength, but half an hour longer, yonder rocks will tell a tale that may prevent thieving Mingoes from ever stealing innocent children hereafter."

The Red Fox took his rifle and turned to go, thereby showing his readiness to humor the summons of the injured scout. Anderson, however, checked their sudden departure.

"You will do nothing rashly, Robert," he conjured the other. "Remember that the life and liberty of your daughter, if not your wife, depend upon the preservation of your own life."

"I shall not forget that, father, rest assured. But I must be stirring to escape the dreadful thoughts that prey upon my mind whenever my body is at rest. We must now move upon the wretches without delay, and if the statement of the Red Fox is correct, of which I have not the slightest doubt, if the garrison is unsuspicious of our surprise, we ought to and shall find no difficulty in overcoming them. Trust me for that, father, and now come on; we have already lost too much time in parleying."

Anderson obeyed, and the two scouts fell quickly into the rear of the Red Fox, who conducted them up the ravine. He, now benefitted by the experience of his first expedition, and in spite of the great secrecy and caution which the nature of the errand forced him to observe, he advanced so rapidly that they soon stood in the heart of the wilderness. It was truly a grand spot; the gigantic rocks looming boldly into the night air, and showing their dim outlines against the starry sky, in spite of thé reigning darkness. The creek contained but little water; but so much was this water lashed by overhanging bushes; so badly was it torn and split by needle-shaped rocks and sharp-edged ledges; so madly did it leap and fall, and tumble over endless precipices, that the ravine echoed with a roar that would have done credit to a mountain stream of first magnitude.

This deafening noise, jarring as it might have been to weaker nerves, was welcome to the three adventurers, as it concealed their advance in a most effectual manner. Even after they had left the bed of the creek, and entered a rocky channel, in which a small tributary spent its short existence, the uproar of the restless stream in the bottom deadened the noise, which was inseparable from their passage over such rough ground.

After a few minutes the Indian left the second stream as he had left the first, and entering the narrow fissure of a massive rock, he commenced an ascent which was nearly perpendicular. The efforts of a few minutes landed him and his companions on a platform which was at least a hundred feet above the bed in which they had so lately crawled. This platform was thickly covered with huckleberry bushes and shrubs of various kinds, affording sufficient protection to a human being in a stooping position. The Red Fox lowered himself on his hands and knees and began to crawl through the bushes, closely followed by the scouts, who displayed an equal skill with the son of the forest in effecting a quick yet noiseless passage through the dense masses of the huckleberries which, though protecting, at the same time hindered their progress.

After a hundred yards or so the rock began to fall off, assuming a rolling form, and descending with repeated ups and downs towards the bottom. This declivity the Indian began to descend, taking great caution not to strike against any loose stone that might lay in the way. At the top of the last swell he stopped, allowing the scouts to come to his side. When they reached the desired position he pointed to the edge of the slope, which was lined with a dense seam of laurel bushes, and huckleberries on its outer rim. After this sign he began to crawl towards this edge, and, having reached it, gazed through the bushes. The scouts, of course, followed, and when their heads were far enough advanced to gain a view into the depth below, a sight met their eyes well calculated to startle them, and make their gaze as stationary as if it had been riveted on the picture below.

The rock to the right swept outward in a semi-circular shape, forming a cauldron of moderate size, whose bottom could be fifty feet below the point they occupied. The lower part of the ledge rose perpendicularly, but at the height of about twenty five feet it shelved out in such a manner as to project at its upper edge a distance of at least twenty feet. In the bottom of this well sheltered cauldron burned a fire of moderate size, lighting up not only all the portions of this edifice of nature's making, but also throwing a red glare upon its occupants. In the immediate neighborhood of the fire sat four warriors, engaged in dispatching a meager supper, and feeding the fire from a heap of dry brush, laying at their side. They were evidently discussing a theme of much interest, for their gestures were as lively as was at all compatible with Indian dignity. Their voices reached the ears of the listeners, but as the distance was considerable they merely struck them like so many meaningless sounds.

Besides this group of warriors there was another in the cauldron, which attracted the gaze of the scouts with even greater power. It consisted of two persons, and was situated in the background near the foot of the encircling wall. One of them was a young man, and the other a little child. In the former the scouts at once recognized the drummer lad (as he was called in the Fort), although his features were not exposed to view. His ungainly body was partly stretched on the ground, and partly propped against the rock, while his head was bent over the body of his little companion, who lay sleeping on a bed of moss, with her head resting on his lap. The sight of his daughter affected Campbell to such a degree that his heart began to throb wildly, and his brain to whirl in a manner calculated to deprive him of the control of all his senses. He had to withdraw his eyes from the affecting spectacle, and the removal of his head from the edge of the ledge was a sign for his companions to follow his example. It was not safe to speak so near their foes above the merest whisper ; so Campbell brought his mouth into the closest proximity to their ears, and said, as softly as possible :

"We cannot attack them from here. The angle of vision is too steep, and we might miss our aim. I noticed there is but one entrance to the cauldron, and we can reach it by creeping down this slope. When there we must take a man apiece, and after firing, rush upon the fourth one and take him alive. Perhaps we can frighten him into a betrayal of the whereabouts of his chief. Now forward."

Suiting the action to the word the scout moved cautiously in the direction indicated, but suffering the young Indian to take the lead. He had witnessed the superior skill with which the Red Fox had passed all the obstacles in his way, and resolved to intrust their further progress also to his care. Nor did the youth disappoint him. So stealthy, and yet so rapid, were his motions; so much judgment did he display in picking out the most suitable places of descent, that the three adventurers stood at the entrance of the cauldron before half an hour had elapsed. Advancing to the edge of the laurel thicket, which lined the cavity, they gazed through the foliage in order to gain a view from their new position. Everything was unaltered. The warriors were still talking, and Peter still bent his head in solicitude over the sleeping child. Things looked favorable, and the invaders prepared for the assault. It would not do to whisper any more, for the slightest sound might have reached the ears of the warriors, and put them on their guard. But as the light of the fire penetrated to their cover they were able to read each other's signs. The Indians around the fire nearly faced them, offering a good mark for their rifles. Campbell stood between his companions, with Anderson on the left and Red Fox on the right. He described a circle with his right hand, and pointed to the Indian on the left, laying his other hand on Anderson's shoulder. The scout nodded a sign that he comprehended. Then Campbell turned to the Delaware, touching him with the right hand, and pointing with the left to the warrior on the other extremity. The Red Fox did as Anderson had done, and Campbell prepared for action. He slowly raised his rifle, and this movement was imitated on the right and left. A second later three deadly muzzles were pointed toward the hearts of three unsuspecting victims. Campbell allowed a few seconds for taking aim, then the low whispered word of command broke from his lips:

"Fire!"

Three flashes, one report, and only one form at the fire remained sitting erect. The fatal messengers had reached the others with such unerring aim that life was ebbing before the consciousness of danger had reached the brain.

"Now!" shouted Campbell, and breaking from the cover he had traversed half the distance to the fire before the remaining Indian overcame his bewilderment sufficiently to think of defense.

"Ugh!" he exclaimed, and springing to his feet drew the tomahawk to hurl it at his assailant. These sharp-edged hatchets were dangerous weapons in the hand of the red man, but in this instance the completeness of the surprise had marred the accuracy of his aim, and the missile sped harmlessly past the head of the scout. Before the Indian had time to draw his knife or think of other modes of defense, the stout arms of Campbell were round his body holding his arms as in a vise, until Anderson and the Delaware came up, and secured the prisoner by binding both hands and feet with a couple of ropes taken from their pouches. The fellow was rudely pushed aside, and then the scouts turned to the place where Peter and the little one were anxiously waiting for the issue of this sudden and unexpected encounter. The girl had been awakened by the reports, and seemed to be more stupefied than frightened by so many repeated shocks upon her nerves. She clung to Peter with all her strength, trembling all over her body in a manner which filled the hearts of the scouts with deep compassion.

"Annie! my darling Annie!" shouted Campbell, his desire for ending her misery overcoming all fear of the evil consequences of too sudden a revelation of their character. "Your father is here to take you home. So cheer up, my child. Don't you know me? Don't you know grandfather and your Indian uncle?"

While uttering these words Campbell had run to the child and snatched her so impetuously into his arms, that she seemed worse frightened than before. Her apparent bewilderment had been the cause of Campbell's questions ; and for a moment the three rescuers actually entertained the fear that the savage treatment which the little one had received at the hands of her jailors, had destroyed the soundness of her judgment beyond recovery. In this, however, they were mistaken, for after her ears had, for a while, drunk in the familiar sounds, her eye began to assume a look of intelligence, and, to the unspeakable joy of Campbell, she suddenly whispered :

"Father !"

"She knows me !" he shouted, and again he pressed her to his bosom, and nearly overwhelmed her with his caresses.

Scenes like this beggar description. Let us drop a veil on it, and take up the thread of our narrative ; at the moment when the sweets and bitters of the reunion had been tasted to the dregs, and the scouts turned to the prisoner, in order to see whether they might succeed in extorting from him any information, which would lead to the discovery of Maghpiway and the other captive, whose recovery was now more ardently desired than ever before. When they reached the place where the Indian was lying on the ground, they helped him to rise, and were on the point of examining him, when an exclamation of the Red Fox caused them to desist, and to turn to the young Delaware for an explanation.

"Ugh !" he repeated ; "my eyes are offended at the sight of a faithless Delaware—the Black Snake has turned traitor."

It was well for the Black Snake—for it was really he that had escaped the jaws of death to fall into the hands of foes hardly less formidable—it is well for him that Campbell was ignorant of the role which he had played in the tragedy ; else nothing—not even the hope of extracting valuable information—could have stayed the hand of retribution, which would have sought and found the heart of the culprit with unerring certainty. As it was the scouts merely echoed the sound of surprise, and Campbell continued :

"The Black Snake, indeed ! Yes, now you mention his name, I can call back the memory of such a person. If I am not mistaken he bore a pretty good report before ; but the Red Feather, no doubt, made him brilliant promises, and succeeded in upsetting his principles by tempting his greediness and love of glory. Well, well, Eve was not proof against the tempter : so we need not wonder that an ignorant Indian would yield to the seducing bait."

Campbell had involuntarily fallen into a meditative train of thought; for a moment he appeared to have forgotten his purpose; but collecting himself he started up and addressed the Black Snake in a very different tone of voice.

"How does it happen that we find the Black Snake in such a scrape?" he asked. "Is it not nearly time that he should leave the evil company into which he has fallen?"

The captive preserved his former silence; there was nothing in his features to show that he had heard the question.

"The Black Snake is obstinate," the scout resumed. "Is it wise in him to irritate the sting which can inflict a wound ?"

Again no answer, unless we may construe as such the contemptuous smile which curled the lips of the captive for a moment or two.

"Let the Black Snake beware !" said Campbell in a threatening tone. "If he will not answer our questions he may compel us to measures which we would rather avoid. Now, the Red Fox here is pretty good at torturing. I have an idea that he wouldn't much object to try his hand on you."

This time Campbell had the satisfaction of seeing his question answered ; although the spirit of defiance which the response breathed did by no means suit his purpose.

"Let the boy try !" said the Black Snake, contempt-uously. "He may tickle the nerves of a squaw—he could not make a warrior quail under his feeble efforts !"

If the prisoner desired to rouse the anger of his captors, he reached his object as far as the Red Fox was concerned. The young Delaware frowned, and it is hard to say what he would have done, if the presence of the scouts had not restrained his passion.

"Don't lad," Campbell admonished him. "Don't you give him the satisfaction of getting angry at his words. He is afraid of being tortured and would like to provoke us

into a rash deed, in order to shorten the period of his suffering. But he is mistaken.''

"Indeed you are mistaken, Black Snake," he continued, turning to the Indian. "Nor is our demand unreason-
able. When you listened to the insinuations of the Red
Feather, you left the path on which an honest Indian ought
to walk. All we ask you now to do, is to return to it.''

"What have you gained by this breach of faith?" he
continued, when the other remained silent. "The loss of
your reputation in the tribe and plenty of hard knocks.
Or am I wrong? Did you get any happier or richer by
your desertion ? If so, my eyes are too dull to see it.''

The Black Snake preserved his moody silence ; yet a
careful observer could have noticed that Campbell's words
began to make an impression.

"It is not too late to return to your allegiance," the
scout resumed. "If the Black Snake desires to do it his
white friends will smooth the way for him. They have influence with the Beaver, and they will use it for his benefit.''

The captive looked more gloomy than before.

"It is too late," was his laconic answer.

"It is not too late," the scout asserted. "What has the
Black Snake done? He has followed the Red Feather because he did not know that the chief meant mischief. He
has adhered to him until he understood his plans; then he
came to his white friends and informed them of his whereabouts. Let the Black Snake do this and Big Jump will
pledge him a favorable reception in his tribe.''

Campbell had proved himself a skillful negotiator ; for
the Indian was on the point of surrendering. He had tasted
the bitterness of exile, and now eagerly seized the opportunity of returning to his home ; which, though a shifting
one, was after all a home. If he hesitated it was merely
for the purpose of securing full pardon for his offenses.

"Will the Big Jump guarantee me full pardon ?"

"He will.''

"In the name of the Delawares ?"

"In their name.''

"In his own name, too ?"

"Yes, Black Snake, I freely forgive you all the injuries you did me, on condition that you make now a truthful statement of the whereabout and intentions of the Red Feather."

"But the Big Jump may learn that it was the Black Snake who decoyed the Wild Rose from her wigwam—will it not alter his resolution ?"

"So you were the wolf that broke into my fold. Well, Indian, it is your luck that you secured my pledge before you made that revelation ; else your chances for old age would now be mighty slim. Still a word is a word, and if you'll tell the whereabouts of the sneaking renegade chief, I shall endeavor to forget that you were instrumental in heaping such misery upon my head."

"The Black Snake will do more ; he will make amends and aid his white friends in their undertaking."

"Well, your aid will not come amiss ; for you have a reputation for both cunning and bravery ; but of that again —the main point is now to know the direction in which to hunt the trail of the renegade."

"The Big Jump is right. He is very wise ; but he will need all his wisdom to bear with composure the evil tidings in store for him."

"Indian, your slowness is excruciating ; can you not speak out like a man ?"

"Let the Big Jump listen, then. The Red Feather is bound for the big lake."

"Lake Erie, you mean ?"

"The big lake that has no shores on the north."

"Lake Erie then—proceed."

"On the shore he expects to find a large canoe to take him across the water."

"Mercy, to Canada ?

"To Canada. He expects to find a kind reception and a home with the Mohawks."

For a moment this new blow made Campbell speechless. Anderson endeavored to work off his wrath and consternation by sundry exclamations, while the Red Fox was bending a look of compassion and sympathy upon the unhappy husband. Peter stood by with his usual vacant stare, and the child on Campbell's arm alone continued to laugh and chatter as before, happily unconscious of a revelation which concerned so much her mourning father.

It was a striking tableau, this group in the rock-bound cauldron, the fire throwing its red glare upon it, and giving it a wild and striking effect.

The confusion, however, lasted but a moment. Campbell was not the man to surrender at discretion, and before the expiration of five minutes he was prepared to meet the emergency. He cut the ropes which up to this time had bound the captive, and said:

"Do you know where the chief intends embarking?"

"At Presque Isle."

"Well, that is fortunate, for we can now make for that point without loss of time. But what about the child? I would give much to have her safely at the Fort in the care of good dame Sullivan."

"Might we not take her to the Seneca village and leave her in the care of Cornplanter?" suggested Anderson.

"We would not have the time, even if I were inclined to give her out of my hands, which I am not."

"Then I see no way but to take her along."

"We'll have to do that, father, and if we take turns about in carrying her, she will not much impede our progress. But now let us plunder the powder-horns and bullet pouches of these fellows, for we may use a heap of ammunition before we are through. I'll fight the united Indians of the Canadas before I give up my wife. So, that attended to, we may as well depart, for time is precious and on the gain or loss of one minute may depend the destiny of poor Mary.'

The Black Snake had meanwhile re-possessed himself of his arms, and under his leadership the party now took the nearest cut out of the rocky fastness.

It is not our intention to accompany them on their rapid journey through the woods, as it is void of any unusual features, and therefore lacks the elements of interest for the reader. Let us, however, rejoin the party, as they break from the woods at the place where Erie is now situated, and cast the first look upon the beautiful sheet of water, which commemorates the name of one of the fiercest Indian tribes. They have no eye, however, for the beauties of the scenery, for their looks are bent upon the ground, following a fresh trail, which after reaching the shore turns abruptly to the left and runs to the point where a low and narrow strip of land connects the peninsula of Presque Isle with the coast. The moist ground shows the foot-prints with great distinctness, and some reeds and blades of grass arising even then from the ground and recovering from the pressure of the rude feet that trod them down, show to a certainty the recent date of the passage of the fugitives.

The chase has been a hot one all the while, taxing the strength of the pursurers to the utmost limit of human endurance; but now that the crisis is approaching, it assumes a fiercer character than ever before. Leaving his daughter in the care of Peter, Campbell throws himself across the neck and rushes into the bushes of the peninsula with a zest that brooks no obstacles. Panting with the greatness of their exertions the others follow in his wake. They care no longer for the trail—they know but too well the point to which it runs.

Rushing, tearing, plunging, they advance in a north-eastern direction, and soon gain a place where the great thinness of the woods indicate the neighborhood of the lake. Campbell is far ahead. It seems as if the intensity of his emotions has made him proof against fatigue and pain, and when the signs above mentioned betray to him the nearness of the lake, he doubles his exertions, and breaks from the cover of the bushes with the impetuosity of the lion ready to pounce upon his prey.

When the trees no longer impede his vision, he casts an anxious, searching glance in all directions; but the sun shines from the west and imbues the water with such a brilliancy that the eyes refuse to act, and involuntarily drop the lashes to guard against the blinding effect.

Now, Campbell screens them with his hands, and thus protected, his gaze succeeds in discovering on the lake, about half a mile from shore, the forms of two large canoes, which are headed northward, and evidently increase their distance from the land with great rapidity.

This sight speaks volumes. One wild cry·wrings itself from the tortured breast of the unhappy man; then he throws himself upon the beach, and covering his face with his hands, bursts into a flood of bitter, scalding tears.

CHAPTER X.

A DIPLOMATE AT WORK.

Campbell's cry rang far off through the air. It also reached the canoes on the lake, and awoke very different sensations in the different persons composing the crew. In Mrs. Campbell's heart it fanned the almost dying spark of hope to a flame: for she had recognized the voice of her husband. So had the Red Feather recognized it; but what had been the source of joy and hope in the bosom of the captive, kindled feelings of a very different nature in that of the chief. He was not only disappointed, and therefore vexed, but these obstinate efforts, this dogged pursuit, gave new nourishment to the hatred he had always borne the scout. His teeth set, his hands clenched, and he felt that to seize his enemy and tear him into a thousand shreds would be a keener pleasure than anything else the earth could then afford.

The rage of Maghpiway, however, was coupled with another and less agreeable sensation—fear. He had concealed his trail with the most cunning devices; but the scout had baffled them all. Was it likely that the man who had followed him through the broad wilderness of Pennsylvania forest, would suffer himself to be checked by a sheet of water? The want of a vessel large enough to cross the lake in would check him a little while; but such a vessel once procured, and the Red Feather might count with certainty on a new pursuit. This never ending chase began to tell on the nerves of the chief, and he who knows human nature will not wonder that sleep fled his eyes, and that he spent the whole night in devising schemes to elude the vigilance of his pursuers.

The night was beautiful, and every stroke of the paddle told on the progress of the canoes. When the morning came, they saw on their left in the far distance the island of Long Point, and right in front of them the main coast in the neighborhood of the Promontory, which now bears the name of West Point. The coast was still several miles off, nor did the chief seem anxious to approach it any nearer just then, for he motioned to the warriors to cease paddling, and beckoning one of them to his side, entered with him into a whispered conversation. The man seemed to be familiar with the coast, for he nodded to the questions of the chief and pointed in various directions with a certainty betokening accurate knowledge. The interview lasted nearly an hour, but so guarded were the voices of the speakers that even the nearest warriors failed to comprehend the meaning of their words. When the conversation closed, the chief motioned the canoe with the captive to come along side of his own. This being done, all the warriors but two were ordered into the other vessel, including the confidential friend of the chief, who had no sooner taken his seat when he assumed command and ordered his men to paddle the canoe in an eastern direction, parallel with the coast. The chief, on the other hand, headed his own craft towards the shore, aiming a little to the east of West Point, and so well did his two subordinates support his efforts, that the canoe shot into the mouth of Grand River before the expiration of another hour.

Maghpiway had never been in Canada, but his informer seemed to have instructed him sufficiently to free his movements from any appearance of hesitation. The progress of the canoe, however, was not so fast now since they had to battle against a strong current. Yet they made considerable headway, and soon rounded the point where the river makes a sharp bend, changing its almost eastern course into one nearly south. About a mile above this point they passed a little island on which they noticed signs of cultivation somewhat above the Indian standard. They saw a good blockhouse and several outbuildings; they saw a large cornfield and cattle grazing in a pasture. These things were certainly out of place at such a spot, but if the chief and his companions felt any surprise they surely did not show it, the betrayal of such a feeling being incompatible with the dignity of Indian warriors. They passed the island without ever turning their heads to view its novelties, and continued their course until they reached a second and larger island two miles further up the river. This island seemed to be the aim of their expedition, for when they reached its lower extremity, they paddled up to it and effected a landing in a little cove well calculated to hold a canoe. After securing the vessel they left the bank and entered a small grove which occupied the entire breadth of the island, and nearly a quarter of a mile of its length. It was soon traversed, and when they emerged from the bushes on the farther end, their eyes fell upon a scene which was as novel as it was attractive. The island was several miles in length, while its breadth varied from a quarter to half a mile. The western or upper end contained a grove similar to the one at the eastern extremity ; but the rest of the island was an open plain, merely fringed with a heavy line of bushes on the two banks. In the center of this plain, stretching from bank to bank, stood a small Indian village, remarkable for the same superior taste and culture which the first and smaller island had betrayed. The number of huts did not exceed fifty, but they were large and substantial enough to deserve the name of houses and to refute the name of savages as applied to the builders. The rest of the plain was devoted to the culture of maize, excepting a few meadows and pastures, on the latter of which several cows were grazing. The whole scene breathed an air of comfort and contentment, and looked more like the habitation of civilized people than of savages. And yet these inhabitants belonged to the copper colored race of North America ; for as Maghpiway and his companions approached the village they saw persons belonging to that race—and only such—lounging, working or playing around their houses or fields. Those lounging were men and warriors, while the workers belonged exclusively to the female sex, a certain proof that the civilization manifested in the surroundings of the people had hardly penetrated beyond the thickness of their skin. Those playing were children, and they indeed were the first to sound the alarm at the approach of the strangers.   Not that the men had not noticed them as soon, or sooner ; but it became their dignity to appear totally indifferent about an event, which, to judge from the secluded position of the village, was hardly of very frequent occurrence.   The visitors walked to the center of the place, and seeing a venerable looking man of advanced age sitting before a cottage, they turned to him their steps and their addresses.

"I greet my Wyandot father," said the Red Feather, in the dialect of that nation.   "May his days be numerous like the pebbles on the shore of the lake."

The old man nodded.

"I thank my brother and bid him welcome.   Is it a peaceful errand that leads him to the village of the Hurons ? "

"My father says it.   If we were enemies we would have chosen the darkness of the night; a foe does not like the sun to shine upon his actions."

"It is true ; my brother is very wise ; has my brother a name ?"

"They call me Turtle Heart in the tongue of the Delawares, and many warriors obey the motion of my hand."

"Turtle Heart is welcome.   Can the Yellow Pine do anything for his brother ? "

"He can.   Let him call the chiefs and the braves of the Wyandots; the Turtle Heart would speak to them in council.   He knows that which will make their hearts glad and sound like music in their ears.   Will the Yellow Pine open his ear to the prayer of Turtle Heart ? "

"Why should he not?   The Wyandots are men ; they have open ears ; they listen alike to the words of the Delawares and the speeches of the Mingoes.   Yellow Pine will do the bidding of Turtle Heart, but the Wyandots have many warriors ; they do not run to the council lodge like children.   It will take time to call the braves ; will my friends meanwhile step into my lodge and refresh their bodies with meat and drink ?   Yellow Pine will show them the way."

The Huron rose and led the strangers into his lodge,

where his squaws soon spread such fare before them as an Indian larder is apt to contain. The host saw that their wants were fully supplied, and then left the lodge to summon the warriors to the council lodge in accordance with the request of his guests. An hour elapsed before he returned; but when he reappeared in the wigwam, he informed the Red Feather that his request had been complied with, and that the warriors of the tribe awaited his coming in the council lodge.

The chief motioned his companions to stay behind, and then followed his host into a building of larger dimensions, in which he found some thirty warriors assembled. We have had occasion to witness and describe the ceremonies of an Indian council before, and shall therefore avoid worrying the reader with unnecessary details. The calumet was smoked with due solemnity, and then the Yellow Pine arose to address the visitors. Red Feather had by chance hit upon the right person, for to judge from the general reverence paid to him, he seemed to be the chief sachem of the tribe.

"My brother has whispered strange sounds into the ear of Yellow Pine; will he now explain the meaning of his words? The ears of the Wyandots are open to receive it."

He sat down again and the Red Feather rose to his feet.

"Turtle Heart comes across the big lake," he began. "He had heard much about the bravery of the Wyandots, and about the beauty of their hunting grounds, he was anxious to praise the former and admire the latter. But a chief must not be curious like a woman, and Turtle Heart would have turned a deaf ear to the prompting of his curiosity, if he had not all at once caught strange sounds floating through the forest. Turtle Heart bent his ear to listen, and he recognized the voices of many Shawanese and a few Yengeese."

He stopped, and the close attention with which the warriors followed his words, showed that he had already succeeded in creating an interest in his communications. After a short pause he resumed:

"What could it signify? The Yengeese never meant

the red man well, and if they whisper in his ear they design mischief. Turtle Heart knew this, and he bent his head to listen to the words of the pale-faces; what he heard made his brow contract, and his eye flash with anger."

Another pause.

"Thus spoke the Yengeese to the Shawanese: 'Let my red brethren listen to our words. The country between the Ohio and the lakes becomes too narrow for the Indian and the white man. The Yengeese cut down the forests, and tear up the soil with iron knives to make the corn grow. They drive the game away on which the red man lives—what will he do? Beyond the father of waters there are no trees; the Shawanese do not like that country; but their white brothers know another in which they may hunt, untrammeled by the axe of the woodman, and the plough of the farmer—this country they will give their red friends.'"

The attention of the assembly increased from minute to minute, and the short pauses of the speaker, instead of lessening the effect of the address, were so cunningly devised as to heighten it. Now the Red Feather prepared to raise their interest to a climax.

"Do my Wyandot friends know where this land lies?" he continued. Turtle Heart can tell them, for he heard the Yengeese whisper the name into the ears of the Shawanese. It lies north of the big lake, there where the hunting grounds of the Wyandots stretch through the forests, where their villages lie in the midst of waving cornfields, where their fathers are buried, where their warriors follow the trail of the moose, and their children play in the shade of sugar trees. There lies the land which Turtle Heart heard the Yengeese promise to the Shawanese."

The effect of these words can hardly be imagined, unless the reader calls to his mind the repeated devices by which the encroaching white man had deprived the receding Indian of his lands; unless he remembers how exceedingly sensitive an often received injury is apt to make us. The Wyandots formed no exception to the rule; they too had been driven from the hunting grounds of their fathers, and the circumstance that the reported movement

was merely an offspring of the Red Feather's imagination,
or rather a willful fabrication of his malignant tongue, did
not lessen the effect of the news on men who received it in
good faith. The insolence manifested in this supposed ne-
gotiation of the pale-faces was too much for mortal stoicism.
even if that mortal boasted of a copper colored skin. A cry
of indignation burst from the lips of almost every warrior
present, and the knives and tomahawks brandished in the
air showed clearly that the Wyandots of Canada at least
would not tamely submit to so flagrant a violation of their
rights.

For five minutes the tumult was such that the Red
Feather could not have made himself heard if such had
been his wish. But he had had his say, and produced the
desired effect and could, therefore, afford to wait for the
abatement of the storm, which his words had aroused.
When order was at length restored, the Yellow Pine, whose
sagacity evidently was in keeping with his age and high
position, arose to say, in reply to Maghpiway's denuncia-
tion:

"My brother has told the Hurons a strange tale. They
knew the pale-faces to be grasping and rapacious; but they
had no idea that their avarice reached across the big water.
The Wyandots thank their brother; they are only a small
band; but they are children of the Eries, and will know
how to repel any invaders that may be bold enough to
claim their inheritance. But is my brother sure that his
ear has caught the true meaning of their words? Has he
any proofs of the strange tale he related to the Wyandots?"

The Red Feather bit his lips. It annoyed him to think
that this old chief should doubt his words; but he would
not have been the cunning chief he really was—the man
for emergencies of all descriptions, if so slight an obstacle
had disconcerted him. He was fully prepared to meet the
objection of the chief, and said:

"He has. He would not have come without them.
Could he expect the Hurons to believe so incredible a tale
if he were not prepared to substantiate his statements with
irrefutable facts? Surely not; the Hurons are wise; they
scent a falsehood far off; let them now listen to the contin-

uation of my story, to see whether Turtle Heart has spoken with a cloven tongue."

He stopped a moment, as if to collect his thoughts, then he continued:

"The Shawanese did not at once enter into a bargain. They loved their own country; they did not know the country which was offered them in exchange. Then it was that the Yengeese put their heads together to deliberate on the best mode of persuading them. At last they said: 'Let us send some scouts into the country of the Wyandots—two Yengeese and two Shawanese, to see the nature of the land, and report to our red brethren on their return.' This was agreed upon, and the four scouts were selected; but in order to blind the eyes of the Wyandots an idiot and a child were added to the party. The scouts invented a touching story, and when they come they will tell it to the Hurons."

Maghpiway stopped; but so powerful was the persuasion of the intense glances riveted on his face, that he felt induced to resume, after a short pause.

"They will tell the Hurons that the wife of one of the pale-face scouts, the mother of the little child, was stolen from her home, and carried into the country of the Wyandots by Maghpiway, a wicked Delaware chief. They will ask the Hurons whether they saw any traces of the robbers, and ask permission to search the country. This will occur before another sun sets in the West; and when the eyes of the Hurons see it, and their ears hear it, then they will know that Turtle Heart has spoken with a straight tongue."

Red Feather stopped and sat down on one of the seats which lined the walls. He was satisfied with the result of his strategy, for when he looked around the circle he saw faces flushed with indignation. After a pause, during which every warrior seemed to have indulged in his own reflections, the Yellow Pine arose and said:

"Turtle Heart has made good his promise; when the Yengeese arrive the Wyandots will know that his tongue was straight. Can my brother tell us their names?"

"I can. Their names have a big sound on the other side of the lake. One of them is a man of nearly fifty summers, but his body is as active and strong as ever, and the years have left no vestige of their ravages. His name is Little Coon."

A murmur passed through the line of warriors, showing that the above name had penetrated to their ears before, and that they were not ignorant of the reputation of the man that bore it. When the murmur had died away Maghpiway continued :

"The second one is in the bloom of his years. He is strong, like the grizzly bear of the mountains, and fleet, like the deer when flying before the bullet of the hunter. He is at home in the water, like the otter, and the squirrel cannot beat him in climbing a tree. His eye is sharp and keen, like the eagle's, and the bullet from his rifle never misses its aim. Have my brothers ever heard of the name of the Big Jump ?"

"Ugh !"

This time the Wyandots did not content themselves with a mere murmur. The utterance of a name so much admired and feared in the wilderness was too much for Indian stoicism, and they broke into the exclamation above recorded. If the pale-faces sent such men across the lake, they surely must be in earnest, and the service of the Turtle Heart assumed a serious character. The Yellow Pine arose to express their sentiments :

"It is well," he said. "The Hurons thank Turtle Heart ; they will not forget that he thought of them in the hour of their danger. He is very wise, and the Hurons have no doubt that he is as brave and strong as he is wise. They place their homes at his disposal ; they would rejoice to have him remain and aid them with his counsel in their strait. He that warned them of their danger, must also be well qualified to avert it. Yellow Pine has spoken."

This was certainly a very civil invitation ; but it did not at all suit the Red Feather. He had put a trap for others, but felt no desire whatever to remain and be caught in it himself. So he arose and said :

"Turtle Heart thanks the Hurons. They are very good, and he would like nothing better than to remain and enjoy their company, and the pleasant life they lead in their beautiful village; but his mission is not yet completed; he must go on and give warning to the Mohawks. When he comes back he will tarry with the Wyandots."

This time no applause—no sign of approbation greeted the ears of Maghpiway. An ominous silence reigned in the circle, and the contracted brows and sinister glances of the warriors induced the Delaware to believe that he had committed a blunder. Nor should he remain uncertain any length of time. Yellow Pine undoubtedly interpreted the feelings of the tribe by saying:

"The Wyandots have nothing in common with the Mohawks—they would not like to share their friends with them. My brother is very wise; does he not know that the Mingoes are intruders themselves?"

Maghpiway now understood the nature of their discontent, and, skillful diplomate as he was, he found no difficulty in shaping his course in such a way as to benefit by the wind, which at first had threatened him ill.

"Turtle Heart knows that the Mohawks are intruders; he knows also that the Wyandots do not love the Mingo. He feels like they do—there has never been much friendship between the Mingoes and the Lenni Lenape. But to be friendly is one thing—to be prudent another. When two evils present themselves, a wise man chooses the smaller. The Mokawks are here, it cannot now be helped; would the Wyandots rather have new neighbors from across the lake than unite with the Mohawks to ward them off? Let my friends consider, and they will see that Turtle Heart is right."

He was right and they could not deny it. Great as their dislike against their stronger, and therefore formidable neighbors might be, they could not conceal from themselves the necessity of their co-operation in case the Americans seriously contemplated an invasion of their territory. So they advanced no further objections to the proposed visit, and suffered the Red Feather and his companions to depart without delay. They provided them with suitable rations, and ferried them to the left bank of the Grand River, the large canoe remaining behind as being

no longer of any use to the travelers.   On the bank
the two parties shook hands, the hosts requesting and
the guests promising a speedy return.   Then Maghpiway and his companions entered the woods and proceeded
in an eastern direction, with a slight deviation to the north,
following pretty much the same course which the Welland Canal feeder now pursues.   They had left the village
at noon, and when the sun set, and the darkness of night
spread over the woods, they arrived at the south-eastern
bend of the Chippewa, where the Welland Canal now
crosses the river.   There they encamped and spent the
night; but when the first streak of dawn stole over the
country, they were already on their way again, for there
were weighty reasons which made it desirable for Maghpiway to reach the village of the Mohawks in good season.

It was situated on the western bank of Niagara river,
opposite Grand Island, about a mile above the mouth of the
Chippewa river; and as its distance from the Red Feather's
last camp ground was hardly twenty miles, he reached its
outskirts before the sun had passed his meridian.   There
was a marked difference between it and the village of the
Wyandots.   While it was at least five times as large, it
lacked the elements of beauty and regularity which gave to
the other the character of order and civilization.   The chief
entered the place without any hesitation, and although his
appearance created some excitement among the squaws
and children, a knowing look in the eyes of the warriors
betrayed the fact that the coming of the party had been
heralded.   Maghpiway at once inquired for Joseph Brant,
or rather Thayendanegea, as the Indians called him, and
received the answer that the chief was in his lodge expecting his visit.   The Delaware, therefore, repaired without
delay to the habitation of the chieftain who had played so
prominent a role in the American revolution, and in consequence of his fidelity to the British cause, became an exile
from the country of his fathers.   When the Red Feather
entered he perceived a broad-shouldered, heavy featured
man who wore a small coronet of silver on his head, and
was attired in the usual hunting suit of the frontier.   He
lay on a kind of lounge and smoked his pipe; but when the

Delaware entered, he laid the pipe aside, and rose to receive his visitor.

"My young men have told me that I might expect the visit of a Delaware chief," he said, extending his hand towards the other.

"They have told you the truth—Maghpiway has come to pay his respects to the great sachem of the Mohawks."

"Maghpiway is welcome. Let him sit down and make himself at home. Is the chief hungry?"

"He is hungry, but he will not eat until he has come to an understanding with Thayendanegea. Does my brother know this belt?"

"Ugh! It was given to a great Seneca chief. How did it come into the hands of Maghpiway?"

"Red Jacket gave it to me to pave my way into the favor of Thayendanegea."

"You could not have brought me a better recommendation. What can I do for you?"

"Let me tell you a short story first. The chief sachem of the Delawares had a daughter. I thought she was a red woman, and loved her; but she preferred a pale-face hunter, and when it was discovered that she was of white birth the hunter took her as his squaw into his wigwam. I was angry then; but I was also very sad, for the maiden had been very dear to my heart. I tried to forget her; but when I thought I had succeeded, her memory returned with greater force than ever. I found I could not forget her. I found I could not live without her, and in the bitterness of my disappointment I formed the resolution to abduct her. In this I succeeded. One of my warriors was ordered to decoy her to the woods, and when she was in my possession I fled northward to the village of the Senecas. I thought I would be safe there, but was mistaken. Her husband threw himself upon the trail and tracked me to the village. He proposed to fight me and I accepted the challenge, but during the night Red Jacket came to my lodge and told me that it must not be; that nothing but a flight across the lake could save me from the wrath of the Yengeese and enable me to keep my captive. I objected, but when he persisted in his demands I had to yield. What could an exiled Delaware do against the dictates of a powerful Seneca chief? Red Jacket favored my escape; he helped me mislead my pursuers so that I could gain a sufficient start to reach the lake. I embarked not a minute too soon; for scarcely had the canoe left the shore when the white hunters appeared in sight and rent the air with their cries of disappointed fury. Now, here I am; I have sacrificed everything to my passion. I am an exile; the warriors of my tribe call me a renegade; but I can bear all my losses if the Wild Rose remains in my possession—will Thayendanegea protect me from the vengeance of the Yangeese?"

The Mohawk chief had listened with great attention. The passing emotions of the speaker had found a mirror in his expressive countenance, showing that he was able to appreciate such a passion and sympathized with it. When the Red Feather had done, he readily offered his hand and said:

"Let Maghpiway rest easy; he is safe in the village of the Mohawks. If the Yengeese come my warriors will drive them back like dogs; but why did my brother pay a visit to the village of the Wyandots? Was he afraid that Thayendanegea is too weak to protect him alone?"

The Red Feather shook his head; his face assumed an expression of malignant triumph, and drawing his lips into a derisive smile. he said:

"Maghpiway did no such thing. The Wyandots are sheep—what could the Red Feather expect from such poltroons? He merely went into their camp to pull the wool over their eyes."

"I do not understand my brother; let him be explicit."

"I stuffed the ears of the Hurons with a big story; I told them that the Yengeese and Shawanese prepared an expedition to cross the lake to deprive them of their territory."

"But why did my brother do that?"

"Thayendanegea will see in a moment. The Hurons asked me for a proof of my story; then I told them that the Yengeese were on the point of sending a scouting party into their land to explore its resources. I described the men, and when my pursuers come they will be received and executed like so many spies."

Brant cast an admiring glance upon his visitor.

"You are a man after my own heart, chief," he said, "and if I had not ample reasons to hate the Yengeese on my own account, I would stick to you merely for this clever trick of yours. Yes, you are safe with me; we shall make common cause, and anything I can do to second you, shall be done, depend upon it. When do you think these scouts will arrive in Canada?"

"As soon as they can secure a craft to cross the water. If they fail in this the Big Jump will swim across, before he abandons the pursuit."

"Ugh! what name did you say there? It has a fearful sound in the ears of the red man."

"I know—does my brother think Maghpiway would have fled before the gambols of a boy or the chattering of a squaw?"

The Mohawk all at once became pensive.

"So you think the pale-faces will arrive without delay?" he asked, after a pause.

"I know it."

"And the Wyandots will finish them as emissaries of the Yengeese?"

"I have good reason to expect it."

The Mohawk shook his head.

"They cannot be relied upon; they are too much under the influence of the white man."

"I have not seen any white men there," Maghpiway said, with the expression of one who doubts.

"Then you did not see the little island below the village?"

"I did; but I failed to perceive white people on it."

"Then the Muskrat must have been absent in his big canoe. But you surely saw Tononqua, the white chief of the Wyandots?"

"I saw no white man in the village," said the Red Feather with a new shake of his head. "Whom can my brother mean?"

The Mohawk in turn looked with surprise upon the Delaware.

"Can it be that my brother never heard of Tononqua the pride of the Wyandots? He is young in years but his hands are strong, his sinews are of iron, and a wise head sits on his shoulders. His skin is white. The Wyandots claim that he was never born : but that he came from the sun in order to restore the tribe to its original greatness. This is a tale of course unworthy of the belief of chiefs ; but there is certainly a mystery about his birth, which has never been fathomed thus far. I, for my part, take him to be some stolen child which the tribe afterwards adopted : but I have no proof whatever for this opinion."

"The words of Thayendanegea are very strange. Where does he think that this white chief could have been while Maghpiway stayed in the village?"

"Perhaps he was out on a hunting expedition. It is his custom to disappear weeks at a time."

"And my brother thinks that he would save the scouts if he should be at home at the time of their capture?"

"I am strongly inclined to think so."

"Then they ought to be sacrificed before his arrival."

"How would Maghpiway do it?"

"Thayendanegea is wise and strong. Could he not send a dozen warriors to the Wyandots to hasten the execution? The pale-faces are the common enemies of the red man—the Hurons cannot but applaud my brothers' zeal."

Again Brant cast an admiring glance at this Delaware, who, a born diplomate, played the intrigues with the skill of a prime minister of some European monarch.

"My brother is right. I shall act on his advice and start the warriors without delay. I see my squaws have prepared some viands for my brother. Let him eat and drink while I go to attend to this affair."

Maghpiway sat down to do his bidding, while Brant turned to the door to leave the cabin. Just as he stepped into the open air a flash of lightning darted across the horizon. It was followed by the rumbling of distant thunder, and when the chief cast a glance at the black clouds which overhung the sky, he knew that a thunder storm of unusual vehemence was brewing.

CHAPTER XI.

WRECKED AND RESCUED.

It is now time to return to those persons whom we left on the shores of Lake Erie in such a deplorable condition. Campbell was still lying prostrate on the ground when his friends emerged from the bushes. Their attention was divided between the scout, who betrayed signs of such unmeasured grief, and the two canoes which were fast receding out of sight. Anderson at once ran to the side of his friend, shook him by the shoulder and endeavored to arouse him by words of comfort and encouragement. Campbell, however, paid no attention to him, and there is no knowing how long the paroxysm of grief would have lasted if left to himself; for all at once little Annie freed herself from the embrace of Peter, and, running up to her father, laid her arm around his neck in a loving manner.

"Papa," she said, lovingly. "Not cry—if papa cry, Annie cry, too."

These words exercised a powerful effect upon the weeping scout. He stopped his tears and arising embraced the child, and showered a profusion of kisses on her head and face.

"No, I will cry no longer, darling," he said, recovering his self-control as suddenly as he had lost it. "You do not wish it and it shall not be. Moreover, we have no time to cry and to lament. If the robber chief imagines that this lake will check my pursuit, he is sorely mistaken. To the very ends of the earth will I follow him if necessary, to recover so loving a mother, so good a wife. Come, friends, let us be up and searching to see whether the beach contains another vessel in which we might start in pursuit."

No sooner had he said this when he plunged into the bushes with a zest which showed that he endeavored to escape, by physical exertion from the maddening thoughts which no doubt continued to assault his mind. The others seconded him, and before five minutes had elapsed, they found the place where the vessels of the Red Feather had been buried. They drove their knives and tomahawks into the sand, hoping to discover another canoe by means of which they might cross the lake. Nor was their attempt a total failure, for the knife of Red Fox struck something hard in the ground, which, on a closer examination, proved to be a birch canoe of the smallest kind. To cross the lake with such a nutshell would in itself have been a hazardous experiment; but the miserable condition of the vessel seemed to put the possibility of such a step entirely out of question. And yet the excited state of mind in which Campbell found himself urged him to make that very proposition to his companions.

"Into the water with her!" he cried. "If this canoe is not as large as theirs, it has at least the advantage of greater lightness. Lift, I say, and shove her into the lake."

The others did not remonstrate—perhaps they thought that facts would prove more weighty remonstrances than any words of theirs. If this was their calculation it proved correct, for no sooner did the canoe fairly swim on the water, when several leaks opened and caused it to fill and sink before their eyes. Campbell looked rather crestfallen, but his impatience would not surrender without another struggle.

"I see it leaks," he said, "but an hour's work will remedy that. We can still be off to-night, I think. Red Fox, you are expert at such things; can't you make this vessel seaworthy without much loss of time?"

Red Fox examined the canoe carefully.

"It is badly damaged," he said. "To make it fit to cross the lake with will take almost as much time as to build a new one. If my brother gives me three times twenty-four hours I can build him as large a canoe as those which even now vanish from our sight."

"Three days, lad? I cannot brook the thought. Come, let us set to work at once and begin repairing. If we all put a hand in, it surely cannot take much time."

The Indian yielded and made all needful preparations
to renew or repair such portions of the canoe as were damaged. To do this he had only his knife and tomahawk ;
but as his countrymen always built their vessels with such
tools, there was no reason why he should fail in this particular instance. Campbell seemed indeed to have no doubt
regarding his ability, the length of time required being the
only point of difference. Campbell made his wishes the
arbiter, while the Delaware was backed by an unimpaired
judgment and the experience of many a similar situation.
The result soon determined the issue in favor of the latter.
Not only had the necessary bark to be collected from a
territory of considerable size, but they were also in want of
pitch which had to be scraped from the pine trees and
worked near the fire in order to close the seams in a proper
manner. When the light of day waned so little had been
accomplished, in spite of their most determined efforts,
that Campbell's hope of effecting a very speedy embarca-
tion was greatly lessened. Although they kindled a large
fire and continued the work of repair by its light, the
restless scout discovered on the break of morning that
another day must elapse, another morning break, before he
could expect to see his burning desire gratified.

We need not dwell on the anxious hours of this long,
tedious delay. They were partly consumed in work,
partly in hunting and preparing game for the meals,
without which the strength necessary for the prosecution
of the work would soon leave them.

On the evening following their arrival on the beach the
work was completed; but impatiently as Campbell advo-
cated an immediate departure, he was overruled by the
calmer voices of the others, and the declaration of the
Delaware that the canoe must be exposed another night
to the drying air before it could be used for the perilous
attempt of crossing the lake. This decided the matter;
and it was only on the second morning that the party
embarked and paddled the canoe into a sheet of water
which is proverbial for its treachery.

It has already been stated that the vessel was a canoe
of the smallest size. So deep indeed did the disproportion-

ate freight sink the side of the frail vessel into the water, that even an inexperienced eye could see that a very small wave would suffice to swamp it. Only if the fairest weather continued could they expect a safe arrival at the opposite shore. But it is not likely that they had a very clear perception of the danger to which they exposed themselves. Great emergencies generally engender bold remedies, and so imbued had these adventurers become with the daring spirit of their enterprise, that they would have faced an almost certain death without flinching, if it had only promised a successful termination of their pursuit.

At the time of their departure the weather was everything they could expect. The sky was blue, the air calm, and, driven by four paddles in expert hands, the canoe shot across the water with a rapidity that promised a speedy termination of their voyage. When the morning advanced the sun began to shine with an intensity unusual at that season. On shore the heat must have been even more intense, for in spite of the cooler lake air, the perspiration stood profusely on the brows of the paddlers. This, however, did not diminish their exertions; nor did their movements or their faces indicate the slightest vestige of fatigue. True, there was a troubled look in the eye of Anderson; but it seemed to originate from a different cause. As the sun rose higher and higher, the sharp eye of the elder scout scanned the horizon in all directions, and when he all at once noticed a dark line in a south-eastern direction, the troubled expression above mentioned stole for the first time into his countenance. He was seen to ply his paddle from that moment with even greater energy; and this, together with the frequent turning of his head, at last attracted the notice of Campbell.

"What is the matter, father?" he inquired. "Is there anything wrong in the sky? You look as if you meant to gaze it down."

"I have no such intentions, Robert. In fact I should like nothing better than to have everything remain up there—for a couple of hours at least—that's up there now. But I fear we shall have more than we bargained for."

"A storm, you mean? Why there's not much danger

yet, I think. Even if we get a flash of lightning and a little shower, that does not of necessity include a hurricane.''

"I know it doesn't, Robert, and nothing would please me better than to be mistaken; but if we ain't going to have more wind in half an hour than will be at all acceptable under the circumstances,—there now! did I not tell you? The storm is sending a squall as the forerunner of the dance that is to come. This will be worse than I anticipated. Friends, recommend your souls to the Almighty; for unless he does a miracle, no one of us will live to witness the termination of this tempest.''

The storm was indeed overriding the heavens with a rapidity in comparison to which the swiftness of the race horse dwindles into a snail's pace. When the eye gazed up the last time the sky was blue and serene, and now, hardly ten minutes later, the heavens were overhung with clouds whose darkness gave them the appearance of a death shroud. The air, so calm a little while ago, became all at once greatly agitated, a heavy sough creeping over the water, and carrying the spray from the paddles ahead of the canoe. A few heavy drops began to fall, descending slantingly into the sea, as if propelled in that direction by the wind.

But this was merely the prelude. Soon the clouds opened their sluices, and sent down such copious torrents, that Campbell summoned the Red Fox to lay aside his paddle and dip out the water collecting in the bottom of the vessel. If he had given that order a minute later no human ear could have heard it; for just then the storm swept with its full fury over the lake. So completely did the heavy clouds bar up the avenues of light, that the persons in the canoe could hardly see beyond its length. The wind grew into a storm; the storm into a hurricane. The occupants of the vessel could not raise their voices against the howling wind; but they succeeded in communicating with each other by signs. Campbell sat in the bow; he knew that the canoe would sink the moment its side was turned to the wind, so he made superhuman efforts to keep the stern squarely against the wind. The others saw and comprehended him, and aided him to the extent of their ability in his manœuvers. Thus the frail little bark sped with the rapidity of the tempest over the waters. As long as the sea was smooth the canoe worked well enough; but when the vehemence of the wind raised the ground swell ; when the short and dangerous waves of the lake began to chase one another, and to tumble their white-caps into the troughs; when the constant passage through these waves filled the canoe up to the rim with water, and caused its frail frame to tremble like a frightened steed: then the most sanguine saw that its career could not last many more seconds, and that the plunge into the great yawning gulf was close at hand. Nor did nature seem inclined to abate the vehemence of her convulsions. The tempest, so furious already, appeared to grow more furious every minute; and the wind, evidently anxious to exhaust its terrors, suddenly assumed the character of a whirlwind, and tore everything with resistless force into its vortex. Now it reached the vessel; in vain did the men stem themselves against such force; the paddles broke like matches in their hands, and before they knew it the canoe was whirled around with a rapidity which threatened to deprive them of their consciousness before the sea would deprive them of their lives.

But, behold! what is this? Are there still miracles performed in spite of all the denials of the incredulous? Or are there monstrous birds living on these lakes of which natural history does not inform us? What else can this huge black body be, which sweeps down towards the doomed vessel with the impunity of a gigantic water bird ? What else this white surface, wing-like extended, in which a portion of the wind is caught, to benefit and further, instead of harming it?

Now it has reached the spot on which the canoe still spins around like a top, preparatory to its last leap into the depth. Over its bow a human being—a white man—becomes visible. He is aware of the perilous position of the vessel's crew, and, watching a favorable moment, grasps the bow with a sharp iron hook, which in turn is fastened to a rope. Meanwhile the mysterious craft continues its course; the rope is strained, but the canoe yields to the force, and a moment afterwards it swims under the gunwale of the larger vessel. But it is full of water, and the person, who has so timely acted the role of a preserver, sees that it is in a sinking condition. So he cries, in English, which has a strongly foreign accent :

"Hurry up, you daire, and come on board. Hand me la petite, de little one—so, c'est bon, dat is right. Now de rest; quick ! quick ! de canoe is sinking !"

So it was, indeed. The party in the boat, bewildered by the whirlwind, and bewildered even more by this startling and providential rescue, had just sufficiently recovered their senses to act upon the urgent summons of their deliverer, when they felt the canoe sinking under their feet. Campbell, in the climax of danger, had snatched his pale and crying child into his arms, obeying, perhaps, more the instinct of nature than any collected thought. He now handed her to the outstretched arms of the stranger, and then, snatching his rifle, clung to the gunwale of the vessel just in time to avoid a watery grave. A few vigorous pulls of his sinewy arms sufficed to land him on deck, where he arrived in time to assist the less active Peter, whose feeble mind had evidently been upset by the recent fright. The other occupants of the canoe had reached the deck nearly at the same time with Campbell, and the bewildered scout had, therefore, leisure to look around and examine the vessel, which had so timely interfered between him and death. It was a sloop about fifty feet in length, and of proportionate breadth, surrounded by a weather-side, under whose shelter the rescued party now couched on the deck, as the pitching and plunging of the vessel put their standing upon their feet out of question. The forecastle contained the only mast of the vessel. The main sail was firmly reefed, the sloop going merely under a triangular foresail, as the fury of the wind did not allow the exposure of a larger sheet. The poop contained the helm, above which a kind of shed had been erected as a protection against the weather. The portion between the forecastle and the poop was several feet lower than the other parts, giving access to the hull by means of doors in the cross walls. The ship was neatly built and painted, creating in the minds of the rescued party an evergrowing wonder at the vessel and its crew. The latter seemed to consist of two persons, the man who had so seasonably reached them a helping hand, and who had now returned to the helm, and another individual whose character and sex could not be easily divined, as a large oilcloth mantle concealed his form from head to foot.

For fifteen minutes the storm continued in all its fury, and chained the owner of the vessel so closely to the helm that he could bestow no attention whatever to the condition and wants of his unexpected guests. At the end of that period, however, the clouds broke as suddenly as they had appeared ; the sun once more sent his animating rays upon the lake ; the wind abated, and nothing but the turbulence of the waters and their own shipwrecked condition, reminded the party on the deck of the recent storm.

The man at the helm now left the vessel to the care of his companion, and approached his guests, who were suffering, more or less, under the effects of an attack of sea-sickness. The sight was amusing enough ; but the man was evidently of too generous a disposition to laugh at the expense of real suffering. Suppressing even the shadow of a smile, he said :

"Dat vas one very big tempeste, I vould say. If my good sloop, la belle France, had not come in de nick of time, you vould now all make food for de fish. It vas a narrow escape certainement."

"So it was," replied Campbell ; "and we owe you a load of gratitude for your clever assistance. But if it isn't too great a breach of manners, I should like to ask you a question. How in creation does this big and stately vessel get on the waters of Lake Erie? Do you understand the art of sailing over such trifles as the Falls of Niagara ?"

The stranger smiled.

"Someting of dat sort, friend," he said, with a genial nod. "You shall know all in good season: but now ve must first tink of giving you one new rig. Cette petite demoiselle, dis little lady is half dead with wet and cold. If you take her to my daughtaire she vill attend to her vants. Ah, you cannot valk ; just hand her to me, Monsieur. I vill not hurt you, ma petite, your fadair come along. Dis is my daughtaire, Monsieur, Mademoiselle Adeline. Ma chere, vill you take dis little von to your cabin, and make her comfortable?"

So it turned out, that the person in the large oil-cloth mantle was a woman. And what a woman! A sweet little face, hemmed in by auburn tresses, peeped out from under a broad-brimmed tarpaulin. As the mantle opened, a neat dress, which would have done credit to a drawing room, made its appearance, and the foot that stole from under it was not larger than that of a good sized child. Everything was as neat and delicate about this young woman as if she had just been taken from a show window of the Boulevards of Paris. The scouts and their savage companions had never seen anything like it, and they now looked upon the apparition with glances which showed that they considered her not the smallest wonder among the host of marvels into which they had suddenly been thrown. The young lady entered upon her father's wishes with great readiness.

"Comme elle est jolie! how pretty!" she exclaimed. "Come, my darling, we will dress the little lady and give her something good to eat."

The child readily entrusted herself to the care of her friend, and the two disappeared through one of the above mentioned doors in the interior of the hull.

"Now, can you take the helm one little vile and hold him dis vay?" inquired the owner of the sloop. "De sun shines varm, and I may as well fetch some eatables up here."

Campbell took the helm and showed himself such an adept in the art of steering, that the captain at once entrusted the vessel to his management and went below for the laudable purpose expressed. When he returned he was loaded with a heavy basket in one hand and a gallon jug in the other.

"So, messieurs," he said, depositing jug and basket on the deck. "Here is eat and drink—now faites votre diner, make your dinnaire. The ham is of my own raising, de viskey of my own distilling and de bread of my daughter's baking—you are velcome to all dat's daire."

The five members of the shipwrecked party were not slow to follow the invitation of their host, who was evidently pleased with the rapidity with which they caused the contents of both basket and jug to disappear. But while their appetite gradually decreased, their wonder at their host and his vessel would not at all abate, so unmistakably did their words and looks betray their curiosity, that the host at last took pity on them and said:

"You are astonished, messieurs, to see me and my daughtaire and la belle France here in dis vilderness? Vell, vell, it is no vondaire and vhen I tell you how ve got here, you vill call it one strange histoire. You know, dey had vat you call one revolution in France and killed de King and de Queen and one great number of noblemen. Now, my mastaire vas one great marquis and de Jacobites came and killed all his children. De poor old man took his money and fled from de country, and I and my daughtaire vent along. Ve would not forsake our kind old mastaire, who mourned ovaire de loss of his family. He was tired of de vorld, and so he buried himself in dis vilderness and ordered one dozaine ship wrights to come and build him La Belle France. Poor marquis! You lived no long to enjoy de vessel. He died vid one broken heart, and three years ago we buried him on one little island in la Grande Riviere near de house he had built for himself. Dat is my story, messieurs."

"And you have ever since remained in this wilderness?"

"I have, monsieur. Vat vould ve do in de vorld? Ve did not vant to leave our mastaire's grave, and den ve had one nice home vid cattle and fields, and many friends amongst de neighboring Indians. Ve feel contented vair ve are."

"But your young and handsome daughter, sir, does she feel no desire to return to the gayeties of the world?"

"She says no," replied the captain, his face assuming a cunning smile. "Ve say, vair de heart is, dair is our home—I tink de heart of mademoiselle is in de vilderness."

He said nothing else, and as Campbell felt delicate about pursuing the subject any further, it was dropped. But as the captain had now gratified their curiosity, he seemed to consider himself entitled to similar privileges, and said:

"But now, messieurs—if you will excuse one question—how could you be so bold as to venture on de lake in such one miserable craft? Vere you so very tired of life?"

"Not that, Captain," replied Campbell. Our story is fully as sad as yours, and as your frank statement has entitled you to our confidence, I shall now confide to you the nature of our errand. Perhaps you can give us both advice and aid in the recovery of her who has been stolen from her home by a demon in human form."

The scout proceeded to give his host a detailed account of what the reader already knows. It soon became evident that the story enlisted the sympathy of the warm-hearted Frenchman in no common degree. He accompanied the thrilling portions with lively gestures, and at times his indignation became so great that he interrupted the speaker with numerous *"sacre,"* *"diable,"* and other spicy words of the French dictionary. When Campbell had finished, the excitable son of Gaul jumped up, clutched his fist and cried:

"But dis is one great shame, monsieur; dis is one unpardonable offense on de part of dat bloody rascal. Here is my hand, sir. I pledge you de support of myself and La Belle France, to recovaire your beautiful wife, la rose sauvage. Ah! ven my daughtaire hears of dis, vill she not veep at the fate of one poor captive!"

In this strain he continued, now giving vent to his indignation at the Red Feather's rascality and anon assuring Campbell of his sympathy and assistance. While he was thus engaged his daughter returned, carrying on her arm little Annie. Campbell hardly knew his daughter. Not only had the child greatly revived under the fostering care of her nurse, and resumed that hilarity and cheerfulness of expression, which is the proper inheritance of childhood ; but her apparel also had undergone a wonderful change at the hands of the little French woman, whose

removal into the wilderness seemed to have in no way impaired the taste for dressing, which the maidens of that country have cultivated with more success than all other
daughters of Eve. The child moreover seemed so taken
with her new friend, that she ceased pining for her
mother, a circumstance of no little importance, if we consider the uncertain feature of the party and the necessity
of the father to leave her to the care of some one besides
Peter, whose ardent attachment to the child would hardly
compensate for his deficiency in judgment. Altogether
this adventure, which had at first threatened the party
with certain destruction, had taken a turn as unexpected
as acceptable. Not only could the scout leave the daughter in the care of mademoiselle Adeline ; but the house of
the Frenchman would serve as an excellent base of operation, to say nothing of the role which La Belle France could,
and probably would, play in the act of deliverance. Under
the influence of these thoughts and calculations the spirits
of Campbell regained their usual buoyancy and he entered
into the movements, views and propositions of his host
with an alacrity, which completed the conquest, which
from the beginning he had made of the heart of the active
little Frenchman.

La Belle France had in the meantime sped on her
northern course with the grace and rapidity of a duck, and
long before evening the captain was able to point out to his
guests the promontory which protected the mouth of la
Grande Riviere on the western side. The company now
gathered on the forecastle and gazed at the panorama of
the coast as it gradually arose before their eyes and to
listen to the lively explanation of Mademoiselle Adeline.
The captain alone remained at the helm, and so well did
he manage the craft, that she not only reached the mouth of
the river without delay, but also proceeded up stream with
nearly the same rapidity, and after doubling the above
mentioned point, shot along side of the little island, which
had excited the curiosity of Red Feather. There the captain cast anchor and shoved out a plank on the bank, inviting his passengers to the hospitality of his home.

CHAPTER XII.

FROM THE FRYING PAN INTO THE FIRE.

If La Belle France had excited the wonder of our friends, the settlement on the island was calculated to sustain it. The fields and gardens were cultivated with superior skill and care, and the buildings, though built of logs, erected with an accuracy which gave them a neat and cheerful appearance. The intervals between the logs were filled with mortar, and the inside walls and ceilings were plastered with the same material, having been procured from the limestone beds of a neighboring hill, as the host explained to his visitors. The floors were made of sawed and planed boards, while the windows contained genuine panes of glass in sashes, which, as the host related, had been made by the same artisans who called the sloop into existence. Nothing but the door locks were wanting to establish the claims of the building to the character of a city structure, and as the absence of locks was indicative of the absence of thieves and burglars, the proprietor had surely no reason to regret this point of inferiority. The chimneys and fireplaces were built of brick, and the range of the kitchen was constructed in so ingenious a manner that Mademoiselle Adeline would have had no reason whatever, to envy the owners of the highly praised cooking stove of the present day, provided, they had been in existence. After examining and admiring the house, the guests paid a visit to the stables and the pastures, where a couple of steers and a few milkcows were indulging in the most luxurient clover.

"This is truly a paradise," Campbell exclaimed, on returning to the house. "I no longer wonder at your resolution to remain here, Mr. —— I fear your name has slipped from my remembrance."

"Perhaps I nevaire told you, sir. Le Blanc is my humble name."

"Well, Mr. Le Blanc, I only meant to say that I understand now why you refuse to return to the turmoil of the world. This is a little paradise and let me express as my fervent wish and prayer, that the serpent may never enter it and destroy its peace, as it did in mine."

This allusion gave the thoughts of the men a serious shade, and when they had returned to the house, the conversation involuntarily turned upon the best mode of recovering the captive. The novelty of his situation had for a little while served as a. counterpoise to the excitement of Campbell, but now when the novelty commenced to wear off, his mind at once returned to and dwelled upon the only engrossing topic of his thoughts. Nor was Le Blanc averse to making the condition of the captive the subject of conversation ; for although he foresaw that any assistance of his in the work of rescue might complicate his relation to the powerful tribe of the Mohawks, and imperil the security of his hitherto peaceful home, he was much too impulsive and generous hearted to hesitate a moment with the offer of his help. The meeting in the room gradually assumed the character of a grave council. Everybody was allowed a hearing and everybody expressed his opinion in as pointed and careful a manner as became the occasion. They all considered force out of the question, the power of the Mohawks being too great to think of a favorable termination of an open contest ; but though everybody counseled strategy, there was considerable difference in the schemes proposed. These schemes all had their merits, all their defects, and the mind of the assembly did not take a definite shape, until at length a proposition of the Black Snake seemed to meet the general approbation.

"Listen to the Black Snake," he said. "He has decoyed the Wild Rose from her home; it isn't more than fair that he should be instrumental in leading her back to it. The Red Feather confides in the Black Snake; let him go to the village of the Mohawks and tell the chief how he escaped from the hands of his captors. He will talk into the ears of Maghpiway so that he cannot hear ; he will strew sand into his eyes that he cannot see. Then he will take the Wild Rose by the hand and lead her to her friends. The Black Snake has spoken."

"And he has spoken well," said Anderson. "If the Black Snake could lead the Wild Rose into the forest, we would surely be strong enough to cover her escape to a place of safety."

"To La Belle France, of course," cried Le Blanc, rising from his seat and flourishing his hand with every appearance of excitement. "You must not tink of any odair place."

"Well, the two ideas together would work excellently," said Campbell. "I accept the offer of our host with gratitude, and that of the Black Snake without hesitation. By doing so, I have an opportunity to show him how implicitly I trust his honor, and how fully I credit the profession of his desire to make amends."

Tne Indian said nothing, deeming it below his dignity to repeat the assurance of his sincerity; but the grateful look which he cast upon the scout was proof that he understood and appreciated his allusion.

"And when is the Black Snake to start?" said Anderson.

"As soon as we can agree upon the other movements," replied Campbell. "Mr. Le Blanc, did you not say that the village lay on the Niagara River?"

"I did, monsieur. It lies on de left bank of de vestairn arm, one big island splitting it just dair. Below de island are de rapids from vich de rivaire tumbles down de bluff."

"I have heard a great deal about these rapids and the falls, and would undoubtedly enjoy their aspect if my mind was not weighed down with care. Could the sloop be safely brought abreast the village?"

"Not without arousing de suspicion of de Mohawks; but I suppose it might be anchored in de odair arm."

"That will suffice, I think. We might receive Mary in a canoe and paddle her around the island, or lead her right across it."

"Exactly, but how vill ve know ven de Black Snake is ready?"

"True enough, we must agree about a signal. Black Snake, what signal could you give to us?"

The Indian thought a moment, then he replied:

"When my brothers hear three times the shriek of the night-owl they will know that the Wild Rose is coming:

when they hear it again, they will find her on the river-bank."

"It is well," said Campbell. "We will go down every night. If the Black Snake fails to meet us the first night, he will surely be there the second."

The Indian stretched forth his hand as if desirous of attracting the attention of the others. When he had succeeded he said:

"Let my brothers not come too soon. Too much haste might imperil all. The Black Snake must first speak with the Wild Rose—this is not easy. He may have to see her many times before he can whisper a word into her ear. The Black Snake will make a fire at the head of the Island; before my brothers see this they need not come down."

"He is right," said Campbell, with a sigh. "This uncertain delay will sorely try my patience, but I suppose it has to be borne. We surely must not take the sloop oftener down the river than we can help. Perhaps it will be best to anchor her at its head, and trust the rest to one or two canoes. Has the Black Snake any other suggestion to make?"

"The Black Snake has spoken."

"Then let him go and eat. I am sure our kind host will give him a meal and fill his pouch with viands for the journey, so that he need not stop for game."

"Of course I vill," replied Le Blanc, jumping up and leading the Indian into the pantry, where Mademoiselle Adeline attended to his wants. When these were satisfied he shook hands with all the men, and then entered a canoe, by means of which Campbell ferried him to the eastern shore. Stepping on the bank, he waived a last adieu to the island, and then glided into the bushes. Campbell, on the other hand, returned to the island, and after he had rejoined the party in the house, Le Blanc remarked:

"I told you already dat dair is one Huron village a little vays up stream. I suppose de people wouldn't like to be drawn into dis scrape, as dey are veak and fear de Mohawks; but it vould certainly do no harm to inform dem of de matter. Vat do you tink of one visit at thair village?"

"I have no opinion either way," said Campbell. "You

are posted on their character, and, therefore, the best judge. If you think that the proposed visit will convert them into sympathizing friends, if not active allies, let us go by all means."

It was decided that the visit should be made. Leaving Peter and the child on the island, the four men entered one of the canoes which belonged to the establishment, and proceeded up stream. As they had supplied themselves with four paddles, the craft fairly flew over the water, and landed them shortly on the beach of the same little cove which had witnessed the arrival of Maghpiway. The large canoe was still there; but as the tribe owned several of that kind, Le Blanc paid no special attention to it. The party passed the same grove we have noticed before, and on emerging from the bushes, the Pennsylvanians could not suppress a slight utterance of pleasure and astonishment at the beauty of the country, and the signs of advanced civilization which met their eyes on every side. Led by Le Blanc they marched to the village, where their arrival received more attention, and caused more commotion than Indians generally like to betray. Not only was there considerable running of squaws and children, but even the warriors would put their heads together and, while whispering, cast such ominous glances at the strangers, that Le Blanc could hardly have failed to notice them if his mind had not been occupied with the object of their visit. Campbell and his associates at once perceived the threatening aspect of affairs; but as they had full confidence in the sagacity of their guide, they did not trouble themselves much about it, thinking that there might possibly be some other cause of dissatisfaction in the tribe.

When the visitors arrived at the council-lodge, there was already a gathering of the warriors in small knots and a murmur like that produced by a hostile invasion of a bee-hive, began to hum in the ears of Le Blanc and his party. The Frenchman now began to see that something was wrong; but as he was on the best of terms with the tribe, and had a clear conscience regarding his dealings with it, he was not at all afraid of the consequences, thinking that there must be some mistake, which a short conference would explain. He, therefore, led his guests into the lodge, whither he was followed by the crowd of warriors, who silently assumed their seats, giving this silence an ominous significance by the sinister expression of their faces. The Yellow Pine was the last one to make his appearance, and when he had taken his seat, Le Blanc arose and said in the language of the Wyandots, which he evidently had acquired during his stay with them :

"The Muskrat greets his brothers ; have they no calumet to smoke with his friends ?"

No answer interrupted the ominous silence of the assembly, and the surprise of the Frenchman changed into alarm.

"What ails my brothers, the Wyandots?" he inquired, in accents of concern. "If the Muskrat has offended them he does not know it. Will his brothers tell him ?"

The Yellow Pine slowly arose from his seat :

"If the Muskrat is the friend of the Hurons," he said, slowly, and in a solemn tone of voice, "why does he bring their enemies into their village ?"

"Their enemies !" Le Blanc exclaimed, with great surprise. "What does my brothers mean? If the Hurons have no worse enemies than these friends of mine, they may rest easy. These men—"

The Yellow Pine interrupted the speaking with an impatient gesture of his hand, a breech of decorum so great in the estimation of red men, that the scouts began to be seriously alarmed for their safety. They had left their rifles at the house of Le Blanc; but even if they had been well armed they could not hope to prevail against such superior numbers. All they could, therefore, do, was to await patiently the further development of things. After the chief had checked the Frenchman in the manner above mentioned, he arose and said:

"The ears of the Hurons have no patience to listen to lies; a wicked tongue is an abomination in their sight."

"But I do not comprehend the Yellow Pine," said Le Blanc, becoming more alarmed. "I have not the least intention to tell my brothers any lies."

"Then the Muskrat tells the lies of others—it is the

same thing.   The Hurons do not want to become the dupes
of a liar, nor the fellows of a dupe."

"But the Hurons have not heard my words; they do not
know what I was going to say."

"The Hurons know everything.   The Muskrat meant
to say: 'This here is the Little Coon; this here the Big
Jump.   They have come into the country of the Wyandots
to recover a squaw, the Wild Rose.'   Is the Yellow Pine
right?"

"He is," said the Frenchman, who was perfectly bewildered by the discovery that the Hurons knew things of
which they, according to his judgment, must be totally
ignorant.   "But if the Yellow Pine knows these things,
why is he angry with his friend, the Muskrat?"

The face of the chief assumed an expression of ferocity.
His eyes shot fiery flashes, and raising his hand in a threatening manner, he cried:

"Because these things are not true.   Who stole the
squaw whom these pale-faces pretend to seek?"

"A Delaware chief by the name of Maghpiway."

The mien of indignation of the chief changed into another of open contempt.   The warriors also looked at one
another with a knowing look and an expression of triumph,
that seemed to say:

"Did we not know beforehand?   Was there ever a more
bare-faced deception?"

"Maghpiway, indeed," cried the chief, with a derisive
smile on his lips.   "Did he not take the captives to the
Mohawks?"

"The Yellow Pine knows everything!" cried the
Frenchman.

"He does," replied the chief; "but the Muskrat knows
very little.   He has suffered himself to be duped by two
cunning pale-faces.   Where is the Red Feather?   The
Hurons know of no such chief.   Where is the Wild Rose?
A vision in the feverish brain of the Muskrat.   Let him go
home and sleep himself sober—these people will remain
prisoners with the Wyandots."

Up to this time the scouts had abstained from interrupt-
ing the conversation.   They did not know the nature of

their offense, and expected to be better able to learn it by listening than by speaking. Now, however, when Campbell heard the resolution of the Hurons to retain him and his companions prisoners, thus threatening to deprive them of every chance of rescuing Mrs. Campbell, he thought it time to rise and ask an explanation. Using the dialect of the Wyandots, which he had learned in his dealings with the Pennsylvania portion of the tribe, he said, amidst the deepest silence of the assembly:

"The Hurons have the reputation of being a just and wise nation. Is it in the nature of wisdom and justice to retain inoffensive strangers?"

This bold question evidently made an impression on the council, but while it increased their respect for the speaker, it was hardly calculated to lessen their animosity. Every eye now turned to the Yellow Pine, who was expected to defend the interest of the tribe.

"The Hurons are both just and wise," he replied, "but that is more than can be said of the Yengeese. They may be very cunning, but justice can not be found in the councils of the nation. Is it just to deprive the red man of his rights and drive him off his land? Is it just to send scouts into the country of the Wyandots and promise their villages to the Shawanese? Let them beware! The Wyandots are just, but they are also brave, and when the hand of the pale-faces is stretched across the water to grasp their rights, they will cut it off."

A sudden light burst upon the mind of the scout. Maghpiway had been here to poison the minds of these people. From what the chief had said, Campbell inferred that the Delaware had foretold their visit, but denied the truth of their real errand, and led the Hurons to suspect some design against their country, or their independence. Much as he hated the crafty Delaware he could not help admiring the readiness with which the chief had availed himself of all the weapons of defense within his reach. He had understood how to touch a sore spot of the Indians, and to make it sorer. Of course the scout could contradict his statement and tell the truth ; but was it not likely that the Wyandots would give more credence to the falsehood of

a fellow warrior, than to the truth of a pale-face? His
heart sank within him, for although he did not consider
the situation very desperate, he doubted his ability to
disinfect the minds of the Hurons in time to counteract
the fiendish designs of the Red Feather upon his wife.
Still the greatness of the interest at stake imperiously
demanded a trial, and so Campbell replied to the imputa-
tions of Yellow Pine as follows:

"If the pale-faces did as my brother says, the Hurons
are right to do what they have threatened; but they have
in verity no such intentions. The Hurons have listened to
the singing of a mocking-bird; it has stuffed their ears
with lies. Do not the Wyandots live under the protection
of their great English Father? How would the Yengeese
dare to invade his dominion? A war would be the consequence. The Yengeese have had enough of war; they
have more territory than they can use; why should they
expose themselves to the dangers of another war with the
powerful British Empire to get still more? Does not my
brother see that this is so? Let him reflect, and he must
perceive that he has listened to the story of a liar."

He stopped and bent an anxious look upon the line of
dusky faces composing the circle. Some looked as fierce as
ever; but others, amongst them that of Yellow Pine, had
become pensive, and wishing to strengthen the impression,
he continued:

"My brothers are wise; can they not see through the
devices of a thief and a coward? He is afraid to meet the
face of men, but he is very expert in stealing women and
children. He stole the squaw of the Big Jump, and fled to
the village of the Senecas. The Big Jump followed on his
trail and proposed to meet him in mortal combat; but the
heart of the renegade belied his skin—it was white. He
led his captive to the country of the Mohawks, but on his
way he stopped at the village of the Wyandots to set the
Big Jump a trap. He was afraid to meet him in combat,
but he was not afraid to tell the Wyandots a lie. A lie
requires no courage; he hoped the Hurons would do a
dastardly deed for him; he hoped they would murder a
couple of pale-faces who had never done them any harm.

Will the Hurons allow a renegade chief to make their name stinking with both Indians and pale-faces?"

Campbell sat down to await the effect of his words. He knew that there is such a thing as overdoing, and therefore rested his case upon what had already been said. The Hurons were evidently puzzled. There was such an air of simplicity and truthfulness about the scout that it was difficult to disbelieve him. While the fiercer and therefore more impulsive members of the council still harbored feelings of enmity against the pale-faces, the older and more prudent warriors began to think that they might possibly have committed the same mistake for which they had upbraided the Muskrat. But to be convinced of a mistake and to acknowledge it are two different things, and as the code of honor of the Indians required no such acknowledgment, the chief considered it best to adjourn the council and reserve the case for another and calmer deliberation. If the prisoners were guilty of the crime of which they had been accused, a careful investigation would make it manifest. If, on the other hand, they should be innocent, a speedy release would follow their captivity and mitigate its sufferings. After a deep, and for the scouts, momentous silence, Yellow Pine arose and said :

"The ears of the Hurons have been open to the words of the pale-face. He has spoken well and his words have reached the hearts of his hearers. But the Hurons have listened to two stories; they know not which is true. The Yellow Pine hopes that the tongue of the Big Jump may be found straight, for the Wyandots have heard great things of him and they would not like him to turn out a liar. But they do not know, and until they can find out the truth, the pale-faces and their Indian friend must remain prisoners in the hands of the Wyandots. Yellow Pine has spoken."

Campbell saw the vanity of any appeal from this decision, so he submitted with good grace to an unavoidable calamity, and said :

"A pale-face squaw is languishing in the hands of a Delaware thief; will my brothers detain us very long?"

"Let the Big Jump rest easy. Before to-morrow night his fate will be decided, for before the setting of the second sun, Tononqua, the king of the Wyandots, will be back amongst his people."

"Ugh !"

This universal exclamation showed that the statement of the chief was unexpected to the warriors. The joyous expression, moreover, which every face assumed, showed that it was welcome news. To none, however, could it have come more acceptable than to Le Blanc. The poor fellow had been completely crushed by the unexpected and threatening aspect of affairs, and only at the announcement of the chief did he begin to recover from his consternation.

"Hurrah !" he cried, jumping to his feet, and paying no attention whatever to the strict rules of decorum adopted in the august assembly of the Hurons. " *Vive le roi!* Long live King Tononqua ! Campbell ! Anderson ! Rejoice, for your captivity is already as good as over. Only one day is lost as yet. Long live King Tononqua !"

The Indians took no steps to curb his delight. In fact the general restlessness of his disposition seemed to have secured for him an indefinite sort of safeguard, the savages no doubt considering as a partial derangement, a trait so foreign to their own nature. He was, therefore, allowed to converse with the prisoners in English as much as he wished. "Take courage," he said, "all will be right yet. Who could have thought dat dis nasty rascal would come and play us such a trick."

"No one, I'm sure. Well, if this king of yours arrives in time, and does not disappoint your expectation, we may be free to act in concert with the Black Snake. But are you sure he will not suffer himself to be influenced by this silly tale? It turned the head of this old chief— Tononqua is young."

"Yes, but he carries one old head upon his shoulders. He will not deny his white blood."

"God grant you may be right. But you had better stop talking now. The warriors are eyeing us as if they did not like this unintelligable jargon much."

"Oh, nevaire mind dem," said Monsieur Le Blanc,

"now dat I know Tononqua is coming, I don't care one bit. He'll tell dem how to treat vite gentlemen, I bet you."

"Well, we musn't overdo the thing, anyhow. As they do not propose to detain you here, you must go back to your house and see to things there. We'll get along well enough for one night, and to-morrow you'll be back, and try your influence on the King—don't you think that is a good programme?"

"I think it is, though I hate to leave you here. But the vomen vould be frightened, dat's de fact, and so I suppose I'll have to leave you. Vell, take heart, I shall be back in de morning, and den ve shall show dese brutes vat it means to play vid de feelings of gentlemen. Adieu, Mon Ami, adieu, Monsieur Anderson, adieu, Le Renard Rouge: depend upon your friend, Le Blanc. To-morrow! To-morrow!"

With these words the lively Frenchman hastened from the door. The captives were shortly afterwards conducted to another and safer prison, and when the night arrived the sun set upon another blasted hope. Would it ever revive again?

CHAPTER XIII.

A ROYAL DECISION.

Hardly had the sun risen on the coming morning, when Le Blanc made his appearance, accompanied by Peter, who assisted in carrying a heavy basket of provisions. When Campbell and Anderson saw this mass of victuals, which would have fed a whole company for a day, they had to smile in spite of their perilous position. Le Blanc took their raileries with genuine French humor.

"Never mind!" he exclaimed, shaking his head with a sagacious smile, "you eat and drink, for vitout eating and drinking, soul and body vill not stay together. You may have to do one heap of talking, and for all ve know, of fighting; and talking and fighting, Monsieurs, makes hun-

ger. Derefore say noting against my basket. De fair fin-
gaires of Mademoiselle Adeline have prepared de viands,
derefore dey ought to taste doubly vell to you."

The three prisoners did no require much pressing, and
dispatched the viands of Miss Adeline with a zest which
spoke well for her culinary talents. Le Blanc left and came,
now paying visits at the various lodges to speak a word in
favor of the prisoners, and anon sharing their durance, to
cheer them up, as he said, and keep their minds from sinking into despondency.

In this way the morning passed away, and Le Blanc
had just left the lodge in order to sharpen his own appetite by a little stroll, as he expressed himself, when, all at
once, he rushed back into the cabin much before the appointed time, with a face all burning with excitement.
The expression of alarm had returned in full strength, and
his voice was indicative of extreme consternation, when he
called out :

"Oh, friends, ve are undone : One dozen Mohawk var-
riors have come to demand your immediate execution.
Vhat will we do? If only Tononqua were here!"

The prisoners were men, but such feelings as those of
which Le Blanc was the prey, are contagious, and for a
moment their stout hearts quailed within them, and the
blood left their cheeks. This was only momentary, however, for no sooner had they recovered from their surprise,
when they gained their self-control, their spirits rising under the blow like the pliant hickory, which roots only
more firmly under the fury of the tossing whirlwind.

"Perhaps you are needlessly alarmed," said Anderson,
"what can a dozen Mohawks do against three times that
number of Hurons?"

"Nor will the Hurons dare to decide the matter in the
absence of the King, his arrival being hourly expected,"
suggested Campbell.

"Perhaps dey vill not," said Le Blanc, "but ven I saw
dese fierce looking savages, I felt one uncomfortable fear

for your safety, and rushed to dis lodge to give you varning."

"It is well you did," replied Campbell, "for forewarned is forearmed. But now you must return to the council lodge and watch the proceedings. Perhaps you can throw in an occasional word which will affect the result. At all events we expect you to report to us from time to time."

Le Blanc promised compliance, and ran from the lodge with the nervous agility peculiar to him. On his way to the council house he was accosted by a middle-aged woman, whose face was free from the exceeding ugliness into which even the fairest beauty of the Indian maiden is apt to wither with advancing age. It possessed even then the remnants of considerable charms, and the eye, which was blue, instead of the black prevailing among the Indians, showed a gentleness, and withal a lustre, which involuntarily charmed the look of the spectator, after it had once been attracted. This squaw stepped into the road of the bustling Frenchman, and although women among the Indians are at least subjects of indifference, and hold a very inferior position, the innate politeness of the Frenchman would not suffer him to repel with rudeness the advances of a being whose red skin could not make him forget that she belonged to the weaker sex. When, therefore, the squaw stopped his progress, he suppressed his pardonable impatience as well as he could, and said:

"What is it, good woman, that you would ask of me? Speak quickly, for my time is measured."

This was said in the Huron language, and, using the same, the woman replied:

"The Bending Willow knows that the Muskrat has but little time; she will not detain him long. Does the Muskrat know the name of the elder pale-face?"

"They call him the Little Coon, good woman."

"I do not mean the Indian name. Does my brother know the name by which the Yengeese call him?"

"Yes, I do; he goes by the name of Anderson."

"And the first name? The pale-faces have many."

"I think they call him David—yes, yes, I am sure now, his name is David Anderson."

The woman seemed to labor under a deep emotion, which robbed her of her speech, and threatened to prostrate her strength. At length, however, she collected herself, and said:

"My friend will pardon a poor Indian woman, if she detains him another minute. Does the Muskrat know anything about his family? Has he a squaw and children?"

"You seem to take great interest in the man," said Le Blanc, still maintaining his complaisance. "The wife of Mr. Anderson is dead, having been killed by your people many years ago. He has two daughters, one of whom was stolen by a red villain, and carried to the Mohawks. That is the reason the poor fellow and his friend are here. Has the Bending Willow any more questions to ask?"

"No, sir, and I sincerely thank you for the information. May God bless you, and him whom the savages now hold in their clutches."

These last words were spoken in English, a circumstance which caused the Frenchman to start in surprise; but before he had time to investigate the matter the Bending Willow had glided into the bushes, and vanished from his sight. At ordinary times the strange phenomenon might have puzzled the Frenchman for hours ; but so critical was the position of his friends, and so valuable every minute of his time that he at once dismissed from his mind every thought which had no bearing upon the present dilemma, and, without delay, hastened to the council chamber. When he entered he found the warriors of the tribe all assembled, and in the far end of the lodge he perceived the forms of a dozen warriors, whom he would have recognized as Iroquois or Mingoes, even if he had had no previous knowledge of their character. There is no denying that in regard to height and symmetry of form the Six Nations outranked all the other Indians of the American continent. But if they excelled them in strength and prowess, they also surpassed them in cunning and cruelty. The twelve Mohawks, at the end of the council lodge, were fine representatives of their race, but if their fine, tall, well-developed bodies would have furnished a dozen models for a copper-colored Hercules, the fierce expression of their faces, and the savage fire of their pitch-black eyes required no great stretch of the spectator's imagination to view in them as many spirits from the fiery regions of hell, come upon the surface of the earth on an errand of vengeance.

When Le Blanc stepped into the lodge the leader of the Mohawks and the Yellow Pine seemed engaged in an animated discussion, for their faces were flushed, and their usual gravity had given way to an excitement, into which the Indian but rarely suffers himself to be betrayed. The Mohawks had demanded, the Wyandots refused, the unconditional surrender of the prisoners. At first the Iroquois had prayed and flattered, but when these gentle means of persuasion had become exhausted, they had begun to demand and threaten. Now a menace is not calculated to soften the feelings of either a white man or a red one, and the Yellow Pine had considered himself called upon to assert and maintain the independence of his tribe. In reality the Wyandots could desire nothing less than war with a powerful neighbor who counted six warriors to their one ; but in boasting of the strength and fearlessness of the Hurons the Yellow Pine only followed the general practice of the world, which is apt to raise a noise just in proportion to the hollowness of the cause.

The speaker of the Mohawks evidently had taken offense at the plainness of the Yellow Pine's language, and when Le Blanc entered the lodge he was on the point of hurling back some bitter invectives.

"The Otter is tired of this," he said, extending his hand with an expressive gesture. "He is tired of following the Yellow Pine in all the windings of his crooked tongue. What is the strength and bravery of the Wyandots to the Mohawks? The Mohawks do not hide themselves like the beavers ; if the Hurons know the path to the villages of the Mengwe, the Mengwe are not ignorant of that which leads into the country of the Hurons. We want no more subterfuges ; we want a plain answer. Will the Wyandots surrender the prisoners, or at least assent to their immediate execution? If their answer is *yes*, it is well ; if it is *no*, the Otter will depart and tell Thayendanegea that he must come and take them himself. The Wyandots have the choice—let them select at once.''

This open menace threatened to bring the difficulty to a sudden crisis. While it intimidated the lovers of peace, it gave umbrage to the younger and bolder warriors, who smarted under the thought that members of a foreign tribe should dare to defy them in their own village. A murmur ran along the lines and deepened as it ran, each murmurer taking heart at the signs of approbation of his neighbor. At last it swelled to so threatening a height that even the rising of the venerable and venerated form of Yellow Pine was insufficient to quell it. Already words of insult, of defiance and of challenge began to rain thick upon the envoys; they would perhaps have been immediately attacked if the sacred nature of their office had not protected them. There was a growing uproar in the lodge, however, and it is difficult to say whether the regard which even the savage has for an embassador, would eventually have prevailed over the indignation of an incensed nationality, if the whole had not all at once taken a strange and unexpected turn by the appearance of a man who stood in the center of the crowd, before anybody had discovered his arrival. No sooner, however, was his presence noted, when it exercised a sudden and almost magic effect. The noise stopped so suddenly that the deep silence which followed affected the assembly like a *douche* of ice cold water coming suddenly upon the irritated skin. Through it floated an element of awe, which showed clearly that no common man had calmed the turbulent waters. While the glances of the Mohawks betrayed both respect and admiration, those of the Wyandots—not excepting the sternest warriors—were lit with an expression of reverence and delight, which bordered on ecstacy.

"Tononqua!"

This word bursting simultaneously from the lips of Hurons and Iroquois, explained the mystery. The king of the Wyandots had arrived, and if personal appearance is the criterion of majesty, the new comer was truly a king. He was a young man yet, hardly over twenty-three. His form was high and stately, excelling as much by symmetry

of shape as by grace of outline. His suit was entirely in
Indian fashion, consisting of a hunting frock, leggins and
moccasins, all made of tanned deer-skin. The frock resembled in shape the Roman tunic, and was held to the body
by a belt of wampum. The leggins were ornamented with
yellow fringes and the moccasins with colored porcupine
quills. Over this suit the king wore a long and flowing
mantle of similar material, which fell in graceful folds upon
his feet and greatly added to the majesty of his appearance.
His head-dress was similar to that we noticed on the brow
of Brant, consisting of a coronet-shaped ring, from which two
feathers arose in a bold and striking manner, adding greatly
to the lofty stature of the king. The hair was of a light
brown, and had been suffered to remain, contrary to the
Indian custom, which demands its removal with the exception of the scalp-lock. It was held from the brow by the
coronet, and fell in rich profusion upon the shoulders. The
face, however, was the crowning feature of the apparition.
It was not only the beauty of the lineaments that made it
so attractive. True, there was a high and noble forehead,
a well shaped nose, a mouth whose lips showed firmness
without betraying cruelty ; a pair of eyes, blue and deep as
the vault of heaven ; but it was the expression of the
entire countenance, the great and noble soul that shone
from out those lucid orbs, which drew the spectator involuntarily towards this man, and forced untutored savages
to his feet with a force more potent than the rod and
scourge could possibly possess. The glance which he now
cast upon the turbulent multitude—turbulent no longer
though—was half wondering, half indignant. It described
a complete circle, and then fastened itself upon the Yellow
Pine with a mute, but nevertheless eloquent query. We
know that the chief had committed no fault, that he merely
lacked the strength of quelling these unruly spirits in the
absence of one more powerful ; but yet he lowered his eye
before the searching glance of the young king, and remained
silent. Then the monarch raised his voice, a voice melodious but deep, so deep that it betrayed the thunder sleeping in its vibrations.

"What is this?" he said, slowly and impressively.

"Have the squaws of the Hurons donned the garb of warriors, to desecrate the sancity of this place? Or have my warriors forgotten that they are men, to scream like noisy women, and half-grown striplings?"

Strange phenomenon! These dusky warriors, some old, some young; some high some low, but all fierce and warlike, like the panther of their woods—they all lower their eyes with the meekness of scolded children. The men, who a few minutes before had flashed up at the insinuations of the Mohawks, now receive without a murmur the reprimand of a man who has barely overstepped the limits of youth. Failing to receive an answer, the king resumed:

"Have my warriors no tongues? Can they find no words to inform Tononqua of the meaning of this scene? Let the Yellow Pine speak. Tononqua has always heard wisdom flowing from his lips, my brother will not now disappoint me."

Thus summoned, the Yellow Pine arose, and, in a laconic, graphic manner, related the events connected with the visit of Maghpiway and the subsequent one of the scouts. Tononqua listened with great attention, and when the Yellow Pine had ended, he pondered on his communications fully ten minutes before he made a reply. We cannot tell the workings of the brain under that lofty brow, but there is no doubt that its reflections were deep and comprehensive. This seemed at least to be the conviction of the Indians, for they hung on his face and lips with a suspense as if life and death depended on his words. And so they did, if not the lives of these warriors, yet those of the three men in durance, who awaited the decision of their fate with becoming fortitude, but an impatience of which no mortal could have divested himself under the circumstances. Le Blanc had forgotten to fulfil his promise, an oversight which the stirring scenes in the council lodge, place in a very pardonable light. He hung with too eager an eye upon every movement of the king to think of relating to his friends the comparative unimportant details of the previous quarrel.

But let me now return to the pensive monarch. Arousing himself from his reverie, he made a motion with his hand and said :

"Let the prisoners be brought in!"

After these words, he took a seat, which had been vacant all the while, even Yellow Pine abstaining from occupying a position, which in the eyes of the tribe, seemed allied with absolute power. When the noise connected with this movement had died away, the old impressive silence resumed its hold upon the assembly, all eyes turning towards the door to catch a glimpse of the men, whose destiny was now to be decided by a word from the lips of the monarch. Hark ! there they come; a shadow darkened the door and a minute later, the three companions in adversity stood before Tononqua. His eye dwelt searchingly upon their features, and to judge from his mien, the examination produced no unfavorable result. Nor was there any reason that this should be otherwise. The three captives were certainly worthy specimens of the types they represented. Anderson, middle-aged and middle-sized, but compactly built, his body wiry and indicative of great endurance ; Campbell, in the prime of manhood, tall and powerful, a true representative of the Anglo-Saxon, as it appeared on the border of the wilderness ; the Red Fox, lofty in bearing and graceful in motion, a perfect model of the Delawares, a tribe less powerful but more agile than the Iroquois.

Tononqua had evidently studied the difficult art of concealing his feelings under the mask of a calm countenance; but if we read that short lived contraction of his lips correctly, his satisfaction at the appearance of the prisoners is tinctured with sadness. What can it mean. Is it possible that this monarch shares with other monarchs the bitter drawbacks of power? Can it be that his feelings and wishes are often overruled by that nightmare of potentates, called policy? Alas! We are afraid that he forms no exception to the rule ; that he pays the toll which greatness imposes upon its votaries: subordination of the individual wish to the iron law of political necessity.

Let us imagine ourselves in his place. Here are his own warriors awaiting his decision as a mandate from which there is no appeal; here the twelve Mohawks, the representatives of a powerful neighboring tribe, which would like nothing better than a fair pretense for extending their dominion over such fair regions. Between them finally the bone of contention, the three warriors, whom he would no doubt like to save, but cannot save except at the peril of the very existence of the tribe. His feelings must not come into play; policy prescribes his movements, and obedient to its dictates Tononqua raises his head.

He actually did raise his head, but whether in consequence of such, or a similar train of thoughts will never be revealed. At the same time he raised his voice and said:

"Tononqua has heard two stories. One of them comes from the pale-faces, the other from Thayendanegea. I know the sachem of the Mokawks—I do not know these white men, who are said to be emissaries of the Yengeese. Can the chief of the Mohawks lie? Tononqua is unwilling to believe it. The pale-faces say that a woman of their tribe is in the village of the Mengwe—did the Otter ever see any traces of her they call the Wild Rose?"

The Otter rose, and extending a hand, replied, emphatically:

"Never did the Otter lay his eye on such a squaw— never did he see any trace of her."

This answer was ambiguous. Perhaps the movements of the Red Feather had been so cautious as really to conceal his captive from the sight of the idle masses, perhaps the answer of the Otter was a mere evasion hiding his knowledge of the presence of the Wild Rose, under the statement that he had never seen her person. However this might be, it fixed the decision of Tononqua.

"The Hurons hear the words of the Otter," he resumed. "So great a warrior cannot speak with a cloven tongue. Let the captives be delivered to the messengers of Thayendanegea."

These words had a different effect upon the different hearers. While the Mohawks received them with a smile of triumph on their lips, the Hurons preserved a silence which looked more like a passive acquiesence in the decision of their beloved monarch than an approval of the verdict. They probably felt that the sentence was a matter of necessity, and therefore abstained from any demonstrations, which could only increase the difficulty of the situation, without altering the issue. On the prisoners the sentence fell like a thunderbolt, but while they tried to bear it with manly fortitude, Le Blanc evinced signs of the greatest commotion. He rushed into the presence of the king, and was on the point of remonstrating against his decision, when an imperative gesture of Tononqua stopped him.

"Let the Muskrat hold his peace!" he said, sternly. "Tononqua thinks before he speaks—his words cannot be changed like the notions of a squaw. The decrees of a chief are like the days of yore, they can never be recalled. Let it remain as Tononqua has decided."

The smile of triumph on the faces of the Mohawks deepened, and they stepped forward to receive the prisoners. When they were on the point of laying hands on them, a gesture of Tononqua stopped them.

"Let the Mohawks delay a moment," he said. "Tononqua gives these captives into their hands, but not without conditions."

"Let Tononqua speak; the ears of the Mohawks are open to receive the words of one so wise and just."

"The Mohawks must not harm the captives on the territory of the Wyandots. Thayendanegea has demanded them of Tononqua; on his head comes their blood if they are innocent."

"Let it be as Tononqua says. The Mohawks will not harm a hair on the heads of the captives while they are on the hunting grounds of the Wyandots."

A gesture of Tononqua's hand indicated that he was satisfied, and the Mohawks produced the ropes with which they meant to tie the hands of their formidable captives, when a bustle at the entrance attracted the attention of the assembly, and initiated a scene so strange and startling, that we must reserve its description for another chapter.

CHAPTER XIV.

STARTLING REVELATIONS.

The bustle alluded to was occasioned by the endeavors
of the sentinels at the door to prevent the entrance of a
squaw, who seemed determined to set at naught the customs of the Indians by forcing her person upon the presence of the warriors when engaged in solemn deliberation.
The guards had probably not expected a very determined
attempt, and therefore made but feeble efforts to exclude
the intruder; for the woman succeeded in breaking through
their line, and rushed into the presence of the king, who
seemed as much astonished at this novel sight as any of
his warriors. Before he had time to address her, and inquire into the cause of such strange conduct, she threw herself at his feet, raised her hands in an imploring manner,
and cried in a voice that trembled with emotion:

"Tononqua will not sacrifice the prisoners! He can, he
must not do it, unless he desires to bring the vengeance of
the Great Spirit upon his head!"

The young king had now recovered from his surprise,
and the tone in which he replied to the conjurations of the
supplicant showed that he was not above the contempt with
which the red man looks down upon the female sex.

"The Bending Willow is sick," he said. "Her blood is
feverish, or she would not intrude upon the deliberations of
men. Let her depart at once, and Tononqua will endeavor
to recollect that she was not well, when she forgot herself
and her position."

These words were well calculated to crush any further
resistance on the part of the intruder; but to the astonishment of the assembly they failed to exercise the least effect.
The Bending Willow maintained her original position, and
instead of quailing before the stern glances of the chief, her
voice rather assumed a lofty and awe inspiring nature as
she replied:

"The Bending Willow cannot do the bidding of Tononqua, for she cannot suffer him to violate the most sacred
laws of nature. She will plead with him until he hears her

prayer, for he whom he would abandon to the hands of assassins, is his *father*, and she who now addresses him in prayer—his *mother*.

With the last words the woman had arisen, and stretched her hand conjuringly towards the king. There was no humble submissiveness in her voice or attitude at that moment. Her figure seemed to rise, and the look she cast upon the king resembled in loftiness that of an ancient seer, when in the act of announcing the will of the gods to the surrounding multitude.

Nor were her words without great effect upon the assembly. So impressive had been her appeal to the monarch, that her rising involuntarily brought all the warriors to their feet, and when she closed her imploration with the startling revelation above recorded, a cry of surprise broke almost simultaneously from every lip. His father! His mother! What could this mean? Still! that not a sound escape their eager ears!

No one in the assembly, however, had been startled as much as he whom the announcement concerned most. What could the woman mean? There had always been a mystery connected with his birth, which he had vainly tried to penetrate. Far as he was from sharing the popular belief regarding his supernatural birth, he was fully resolved to execute the mission with which this belief intrusted him, and had therefore taken good care not to shake the foundations of a faith which was so apt to second him in his efforts. And now this woman announced herself as his mother, and pointed as his father to a man whom he had just delivered into the hands of the Mohawks, a step fully equal to signing his death warrant.

These thoughts ran through his brain with the rapidity of lightning. Gladly would he have withdrawn from the crowd to ponder on the startling revelation, and on the best steps to pursue in this emergency, but it is the fate of kings to have the eyes of the multitude centered upon them, and to form their decisions with a readiness calculated to engender many an injustice. Tononqua knew himself the subject of the keenest attention, and without allowing a pause to intervene between the words of the Bending Willow and his answer, he replied:

"Is the Bending Willow mad? What is Tononqua to think of her words? Is there any truth in them, or has the Great Spirit destroyed her reason?"

"Her reason is sound, her words are truthful, the Bending Willow will prove them before the whole tribe of the Hurons."

"And what proof can she produce?"

The woman pointed to the Yellow Pine.

"That chief knows all; if he is an upright man, if he expects to enter the blessed hunting grounds where the virtuous Indian sojourns after death, he will testify to the truthfulness of my statement."

All eyes now bent upon the venerable chief, who was evidently the prey of considerable confusion. There seemed to be a struggle in his breast between a natural love of truth and grave considerations of state demanding a denial. When he failed to reply at once, Tononqua looked at him with a searching glance, and said:

"Has my father not heard the words of the Bending Willow? If they contain the truth why does he hesitate to acknowledge it? Let the Yellow Pine speak."

Thus addressed, the chief had no choice. The glance of the king more than his words had reached his innermost soul, and laying his hand upon his bosom, he replied:

"Tononqua demands it, the Yellow Pine cannot refuse. He has grown old in honor, his tongue has always been straight, it cannot now twist and bend, though the truth be an injury and the lie a blessing. *Tononqua is the son of the Bending Willow.*"

Another exclamation of surprise on the part of the Hurons followed this confession. The eyes of the woman sparkled, and a glow of pride and love lit up her countenance. She turned again to the king, and said:

"Does Tononqua hear? He is my son, my darling son, whom I had to love in secrecy, and therefore, perhaps, loved with double fervor. Does Tononqua's heart not yearn towards his mother? Is there no voice in his breast that tells him when his father is drawing near? Behold him there! Will Tononqua tarry any longer to push back the rude hands which dare to touch the sacred person of his sire?"

After this conjuration she made a few hasty steps towards Anderson, and said, with outstretched hands, in the English language:

"And you, David, do you not recognize your poor Mary, whom a cruel fate snatched from your side four and twenty years ago? Oh, tell me, is there still a spot in your heart which beats for me, a place in your breast where I may rest, after long and weary wanderings? Speak, David, let me hear the sound of a voice which has not greeted my ear for many a gloomy day."

The scouts had fo'lowed the development of the above related events with as much suspense as all the others. When the startling revelation of the Bending Willow implicated them so strangely in the family drama, their interest deepened as a matter of course, and the last ten minutes Anderson had stood like one in a trance, now looking with breathless suspense at her who had proclaimed him the father of a son, of whose existence he had not had the slightest knowledge, and anon feeling his own forehead to convince himself that he was not the victim of a tantalizing dream, or the prey of a raging fever. When the woman at last accosted him in English and claimed to be the wife whose bones and charred remains he believed to have been buried twenty-four years ago, his bewilderment reached its climax. The lodge swam before his eyes, and he had to grasp the arm of Campbell to keep from falling. Through all the confusion, however, he heard and recognized the voice of his long-lost but never forgotten wife. When he had succeeded in regaining the control of his limbs, he made a step towards her, and exclaimed:

"Mary, can this be? You, Mary, whom I have thought dead and buried all these years? You, Mary, the mother of my daughters?"

"Of Mary and Rosa, David. I am indeed your own wife, your Mary, who lived with you on the western slopes of the Allegheny mountains until the cruel Indians dragged me away. If Grace were here, she surely would recognize poor Mary Anderson. Oh, God, must I also bear this trial, to be denied by my own dear husband?"

"No, Mary, speak not so!" cried the scout, springing forward, and drawing the weeping woman into his embrace. "Deny you, how can you misjudge me so? Has not this great joy undone me? Must I not first comprehend that this is truth and not fiction; reality and not some delightful delusion; a dream, from which I will, sooner or later, awake?"

"But it is no fiction, David," she exclaimed, looking lovingly into his face. "It is no dream, but rather the glorious morning, which closes a long spell of gloom and darkness. You need no longer fear any harm from these people, for he who rules them is my *son*, *your* son, *our* son. Does it not, in a measure, indemnify us for our suffering, to have a son like him? Look at him! He is the King of the Wyandots : but royal as his station is his body, lofty and dignified his soul. Go, shake his hand, and feast your eye upon your noble boy!"

She drew him to Tononqua, who had watched the scene of recognition with changing emotions. He felt convinced that the Bending Willow was his mother, and he had no reason to doubt that Anderson was his father; but while he indulged in that delight, which the discovery of his parents could hardly fail to engender, he could, on the other hand, not help experiencing a slight displeasure at the disappearance of that nimbus, which had hitherto surrounded his person in the eyes of the Hurons. He was no longer an inhabitant of the sun; he had sunk to the low condition of being the offspring of a race on which the Hurons looked with jealousy, if not with hatred. If he would still maintain his high position, he must do it solely by the exercise of those wonderful gifts and talents which had excited the admiration of all who knew him. While he resolved to acknowledge his parents, and to pay them all the tribute of respect and love to which they were entitled, he was equally determined not to relinquish his position, and to be from his own free choice that to which hitherto tradition had stamped him—the deliverer of the Indian race, the inaugurator of a new era in which the red man would combine the simplicity, strength and prowess of his race with the culture and education of the pale-face.

These thoughts rushed through his mind while his parents were engaged in filling up the chasm, which the separation of many years had left between them. When they now approached him he laid aside the sternness, which the Indians demand of their warriors, and received them with a smile so gentle and affectionate, that their hearts leaped out towards him, and their eyes shone forth a proud satisfaction at the possession of such a son. He extended his hands towards them, and said :

"My parents are welcome in the lodge of Tononqua. His treasures are their treasures; henceforth no trouble shall cross their path. Their enemies shall be his enemies, and if the prayer of Tononqua prevails with his brethren, the Mohawks, they will follow his example. Thayendanegea cannot expect Tononqua to deliver his own father for torture."

"There are two more captives," replied the Otter, with a sullenness which plainly indicated how much he was dissatisfied with the turn of affairs.

"My son, you must not give them up," said Anderson, "they are as innocent of the crime of which they have been accused as you are yourself. Nor are they strangers to our family. This Indian is the foster brother of your sister, and in this scout you see her husband. I could not consistently accept a favor which is denied my friends and comrades."

"They will be treated like my father," said Tononqua. "When I first listened to two stories, I did not know my father. I was excusable for taking the word of Thayendanegea in preference to that of strangers. Now I know better; I know that Tononqua's father could not lie. I do not say that the tongue of Thayendanegea is crooked; I say he is mistaken. When his messengers have rectified his mistake, he will rejoice that Tononqua has recognized as friends the persons whom Thayendanegea considered to be his foes. Let my brethren depart in peace, and deliver my best wishes to the sachem of the Mohawks."

Thus dismissed there was nothing left for the Mohawks

but to depart. They were evidently in a surly humor, and the Otter considered himself called upon to give expression to his feelings before he left the lodge.

"The Mohawks are going," he said. "They do not wish to tarry where they are not welcome. They expected to take some prisoners along. The word of Tononqua had awarded them to the messengers of Thayendanegea; but when they prepared to lead the captives away they discovered that Tononqua has two tongues, to say *yes* with one, and *no* with the other. It makes no difference, but the Otter shall tell Thayendanegea what he has seen—may be the sachem of the Mohawks will come in force to take by compulsion what was denied to persuasion; let the Hurons beware!"   .

Tononqua smiled.

"The Hurons are not afraid," he answered. "The Otter forgets that he does not speak to women. Tononqua desires to live in peace with all his neighbors. When Thayendanegea comes as a guest he will be welcome in my lodge—if he comes as an enemy, Tononqua will know how to repel him. Let the Otter say nothing further, he wastes his breath on deaf ears."

This hint was too plain to be mistaken, and the Iroquois at once withdrew from the lodge. Their departure seemed to take a weight from every heart, for the restraint of a formal council was at once relaxed, and the assembly broke up into knots and smaller circles, which entered into an eager discussion of the recent occurrences. The revelation of Tononqua's origin seemed to have done him little harm. If there was any ill-will harbored in the hearts of the Hurons, they surely did not show it in their faces, their eyes hanging on his form with the old expression of love and reverence, whenever they had occasion to turn their looks in that direction. Tononqua himself requested his parents and their friends to follow him into his own lodge, and no sooner had the party reached the seclusion of its walls, when his Indian restraint yielded still more to the impulses of his affectionate disposition. He received and returned his mother's caresses, and asked her to give him an explanation of the curious circumstances which had produced this mystification. Campbell was equally anxious to learn her adventures, and in order to satisfy their pardonable curiosity, she told them her story :

"You know, David," she said, "that our home was attacked by the Mohawk Indians during your absence. Grace was in the woods with little Rosa, so I and Mary were the only members of the family in the house. Several of the neighbors, however, had taken refuge in the building, and when the Indians came they found a rich field for their murderous weapons. I had crouched into a corner, holding Mary in my arms, but all at once the child took fright and started for the door. Before I could recover her she was seized by an athletic Indian, and carried from the house. Her shrieks overcame my fear, and with the cry, 'my child ! my Mary !' I rushed from my cover in pursuit. Suddenly I was seized by the hair and dragged so rudely to the ground that I swooned in pain and terror. I had an indistinct recollection of being dragged over the ground, and when I recovered my senses, I found myself lying in the forest, with a fierce looking Indian stooping over me, his bloody tomahawk ready to do the work of butchery in case I should prove contrary or burdensome. Often have I wished since then that the Mohawks had killed me at that moment. I would, in that case, been spared many miseries; but on the other hand I would also have lost the comforts of to-day, which indemnify me for all my troubles. The Indian summoned me to arise and follow him, and as the love of life prevailed over my repugnance, I obeyed his order and suffered myself to be led away from home and friends. I believed my dear ones all butchered then, else I might perhaps have offered greater resistance to my captor. He traveled all by himself, an indication that he did not fancy the company of his fellows. At first this did not strike me as strange, but when after a week's travel we reached the shore of Lake Erie and my captor requested me to enter a large canoe which he drew from a cover, I began to fear that he meant to take me to Canada, and that such a step would result in long, if not endless, captivity. Then it was that I endeavored to resist ; but what could I, a weak, forlorn woman, do against a strong and unscrupulous warrior? He finally enforced his orders, and the next evening saw me on the coast of Canada. Here the movements of my captor became less guarded. He ascended this river and landed in this very village. It looked different at that time, and another chief held sway over the tribe. His name was Teyetaw, and I soon learned to my sorrow that my captor had sold me to this chief, whose sole property I then became in accordance with the customs of the people amongst whom an adverse fate had thrown me.

"Teyetaw was not a bad man and his people were devotedly attached to him, but to me he became an object of terror, because he molested me with his importunities and insisted that I should follow him as his squaw into his wigwam. This I was determined not to do, preferring death to such a state of wretchedness. Nor was my resolution left untried ; many a time was the scalping knife pointed at my heart in those days ; many a time the tomahawk lifted up to dash out my brains when my refusal had roused the fierce anger of the chief. But the knife was always withdrawn, the tomahawk lowered, and gradually Teyetaw ceased to persecute me with his hateful offers. This change was partly due to Kawissa, his sister. Kawissa had taken me from the beginning into her favor, and when I told her after the expiration of five months that I would soon be a mother, she conducted me to a place of seclusion and security, and nursed me during the period of my confinement. Two weeks had passed off since the day on which I had given birth to my boy, when all at once Teyetaw appeared in our refuge. He had tracked our footsteps and found our hiding place. The sight of my child roused his jealousy to such a degree that he insisted on killing it. Only the earnest intercession of Kawissa saved its life ; nor was the forbearance of the chief unconditional. His disappointed passion was bent upon revenge, and as he was prevented from reeking it upon the infant, he poured it out upon its mother. Ordering us to remain at the same spot, he withdrew, and one week afterwards returned with the Yellow Pine. To him I had to deliver my child. No tears, no prayers, no conjurations availed against the stern resolution ot Teyetaw. All I could obtain was the promise that the child should not be harmed, and that I should, sooner or later, be suffered to see it again. Never, however, was it to be mine again, and I was threatened with instant destruction for myself and child if I claimed it publicly before the tribe. Teyetaw kept his promise. After the expiration of two years, the Yellow Pine appeared in the village with a beautiful boy whom he proclaimed as a gift from the hands of the Great Spirit. He pretended to have found him in his lodge on awaking from slumber. He alleged, moreover, to have had a dream in which the Great Spirit had spoken to him, informing him that this boy would in a future day become the deliverer of the Hurons and the restorer of their ancient greatness. My heart yearned for my child, but fearing the vengeance of the chief, I abstained from claiming him, contenting myself with seeing and loving him and reserving for a future day the revelation of my claims upon his love and obedience. I would then tell him of his father and the great American nation beyond the lakes ; but although Teyetaw died and Tononqua assumed his place, I delayed my communication from day to day. Need I tell the reason ? I feared that my revelation would destroy the nimbus around the person of my son, and that he might spurn the mother who would plunge him from the position of a heaven-born messenger, into the abject condition of a homeless, fatherless creature, which required the assistance of the Hurons instead of lending them a supernatural aid in recovering wealth and power. Tononqua grew from boyhood to youth, from youth to manhood, and still my secret remained buried in my heart. Heaven knows whether I would ever have found strength to reveal it, if your arrival and desperate plight, David, had not brought on a crisis. That is my story. I thank the Almighty for sparing my own life and giving me an opportunity of saving yours. But now you must make haste and tell me everything concerning you. How have you fared? Where are you living ? What has become of Rosa and Mary? You see I have a hundred questions to ask and shall have no peace until you have satisfied my craving after news concerning you and our daughters."

Anderson at once complied with her wish and an hour was spent in lively conversation, in asking and answering questions, in soliciting and giving information about the hundred and thousand things which only gain interest by their connection with friends and relations. When the first excitement had died away and the mutual thirst for news had been satisfied, the conversation involuntarily turned upon the perilous position of Mrs. Campbell and the best mode of rescuing her. Tononqua was informed of the preparations which had already been made to that effect and he gave them his hearty approval.

"If my friends can rescue her by strategy," he said, "Tononqua need not lend his assistance. He would rather not. He loves his parents; he shall undoubtedly love his sisters when he sees them; but he is also under great obligations to the Hurons. There is even now danger of a rupture with the Mohawks—if Tononqua were found on the trail of the Wild Rose, Thayendanegea would surely unearth the hatchet. The Wyandots are few; the Mohawks numerous as the leaves of the forest; the bravest must yield to superior strength. Tononqua would rather remain at peace with the Mohawks."

"And Tononqua is right!" said Campbell, "it is enough if he allows us to fall back upon his strength in case of failure."

"If cunning should not prevail, the arm of Tononqua will be ready to strike a blow. Does that satisfy his friends?"

"It does, my son. And now let us return to the habitation of Le Blanc. When the sun sets, we ought to be on the move to second the efforts of the Black Snake. Will Tononqua accompany his parents?"

It was strange to hear the scout speak in that way to his son, but habits are the result of years and cannot be broken in a day. Although Tononqua's skin was white, his thoughts, costume and manners were those of an Indian, and as such did Anderson accost him. He knew full well that love is more apt to be engendered by gentle-

ness and yielding kindness, than superciliousness and contempt. Tononqua evidently appreciated his indulgence,
and the newly discovered relationship had every appearance of producing that mutual affection which is as much
the result of habit and deportment as consanguinity. "Let
my parents excuse Tononqua to-night," was the reply of
the young chief. "The Hurons are in commotion like the
bees when swarming; it would be imprudent to leave the
village now. But Tononqua will come to see his parents
soon ; if the coming day brings no disturbance, Tononqua
will show his face at the wigwam of the Muskrat."

With this reply they had to content themselves. Nor
did they, in consideration of the circumstances, blame the
resolution of their son. His relation to the tribe had
entered into a new phase, and although he was the subject
of general affection, a false step might easily alienate the
monarch and his people. When the party left the village,
he accompanied them to the cove and saw them enter the
canoe. Then he waved his hand, and when the boat began
to obey the paddles and the current, he turned and walked
back to the village, which lately had been the scene of such
startling events.

CHAPTER XV.

PRELIMINARY MEASURES.

It was about five o'clock when Le Blanc and his guests
reached the smaller island. The discovery of Mrs. Anderson and the rescue from a great peril had considerably
elated the spirits of the party, and although they did not
close their eyes to the fact that the captivity of the Wild
Rose left still a very difficult task to be executed, the recent
success encouraged the hope and belief that this enterprise
too would be crowned with the desired result. But while
they looked into the future with hopeful eyes, they lost not
a moment to bring about the hoped for issue, and after an
affectionate farewell to Mrs. Anderson, made hasty preparations for an immediate departure of La Belle France.

The sloop was merely fastened to the bank by a couple of ropes, which had been wound around some trees, and no sooner were these ropes withdrawn, when the craft yielded to the force of the current and began to float down stream. The wind came from the north-west, blowing almost parallel with the course of the river, and as the greatly augmented crew facilitated the handling of the sails, the large sheet of the mainsail was soon spread to the breeze. This course, dead before the wind, was by no means calculated to display the sailing qualities of the sloop; but since the current was in her favor she succeeded, nevertheless, in making twelve knots an hour. When the change of the river to a southern course allowed the craft to receive the wind a little on the right, her speed at once increased to fifteen knots. The scouts could not help praising her fine sailing qualities, and the eulogies bestowed upon his vessel pleased Monsieur Le Blanc as much as if they had been bestowed upon his own personal qualities.

"Yes, yes," he said, smiling proudly. "La Belle France does vell enough now ; but dis ain't her best yet. You ought to see her under full canvas before a stiff breeze, taking her one little bit abaft de mast. I have seen her make as many as seventeen knots dat vay."

His passengers were fully satisfied, however, with this speed, and they even seemed to think that it would slacken the moment the current ceased to second the propelling power of the wind. In this, however, they were mistaken ; when fairly in the lake, and as their course now was a due eastern one, the breeze again struck the sloop in the most favorable manner, allowing the mainsail, the foresail and the top sail to receive it in full force. The cool evening air moreover stiffened the breeze, and so La Belle France skipped over the waters with a grace and swiftness which delighted her owner and secured at least the approbation of his friends. There was no special reason for speed, because the Black Snake had intimated that he would hardly be ready the first night ; but then it surely would do no harm to be at the post at an early hour, and there is moreover a charm in rapid motion which even the most philosophical can hardly resist.

The distance from the village to the head of the Niag-ara river was about forty miles, but so well did La Belle France do her duty, that the eighth hour of evening was not fully spent when she reached the island a few miles be-low the present site of Buffalo. The days of summer in the northern latitude are long, and there was sufficient light in spite of the lateness of the hour to moor the sloop under the banks of that island. While on the way they had fully discussed the question whether it would be better to leave the sloop at the head of the river, or to take her abreast of Grand Island, and they had finally decided against the latter measure. The greater safety which the presence of the sloop might afford further down the river, in case of a discovery of Mrs. Campbell's flight, was more than coun-terbalenced by the unwieldiness of the craft in such a nar-row channel and the impossibility of removing her from the river in case of a contrary wind. The vessel might in such an instance not only become a total loss, but even prove a trap for everybody on board. So she was to remain abreast the island with Anderson and Le Blanc as guard, while Campbell and the Red Fox were to start without delay in a canoe and to reconnoiter the river, its banks and islands, partly to be acquainted with the character of the region for future emergencies, partly to look for signs from the Black Snake, in case that ally should have succeeded in pushing the rescue beyond his expectations.

It was nearly ten o'clock when the canoe with the two adventurers pushed into the current. It was a solemn hour and a solemn occasion. The sky was covered, only here and there a solitary star twinkling through the rents of the clouds. The river could only be distinguished from the leafy banks by the streak of somewhat less intense obscu-rity running through the pitchy darkness. The two occu-pants of the canoe had never been on this river before—if river it can be called—but they had heard so many mar-velous stories concerning the mad leap it takes into the abyss below, and the desperate hurry with which it speeds towards the awful precipice, that they were inclined to overrate the danger they would have to face in case their mission took them near the cataract. Under the circumstances we need not wonder if they maintained a rigid silence, for it agreed not only with their interests but also with their inclinations. They used the paddles softly and slowly, speed being undesirable, and thus reached the second island, which is smaller than the first one, but of a very similar nature. Le Blanc had given them the direction to leave all the islands they should come to on their right, and obeying this injunction they passed on until but a short distance below the island above mentioned, a small fire met their view. The fire was so exactly in their course that they at once judged it to emanate from an island. Could it originate with the Black Snake? From the instructions of Le Blanc they knew that this must be the very point of which the Black Snake had spoken. Yet it was so improbable that he should be there already, that they were inclined to consider the fire as the work of somebody else, and the coincidence, though startling, as purely incidental.

Still, the presence of the friendly Delaware at the point, although improbable, was by no means impossible, and for that reason the scouts resolved to make the trial. True, the signal of an owl's shriek had only been agreed upon as the part of the Black Snake's role, but if the latter was really there, our friends were sure that such a shriek would bring a response. The signal was entrusted to the Red Fox who imitated the nocturnal bird with such fidelity that even Campbell would have been deceived had he not known the origin of the sound. Three times did the plaintive shriek tremble through the night air, and hardly had the last sound died away, when the response came across the water, emanating evidently from the neighborhood of the fire, and limiting the shrieks to the number of those which had started from the canoe. This caused the scouts to believe that the Black Snake had really reached the island at so early a time ; but to make the matter sure the Red Fox gave one more shriek. This in turn was responded to, and now the two scouts no longer hesitated. They dipped their paddles once more into the water and headed the canoe in the direction of the fire, cautiously approaching the shore.

"It may be a snare," Campbell whispered to his companion. "Keep your eyes open and weapons ready."

When the canoe grated on the sandy beach, which projected a few feet beyond the bushes, a shadow passed across it.

"Ugh!"

This sound, more whispered than spoken, had hardly reached the ears of the scouts, when they perceived a human figure walking towards the canoe. It was the expected Delaware.

"The Black Snake is very punctual," said Campbell, "he is better than his promise. Is the Wild Rose in his company?"

"The Wild Rose is in the village of the Mohawks. She will be here to-morrow night."

"Then the Black Snake has spoken to her?"

"He has whispered into her ear. If my brother will give the Black Snake a seat in the canoe he will tell him all about it. The woods have ears; let my brother paddle the canoe up stream."

This was apparently a superfluous caution; but Campbell thought it was better to be on the safe side than on the other, and so complied with the desire of the Delaware. When the canoe had reached a point where it was an equal distance from the two banks and the head of the island, the two paddles with a moderate effort kept it stationary. The Black Snake saw that they were ready to receive an account of his proceedings, and without waiting for a summons he began:

"When my brother had paddled the Black Snake across the river, he turned his face towards the east and never stopped until he reached the river which tumbles over a precipice. The canoe of my brothers is now riding on its waters. He struck it a little below the head of this island, and when he saw how large it was, he knew which way to look for the village of the Mohawks. He had to follow the course of the river to reach the lodge of Maghpiway, but when he was on the point of turning to withdraw from the dense bushes of the bank, his eye fell upon a canoe which had been caught by the branches of a willow and was riding on the water. Then a thought struck the mind of the Black Snake. He had already invented a tale for the Red Feather. He intended to tell him that he had been taken across the big lake by the pale-faces, and escaped from their custody while a prisoner on the island of the Muskrat. But the Red Feather is a cunning chief. He might have asked many questions of the Black Snake; his eye might have read in the depth of his soul. Could the Black Snake not invent a better tale. There was a canoe, it had floated from the lake ; could he not say that he found it on the southern shore, and used it to reach the village of the Mohawks? The Red Feather might then ask questions; the Black Snake would not be afraid to answer them. He stepped into the water and entered the canoe. There was a paddle in the bottom; this was well, or he could not have told his story. He loosened the craft from the bushes and followed the current of the river; it took him to the village of the Mohawks before the sun climbed half the heavens. When he entered the lodge of the Red Feather, the chief cried, 'Ugh!' He was much astonished to see the Black Snake, and began to ask many questions. It was well that the Black Snake had a good story to tell or he never would have blinded the eyes of the chief. He told him that the pale-faces had surprised his camp and killed his companions. He told him that the Black Snake alone had escaped in the woods, and that he had commenced the long walk for the village of the Mohawks. He told him that the sun had three times set and risen before he reached it. Two days brought him to the shores of the big lake. There he saw a small party of Senecas fishing. When the night set in he crawled into the camp and took their canoe. Then he paddled along the southern shore until he reached this river. He was glad to see it, and ride on its current, for he had paddled long and hard, and his arms were tired. The current took him to the village of the Mohawks; he was glad to reach it, and rest in the lodge of the Red Feather. The chief thought it was a good story, and he laid meat and firewater before the Black Snake to eat and drink. He said he was glad to see a Delaware; his warriors belonged to

the Shawanese, the Wyandots, the Six Nations; Maghpiway would rather trust a Delaware than any of them. He
wanted the Black Snake to eat and drink, and then go to
the lodge of the Wild Rose to keep an untiring watch.
The Black Snake must never close his eyes in day time, he
said, and when he slept it must be on the threshhold of her
lodge. He must roam the woods and watch the river for
any movements on the part of the pale-faces; for the chief
was sure they would, sooner or later, renew their attempt
to rescue the prisoner, in case the Mohawks in the village
of the Hurons should fail to secure their scalps. Has the
Big Jump not seen their faces?"

"He has, my good friend, and their knives were nearer
his heart than he at all relished. I will tell the Black
Snake in good season ; let him now proceed, and report his
meeting with the Wild Rose, and the arrangements he
made with her concerning to-morrow's enterprise."

"It is well ; let my brother listen. Maghpiway led the
Black Snake to the lodge of the Wild Rose. It is not in
the village, but on a little island below this large one.
From it one can hear the distant thunder of the cataract.
The lodge of Maghpiway's braves is also on the island, and
the Wild Rose cannot flee as long as the eyes of these warriors are open. The Black Snake must see whether his
cunning cannot close them."

After a short pause, the narrator resumed :

"Maghpiway did not go into the lodge. He fears the
tearful eyes of the Wild Rose, and his heart quails before
her look of reproach. The Black Snake entered it alone ;
he saw the white squaw lying on her couch the very image
of despair. Then it was that his conscience smote him,
and he felt an intense desire to repair the injury he had
done. When the Wild Rose heard his step, she looked up.
He saw that she knew him, for her eyes were full of wrath,
and when she spoke her words breathed fire. She blamed
the Black Snake for being the author of her misery, and her
voice was loud enough to reach the warriors without. It
was well, for, although the words of the Wild Rose burned
the heart of the Black Snake, they stuffed the ears of Maghpiway's braves with a false tale. If the Wild Rose hated

the Black Snake with such a hatred, could the Black Snake possibly be her friend?   He told her so, he said :

"Let the Wild Rose pour forth her wrath upon the Black Snake to blind the eyes of his companions.   If she scolds him they will not know that he is her friend !"

"She started up.

" 'Her friend !' she said. 'When and where did the Black Snake show himself my friend?' "

"He did not, so far, but he has repented of his deeds. He has joined the pale-faces to break the bonds of the Wild Rose. But why does she not raise her voice in anger? The ears of the listening braves must be stuffed."

"The words of the Black Snake affected the Wild Rose as the rain does the wilting flower. They brought hope into her heart, and a smile upon her lips; but the Wild Rose is as cunning as she is beautiful; she took the hint of the Black Snake and broke forth into a new torrent of abuse. While her angry words sounded through the lodge, the Black Snake whispered his designs into her ear. To-morrow night the Wild Rose will be ready to follow him through the woods. The Black Snake has spoken."

"It is well," replied Campbell, "the Big Jump has a good memory for the injuries of his foes, but he has a better one to remember the services of his friends. He will never forget those of the Black Snake. Has my brother already laid his plans ?"

"He has not, he wanted first to listen to the words of the Big Jump. Whither does my brother wish me to conduct the white squaw?"

"Tell me something about the character of the place first. Is it difficult to cross from the small island to the large one?"

"It is not. The channel is narrow, and a few strokes of the paddle would send a canoe across."

Campbell reflected a while; at last he said :

"Let my brother listen now, for the words of the Big Jump must not be forgotten. At twelve to-morrow night a canoe with three warriors will hover near the head of the island, on which the Wild Rose is confined. The cry of the owl thrice repeated will bring the canoe to the shore to receive the squaw and the Black Snake."

"It is well," said the other. "Let my brothers paddle the canoe back to the island. The night is short, the way long, and the Black Snake must be at the village before his absence can arouse the suspicion of the Red Feather."

"My brother is right, but before he goes let him listen another minute. We shall leave a second canoe concealed at this place. If there should be any pursuit, and the party be compelled to separate, let the Black Snake adhere closely to the Wild Rose, and lead her across the island to this place."

"It is well."

"Let him then embark in the canoe and go up the river to reach the large vessel of the Muskrat. Does he know the long narrow island at the head of the river?"

"The Black Snake has seen it."

"Well, the vessel of the Muskrat lies on the eastern bank. I hope to join my brother there, if not sooner; but if any thing should befall me and the Little Coon, the Black Snake must go with the Muskrat to his home, and take the child and her mother back to Fort McIntosh. He must also take a squaw that lives there, the Bending Willow, for it has been discovered that she is the mother of the Wild Rose, and the wife of the Little Coon."

"Ugh!"

"I shall tell the Black Snake all about it when he has more leisure. Now he is in a hurry, we shall take him to the head of the island."

When the canoe grated on the beach, and the Delaware stepped out, Campbell struggled a moment with himself, then he said:

"Will the Black Snake carry the affection of the Big Jump to the Wild Rose? Let him tell her that he will be there to-morrow night, to rescue her from the clutches of the Red Feather, or die in the attempt."

The Indian made a motion with his hand, to indicate his compliance with the wishes of the other. Then he walked away, and disappeared in the bushes. The two scouts on the other hand shoved the canoe back into the river, and returned to La Belle France.

CHAPTER XVI.

FREAKS OF FORTUNE.

The village of the Mohawks was perhaps seventeen miles away from the island to which the sloop was moored; but as there were many warriors in the tribe who started almost daily on hunting and fishing excursions, it was considered too risky to leave the vessel at its present anchorage. Not that there was any danger of an attack by the savages—the Mohawks were just then at peace with all their neighbors—but a casual visit of theirs in the neighborhood would betray the presence of the vessel, and certainly arouse their suspicion as to the cause. The Mohawks might anticipate the meditated effort, and take measures to cut off every chance of success. Le Blanc therefore immediately set to work to leave the river, and spend the balance of the night and the whole coming day at a remote section of the lake. The bow of the vessel was looking down stream, and the sloop had, of course, to be turned before they could accomplish their purpose. This was effected by loosening the rope which held the stern to the bank, and by pushing the vessel, by means of long poles, into the river. The current soon began to work upon the sloop, and as the bow was securely fastened to a projecting tree, the stern, of course, swung around, causing the craft to head towards the lake. Before she had reached her present moorage Le Blanc had dropped a little anchor into the river, so that it lay nearly a hundred yards above the head of the island. When the stern was three-quarters down the stream, the rope which held the bow was rapidly withdrawn, and the men began to pull with all their force at the line, which was attached to the anchor. As the latter lay south-east of the vessel, the tendency of the stern to swing around to the bank was effectually checked, and the craft was entirely free from the island. While two of the men continued to take in the line, Le Blanc and one assistant hoisted the sail, and no sooner was the vessel above the head of the island, when she began to feel the fresh north-western breeze, which filled the sail and drove her so fast up stream that the crew had to use the utmost diligence in securing the anchor before she would speed past the spot at which it lay. They succeeded, however, in raising and fastening it to the proper place, and then they hoisted the additional sails, and had the satisfaction of seeing the sloop shoot into the lake with a rapidity that promised to leave its eastern terminus far in the distance.

The rapid motion did Campbell and his friends good. Used to dangers and emergencies, as they were, they could not help feeling a certain restlessness and nervousness at the thought of the attempt, which was to decide the destiny of one so dear to them—and consequently, in a measure, their own fate—before the expiration of the next twenty-four hours. To lie still would have been almost intolerable ; the rapid sailing of the sloop and the active assistance which they now and then had to give to Le Blanc engaged their attention, and withdrew their thoughts from the all absorbing subject of interest.

At first the sloop followed a southwestern course, until she had reached a place due south of Long Point, near the Pennsylvania shore. Then she tacked and headed towards the northeast, aiming at the mouth of Grand River, which she reached about eight o'clock in the morning. As the wind blew down the stream she merely proceeded to the point so often mentioned, where the river changes from an eastern to a southern course, and cast anchor. The captain and his passengers lowered a canoe, and by means of it paddled to the island. They were received with every manifestation of satisfaction, and when Mrs. Anderson learned the prospects of a speedy and successful termination of the work in store, she felt happier than she had for many years. To crown her contentment, Tononqua, at noon, also made his appearance at the island. It was a happy meeting, so happy that Campbell sometimes felt a scruple at his unusual cheerfulness, and would not accept the hope of a speedy reunion with his dearly loved wife as a balm for his troubled conscience.

The day passed rapidly, and at four the two scouts, the Red Fox, and Le Blanc re-embarked on the canoe to begin their perilous undertaking. Half an hour afterwards they were on board the sloop; the anchor was weighed, and with

the same favorable wind, the distance to the head of Niagara River was traversed without mishap, and the island
reached about the same time as the night before. This
time the sloop was anchored in the middle of the channel,
to provide against a sudden seizure in case of pursuit. A
light anchor was thrown into the water, the line of which
was fastened to the bow, so that the sloop could ride in the
current with the bowsprit headed to the lake. The sails
were left unfurled, so that the labor of a minute would expose them to the breeze, and a sharp ax was placed on the
forecastle to clip the anchor line, in case there should be no
time to weigh the anchor in the usual way. This done,
two canoes were lowered into the water, and supplied with
the needful paddles, ropes, and other utensils belonging to
the equipment of such crafts. To these were added a basket with provisions, to provide against hunger in case of an
unexpected prolongation of the expedition, and when the
night had deepened sufficiently to guard against discovery,
the canoes were unfastened, and began to float slowly down
stream. One was occupied by Campbell and Anderson, the
other by the Red Fox, Le Blanc having remained on board
the sloop as an indispensable guard. The three adventurers at once plied their paddles, and proceeded to the head of
Grand Island, where the canoe of the Red Fox was concealed in the preconcerted manner, the Indian joining the
scouts in the other.

It was now between nine and ten o'clock, and as they
were not expected before midnight, they could use all the
circumspection necessary for so difficult an enterprise.
They chose the left and shorter arm of the Niagara, the
island in question lying in its channel, according to the information obtained from the Black Snake. It could be
seven or eight miles from the place where they had left the
canoe, and as they had more than two hours to make that
distance in, no hurry need enter their calculations. The
current alone would have floated them that far in that
time; but as the cautious use of the paddle would produce
no noise, and too early an arrival was greatly preferable to
a tardy one, they dipped the blades into the flood, and thus

doubled the progress of the craft. It was already very dark, and as the sky had clouded up in the afternoon, there was a prospect that the darkness would deepen as the hours advanced. The river was, of course, less obscure than the woods, and of the river again the middle received much more of the faint light diffused in the air than the sides, which were buried in the dense shade of the fringing trees and bushes. In this shade the scouts pursued their way, straining not only their eyes to penetrate the darkness for anything unusual which might turn up in front, but exercising their senses generally to discover the trace of any foe, either in the woods or on the river. In this, however, they failed; nature seemed buried in sleep, and so deep was the reigning silence, that even the slightest noise became audible, and penetrated to a considerable distance. The rustling of the flood against a dipping branch, the chattering of a squirrel, the jumping of a frog into the river, or the musical note of another, struck against the ears of the scouts with a distinctness which startled them, and filled them with the apprehension that their progress might betray itself in spite of the greatest caution. When they had reduced the distance to the village three miles, their desire for secrecy overcame their wish for speed, and drawing in their paddles, with the exception of one, which served as a rudder, they allowed the canoe to float with the current.

They were now entering the precinct of their foes in the true sense of the word, for, although the Mohawks were at peace with the whites, an invasion of their territory like the present, with an attempt such as meditated by the scouts, would surely provoke their enmity in no small degree. The canoe entered upon ground where they lived in masses, and every second might precipitate its occupants into an ambush, if the Black Snake had played false, or if the Red Feather had formed the slightest suspicion of the time or the locality of the attempt.

On the canoe floated, the silence becoming now so deep as to be almost painful. Through it, however, broke a far-off rumbling sound like distant thunder; it was the echo of the mighty waters taking the mad leap into the abyss, which intersects the course of the Niagara River. This sound originated from a marvel of which the scouts had heard, without knowing its exact character.

Suddenly, however, the thoughts of the scouts were recalled to reality. A feeble light, like the red glare of a dying fire, sent its rays through the bushy seam of the left bank across the water, touching up the bushes of the left bank with spots of a reddish hue, and causing the canoe to seek the deeper recesses of the shore. Campbell seized an overhanging branch, and thus suspended the motion of the vessel, then the three looked across the river to see whether they could notice any signs of life near the fire. In this they failed; the fire was either deserted, or the party around it maintained so deep a silence, and so immovable an attitude, that no sign of their existence escaped across the stream. One thing, however, the scouts discovered in the light of the fire. Its rays pierced the bushes of the opposite bank for several hundred feet, and those farthest down the river cast their lurid shine upon the head of the very island of which the adventurers were in search. This was a fortunate discovery, for so deeply overcast had the sky meanwhile become, that the darkness was almost tangible, making a sudden precipitation of the canoe upon the island so probable, that nothing but this timely warning prevented it. But what had warned them, might warn the foe, and the scouts therefore perceived, with great satisfaction, that the light was rapidly fading away. Nothing could be done until the fire had completely died out, and as full thirty minutes had to elapse to bring the hour of midnight—according to the calculation of Campbell—he resolved to await the signal of the Black Snake in the present cover. As the neighborhood of the foe forbade communication, the management of the expedition had previously been put into the hands of the younger scout, and it is his movements, therefore, we have to watch.

Thirty minutes elapsed, thirty more followed in their wake; but when none of them brought any signal from the island, the scouts began to be apprehensive that something had prevented the Black Snake from the execution of his original plan. It would have been a great mortification of their feelings to return without the Wild Rose, but as it would not answer to risk the final result of the enterprise by a bold and independent action of their own, Campbell was just trying to resign himself to the possibility of a temporary disappointment, when all at once the cry of the owl arose from the island. As these birds were numerous, the sound might have originated with a real one, and the scouts, therefore, with beating hearts, listened for a repetition. There it came, and after a short pause a third hoot trembled through the night air. Would it be repeated? No, everything was still, and letting go the branch, Campbell once more surrendered the canoe to the influence of the current. The distance to the island was not over 200 yards, and the current would soon have taken it there, but as the river split on its head, and flowed in two directions, the paddle was necessary to guide the course of the vessel. It was, moreover, desirable to reach the island in the shortest possible time, as there was no knowing how soon the flight of Mrs. Campbell might be discovered. So all the paddles were lowered into the flood, and the canoe propelled with a rapidity which brought it to the desired spot before a minute had elapsed. The island ran out into a low sandy point, and at its head the paddlers arrested the motion of their vessel, allowing its bow to grate slightly on the ground. At this moment the light sound of approaching footsteps struck their ears, and they listened for the fourth and last cry of the owl, which was to announce the arrival of the fugitives on the beach, when all at once the footsteps stopped, and other sounds of an alarming nature penetrated through the night.

"Ugh!" the scouts heard somebody exclaim, so loudly and with such elements of wonder and surprise in the voice that *he* surely was not interested in the secrecy of the flight. "What does my brother mean? Is the Wild Rose——"

At this moment the voice stopped abruptly, and a loud rustle in the bushes betrayed to the listeners in the canoe that a struggle had commenced on the island. Campbell was already on the point of leaping on the bank, when suddenly two figures rushed from the bushes and looked around as if in quest of some expected object. The erect form of Campbell evidently met their gaze, for they hastened to the edge of the canoe and a deep voice said in low and hurried accents:

"Let the Big Jump hasten! A cursed Mingo was in our way and the knife of the Black Snake had to silence him. But the camp is aroused and in a short time two hundred Mohawks will be on the trail."

It was evident that he said the truth, for even at that minute a shout arose from the island which awoke a ready echo in the village and caused a cold sensation to creep over the nerves of the party. There was no time now for an affectionate greeting; no time for tender words and loving caresses. Not a word was spoken. Mrs. Campbell and the Black Snake took their seats; the canoe was shoved off the sand and turned, and the next moment four paddles forced it up stream with a rapidity which bid defiance to the power of the current. But while the canoe sped up stream with remarkable swiftness, the night gave birth to signs of life on the left bank of the river, which were calculated to try the nerves and hearts of the stoutest and most courageous. The first yell emanating from the island had initiated others on the bank, which embraced in loudness, hideousness and variety, all that an Indian throat can accomplish. It rose and fell, now dying to a faint angry murmur, and anon taking new life from an isolated yell, swelling to more than its original compass and fury. In addition to this, hurried footsteps could be heard proceeding up and down the river, while paddles were thrown into canoes, indicative of the intention of the tribe to pursue the invaders by land and water. If the reader adds to this tumult the vivid flash and sharp crack of the rifles, the angry hiss of the bullets fired at random, he will receive a lively impression of the uproar, through the midst of which the fugitives now made their way. They retraced their previous course, remaining as near the eastern bank as possible and propelling the canoe as fast as the necessity of secrecy would permit. The sign of enemies, however, that hurried past them on the western bank, multiplied from minute to minute, giving rise to the apprehension that they would intercept the advance of the fugitives, either by means of some canoes or by manning the small island above. In addition to these alarming signs ahead, there were others coming from the rear. The Mohawks had evidently succeeded in manning half a dozen canoes and started in hot pursuit of the fugitives. As their number and strength gave them confidence and, as in addition to this, speed was much more of a consideration to them than secrecy, they came up stream in rather a noisy but, at the same time, effective manner. The strokes of their paddles sounded more and more distinct in the ears of the fugitives, and the apprehension that a change of operations would before long become necessary, at length ripened into conviction.

"Hold the canoe towards the bank, father," said Campbell, as soon as he had formed his resolution. "We'll have to take to the island and try to reach the other canoe, or, in the worst case, endeavor to aim for the American shore. The imps are in front and in the rear, and if we remain much longer where we are, they will spring a trap on us, as sure as I am living. So that will do. Now, Mary, give me your hand and take a leap. Red Fox, will you give the craft a good push to make it spin across the river? The Mohawks must be led to think that we took to the mainland instead of the island."

"The canoe is too light to go far ! Will the Big Jump let the Red Fox take it across and follow the trail of the Mengwe? He can join his friends at the big canoe."

"The idea is not bad, but it is very bold! Is the Red Fox sure that he will not allow his zeal to run away with his judgment? The Wild Rose cannot afford to lose her brother."

"The Red Fox will be cautious like the Beaver !"

"Well, let him go, he knows the language of the Mohawks, they will not know him in the night."

This point decided, the fugitives hastily entered the woods, which covered Grand Island as thickly as the mainland. The Red Fox, on the other hand, began to paddle the canoe across the stream. He effected the passage with such rapidity, observing at the same time the needful caution, that he reached the western bank unobserved, landing only a short distance below the starting point. He fastened the canoe to an overhanging branch, taking care to make its position as conspicuous as possible. Then he ascended the bank and concealed himself behind a dense bush to observe the movements of his foes. Hardly a minute elapsed without some warrior hurrying by as fast as the darkness of the night and the denseness of the woods would have permitted. All at once the tramping of many feet announced the arrival of a larger party. Now was the time for the Red Fox to act, for there was not much danger of discovery in so large a crowd. Slipping adroitly from behind the bush, he joined the Mohawks, who were too eagerly bent upon the execution of their designs to pay any attention to the silent figure in their midst. They continued their hurried walk for fully three miles, breaking into a run when the open character of the woods would permit. At last, however, they reached a place where all the scattered forerunners seemed to have come to a stop, for judging from the hum of voices and the many shadows flitting through the trees, the Red Fox felt convinced of the presence of fully two hundred Mohawk warriors. A few tardy ones continued to arrive, but with the exception of these, the strength of the tribe seemed to be collected on this spot. In this belief the Red Fox was strengthened by the subsequent movements. The bustle among the warriors came to a sudden termination, and the silence which followed seemed to indicate that some decisive measure was to be carried out. In this expectation the Delaware was not disappointed. Standing incidently in the center of the crowd, he found himself suddenly and against his own wish, the center of a narrow circle which surrounded Thayendanegea, the sachem of the Mohawks. To retreat was impossible, as all outsiders pressed towards the center and held the members of the fortunate inner circle as in a vice. All at once the chief raised his voice:

"Let my warriors listen," he said, with a voice which, though low, was distinct and could therefore be heard by all for whom the words were intended. "The pale-faces have broken into our village. They have robbed the

squaw of one who had claimed the hospitality and protection of the Mohawks. This ought not to be; the Mohawks ought not to let the pale-faces escape from their
territory. If caught, they will feel the vengeance of an
insulted tribe."

He stopped a moment, then he proceeded:

"Let my young men extend a line across both branches
of the river, to cut off the retreat of the pale-faces, which-
ever way they come. Fifty may scatter on this bank toward the west; fifty on the side belonging to the Yengeese.
Twelve may occupy the head of the big island, and twelve
garrison each one of the little islands in the river. Let my
young men hasten. He that brings me a pale-face, dead or
alive, shall be honored in the sight of the Mohawks."

The crowd suddenly scattered, a portion pushing
through the forest in a western direction, the balance,
by far the largest number, hastening to the bank and
plunging into the river in order to reach the stations assigned to them. The Red Fox took care to join the latter
division. With it he first swam to the little island before
mentioned, with it he afterwards proceeded to the larger
one, at the head of which the canoe of the fugitives was
concealed. He had now obtained his purpose, and as it did
not suit him to advance to the island in the eastern branch,
or worse, to the shore beyond, he considered it his interest
to disappear as stealthily as he had advanced. This step
was effected without difficulty, and after the large body of
the Mohawks had continued their advance, the Red Fox
carefully followed in the wake of the twelve warriors who
had been ordered to assume a position at the head of the
island. Fortunately, this head was rather bare of bushes,
so that the Mohawks preferred a position a little further
north-west, which was densely covered by underbush,
forming a natural ambush upon any party that would attempt to reach the head of the island. The canoe was concealed an equal distance from the point, but on the eastern
bank, so that the cover of the vessel and the ambush of the
Mohawks lay in a line running due east and west, and at a
distance of a hundred feet from one another. Upon this the
Red Fox based his plan. After he had gained a correct

knowledge of the position of the Mohawks, he proceeded nearly half a mile down the island until he reached a place where it became too broad to send the voice to both shores. Here he raised the hoot of the owl at intervals of five minutes, and in the pauses listened with the greatest attention for a response. He had been at the station fully an hour without receiving any encouragement, and was already reflecting on the policy of changing his position, when he imagined he heard a faint response from the northeast. Again he gave his signal, and again he received an answer, the sound becoming a little more distinct than before. This induced him to give his next signal somewhat nearer the place from which the cry came, and this experiment proved so successful that the next hour saw him reunited with the party. Campbell had felt considerably alarmed about his safety, and his satisfaction at his sight increased, when the young Delaware gave him the valuable information which he had obtained by means of the risky undertaking.

"So the imps are stationed on the western bank," he said. "Well, then, we shall give them a wide berth, and hug the eastern one. There is land enough for the white man and the red one. Why should we fight about so narrow a strip?"

The humorous touch in this remark was the best proof of the animating influence which the rescue of his wife had had upon the scout. He seemed cheerful and sanguine of success, and as far as his own ability of attacking or defending was concerned, it could truly be said that the recovery of the Wild Rose had doubled both his strength and cunning. He now headed the party, which advanced towards the critical point, in single file, Mrs. Campbell being next to her husband, and Anderson bringing up the rear. Everything went well until they reached that portion of the eastern bank, the bushy seam of which had gaps, these gaps increasing in width as they advanced towards the cluster of bushes under which the canoe lay concealed.

The light had meanwhile become somewhat lighter, the clouds had broken and the stars were here and there shining through the fissures. Still it was sufficiently dark

for all purposes, provided the Mohawks had not changed
their position. This was not very likely, nevertheless
Campbell doubled his precaution in traversing the last few
steps to the longed for goal. He stopped every half minute
and listened; he bent his keen searching glances in every
direction, and endeavored to penetrate the darkness for a
suspicious sign; but everything remained quiet, and when
he at last reached the cover of the canoe, he flattered himself to have overcome the greatest obstacle to a successful
termination of the flight. The Black Snake and the Red
Fox now stealthily entered the river, and shoved the canoe
to a place where the party could easily embark. Mrs.
Campbell entered first; she was followed by her husband,
while the two Indians remained in the water on the two
sides of the vessel, in order to steady it and prevent all
noise during the embarkation of the others. Anderson was
the only one remaining on shore. He also prepared to step
into the vessel, when all at once a dark figure leaped
against him and threw him to the ground. At the same
time a fierce yell broke the stillness of the night, followed
by a dozen on the island and a hundred on the shores. The
onset was made parallel with the bank, thus precipitating
the scout upon the land, instead of the water. It had moreover been executed with such a force,, that it threw both
the assailant and the assailed out of the reach of the party
in the boat. For a second Campbell was stupefied ;by the
suddenness of the attack, but when he recovered and saw
the perilous situation of his comrade, he, arose and was on
the point of leaping to the shore, when a foreign force con-
trived to prevent him. The two Indians being nearer the
shore, were better able to judge of the situation. They saw
that a dozen Mohawks were on the point of making a dash
at the boat and its crew. The bravery of the Indians is always tempered with prudence; to throw their lives away
without any chance of success, is with them not valor but
folly. They saw that to remain would be to imperil the
lives of all of them, or at least to bring about a universal
captivity. This they wanted to prevent, and without any
mutual agreement or consultation, they pushed the canoe
into the water with all the strength they could command.

No sooner was the vessel in motion, when they themselves jumped in and seized a paddle to increase the distance from the shore. This in a measure checked the movement of Campbell ; but he might after all have taken the fatal leap, if a pleading voice at his side had not exclaimed, imploringly :

"Oh Robert, do not leave me !"

At this moment the voice of Anderson sounded from the shore.

"Be off Robert," the noble fellow cried, "the island swarms with Mingoes, and by landing you would only imperil yourself and Mary. Give my love to———"

The voice suddenly stopped as if the speaker had been checked by a rude slap on his mouth or some other summary measure. The attempt at communication was not repeated on the part of Anderson at all events, and as the danger of an immediate capture increased rapidly, Campbell at last gave his reluctant consent to flight. He could not abstain, however, from encouraging a man whose relationship to his wife was the slightest claim to his love, friendship and assistance. He had been his fast friend for many a year : his constant companion for many a chase in peace and war, and Campbell would not withdraw now without assuring him of his assistance to the last extremity.

"Farewell, father, for to-night," he cried. "If I live you will soon hear from us. Keep up your heart and look for signs !"

It was well for the fugitives that the Mohawks on the island had no guns with them; else a volley fired at random might have done execution, the distance being so short and the station of the boat so plainly indicated by Campbell's voice. As it was, the Mohawks on the banks discharged their rifles without effect. Not a single bullet hit either the canoe or the occupants ; but some of them passed in such uncomfortable proximity that Campbell felt no desire for directing the aim of the Mohawks by further utterances. He knew, moreover, that there was no time to be lost if they wanted to evade a repetition of the ambush, and dipping his paddle in the flood, he cautioned the Indians to aim at noiselessness as much as speed. Three

oarsmen of such strength and skill soon told on the progress of the canoe, which glided over the water with a
swiftness excelling the most rapid walk and nearly equal-
ling a moderate run. The Mohawks might possibly reach
the anchorage of the sloop at the same time with or even
before the fugitives, but while on the one hand it was
hardly probable that the savages were informed of her
whereabouts, the chance of an escape was still very fair,
even admitting such a knowledge on their part. The sloop
was large, and if a chance shot should hit the hull, that was
very different from hitting a canoe. Ten minutes would
suffice to put her in motion and— farewell to all chances of
the Mohawks ever reaching her.

Thus ran the thoughts of Campbell and his friends, and
so secure did the scout begin to feel, that he suffered himself to ponder upon the rulings of an adverse fate, which
deprived him of his best friend, at the same moment when
it restored to him a lost wife. From these reflections, however, they were startled by sounds of paddle strokes in the
rear—the canoes of the Mohawks were coming up a second
time and evidently gaining on them !

The canoes! the flurry and excitement of the chase had
caused them to forget the canoes. These fatal vessels at
once changed the aspect of affairs. If they should overtake
the fugitives while in the canoe; if they should reach the
sloop before it was fairly under way, then all their previous
efforts would be vain.

The only chance of safety was now in the quickness of
their progress. The bullets of the Mohawks on shore were
less formidable than the paddles of those on the water. If
they had thus far combined secrecy with speed ; they now
sacrificed secrecy to speed, and in consequence greatly increased the swiftness of their vessel. Even the Wild Rose
took a paddle, and so well had she retained the knowledge
of a previous accomplishment, that the scouts at once felt
the influence of her aid. Yet the formidable canoes came
nearer and nearer, and Campbell could not abstain from casting now and then an anxious glance behind, to see whether
the pursuers were near enough to check their progress by a
well aimed bullet. In this expectation, however, he was

fortunately disappointed, the sound of the paddles reaching much further in the stillness of the night than during the busy day time. But if the canoes of the Mohawks were not near enough to be seen, they were certainly as near as was at all desirable, and Campbell looked impatiently ahead to see whether the island would not soon loom up in the night.

Fortunately the distance was not great, and all at once a darker shadow on the water betrayed the neighborhood of the eagerly expected island. There was no time for deliberation. The channel between the island and the eastern shore was rather narrow, and by choosing it, the canoe might have to run the gauntlet of fifty Mohawk rifles; but the sloop lay in that channel, and to round the head of the island and to approach the vessel from the front would cost precious moments, which would perhaps decide their fate.

These reflections decided the course of the scout.

"To the left!" he whispered to his companions, and a minute afterwards the canoe shot into the channel above mentioned. The darkness was deeper there, compensating in a measure for the greater proximity of the shore. Campbell held the exact middle of the channel, for if the savages were really on the shore, there was no reason why they should not also be on the island. The latter was long and narrow, its length amounting to nearly a mile. This distance the party had to traverse with the constant expectation of a volley from either shore; but nothing occurred until they reached the immediate neighborhood of the sloop. Campbell had previously arranged with Le Blanc that the cry of the owl should be the signal of their arrival, and when the hull of the sloop rose darkly from the lighter background of the lake, the Red Fox with his usual skill uttered the well-known hoot. It was at once answered from the sloop; but either did the performance of the Frenchman lack the necessary smoothness or the frequency of the signal had aroused the suspicion of the Mohawks; however this may be, the second hoot had hardly been uttered, when a savage yell of many voices broke from the shore and island at the same time, seconded by a volley that once more caused the bullets to fly around the heads of the fugitives in rich profusion, without harming, however, either their persons or their vessel.

"Just in time," muttered Campbell. "Five minutes later and the sloop would have been theirs. Now for a last pull, lads. Take the larboard, for unless I am much mistaken the bullets flew thickest from the island."

Larboard it was, and a moment afterwards the canoe shot under the hull which protected it at least on one side. Before the Mohawks had time to reload, the party was on board the sloop.

"Back at last!" cried Le Blanc, in joyous but excited accents. "And brought your wife along? Den let me vish you luck."

"Not now, my friend, not now. If you value your sloop—yes, if you value your life, get the vessel out of the river. The Mohawks are coming up in a dozen canoes and will be here in a minute. So you see we have no time to lose."

The Frenchman started.

"Pull in de line den!" he cried, "all of you. Ven you come to the anchor, clip de cable. I'll set de sail."

Campbell and the two Indians rushed to the forecastle and commenced to haul in the line with such dispatch, as men will use when they know their lives depend on the effort. It was very difficult to overcome the weight of so large a body; but that accomplished, the vessel began to move up stream with moderate rapidity. The sail now commenced to flap in the air, and when the sloop passed the head of the island, the breeze filled the canvas and facilitated the efforts of the scout and his companions. At this moment the Wild Rose exclaimed:

"Watch, Robert! I hear somebody in the water."

"Keep on pulling," the scout instructed his assistants.

"When the line shortens take the ax and clip it."

After these words he picked up a heavy staff and hastened to the center of the sloop where his wife was standing. Nor was he a moment too soon; for hardly had he arrived at her side when several dark objects were seen above the weather-boards. Without hesitating a moment he dealt the highest one a blow that made it disappear.

The second figure was dispatched by a vigorous thrust of the same weapon, and then the splashes of these involununtary divers on the water were followed by half a dozen voluntary ones. This side of the board cleared, Campbell sprang to the other side and came just in time to apply a stunning blow to a savage who had climbed the weatherplank and was in the act of springing on the deck. The blow knocked the intruder senseless, and as his motion had been inward, he fell upon the deck, receiving another heavy concussion from the fall. Campbell had no time to ascertain his condition, for the appearance of new assailants above the plank claimed all the attention he could spare. The capture of Anderson had filled him with rage as well as sadness, and his blows were dealt with a vehemence truly terrific. Every second a dull crushing sound betrayed the contact of the club with the skull of some unfortunate Mohawk, and five minutes after the cry of warning the assault of a heavy force of savages had been beaten off by the strength and prowess of a single man.

"Saved again!" Campbell cried to his wife, and then hastened back to the forecastle. When he arrived there he found that the cable had been clipped and that the sloop was making headway against the current by the pressure of the wind alone. On the narrow confines of the river the influence of the breeze was but feebly felt and the progress of the sloop therefore so slow, that the scout took fresh alarm at the thought of the pursuing canoes and the probability of being overtaken and attacked by superior numbers, before they could avail themselves of the speed and other points of excellence of the sloop. In the heat of the recent fray he had forgotten all about the formidable foe on the water; but now the thought and fear of them returned with double force, and he summoned the two Indians to accompany him to the stern, as that part of the vessel was most exposed to the attack of the party in the canoes. Again they were in good season. The obscurity of the night was gradually wearing away, and the approach of the enemy was therefore not only heralded to them by the instrumentality of their ears, but also by that of their eyes. They perceived the dim outlines of eight large canoes, in each of which there was a crew of six warriors. This formed an overwhelming force of nearly fifty warriors, who seemed determined to take the sloop at all hazards, for at the sight of the vessel they sent a savage yell into the air, and doubled their efforts to reach its side. They must certainly have been aware from the previous desperate resistance of the crew that the sloop could not be taken without heavy loss; and the determination with which they pushed their pursuit notwithstanding, betrayed the fury into which the losses hitherto sustained had driven them. Campbell and his companions knew that no quarter would be given, and they therefore prepared for a combat unto death. Campbell put a knife into Mary's hand, and said:

"If I fall this will show you how to follow me."

"I'll make good use of it, Robert," she replied with a courageous smile, "the Mohawks shall not retake me alive."

"But do not act rashly, dearest. Remember that this is merely for an utmost strait. Could you hold the helm, so as to keep the vessel on its course?"

."Certainly, Robert. I can and will do anything to succor you."

"Then take your post, dear Mary, to give Le Blanc a chance to aid us. Ready, lads, the rascals are gaining steadily; another minute will teach our bullets the way to their hearts. What are you doing, Le Blanc? Don't go, for we can hardly spare your rifle."

"Vell, de vind is freshing up. If I hoist another sail may be ve could give de imps de slip."

"If that is so, captain, hoist it at all events; but guard your body, for if they learn your purpose, they will surely bang away at you."

"Vell, dat cannot be helped," said the little Frenchman, with a coolness which gained the scout's respect. At the same time he ran to the forecastle and began to tug away at a pulley, by means of which he managed to raise his topsail. It soon began to move, a circumstance which did not fail to attract the notice of the pursuers; for they yelled more lustily than ever and sent a serious remonstrance in the shape of a dozen bullets; which passed the captain in an alarming proximity. The night had by this time given away to dawn, and the erect figure of the Frenchman, on his elevated position, could be readily distinguished by the Mohawks, who were at that moment no further than sixty yards from the vessel. Thus far Campbell had retained his fire, but when he saw the danger to which Le Blanc was exposed, he took aim and bid his companions do the same. On the word fire, three bullets sped from the sloop on an errand of death, for three Mohawks dropped their paddles and took a frantic leap into the water preparatory to the great leap into eternity. This loss, however, did not check the progress of the canoes ; it only made the yells of the warriors fiercer, their strokes more telling, and their fire at the captain hotter. The latter had meanwhile succeeded in raising the topsail, and he now ran to another pulley to hoist the front sail. This brought him nearer to the bow and exposed his body in even a higher degree than before. The bullets continued to fly around him as thick as the hailstones in a storm ; but although his cap was knocked off and his suit cut in several places, he persevered undaunted and unharmed to the end. When the foresail was in its place, he picked up his cap again, swung it around his head and broke into a hearty cheer. And well he might, for not only did the sloop approach the wider margin of the lake, where the wind blew with greater strength and steadiness; but the newly expanded canvas caught a greater portion of the breeze and therefore increased the velocity of the sloop. Campbell observed with great satisfaction that the canoes no longer gained on them, in spite of the most desperate efforts of their crews. They even began to fall back a little, although they seemed to persuade themselves to the contrary, and continued to row after the receding sloop with all their might. If the scout had been of a bloodthirsty disposition he might now have continued to sacrifice a number of his foes to his fury ; but the previous excitement had died away, and he not only abstained from firing upon a foe which could no longer harm him, but also prevented his dusky companions from yielding to their more savage impulses.   With his eye at a knot-hole in the weather-planks of the stern, he watched the movements of the foes who seemed to have at length become convinced of the vanity of their efforts, and vented their disappointment in one last yell of rage and a volley from their rifles. At this moment an exclamation from the lips of Mrs. Campbell caused the scout to look around. He turned just in time to see that the Mohawk who had been stunned by his blow some time ago, had recovered and was on the point of leaping over the weather-plank into the water. Campbell endeavored to reach him by two or three powerful leaps, but he came too late. When he reached the spot where the Indian had lain, the figure of the latter just disappeared in the water.

"Confound the villain," cried the scout, seeking at the same time the shelter of the weather-planks against the re-opened fire of the Mohawks, who had evidently perceived the movement of their countryman, and now desired to protect him. "Confound him, I say. I would rather have lost my best rifle than this sneaking Mingo. I calculated to keep him as a hostage for the good behavior of his kins-man toward Anderson, and now he has taken to the fishes. Well, I wish them luck to the savory morsel."

The suggestion embodied in these words, however, proved fallacious, for instead of sinking the Mohawk again rose to the surface, and struck out for the canoes of his com-panions, who paddled towards him to facilitate his efforts. Campbell could easily have sent a bullet through his head, but the same humanity which had before induced him to abstain from unnecessary bloodshed, now saved the life of a person whose living body he would have liked to secure, but in whose death he felt no interest. When the swimmer reached the canoes a shout of triumph arose from the lips of the Mohawks; then they turned their canoes, and pre-pared to return to the shore, while the sloop shot through the water with an ever increasing velocity, and soon left the scene of the recent struggle far behind.

CHAPTER XVII.

A MODEL KING.

When the La Belle France glided up to the island in the Grand River, a little before noon, the passengers were received with a strange mixture of joy and sadness. While Mrs. Campbell embraced her newly found daughter with that delight which only a mother can comprehend, who recovers her child after the separation of nearly a quarter of a century, she could not, on the other hand, help weeping at the capture of him whom she had merely found to lose again. Through her sadness, however, hope threw its rays; she looked towards Tononqua for help and comfort, and when Campbell announced his intention to visit the king, and inform him of the capture of his father, she confirmed him in his resolution, and urged him to depart for the village of the Hurons without delay. Mrs. Campbell, of course, shared the feelings of her mother, but although she was equally anxious to see the captive liberated, she could not help remembering that he who was now going to stake his life on the recovery of her father, was her husband, and the father of her child. The ride on the sloop from the river to the island had been fraught with too much happiness to let her contemplate a new separation with indifference. Still, apprehensive as she was of the consequences of his errand, she did not find it in her heart to retain him one minute over the time which he had fixed for his departure. So after caressing little Annie for half an hour, and refreshing himself with the bountiful supplies of Adeline's larder, he went to the canoe where the Red Fox and the Black Snake already awaited him, and proceeded to the village of the Delawares. It was evident from the looks of the people that the arrival of the sloop was already known, though they were probably ignorant of the issue of the expedition. Of this Campbell became convinced when he stepped into the presence of Tononqua. The young chief received him cordially, shaking his hand, and saying:

"My brother is welcome; has he freed the Wild Rose from the clutches of the Mohawks?"

"I have, but though I have reason to rejoice at her recovery, there is sadness in my heart at the loss of a friend. Tononqua's father is in the hands of the Mengwe."

"Ugh! was there no one near the Little Coon?"

"I understand your question, Tononqua; but if you will listen to my story you will find that no one was to blame."

The scout now gave the chief a concise narrative of last night's adventures. Tononqua listened with intense interest, and when Campbell had finished, he reflected long and deeply on what he had heard. At length he raised his head, and said to the scout:

"Let my brother come with me, I want to address the warriors of the Hurons."

With these words he led the way from his lodge, and as the tribe was small and, moreover, expectant of a similar movement on the part of the chief, five minutes were sufficient to gather all the warriors around him. He did not lead them to the council lodge, but preferred to address them on the commons, situated in the centre of the village. The squaws and children construed this evidently as a permission to listen to the words of the king, for they formed a second and outer circle behind the warriors, who had grouped themselves around Tononqua and the scout. In all there seemed to be about two hundred persons present, one-fifth of whom were capable of bearing arms. Everybody maintained the deepest silence, even the children learning thus early the difficult art of self-government. The eyes of the whole tribe hung on the face of Tononqua, who seemed to be the prey of an inward struggle. At last, however, he opened his lips and said :

"Let the Hurons listen to the voice of Tononqua, for he would want his words to sink into their hearts, and penetrate to the seat of their understanding. The Hurons have always been very good to Tononqua. They gave him the best of everything, and when he raised his voice to speak they divined his meaning, and obeyed his words before they were uttered. This, however, was because they thought Tononqua had descended from the sun to make them great and happy. If they had known that he was the child of a pale-face, the offspring of a Yengeese they might have spurned the thought of doing him homage, and refused to obey his commands. Tononqua labored under the same mistake, he did not deceive the Hurons, but was like them deceived. Now, however, he knows better ; he knows that he has no right to the position to which the Hurons have lifted him, to the allegiance which they have so cheerfully vouchsafed to him. He lays down his crown, and begs the Wyandots to consider it as a free gift, which they are at liberty to bestow upon him whom they consider the worthiest of the nation."

Suiting the action to his words he took off the coronet we have described, and laid it on the ground at his feet. As his silence seemed to call for a reply the Yellow Pine stepped from the circle of the warriors, and said :

"The Hurons have heard the words of Tononqua. They are deeply moved. If he did not descend from the sun he surely has the virtues of the children of that body, which gives us light and heat. He is brave, but the Hurons are no cowards; he is wise, but the Wyandots are no fools amongst the red men. But he is more, he is guileless like a child, and that alone raises him above all others, and makes him worthy of ruling over warriors. He has laid down the coronet because he is not the child of the sun; the Yellow Pine bids him take it up again, because there is no one as worthy in the tribe to wear it as Tononqua. If there is one amongst the warriors of the Hurons who dissents from me, let him step forward and protest."

Not a movement became visible in the ranks of the braves. Tononqua was evidently touched by this unanimous reappointment ; but he seemed still scrupulous about accepting the restored dignity, for he raised his hand and said :

"The Hurons are very good, and Tononqua thanks the Yellow Pine for laying bare their hearts, but they have not heard all Tononqua has to say. He has found the authors of his life ; he has a mother who claims his love, a father who is entitled to his protection in old age. The Great Spirit has made the child dependent on the parent. Tononqua means to obey his command. His father has fallen into the hands of the Mengwe—if the Hurons reinstate him into power he will use it to rescue the captive."

At this moment the Hurons manifested symptoms of an intention to rush upon the person of their chief and to offer their assistance in the contemplated enterprise, but Tononqua raised his hand, and so perfect was the control which this extraordinary being exercised over the fierce inhabitants of the forest, that this gesture instantaneously checked the movement. One foot advanced, the right hand at the tomahawk, the warriors stood the living image of suspense and expectation.

"Tononqua understands the generous impulse of his friends," the chief continued, "but had the Hurons not better count the cost before they act. Are they fully conscious of what it means to make war upon the Mohawks? Before Tononqua knew that one of the white strangers was his father, he listened to the voice of policy, for it was his duty to protect the interests of his people. He knew the innocence of the prisoners, and yet he delivered them into the hands of Thayendanegea, laying on *his* shoulders the responsibility. Then it was that the Bending Willow opened Tononqua's eyes; he was no longer at liberty to deliver his father and his father's friends to the vengeance of the Mohawks. He is not now at liberty to choose his movements—duty compels him to stake his life on the rescue of the Little Coon. With the Hurons it is different. They are under no obligation to the pale-face prisoner, they are under none to Tononqua, for he has released them. If they war against the Mohawks they may meet certain death; they may see their fields devastated, their homes destroyed, their cattle slaughtered, their mothers, wives and children butchered and scalped, or carried away into a galling captivity; are the Hurons prepared to carry their allegiance to Tononqua to such extremes? If they turn from him he will be the last to reprove them. Tononqua repeats his warning, let them consider while it is time."

But the Hurons were evidently disposed to disregard this disinterested counsel. They could no longer restrain their desire to show the ardent affection they bore their young and noble king, to prove to him that with them the sense of honor and the love of glory weighed more heavily than the love of life and its pleasures.   They rushed in a body upon the person of Tononqua, their knives and tomahawks glistened before his eyes, and a confused mass of yells, cries, conjurations, and exclamations conveyed to his ears the fact that he could count upon the fidelity of these true-hearted children of nature to the last breath in their bosom, the last drop of blood in their veins.   The women and children were affected in a similar manner. They joined in the tumultuous clamor, and so much had a warlike spirit seized the boys that they rushed upon a half-grown sapling, and rapidly divested it of its leaves and branches.   While some were engaged in this manner, others procured red paint, and with great dexterity daubed the naked trunk with a blood-colored dye.   By this time the tumult had somewhat abated, and the warriors were prepared to take the hint from the boys, and formally declare their intention to enter upon the war-path.   The chief took his tomahawk and, walking up to the painted sapling, buried the edge in the wood.   He was followed by all the warriors, who advanced to the tree one by one, according to rank and age, and dealt it such tremendous blows that the splinters soon began to fly right and left. In addition to this they indulged in the most savage howls and frantic menaces against some invisible, imaginary foe, until the sapling disappeared, and their exhausted nature demanded a cessation of the sport.

The Hurons had now solemnly declared their readiness to enter upon the bloody path of war.   As they had caused the tree to sink beneath their blows, so they were determined to strike their living foe with the sharp edge of their hatchets.   But to make war successful there must be a plan, and the bravest and wisest warriors now put their heads together to deliberate upon the contemplated expedition.   The tribe mustered forty warriors who were fit to take the field.   There were twenty more capable of bearing arms, but these were either too old or too young to endure the hardships and fatigues of long and forced marches, and to these the defense of the village was entrusted.   As it lay on an island, a small force was deemed sufficient to hold it against an invading force; but in case a night attack should eventually prevail, Tononqua gave orders that the most valuable property should be stored away in the canoes, and that the entire population should beat a retreat as soon as the village became untenable. The lower island was smaller, and therefore more easily defended, but if superior numbers should enforce its evacuation also, the leader of the homeguard was directed to continue the flight to the island of Long Point, whither the Mohawks would surely be unable to continue their pursuit, for want of vessels.

This being arranged, the warriors who were to join the expedition, prepared for an immediate departure. They were ferried across the river by those of their comrades who belonged to the garrison, and once on the opposite shore they rapidly vanished in the woods under the lead of Tononqua and Campbell. The latter had hardly expected so early a departure, and therefore failed to take leave of his family, but the speed of Tononqua was too much in accordance with his own impatience to stay behind on that account. The Yellow Pine, to whom the command of the garrison had been intrusted, had received orders to take the farewell of Campbell and Tononqua to the women at the house of Le Blanc, and also instructions regarding the movements of that individual himself. He was to take all the members of his household on board his sloop, as the anticipated hostility of the Mohawks would make the island too insecure a place of residence. He was to cruise on the lake, and to approach the head of Niagara River once in the morning and once at night. He was warned, however, not to endanger his vessel and his passengers by entering the river itself, but advised to give both river and shore a wide berth, and listen to no signals whatever, unless he had the evidence of his eyes and ears that they did not emanate from the enemy. With these instructions, which they knew the faithful Frenchman would carry out to the letter, the two leaders turned their backs to their homes with all the composure which the followers of the fickle god of war can summon. While they led their division forward with all due speed, they sent half a dozen scouts in advance of the main body to reconnoiter the country, and advance near enough to the village of the Mohawks to inform themselves of Anderson's whereabouts and condition. The Red Fox was eager to join them and, as Campbell had justly a high opinion of both his valor and discretion, he granted his request. The scouts set out at a slow run which would soon have put a white man out of breath, but which did not at all molest men who had been inured to similar exercises from their very infancy. Considering the entangled nature of the woods, it is very doubtful whether a horse could have excelled, or even equalled them in speed. In this instance swiftness was absolutely necessary, for the village of the Mohawks was, as the reader knows, thirty miles from the island of the Wyandots, and as the sun had passed his meridian, and the reconnoitering of the hostile territory must necessarily be done during the night, the Red Fox and his companions had no time to lose.

We let them go on their dangerous errand, and accompany the larger body of the Hurons through the forest. Although they were not quite so much in a hurry as the scouts, yet they showed considerable expedition, for when the night broke in, they had traversed two-thirds of the distance to the village, and reached a little island in the river, which empties its waters into the Niagara a few miles above the cataract, and is now known by the name of Chippewa. On this island the party encamped to take a hasty meal, and await the arrival of the scouts. The island was chosen to give greater security against an attack, for, although the Hurons calculated to surprise the Mohawks, the tables might be turned on them, and like prudent men they prepared for emergencies.

Soon the last vestige of light faded away, and no noise or motion upon the island betrayed the presence of so formidable a body of warriors. They all slept excepting the two leaders, and the sentinels who had been placed to guard the avenues of the position. The former sat in close conference, and discussed the details of their undertaking, although their voices were so low as not to spread beyond the circumference of a few feet. The night wore on, and the chiefs also relapsed into the silence which was the impress of everything around them, but yet no sleep entered their eyes, and, when towards three o'clock the scouts returned from their expedition, and approached the island, Campbell and Tononqua needed no summons to be ready for their report. The fine qualities of the Red Fox evidently had secured him the command of the expedition; at least there seemed to be a tacit agreement now amongst the scouts to let him be the mouthpiece of the party, and when Tononqua requested him to speak, he said:

"The warriors of Tononqua have been very successful. They have also been very good to the Red Fox. They looked to him for council, and when they asked his advice, hd told them what he thought they had better do. He bid them scatter in the neighborhood of the Mohawks, and reconnoiter the village from every side. They adopted the plan of the Red Fox. After agreeing upon a time and point of rendezvous, they parted and crawled into the village of the Mohawks. The Mohawks are very dull; they are owls by day, but they are no owls by night, for they could neither see nor hear. The Red Fox crawled into the very midst of their village. The warriors were asleep, even the very guards nodded on their posts. They had been talking too much during the day. A few squaws were awake; they had been talking too, but they have longer tongues, and were still equal to the work. The Red Fox cares but little about the gossip of women; but the voices of the Mohawk squaws were music in his ears. He listened with close attention, and harbored their words in the depth of his heart. They spoke about a great council which had been held during the day, and about the war dance which had been danced. They said that to-morrow a war party would start for the village of the Wyandots."

"Ugh!"

This low exclamation from the lips of Tononqua was more a matter of habit than a sign of excitement. He had expected a similar movement, and the confirmation of his suspicion could not now surprise him.

"Did the Mohawk women mention the time of departure?" he inquired of the Red Fox.

"They did not, but they stated that a Yengeese prison-

er would be burned at the stake when the sun climbed half
way up the sky. The tribe would first enjoy the sight, and
then depart."

"Ugh!"

This time the sound came both from Tononqua and
Campbell. To tell the truth they had hardly expected anything else, but they had buried the thought so deeply in
their bosom that they hardly recognized it when the note
met its counterpart in this communication.

The rest of the report was comparatively unimportant.
The Mohawks contemplated an attack upon the Huron village, and intended to burn Anderson at the stake. That
was surely enough of news, both welcome and un-
welcome. While the account of the perilous situation of so dear a friend and relative shocked the
feelings of Campbell and Tononqua, it raised to the
highest pitch their determination to strain every
nerve for the prevention of the dreadful tragedy in
which the scout was to play the principal role. On the
other hand the account of the intended invasion of their
homes served to fire the zeal of the Hurons, and give a personal character to a strife into which they had thus far
merely entered for the sake of their leader. Besides this it
was to be hoped that the prospect of and the participation
in the great spectacle of the morning would blind the Mohawks against the approach of a foe whose very weakness
would secure him against the suspicion on the part of the
Mohawks of the contemplated surprise. On the whole the
auspices augered well, and when the chief had aroused his
warriors, and carefully instructed them regarding the details of the impending assault, the whole body broke up,
and advanced towards the Mohawk village with a secrecy,
a skill, and withal a determination which deserved, if they
did not secure, success.

CHAPTER XVIII.

A DOUBLE SURPRISE.

There was considerable bustle in the village of the Mohawks as the sun on the following morning slowly began his course across the heavens. The great council of the previous day had decided the fate of the pale-face prisoner, and promised the Mohawks a spectacle towards which they now looked with great impatience. The loss of the warriors who had fallen in the memorable night struggle, above described, had galled them to the quick, and filled them with a thirst for vengeance which their chief could not have resisted, if he had desired to do so. He had, however, made no effort to this effect, unless we can construe as such the postponement of the execution, and the departure of the expedition a whole day longer than necessity required. The younger warriors of the tribe had murmured against this arrangement, and, although the chief had carried his point, the Mohawks now looked for the beginning of the cruel sport with an impatience which augered little good to the fate of their victim.

At last the hour of nine was drawing near. The center of the village had been prepared for the savage performance. The ground had been cleared of all obstacles, and a stake erected, to which the unfortunate prisoner was to be tied. Around this spot the tribe now began to gather, the warriors forming the inner circle, and the women and children crowding behind them, and exercising all their ingenuity to obtain a glimpse of a spectacle which was so much in accordance with the feelings of their savage nature. The chief was with the warriors, and at his side stood Maghpiway, his honored guest, and the author of so much misery. When the appointed hour arrived the signs of impatience increased in such a measure that Thayendanegea thought best not to trifle with a passion which, like a two-edged sword, was apt to wound in two directions. He motioned with his hand, and a minute afterwards Anderson was led into the circle.

To say that the scout was unaffected by the prospect of

such a horrid. end, would be to say that he was more than
human. He was pale, and at the sight of the stake, which
would soon witness the agony of his quivering limbs, when
exposed to the heat of the fire and inroads of cutting steel,
an involuntary shudder ran through his frame. This weakness, however, was of short duration, and if the scout did
not exhibit the vaunting spirit in which the red man
glories on such occasions, he was equally far from dejection
and despair. He suffered himself to be led and tied to the
stake without a single word ; for he knew beforehand that
nothing he could say would swerve the savages from their
purpose. He knew that they would glory in his supplication, and though his color and his religion forbade him to
meet death with ostentatious boasting, he was equally determined not to lower himself to any steps which would
subject him to the contempt of the savages without securing their compassion.

There was perhaps another circumstance which enabled
him to meet this prospect of a horrid death with becoming
firmness. He firmly expected and believed that Campbell
would not let him die without some desperate attempt at
rescue. He also hoped that Tononqua and his Hurons
would join in such an attempt; and, although the previous
night had failed to bring his deliverers, although he would
soon be subject to tortures under which human nature
could not possibly endure, he still looked with unshaken
faith for the arrival of his friends. Nothing in his mien,
however, betrayed such a hope ; he was prudent enough to
abstain from casting anxions glances into the woods, for
these glances would surely have frustrated his expectation
by betraying them. He suffered himself to be tied to the
stake, and when a Mohawk placed himself in his front,
ready to commence the sport by throwing the tomahawk
as near to his head as possible without actually cutting it,
he only employed his ears in listening for propitious sounds
from the woods, and met the eye of the Indian with a
steadiness of gaze which reflected a mind merely occupied
with the thoughts of meeting death with becoming firmness. He knew the customs of the Indians too well to fear
for his life during the first half hour of the trial. They

valued their chance for sport, and consequently the life of their prisoner, too highly to throw it away at the very commencment of the trial. Anderson knew that the Indian before him must be very expert in the use of the tomahawk, else the warriors would not have given the life of the captive into his hands. He therefore awaited the hurling of the weapon with a composure which had less merit than one uninitiated would have supposed, although the throwing of the hatchet was at best an uncertain thing, and the slightest twist of the hand or arm would suffice to bury the edge in his brain, instead of the tree, as intended.

The Indian, however, did not throw at once. He changed his position repeatedly, and several times caused his arm to sink again, when everybody expected the deadly missile to whirl towards the mark. These feints were made to worry the prisoner, and allure him into the betrayal of a sudden weakness. Anderson, however, was too expert to be caught in such a snare, and kept his gaze riveted upon the eye of his adversary with so much calmness and steadiness, that the Mohawk saw the vanity of his attempt, and with a quick motion hurled the hatchet. It struck the stake about one inch from Anderson's right temple, grazing, but not cutting, the ear. This was a skillful throw, and a unanimous yell from the lips of the spectators evinced their delight and satisfaction. The successful brave stepped back, and another warrior was on the point of taking his place, when, all at once, another missile whistled through the crowd, and another shout rent the air, whose effect upon the tribe was in exact proportion to its suddenness and unexpectedness. The missile found its way through the crowd, and cut the eagle feather from the coronet of Thaendanegea. The shout, however, came from a dozen places in the woods, and before it had died away, a dozen dusky forms appeared in the opening, and, with uplifted rifles, dispatched a dozen bullets into the crowd. None took effect, because none was intended to take effect; but this circumstance was overlooked in the excitement of the moment. The Mohawks saw nothing but the forms of the invaders; they thought of nothing but the fact that their village had been attacked, attacked by a handful of men who thus added insult to injury. They were incapable of reasoning, they could only feel, and what they felt was a burning desire to wash out the insult in the blood of the invaders. Before their chief could speak, before they could even form anything like a concert of action, the warriors of the tribe were seen to plunge towards the spot where a moment ago their assailants had become visible. The women and children scattered before them like the chaff before the wind, and a moment afterwards the prisoner stood alone in the center of the commons.

Then it was that the Mohawks were astounded by another phenomenon. The part of the forest which lay opposite to the invaded portion, suddenly became alive. Human forms seemed to spring from the ground. In deep silence, but with mighty leaps, they bounded towards the stake, and before the Mohawks had well seen them, before they had the least idea of the meaning of the movement, the bonds of the captive had been cut, a rifle and knife had been pressed into his hands, and he stood surrounded by thirty warriors, a free man and a warrior himself.

When we say he *stood*, we do not mean to say that he *stayed* there very long. He heard somebody cry: "On for the river !" and before he was fully aware of the fact, he was caught in the dash which his liberators made for the bank. They rushed over the commons, they passed the huts, they plunged down the bank, they jumped into the canoes which lay there in profusion, and paddled for the island in the river before the Mohawks had time to recover from their consternation. This assault had come so suddenly that they had had no time to count the number of the assailants, and these assailants had vanished so rapidly that they had no time to intercept their flight. Only when the Hurons were in the river, carrying with them the prisoner so boldly recovered, the duped Mohawks seemed to awake to a sense of their position. Yelling madly, they discontinued the pursuit of the smaller party, and hurried to the river bank to discharge their rifles after the members of the larger one. An excited hand, however, dispatches an insecure bullet, and as the Hurons were, moreover, somewhat protected by the dense bushes growing on the bank, a few insignificant scratches were all the injury they received. Before the Mohawks had time to load again, they had reached the island, which had but lately served as a prison for the Wild Rose.

CHAPTER XIX.

A SALTO MORTALE.

On leaving the shore the canoes of the fugitives had scattered in every direction. This was the order of Tononqua. A condensed flotilla would not only have presented an excellent aim for the rifles of the Mohawks, but also probably provoked an united attack. This Tononqua and Campbell desired to avoid. Although they had hoped and managed to accomplish the rescue of Anderson by a bold *coup de main*, they were too sensible to promise themselves a lasting success of their arms against an enemy so overwhelmingly superior. Their warriors had therefore received the order of retreating in small divisions across the Niagara and unite on the American side in the neighborhood of the falls. By preserving a broken front before their foes, they hoped to break, also, their forces into fragments and thus neutralize the advantage of superior numbers until they were better prepared to fight against them.

The island on which the Hurons had now landed was fully a mile long, but as the current had swept them down stream their force was scattered on the lower half of that distance. Campbell and Anderson had been separated from Tononqua in the hurry, and as there was no time to be lost in a useless search, they postponed it until a more favorable time. They had not even spoken to one another, and only when they jumped on the bank of the island, did they take time to shake hands together and express their satisfaction with the lucky issue of the bold enterprise.

"I knew you would not desert me," said Anderson, "although my chances looked mighty desperate. But

what is to be done next? We can't hold this place against
the Mohawks."

"I know we can't," said Campbell, and then proceeded
to explain his plan. "We mustn't stay a moment longer
than we can help, for once cut off from the opposite shore,
we may as well say our prayers and prepare for a jump
into the cataract."

"Then why not start at once? The Black Snake told
us there were plenty of canoes on the other side of this
island."

"Exactly. Only let me scare that imp a little who
paddles so boldly across the channel. I do not want to
hurt him either, for Tononqua thinks if we abstain from
spilling blood, this quarrel can sooner or later be made up.
A little scare, however, can do the fellow no harm.
There it goes. Do you see how he starts? He turns his
craft, and that is all I wanted. So, now, let us go forward
at once."

With these words the two rushed into the woods, keeping a south-eastern direction, so as to reach the opposite
shore of the island as far up stream as possible. They
knew the force of the current and had no desire whatever
to form too intimate an acquaintance with the rapids and
falls of the Niagara. As the island was long and narrow
they soon reached the looked-for eastern bank. After a
short search they were so fortunate as to secure a canoe,
in which, however, they found only one paddle. As time
pressed, and one blade in the hands of such skillful oarsmen sufficed to take them safely to the other side, they
started at once, proceeding in a south-easterly direction,
heading for a little island in the middle of the river. The
current was strong, but the skill and strength of such oarsmen soon brought them to the desired spot where they once
more sought the shelter of the woods. While they recovered their breath, of which the violent struggle against the
current had in a measure deprived them, they looked
around to learn the exact state of the conflict, and the situation of the respective parties. Let us gaze with them to

post ourselves on matters, the knowledge of which is necessary to comprehend the following narrative.

The point on which the two scouts stood was nearly abreast the spot whence they had started. South of it at a distance of more than a mile they discovered something which hardly deserved the name of island, but looked more like a long and narrow ledge or reef. Between the island and this ledge lay the passage to the American shore, and on it their eye now discovered nearly a score of canoes, all striving to reach the eastern bank, but being farther from or nearer to it according to their skill in rowing or the number of paddles at their command. Thus far the Mohawks had not made their appearance, but if the scouts failed to see any symptoms of their foes, they were equally unsuccessful in discovering any signs of Tononqua. In none of the canoes did they observe a figure which could at all be compared to that of the king, in height and stateliness, and yet the great majority of the Hurons were now in sight. What could it mean? Had anything befallen him? Had his generosity induced him to remain in the neighborhood of the Mohawks until all the chances of flight had been exhausted? This would never do. They could never think of continuing the flight as long as Tononqua was in the midst of his enemies, and Campbell was on the point of pushing the canoe into the flood in order to return to the island, when an exclamation of Anderson induced him to arrest his motions and look in the direction pointed out. What he saw was calculated to interest and excite him. The chief for whom they had looked so long and anxiously, had at last made his appearance, but with him a dozen hostile canoes had shot out into the river. Some of them were above, some below him, and of the former two had the advantage of larger crews and thrice the number of paddles. Tononqua was all alone, but as he only had one paddle, a companion would have been more of a burden than of an assistance, excepting in case of a close encounter. The canoes above him seemed merely bound to head him off and thus drive him into the hands of their companions below, and the latter strained every nerve to be ready for the reception. Tononqua handled his canoe splendidly, but the vessels above gained so much of a start of him, that he changed his course slightly to the north-east in order to have the benefit of the current and to compel his pursuers to a similar movement. In this, however, he failed. The Mohawks evidently considered their companions below a match for all the skill and strength he could bring into play, and continued their eastern course in the expectation of gaining enough of a start to cut him off entirely. Now was the time for Campbell and Anderson to give Tononqua a sign of their presence. The two foremost canoes of the Mohawks had come into rifle shot distance of the point on which the scouts were stationed, and willing as they would have been under other circumstances to honor the wishes of Tononqua and spare the lives of the Mohawks to their utmost ability, they felt that the perilous position of the king required energetic measures, and that the Mohawks would care little for the demonstrations of men whose bullets never hit the mark. So they took a careful aim, and when they pulled the trigger the rifles spoke the death sentence of two Mohawks.

The deadliness of their aim seemed to have deprived the Mohawks of all further desire of coming in closer contact with the scouts, for they suddenly turned their crafts and paddled back to the island near their village, with all the speed of which they were capable. This movement freed Tononqua of his most formidable adversaries, and enabled him to advance in a direct line towards the scouts. His foes, however, followed in hot pursuit, and in one of the foremost canoes the scouts recognized their inveterate enemy, Red Feather. Perhaps the rage over the escape of the Wild Rose had made him desperate ; perhaps he wished to acquire the reputation of a great warrior in the estimation of his new allies ; however this may be, he certainly showed a daring bordering on recklessness. As he had a Mohawk in his canoe, who assisted him in propelling the same, he rapidly gained on Tononqua, and the scouts expected every moment to see him take his rifle and discharge the same at the king from a distance calculated to make the shot fatal. They, in their turn, had rapidly approached the combatants, and when Campbell saw from the movements of the Delaware, he said, hurriedly:

"Steady, father! I see the rascal is going to fire, and I must venture a shot at him, though the rifle will hardly carry a bullet that far. Steady now!"

He had certainly no time to lose if he wanted to anticipate the Red Feather, who was even then raising his rifle to fire the bullet which, according to all probabilities, was destined to end a noble life. Tononqua seemed indeed aware of his danger; but what could he do to avoid it? To cease paddling and conceal himself in the bottom of the canoe would have checked his flight and caused him to drift towards his foes and the even more dangerous rapids whose uproar began to sound from a startling vicinity. In this strait he might well congratulate himself that a trusty friend was near, whose skill with the rifle was sure to accomplish anything in the reach of possibilities. He raised his weapon with that rapidity peculiar to him, and pulled the trigger before the Delaware had succeeded in drawing his bead upon the king. After a moment of breathless suspense, the report of Red Feather's rifle followed; but it appeared to the falcon eye of the scouts as if Campbell's bullet, and not his own effort, had discharged his weapon, for the barrel was slightly knocked aside, and the bullet sped harmlessly past Tononqua's head. At the same time the Delaware uttered a cry of both rage and pain, and the scouts saw that his right hand had been helplessly disabled. At the same time the Mohawk, who shared the canoe with the Red Feather, ceased paddling, as if inclined to assist his companion. Campbell was on the point of discharging a second bullet with more deadly aim at the pursuers, when the actions of the king caused him to desist. The young monarch evidently deemed the moment propitious to strike himself a blow at his foes. After a few powerful strokes of his paddle, which propelled the light craft on its course, he raised the rifle and discharged it with deadly effect, for a few moments afterwards the companion of Maghpiway was seen to rise, throw up his arms and then fall backwards into the flood, which at once closed over the lifeless body.

A crisis was fast approaching. The combatants were now about the middle of the river, and the neighborhood of the rapids made it imperative to reach either shore, in order to avoid their fatal embrace. The Hurons strained every nerve to reach the American shore, and if the Mohawks did not wish to imitate their example, a step which the presence of their foes might make rather dangerous, they must turn their canoes, without loss of time, and head for their own shore or be inevitably drawn into the horrible vortex below. See! they have already chosen the latter and more prudent alternative, directed perhaps more by the prudence of their chief than a lack of courage. Brant had recently felt the strong hand of the Union, and might well hesitate to invade its territory. At all events, he uttered the signal which called the canoes of his warriors back to the western bank.

So rapid had been their retreat that Red Feather was left to his own resources. He was, as we have seen, a few hundred feet in advance of his party—a circumstance calculated to hide from the Mohawks the exact nature of his injuries. When they at last perceived his canoe rapidly gliding down the current, they were too far to rescue him, as such an attempt would have inevitably drawn them into the rapids ; but while they continued their frantic efforts to reach the shore, they gazed, horror-stricken, upon the Delaware, who was rapidly drifting towards a fate as certain as it was appalling. True, he made desperate efforts to force his craft with one hand to the shore ; but the current, which became stronger every moment, made all such efforts idle, and seeing this, the chief soon ceased them altogether.

We know that, bad as this man was, cowardice did not number amongst his vices. He knew that the eyes of friends and foes were centered upon him, and while the wish not to disgrace the former was certainly a strong incentive to display true heroism, the desire of defying the latter had certainly much more influence in shaping his conduct. He arose to his full height and maintained this position as long as the smoothness of the current would allow him. When the madly rushing rapids received the frail craft, and tossed it like a nutshell in every direction, he had to sit down, and the spectators now and then lost sight of him, thinking on such occasions, with a sigh of relief, that the hungry waves had swallowed him. The very lightness of the canoe, however, enabled it to ride its mad career in safety to the very end. Now it had reached the yawning precipice; the tall form of the chief was seen to arise, and with one wild shout of defiance, which arose even above the thunder of the cataract, he and his craft disappeared in the clouds of spray never more to be seen again.

CHAPTER XX.

CONCLUSION.

This horrible death seemed to have hushed the very Nature into an ominous silence. When the two parties had reached their respective banks, they disappeared in the bushes, and a whole hour passed by without bringing any continuation of hostilities. Tononqua and his friends benefitted by this respite, and prepared for the renewal of the struggle which, in all probability, would soon begin. They collected and posted their forces in the most advantageous position, and were on the point of dispatching scouts up the river bank to guard against a secret transit of the foe at a place further south, when, to their surprise, they saw a canoe start from the opposite bank in which no less a personage than that of Brant was seated. He was accompanied by only four warriors, who paddled the canoe with such swiftness across the stream that the intense suspense with which the Hurons watched these proceedings, promised to be of but short duration.

When the canoe of the Mohawks was about one hundred yards from the American shore, Brant signaled his companions to cease paddling or rather to keep the canoe stationary, and then raised a green branch as a token of his peaceful intentions and his desire to parley with the Hurons. Upon this, Tononqua stepped from the bushes, and no sooner had Brant observed him, when he motioned his followers to resume their labors, and a few minutes later stepped upon the shore. He showed a fearlessness which was perhaps based upon his own strength, perhaps upon the well known character of Tononqua. As he advanced towards the Huron, his mien was serious but not unfriendly, and offering his hand to the young monarch, he said:

"A cloud had arisen between my brother and myself, but it has glided down the rapids and disappeared behind yon cataract. A cunning Delaware had stuffed my ears with lies and set my heart against the Wyandots. My warriors have suffered severely for my folly, and the braves of my brother have sent many of them to the happy hunting grounds beyond the grave. But they are not to be blamed, and Thayendanegea bears them no ill will. To prove this he proposes to bury the hatchet—is Tononqua satisfied?"

"He admires his brother's generosity, and nothing could be more in accordance with his wishes. Henceforth a bond of friendship shall tie the Mohawks and the Hurons, and deeds of kindness shall bring this feud into forgetfulness."

"It is well; my brother may use the canoes he has taken to reach the big canoe of the Muskrat, and if he will listen to the advice of a friend, he will lose no time in departing. The village of the Mohawks contains many hot-headed young warriors, and if the Wyandots tarry, there might be encounters leading to further bloodshed. Tononqua is wise enough to understand his brother."

There was, indeed, no difficulty in comprehending that grave reasons of policy had wrenched these concessions from the proud sachem of the Mohawks. Probably the fear of complications with the United States was aided by the apprehension of provoking the displeasure of the English government. Whatever these considerations may have been, they had sufficed to recall the chief from that sudden outbreak of passion into which the fiery invectives of Maghpiway had stirred him, and brought about these offers of peace, so humiliating to a haughty spirit. But while Tononqua saw the motives, he was not slow in accepting a proposition so advantageous to his tribe. So he assured Brant of his readiness to enter upon his views; and no sooner had the Mohawk departed for his village, when Tononqua ordered an immediate embarkation, bidding his followers to commence the trip up the river. It was now about two o'clock in the afternoon, and using due dispatch, the flotilla reached its head just when twilight began to spread its somber veil over the landscape. The sloop was seen cruising at the distance of a mile or two; but the firing of a rifle, and other signals soon brought it to the spot. The canoes were then surrendered to the care of a young Mohawk, who had accompanied the party for that purpose, and this accomplished, they all boarded the La Belle France, where they were received with manifestations of the most unbounded delight. Mary threw herself into the arms of her husband with a sigh of relief, showing plainly how much she had suffered during his absence on such a perilous expedition. To Mrs. Anderson, on the other hand, it appeared as if she had found her husband a second time, and the feelings of anguish that had tortured her during his short but dangerous captivity, now seemed to her like a heavy ransom paid for his recovery. The voyage to the home of Le Blanc was spent in the communication of events, and the exchange of happy thoughts, and before they knew it, the sloop had anchored at the island in Grand River. Soon the news of the successful termination of the expedition reached the village of the Hurons, and threw its inhabitants into a fever of excitement fully as intense as that which had seized the pale-faces. Everybody walked about as if in a state of intoxication, and a full week elapsed before the little community sobered down and events began to flow in the calm bed of everyday occurrences. Then only it was that the plans for the future began to take a definite shape. Anderson and Campbell declared their determination to return to Fort McIntosh, whither their wives and little Annie would, of course, accompany them. As to Tononqua, they tried hard to induce him to join their fortunes; but not only did they fail in this undertaking, but were finally compelled to acknowledge the correctness of his reasons. Though of white origin, he had received an Indian education, which disqualified him for a closer intercourse with the white race, and live in the settlements. Among the Wyandots, on the other hand, he felt at home, to say nothing of his conviction that he had to fulfill a mission among them, and that it was his duty to lead them onward in the path of civilization, which they had entered with such flattering prospects of success. His friends, however, remained sufficiently long to honor with their presence the rites which united him and Adeline in the bonds of matrimony. Then, at last, after many affectionate embraces and many mutual promises of frequent visits, they took their departure in La Belle France, as Monsieur Le Blance insisted upon depositing them safely on the Pennsylvania shore. Thence, after a last cordial farewell to the warm-hearted Frenchman, they started upon their journey to the Fort, using as much as possible the more convenient water routes. Nevertheless, they were pretty well tired out when they at last reached their place of destination, where they were received with the loudest demonstrations of joy and satisfaction. Their arrival ended a period of painful anxiety, which their long absence had engendered in the hearts of even the most hopeful. The marvelous adventures of the expedition, and especially the almost miraculous recovery of Mrs. Anderson, formed the theme of conversation many a long winter evening. The relations with Tononqua and Le Blanc were kept alive, according to previous agreements, and when the young monarch paid his first visit to the Fort, he created as powerful a sensation as many a mightier potentate of the Old World. All the persons of our narrative reached the high old age which their simple mode of living is apt to procure; but although their occupation and their residence on the perilous border brought them many more adventures in the course of time, they were never again exposed to such soul-stirring trials of endurance as those we have endeavored to depict in this narrative.

THE END.